Born in Lincolnshire in 1912, educated in Sussex before enterir he gained an LL B with honours in 1937.

He joined the Royal Horse Artillery during World War II, and served in Europe and North Africa, where he was captured and imprisoned – an experience recalled in Death in Captivity. After the war he worked in a law firm as a solicitor, and in 1952 he became a partner.

Gilbert was a founding member of the British Crime Writers Association, and in 1988 was named a *Grand Master* by the Mystery Writers of America – an achievement many thought long overdue. He won the *Life Achievement Anthony Award* at the 1990 Boucheron in London, and in 1980 was made a Commander of the Order of the British Empire.

Gilbert made his debut in 1947 with *Close Quarters*, and has become recognized as one of the most versatile British mystery writers.

BY THE SAME AUTHOR
ALL PUBLISHED BY HOUSE OF STRATUS

Inspector Hazlerigg Series

Close Quarters		1947
They Never Looked Inside	alt: He Didn't Mind Danger	1948
The Doors Open		1949
Smallbone Deceased		1950
Death has Deep Roots		1951
Fear To Tread	(in part)	1953
The Young Petrella	(included) (short stories)	1988
The Man Who Hated Banks and Other Mysteries		
(included) (short stories)		1997

Patrick Petrella Series

Blood and Judgement		1959
Amateur in Violence	(included) (short stories)	1973
Petrella at Q	(short stories)	1977
The Young Petrella	(short stories)	1988
Roller Coaster		1993
The Man Who Hated Banks	(included) (short stories)	1997

Luke Pagan Series

Ring of Terror		1995
Into Battle		1997
Over and Out		1998

Calder & Behrens Series

Game Without Rules	(short stories)	1967
Mr. Calder and Mr. Behrens	(short stories)	1982

Indivudual Works

Death in Captivity	alt: The Danger Within	1952
Sky High	alt: The Country House Burglar	1955
Be Shot for Sixpence		1956
After the Fine Weather		1963
The Crack in the Teacup		1966
The Dust and the Heat	alt: Overdrive	1967
The Etruscan Net	alt: The Family Tomb	1969
Stay of Execution and Other Stories	(short stories)	1971
The Body of a Girl		1972
The Ninety-Second Tiger		1973
Flash Point		1974
The Night of the Twelfth		1976
The Empty House		1979
The Killing of Katie Steelstock	alt: Death of a Favourite Girl	1980
The Final Throw	alt: End Game	1982
The Ninety-Second Tiger		1984
The Long Journey Home		1985
Trouble		1987
Paint, Gold, and Blood		1989
Anything for a Quiet Life	(short stories)	1990
The Queen against Karl Mullen		1992

MICHAEL
GILBERT

THE MAN WHO HATED BANKS
& OTHER MYSTERIES

HOUSE OF
STRATUS

This edition published in 2011 by House of Stratus, an imprint of
Stratus Books Ltd., Lisandra House, Fore Street,
Looe, Cornwall, PL13 1AD, U.K.

www.houseofstratus.com

Typeset by House of Stratus.

A catalogue record for this book is available from the British Library
and the Library of Congress.

ISBN 0-7551-1921-5

INTRODUCTION

Of the four characters who play, in turn, the principal part in this collection of stories, the first in the field, by a long chalk, is Hazlerigg, who featured in my crime novel *Close Quarters* playing, on that occasion, second fiddle to his own assistant, Detective Sergeant Pollock.

This, my maiden effort, appeared in 1947, though most of it was written before I disappeared into the Army in 1939. Judging by his rank, which was at that time Chief Inspector, and argues an age of forty or more, he must, by now, be over ninety, which may account for the fact that not much has been heard of him lately.

He was what you might call a standard pattern policeman, and I have a feeling that the late Julian Symons would have considered him to be "humdrum." It was with this adjective, you may remember, that he insulted many of the leading lights in the crime story field of the early years of this century.

I find the thought encouraging.

It is the fashion nowadays for the author to penetrate deeply into the characters and feelings of his policemen; their family quarrels and upsets, their psychological backgrounds, their secret ambitions and phobias, all are laid bare for us. The great American writer Professor Jacques Barzun objected strongly to the practice. "Am I a couch?" he demanded.

I side with Barzun. Let your policeman get on with his job. And for many years, and through many novels and short stories, Hazlerigg did just that.

Henry Montacute Bohun, solicitor and partner in the Lincoln's Inn firm of Horniman, Birley and Craine, made his first appearance in my book *Smallbone Deceased,* which appeared in 1950.

It fell to him to play the part of detective in this book, and in a number of short stories which appeared in *John Bull and Argosy,* two excellent short story magazines, now both deceased. Since I had, myself, just become a partner in a Lincoln's Inn firm of solicitors, people were not slow to suggest that Bohun was me in disguise. This was far from correct. I sleep excellently at night and have never felt any desire to dabble in real life crime. My criminals all come from my pen.

Bohun's detective activities arose by chance.

Since he suffered from a form of para-insomnia which never allowed him more than two hours sleep each night, and sometimes none at all, this left him with a lot of time on his hands which he spent, as another man might puzzle over an unsolved clue in the *Times* crossword puzzle, in thinking out answers to the problems which he encountered either from his growing friendship with Inspector Hazlerigg, or from his job as a solicitor.

In saying this, I do realise that there may be solicitors whose thresholds are never crossed by crime, potential or actual, but I don't suppose there are many such. For the most part, when they encounter a criminal matter, they are ready to pass it on to Counsel, or even to the police. Horniman, Birley and Craine preferred to take in their own dirty washing.

Former Detective Chief Inspector Mercer plays the leading part in a book called *The Body of a Girl*, which was first published in England and America in 1972.

He once shared with Hazlerigg the rank of Chief Inspector, but this is almost the only thing that he did share. While Hazlerigg plays the game according to the rules. Mercer is prepared to bend any rule that gets in the way of his single-minded pursuit of his objective. Hazlerigg is monogamous. To Mercer a girl is somebody to be enjoyed and forgotten. Their difference must be apparent to a perceptive reader when Mercer is described: "A lot of dark hair, worn rather long, and a thick, sensual face, his appearance not improved by a puckered scar which started at the cheek-bone and gathered up the corner of the left eye, so that it seemed to be half closed!"

He was going to get his revenge for that scar whatever the cost.

Last, but by no means least, comes Patrick Petrella, who first saw book publication in 1959 in *Blood and Judgment,* although many of the short stories are earlier. Son of a senior Spanish policeman and an English lady, fluent speaker of Arabic, knowledgeable about vintage wines and the mechanism of locks.

I have described elsewhere how he arrived, and hope that I may, for once, quote my own words.

"Patrick Petrella was conceived in church. It was a drowsy summer evening and the preacher had reached only the midpoint of his sermon. It was not an inspired address, and I turned to the hymn book for relief. I opened it at the lines of Christina Rosetti, 'Who has seen the wind. Neither you nor I. But when the trees bow down their heads, the wind is passing by.' And later, 'Who has seen the wind. Neither I nor you. But when the leaves hang trembling, the wind is passing through.'

"And there, quite suddenly, it was. A working class family, wife and children, sitting in their front room being talked to by a visitor (parson? social worker? policeman?) but remaining totally unresponsive. Answering in monosyllables. Trembling. Heads bowed down. Why? Because they know, but their visitor does not, that there is a monster in the back kitchen. Their father, a violent criminal, had escaped that day from prison and is hiding there. At that moment their visitor (he is now quite definitely a policeman, and a youngster at that) recalls the poem and realises the truth."

In that short sequence a complete character is encapsulated.

A young policeman, in his first posting, sufficiently interested in his job to visit the wife of a man who was serving a prison sentence, sufficiently acute to notice the unnatural behaviour of the woman and children, sufficiently imaginative to deduce the reason for a simple, furtive glance at the kitchen door; above all a young man who read and could quote poetry.

Almost everything that happened afterward was as traceable to their first conception as is the character of a real person to the accidents of the nursery and the schoolroom.

So there they are. Four different characters, deployed for your pleasure.

Michael Gilbert Gravesend, Kent November 1996

BACK IN FIVE YEARS

(As Told by Chief Inspector Hazlerigg)

IN THE EARLY THIRTIES, when I was a junior inspector attached to the uniformed branch in a North London division, there were a number of known counterfeiters at work in London. I don't mean that we knew their names and addresses, for they tend to be shy people, but a surprising number of facts about them and their products were filed and tabulated at the Criminal Records Office and in the M-0 file.

There were forgers of Post Office Savings books, and there were those who specialized in passports and share certificates. But the kings of the trade were the forgers and utterers of banknotes. And the king of them all was a certain shy, unobtrusive genius who manufactured the "Beauties."

His identity was, of course, a mystery. He was known to us only by his £1 notes, finely etched and most scrupulously printed.

In a lot of ways they were a better product than the stuff being turned out by H.M. Mint. That young lady who sits up in an inset in the top left-hand corner (on the genuine pound notes she looks rather a pudding-faced young person) – well, in his productions she was a miracle of dignified beauty. That's why we called them "Beautiful Britannias," or "Beauties."

And you can take it from me that there wasn't a policeman in the Metropolis who wouldn't have given his belt and buttons for a chance to lay hands on the artist.

However, as it happens – and as it happens in most police work – it wasn't one man or even a few men who got on the track of the forger. When this happy event finally came to pass it was the result of a combination of luck and instinct backed up by the hard, slogging work of a great number of people.

We had regretfully decided that in the case of the Beauties we were up against one of those rarities in the field of crime – an entirely solitary and single-handed operator; a man with at least one god-like attribute, the strength which is said to come from loneliness.

He must have made his own plate – it may have taken him a year or more of patient trial and error, cutting, smoothing, and sizing. He even had a rotation system which enabled him to change the numbering.

But it was his method of distribution that put him at the top of the class.

Having printed a number of very excellent pound notes, he rationed himself to about twenty a week. These he would cash personally, going to shops and post offices all over London, and never to the same one twice. He would purchase some small object costing not more than a few pence or a shilling, pay with a pound note, and pocket the change. The system was laborious, but almost foolproof. And, but for one small thing, I really have my doubts whether we should have got on to him.

The thing was he had a weakness for pawnbrokers. Perhaps it was because pawnbrokers' shops are places which have a wide variety of things which you can pick up for a small sum; and they are usually rather dark and not very crowded and don't make difficulties about change. Anyway, it proved his undoing.

For pawnbrokers, as you may know, are people who like to work very closely with the police. There's nothing underhanded about it. It just happens to pay both sides. There's a Pawnbrokers' List of Stolen Articles which we publish at Scotland Yard, and most pawnbrokers make a practice of reporting anything suspicious to the local station. The local police, in return, keep a special eye on their shops, which are a tempting target to the light-fingered fraternity.

Well, over the months and years, reports piled up of these pound notes being received by pawnbrokers. So, just on the chance (that's a phrase which features pretty prominently in police work), a letter was sent round to all pawnbrokers saying that if they should happen to notice a man or woman coming into their shop who wasn't a regular customer, and who wanted to make a small purchase and proffered a brand-new pound note for it, then would they please make a careful note of his description, etc., etc.

After a time the descriptions started to add up. It was extraordinarily fascinating, sitting back in an office watching a living person being built up out of fractions, watching his features line themselves in, and his identity declare itself.

We got a picture of a man, middle-sized to small, plump, soft-spoken, with white, pudgy hands, strong black hair and weak, rather peering eyes. His clothes naturally varied from time to time and from place to place but the essentials were the same.

A very wide and elaborate net was then spread. I won't bore you with all the details, but you can gather the scope of it when I tell you it meant stationing policemen within call of almost every pawnshop which had not yet been visited and arranging a simple system of signals with the pawnbrokers themselves.

And that was how, at the beginning of June, 194– , the police at last caught sight of Mr. Mountjoy and followed him discreetly home to 14 Malpas Street. This proved to be a small shop in North London, with living quarters attached, and an independent flat over it.

Some further facts now came to light. All seemed to point to the one conclusion. To start with, Mr. Mountjoy's business was that of a one-man printer and typemaker; very suitable, we felt, allowing its owner to possess and operate various small machines and lathes without exciting suspicion. Then again, he was a solitary man, who, according to Mr. Crump, of 12 Malpas Street, his nearest neighbour, spent much of his time out of his shop, apparently on journeys round London.

"Looking for commissions, I expect," said Mr. Crump. "Not that he seems to get much work. Manages to do very well for himself, none the less."

I was in charge of these local inquiries, and sensing a certain amount of rancour in that last remark, I guessed that there might be some trade rivalry. Mr. Crump was a newsagent and printer himself. However, he was unable to help me much, because he didn't know very much. But he did say that Mr. Mountjoy seemed to do a lot of work at night.

In some trepidation, because we didn't want to expose our hand too soon, I tried Mrs. Ireland, who lived in the flat over Mr. Mountjoy's shop. She was a middle-aged party, intensely respectable and slightly deaf. I visited her one morning in the well-worn disguise of an inspector of gas meters, and found her surprisingly willing to talk.

She, unlike Mr. Crump, had the very highest opinion of Mr. Mountjoy. Possibly he *was* one who kept himself to himself but there was no harm that she could see in that. Better that than clumping about sticking your nose into what didn't concern you. This, I gathered, was a back-hander at Mr. Crump, whom she didn't like. Unfortunately, her deafness prevented her from being able to corroborate the story of night work.

Well, there it was. You now know all that we knew at that point and you can see how we were fixed. I had no doubt in my mind. The description fitted. The setup was exactly what we had imagined. The printer's shop – the night work – the journeys round London.

There was only one thing to do – take a search warrant and chance the odds.

Accordingly, on Midsummer Day, 194– , just after four o'clock in the afternoon, I took Sergeant Husband with me and walked over to Malpas Street to put the matter to the test. And as I turned into the road the first thing that struck my eye was that damned notice and I realised that we had missed our man. How narrowly we had missed him became apparent as we pursued our inquiries.

The notice? It was pinned to the door of the shop. Written in a copperplate hand on a neat white card, it said: *BACK IN FIVE YEARS.*

No. 14 was the end house of a block of seven. It had the shop entrance in front, and an independent side entrance which led up to Mrs. Ireland's flat.

Now the curious thing was this. Five minutes before we had

arrived, several people had seen Mr. Mountjoy come out and pin that notice on his door. But after that no one could say which way he had gone. This didn't all come out at once, but inquiries in the street, then and later, only deepened the mystery.

For instance, Mrs. Ireland had been sitting at her window, which overlooked the point where the side street joined the main. Although she might be deaf, she certainly wasn't shortsighted and she happened to have been keeping her eyes open for the postman. She was prepared to swear that Mr. Mountjoy had neither passed the end of the side road nor gone down it.

Suppose, therefore, he had turned to the left outside his front door? But Mr. Crump in No. 12 and the barber in No. 8 had both been in their shops the whole time and were positive that he had not gone past them. Had he gone back into his shop or the living room behind it? But these were most undeniably empty, and had, besides, the sort of "packed up" appearance of rooms whose owner has left them deliberately. The gas and electricity were turned off, the larder was empty.

There was a door leading into the garden, and this was locked. That, by itself, didn't prove anything, of course, but the garden was a dead end. There was a very high, glass bottle-topped wall on the street side, the blank elevation of another house at the end, and a garden full of little Crumps on the right.

Mr. Mountjoy, in fact, had walked into the street, pinned up his famous notice, and then dematerialised.

But, unlike the conjurer's lady assistant, he not only disappeared, he stayed disappeared. And that is not such an easy thing to do – not in this country, anyway, especially when the police are on the lookout for you and have your full description.

However, as with everything else, Mr. Mountjoy managed it competently enough.

The police force, like the Army, believes in moving its executives around, and it wasn't until well over four years later – nearly five – that I found myself back at the same North London police station, attached this time to the plainclothes branch.

One of the first places I visited was Malpas Street, and there, still, was the notice: *BACK IN FIVE YEARS.*

In a district like that you'd have imagined that it would have been torn down long ago. But it hadn't.

I gathered, in fact, that it had become a sort of local tradition. Mr. Mountjoy had always been a mystery man to the neighbourhood, and his reputation had been nowise diminished by his dramatic disappearance and the interest of the police in his whereabouts.

There was a strong local feeling, amounting almost to an obsession, that five years after his disappearance (on the very day and at the very hour) Mr. Mountjoy would reappear and take that notice down again.

What would happen then no one could suggest.

I asked the station sergeant about the place. For instance, why hadn't it been re-let or taken over by the authorities? Mr. Mountjoy, I gathered, owned the building but the taxes must be mounting up and anyway it was a nice little shop and living quarters. We didn't talk about requisitioning in those days, but we had some powers. Apparently, however, all this had been foreseen by Mr. Mountjoy.

The day before he disappeared he had handed Mrs. Ireland a sum in notes (genuine ones this time) sufficient to deal with all foreseeable expenses *for exactly five years.* At the end of that time, he said, if he hadn't come back she could sell the house and keep the proceeds. And he had even executed a legal document enabling her to do this.

In short, she was to wait for him for five years, and at the end of that time, like the frog in the fairy story, she was to have her reward – unless the fairy prince had reappeared to claim his own.

It sounded pretty fantastic to me.

The next thing that happened, about three weeks later, was the arrival at the station of a badly worried Mr. Crump, with a tale that No. 14 was haunted.

He was so clear about it that we gave more attention to his story than the police usually accord to psychic manifestations. Also, of course, we were interested in that particular house.

"Scraping, cutting, and emery-papering," said Mr. Crump, his great red face moist but earnest. "Every night – about midnight or one o'clock. Just like he used to. I don't like it. Nor the wife don't like it. She's talking of moving if it isn't stopped."

"Did you go down and look in?" I asked. "Was there a light on in the shop?"

"Of course there wasn't no light on," said Mr. Crump. "Hasn't the electricity been cut off? I've told you, it's not yooman, this noise isn't."

When I suggested that it might be rats, I thought Mr. Crump was going to detonate, so I hurriedly promised him that we'd look into it and he departed.

We had the keys of the shop, so I let myself in that evening, going after dark to avoid causing any undue stir. I took a torch and made a thorough investigation. It was obvious no one had been there. The dust was inches thick over everything, and the place – well, it *smelt* deserted, if you know what I mean.

When I came out I found half Malpas Street gathered outside armed with sticks and bottles. Apparently a small boy had seen my torch flashing and the crowd were just summoning up courage to break in and lay the ghost when I stepped out.

After that, of course, there was no stopping the stories.

Mr. Crump appeared about a month later with an ultimatum.

Either the police "did something" or he was going to clear out himself. He couldn't stand it any longer. His wife had already gone on an indefinite visit to her married sister and trade was falling off. The sinister reputation of No. 14 was beginning to corrupt No. 12.

"All right," I said at last. "I'll come long myself tonight and we'll both listen."

When I came off duty at about half past ten that evening, I walked along to Malpas Street and Mr. Crump let me in. We sat in his parlor, which was on the first floor overlooking the street, and we drank beer and talked for a bit, and at midnight, at my suggestion, we turned the lights out and made ourselves comfortable in chairs near the window.

After a bit I must have dozed, because I woke up to feel Mr. Crump gripping my arm.

He said nothing, but I gathered from his breathing, which he was trying to control, that something happened.

Then, in the stuffy blackness of the room I heard it, too. It was a thin intermittent burr, which sounded like a very sharp edge cutting across some tough substance. Then came the sound of scraping, and then the cutting started again.

I jumped up, leaped at the door, nearly broke my neck on the stairs, and three seconds later I was out in the street. I had my key at the ready and I snapped open the door of No. 14 and switched on my torch.

There was no one there. Nothing had been disturbed at all. There wasn't even the trace of a rat or mouse paw in the dust. I hadn't thought that there would be. There had been something indefinably human about that sound.

When I got back to Mr. Crump, I found he had turned on the light and poured out some more beer. He seemed much more cheerful. I think that half his trouble had been that no one believed his story.

Also, as we were finishing our beer, he said something which surprised me.

"Thanks be," he said. "I've only to put up with it for one more week."

"What do you mean?" I asked.

"Work it out for yourself," he said. "It's the seventeenth of June. Four years and 51 weeks ago he left. Said he'd be back in five years. Very methodical man was Mr. Mountjoy."

I could find no comment to make.

It was quite illogical and fantastic, and I felt that we were making fools of ourselves, but in the end I agreed, weakly, to post two sergeants to watch the back of the house while I kept an unobtrusive eye on the front.

If Mr. Mountjoy was going to maintain his reputation for punctuality he was due in the street at four o'clock in the afternoon. Accordingly, at five to four I turned the corner at the far end of the road and started strolling nonchalantly towards No. 14, stopping every now and then to look in at the various shop windows.

It was a true midsummer day, warm and windless, and the children were still in school, so that by Malpas Street standards it was almost quiet.

I looked at my watch and saw that it was just short of four o'clock. And Malpas Street was still most definitely empty.

At that moment, in the warm summer silence, I heard it again. I want to be quite clear about this. It was exactly and undeniably the same sound that I had heard that night when I sat up over Mr. Crump's shop. But it did not come from No. 14.

It was from the same side of the street but much lower down.

I moved cautiously along until I could locate it. It came from the barber's shop at No. 8, where Toni Etrillo, the barber, was shaving one of his swarthy compatriots. The burr and the rasp as the razor passed across the strong black stubble – these were unmistakable.

And in that moment the secret of Mr. Mountjoy's disappearance became as abundantly clear to me.

The first thing I did was purely symbolical. I took out my knife and levered out the tack which held up that notice. I was about to tear it up but thought better of it and dropped it in my pocket.

Conscious that a dozen pairs of eyes were watching from curtained windows, I went round into the side street and rang Mrs. Ireland's doorbell.

When she opened the door I didn't do anything dramatic; I just beckoned her out into the street and signalled to one of the sergeants to accompany us, and we all walked back to the police station.

For the greater part of the way we were silent, but I felt, in justice, that one thing had to be said.

"A marvellously well kept-up impersonation, Mr. Mountjoy. It's nothing new for a man to dress as a woman, and I have even heard of cases before where a landlord became his own lodger. But – it's a great mistake for any man to do his shaving last thing at night."

John Bull, December 18, 1948.

A NEAT, COLD KILLING

ON THE NIGHT OF MARCH 15TH, a night of fog, Lou Rowley (whose other name was Cab Rowley or Rowley the Roller) was shot down in a street in Islington.

A constable who heard the shots, but arrived too late to do much about it, got on the telephone and a squad car brought Inspector Hazlerigg from Barley Lane Police Station. Hazlerigg was the Divisional Detective Inspector of Q Division at that time and all crimes in Q Division were his crimes.

He had the head lights of the car turned on the sprawling body and saw that Rowley was still, incredibly, alive. He also saw that it would be impossible to move him far, and the police doctor, who arrived a few minutes later, supported him. Rowley was therefore carried with minute, painstaking care into the nearest house and placed on a sofa.

Four bullets had gone through him, two under the stomach and two through the chest, and one of them had almost severed the spinal cord paralysing speech and movement, so Lou Rowley lay for six hours, impotence and hatred in his eyes, unable to speak or write the name of the man who had shot him.

The tips of his fingers scrabbled once or twice against the rough sofa cover and the detectives and the doctor leaned forward hopefully, but that was all.

Just before three in the morning he died.

The Superintendent went home to bed and Hazlerigg started a search for the ejected cartridge cases. The street had been cordoned, and he found them all in the end, and took them down himself to the laboratory at Scotland Yard where the experts did a lot of work on them.

The bullets, in fact, were almost the only thing they had got to work on. It was a quiet, neat, cold, professional killing, with no loose ends at all.

"Rowley was in the stolen motorcar game," said Hazlerigg later to his assistant, Detective Sergeant Pickup. "There were at least three competitors in the business, any of whom could have wanted to cut him. I think we've checked them all three pretty thoroughly—"

"Ernie Morris was at the cinema – so he says. Heinie Jacobs was having supper at home with his wife – so he says, and so his wife says. Smiler Martin was playing cards with two friends – so they all say."

"In fact, it might have been any of them," agreed Hazlerigg.

And there the matter rested. The case was not closed because murder cases are never closed, but life went on in Q Division and a certain amount of dust gathered on the file.

Every police division in London has its great grandfather criminals, oldest inhabitants in the world of crime, rather pathetic figures, grizzled and broken by repeated descents into the grey undersea of penal servitude; men who have still not learned, despite a lifetime of object lessons, that crime is a disease and not a vocation.

Slater Joe was such. Though police records usually referred to him as Joseph Slater, in fact he had no surname, or if ever he had one he had lost it, with other things, in the far-off days of his infancy. "Slater," as will appear hereafter, was by way of being a reference to his professional activities.

Hazlerigg, on one of his endless rounds of routine visits, found the old man on his bed in an attic in Tool Street.

"Howde, Inspector," said Slater, "what can I do for you?"

"Nothing, Joe. Just keep on the straight and narrow." His eyes wandered speculatively round the room. There were hardly two sticks of furniture.

"My nose is always clean," said the old man. "I've never once been inside but I've been jobbed."

"How many times have you been inside, Joe?" asked Hazlerigg curiously.

"Thirty-nine times. Plants every one of them. I'll make it forty yet," he added illogically.

Hazlerigg said nothing. It was clear to him that the man was dying.

Late that night he had cause to think of Joe again, when he was called from his bed by an urgent message from the police station. Hazlerigg had the bottom floor of a small house in Carver Street. It was connected with Barley Lane Police Station by two lines, one of which the ill-disposed cut from time to time but the other of which was so deeply buried that they never got down to it.

"Slater's on the loose," said the desk sergeant.

"Loose," said Hazlerigg. "When I saw him this morning he didn't even look road worthy."

"He's raising hell, sir, down in that lodging house—"

"Who do you think I am," snarled Hazlerigg, "the district nurse?"

Nevertheless he climbed wearily into his trousers and, since it scarcely seemed worth calling out the squad car he rose round to Tool Street on his old pedal cycle.

He heard the noise from halfway down the street. When he got into the attic he was shocked at what he saw. Slater Joe, an unnatural flush on his cheeks, his thin white hair fuzzing up in streamers from his head, was being held, with difficulty, by two women. A young constable was trying to remonstrate with Slater, whilst making notes in a very new notebook. He was clearly out of his depth.

"—" screamed the old man, "—and—"

"Behaviour whereby a breach of the peace—" began the young constable hopefully."

"—you and—you. You want me to smarten you up. You want an old timer like me to keep you on your toes."

With a convulsive effort Slater freed his arms and jumped for the wash hand stand. He jerked open the drawer and as he swung round they saw he had a gleaming black Luger pistol in his hand.

The constable was plainly making up his mind to chance a heroic death when he felt a grip on his arm.

"Don't do anything silly," said Hazlerigg. "Your recruit training cost the state seven hundred pounds. You don't want to throw all that away on a crazy old coot. You go round one wall and I'll go round the other. Take it very steady."

Slater, in fact, put up very little opposition to this pincher movement. The fire seemed to have died, and he dropped the gun just before Hazlerigg got hold of his arm.

"That wasn't clever, Joe," said Hazlerigg. He picked up the automatic. It was loaded all right, and the safety catch was off. "You'll have to come along with us. It looks as if you may be making your fortieth trip after all."

Hazlerigg, however, was wrong. Slater Joe was taken along and lodged in the police infirmary; and before Hazlerigg got up for his breakfast the next morning a judge more prompt than any Justice of Quarter Session had called Joe to his account.

The office of a Divisional Detective Inspector is not likely to be a large or luxurious apartment. The whole Criminal Investigation staff at Q Division, Inspector Hazlerigg, Sergeant Pickup and two or three detectives (the number varied) lived, at that time, in two rooms and part of a corridor at the back of Barley Lane Police Station.

Nevertheless, to Hazlerigg the room was home. The scene of much routine work, many small triumphs, a few major disasters. The daily bread of a Divisional Detective Inspector. To this room he called Pickup a few days later and showed him a message. It was from Records at Scotland Yard, and like most communications from that august body, was brief and to the point.

"Test shots from Luger automatic handed in by you correspond in all particulars, striker point, striations and ejector marks with cartridges used in Rowley killing."

"Do you mean to say," said Pickup, "that that old goat—"

"No," said Hazlerigg. "I think not." He thought for a moment. "Have a word with the desk sergeant would you, and ask him if Slater said anything at all about that gun when he was brought in here to be charged."

Pickup was back in five minutes. "Here it is, sir," he said. "For what it's worth. Accused when asked where he had obtained the firearm said well, we can leave out the first part, that's just Joe's usual bird song. Then he said, 'On the Foreigners. I got it on the Foreigners.' He said this twice. What does it mean, sir?"

"I wouldn't go so far as to say I know what it meant," said Hazlerigg. "But I'm getting an idea about the shape of it. I've been doing some work on Joe's records. Do you know what most of his offences were? Stealing out of empty houses. He was an agile old boy, and as often as not he went for the lead on the roofs – the gutterings – that's how he got his name. Slater. You see it?"

"Not yet," said Pickup.

"You saw that gun, didn't you? It was a nice gun. A Luger Special, with the long twelve-bullet clip and night sights. It must have come home in someone's kit-bag at the end of the war. The man who had a gun like that wouldn't want to throw it away."

"I see, sir. You mean the man who killed Rowley was too fond of his gun to chuck it in the Thames. He hid it, as he thought, in a safe place."

"That's it. Some special hiding place, right in among the rafters. You'd probably never find it, from underneath. But old Joe, on one of his nightly prowls, ripped off the lead *from on top.*"

"Then if we knew where Joe was that night."

"We do," said Hazlerigg. "We do. He was on the Foreigners."

"What's that, sir? Thieves slang? What does it mean?"

"I haven't the least idea."

"We might put a ghost in to try and pick it up."

"I think you've got something there," said Hazlerigg.

Thereafter a number of strangers came and went in that district. They blew up tyres at garages and carried trays in tea shops and one of them spoke at great length on street corners about the new Millennium and the Fascist State. They all seemed well supplied with money for the buying of rounds of beer and they were good listeners. Reports from them reached Inspector Hazlerigg from time to time.

"I think Heinie Jacobs is out," he said to Pickup. "The other two, Smiler and Ernie Morris, have ganged up on him. They've beaten hell out of one or two of his employees and he's shut up shop."

"He still might have shot Rowley before he went out of business."

"Well, he might," agreed Hazlerigg. "But I think it was one of those two strong-arm merchants."

At about this time, too, Ron Atkins appeared. His record in Q Division was short but colourful. He was charged with driving at excessive speed down a one-way street and, having apparently no money to pay his fine, took seven days. On the afternoon of his release a constable cautioned him for parking a lorry on the wrong side of the road, whereupon he got out and hit the constable in the eye. Reward, one month, without any option this time. When he came out from this he drifted by easy degrees into bad company and was seen going about a good deal with Lefty Moran and Tom Collins, two lesser members of Smiler Martin's happy family.

One night in late November some months after the events narrated above, Atkins was sitting in the saloon bar of the Green Man, drinking with his friends. Apart from Lefty and Tom there was present a certain Charlie Lewis, who was known to the initiated to be Smiler Martin's second-in-command. No doubt it was the result of the general bonhomie inspired by the presence of such a distinguished person which emboldened Atkins to make a suggestion to his friends. The question had arisen, as it will arise sooner or later in the best drinking parties, as to whether a change of scene might not be a good idea.

Various possibilities were examined and it was then that Atkins put forward his contribution.

"Why don't we have the next one at the Foreigners?" he said.

The silence which greeted this innocent suggestion was remarkable. It was Charlie Lewes himself who finally answered, and it might have been observed, had there been anyone else in the saloon bar to observe it, that his right hand was in his jacket pocket as he spoke.

"Quite an idea," he said. "Yes, why don't we?"

"We've got a car outside," said Lefty Moran thoughtfully.

"What are we waiting for then?" said Lewes.

A small person in the four-ale bar, who had been listening to this conversation through a convenient crack in the partition, slipped out at the same time and made his way hastily to a call box.

"They've got Pollock," said Hazlerigg.

There was a hastily summoned conference in his room. Two Flying Squad cars were standing by in the alley outside.

"He's been calling himself Atkins. He was getting in very nicely with the Martin crowd. Apparently tonight something went wrong. I've just had Mousey Williams on the phone."

"Has he been followed?" said the Superintendent.

"We had him covered, sir," said Hazlerigg. "But they took him off by car. Our man was shaken off here." He put a finger on the map. "They were making for the canal."

"So you don't know to within six streets each way where they've gone to earth."

"We could comb that area, but it might take twenty-four hours."

"If I know Martin," said the Superintendent, "Pollock will be past caring by then, even if you did find him."

It was at that moment that Hazlerigg had his inspiration.

He said to Pickup, "Get a list of all the cafés, shops, and public houses in those streets."

Police headquarters have odd but effective sources of information and in a few minutes the list was there.

"'Rising Sun,' 'Crown & Thistle,' 'Ace Café,' 'Domino Tea Shop,' 'The English Bard' – There it is."

"English Bard," said the Superintendent. "I don't see—"

But Hazlerigg was already halfway down the passage.

The English Bard is a sordid remnant of what was once quite a nice little canal-side public house. In fact, it is half a public house, having been sliced in two by a bomb in 1943. The brewers who owned it had done some temporary repairs and then left it to rot quietly.

It was easy to see how Smiler Martin, who was doing most of the talking, had acquired his name. He was a large, genial, blond person and the electric light glittered back expensively from his 18-carat smile.

"Do you see the joke," he was saying.

"Not yet," said Pollock.

"About the name?"

"In a way," said Pollock. "English barred. Foreigners only. That sort of thing."

"The real joke," said Smiler, "was *how did you know about it*? That's the real joke."

"Oh, these things get round."

"Like hell they do. Only six people ever knew that name." (Martin was wrong, of course; he had forgotten the late Slater Joe, who knew all the catchwords in the world of crime.) "When you came out with it like that – well, it was a plain tipoff, wasn't it?"

Pollock said nothing. He was listening, hard, to something that seemed to be happening in the room underneath.

"You weren't one of us." Martin flicked an expensive cigarette lighter on and off thoughtfully. "So you must have been a nosey little slop. An undercover boy. That's right, isn't it?"

Pollock still said nothing.

"Well, if you don't want to talk," said Martin, and his smile was broader than ever, "we could try a little of the well-known heat treatment."

"I wouldn't do it," said Hazlerigg from the doorway. "Really I wouldn't. Now don't start looking for guns. I've got fifteen men on the premises and another twelve on the street. The odds are too long."

Even as he spoke the room was filling with policemen.

"Alfred Martin," went on Hazlerigg, "I am charging you with the murder on the night of March 15th of Louis Rowley."

Which is really the beginning and end of this story.

Reveille, January 27-29, 1950.

TICKER BATSON'S LAST JOB

LONDON HAS BEEN THE SLOWEST to rebuild of all capital cities. Stand at the junction of High Road with South Street and you will still look over an area of devastation. Low walls of yellow brick, like the bases of demolished honeycombs, acres of bindweed, hiding the rusty metal.

Among it all one freshly-painted notice still proclaims: *BUSINESS AS USUAL*. That is the High Road Safe Deposit.

Nor is this "Business as usual" notice difficult to understand, since the essential portions of this undertaking – the guts, as it were – lie between 30 and 80 feet below the surface.

Like the seven circles of Dante's Inferno, the richest and most valuable deposits stand lowest in the descending scale.

The bottom two storeys, which are mostly used by banks for the storage of surplus currency, were constructed with the additional protection of a subterranean "water jacket."

The cement walls that surround them were built "double" with a fair-sized hollow space between them. This space was then filled with water.

At the height of the blitz the authorities decided that it would be safer to remove the water. It has never been replaced.

Early this year Messrs. Up-to-Date Office Properties, who owned most of the surface space under which the safe deposits lay, started rebuilding.

Early in the morning and late at night the automatic drills of their clearance squads beat out a devilish tattoo, and the steel fingers of their automatic excavators reached deeper and deeper into the earth – to the considerable satisfaction of Ticker Batson, king of the safebreakers, who was in favour of all the covering noise he could get.

"Ticker" was a nickname he had had before the Army, but he had plenty of others. The one he liked least was Dynamite Bill. After all, as he said, a man has his pride. He had never in his life tried to blast a safe with plain dynamite – which would be a silly thing to use anyway.

Undoubtedly, though, he understood the natures, the uses and the abuses of explosives.

At first he worked almost exclusively with gelignite, which is rather like a mixture of dynamite and toffee.

Later he became attached to commercial tonite. He said it blew a cleaner hole. It was with a single plastic charge of tonite that he took the lock out of the safe of the West London Ice Stadium two years ago.

So certain and so professional had his touch been that Inspector Hazlerigg – he was D.D.I. of Q Division at the time – took one look at the damage and said: "That's Ticker."

Now, determined to pull off one last stupendous job and retire on the proceeds, Ticker had hired an office near the High Road Safe Deposit (under the original name and title of "Jones, Agent") which gave him sole use of a sub-basement storage room.

Mr. Jones may not have appeared to entertain many clients in his office by day, but he certainly spent a lot of time in his underground store.

On occasions, indeed – had there been anyone interested enough to observe it – it would have been noticed that he entered the room in the evening and did not emerge until the following morning.

It was about this time that the U.0.P. discovered that it does not always pay to hustle.

One morning – work had been in progress for about three weeks – a War Office shooting brake drove up to the foreman's office and a Staff Officer got out. The foreman listened to the Staff Officer, hurried back into the hut, and made a telephone call.

At the other end of the line a stout gentleman, who was about to go out for his morning coffee, swore when he heard the words "unexploded bomb," and dialled a number.

A director was contacted as he was leaving his house at Weybridge and in a surprisingly short time had been driven to the High Road site. The War Office car was still there.

"I can't understand it," said the director. "Yes, I did know that you couldn't excavate a blitzed site without a War Office clearance, but surely—"

"Mightn't it be a good thing to stop those drills?" suggested the Staff Officer.

"Yes, of course."

The foreman left the hut and shouted an order. One by one the drills and the excavators slowed down and stopped. Even the picks and shovels ceased to ring. A great silence settled.

"How long will you be?" asked Inspector Hazlerigg.

"Difficult to say." The speaker was a very young, very blond, very serious subaltern of Royal Engineers, who wore the Bomb Disposal flash on the upper arm of his neat battledress jacket.

"How deep would she go?"

"That's difficult to say, too. If she went in close to that outer wall"— he pointed to the sheer concrete casing of the safe deposit which the excavations had laid bare—"she might go a long way. Once the earth's been disturbed, you see . . ."

"Twice as far as they've gone already?"

"Might be."

"I suppose there's not much chance she could be active after all that time?"

"You never know," said the subaltern. He thought for a moment and added: "I don't suppose she liked all this drilling one little bit . . ."

By nightfall the hole gaped blackly under the arc lamps, and the only noise was the clanking of the bucket hoist and a very distant, very quiet chink of steel shovel against stone. A head appeared.

"We seem to be on to something, all right."

The subaltern sounded tired, but cheerful.

"It's quite a setup when you get down. There's a sort of ledge – it's a shelf really – running out from the foot of the wall. I thought at first we'd struck the actual foundation of the wall, but it can't be that – it's hollow."

Hazlerigg had his torch on a roll of plans which he had borrowed from the manager of the safe deposit.

"I think you're breaking into the old water jacket," he said. "It's all right. You'll find it's quite dry now. If the bomb went in there it shouldn't be difficult to spot it."

There was a muffled cry from the bottom of the shaft and the subaltern bent his head to listen.

"We're in," he said. "Get me one of the knotted ropes and a pick helve. I'll go down first and poke around."

"Do you mind if I come with you?" asked Hazlerigg.

"On your own head," said the subaltern.

After a breathless five minutes both men were standing inside the "water jacket."

It was like a narrow, very roughly finished, semicircular, underground subway. The floor was uncemented rubble. It was not exactly airless, but it had the unhealthy, breathless feeling of some old tomb unexpectedly thrown open.

The subaltern had unconsciously lowered his voice.

"What a hole," he said. "And, my God, there she is."

The bomb looked enormous.

It lay, half on its side, in a drift of rubble.

"Must have gone clean through the casing into the drink." Again it was the subaltern. Hazlerigg's mouth was too dry for speech. "When they drained the water away it just came down on to its side."

Hazlerigg still found nothing to say. He was overcome by the mere bulk of the bomb. He had never looked at one before, not at such close quarters.

"Funny to think" said the subaltern, "that we're the first people to set eyes on her since she left her bomb rack in 1940."

The silence which succeeded this remark was unexpectedly broken.

A quiet, a deferential cough sounded behind them. Both torches swung round. Seated on a pile of rubble, blinking up at them, was a little, dust-covered old man.

Hazlerigg found his voice at last. "Ticker?"

"That's right, Inspector."

"What—?" The torch swivelled up the wall, and showed the newly-cut entrance of the tunnel. "I see. Moling again."

"Just ferreting around," said the old man. "No harm done, I hope." The note of determined cheerfulness in his voice lowered the tension, and Hazlerigg grinned.

"If that isn't felonious intent," he said, "then I'm the Commissioner of Police for the Metropolis. Never mind that, I'll think about you in a moment. We've got a job here."

"Beauty, isn't she?" said Ticker.

"Yes," said the subaltern. He seemed quite disinterested in Ticker's sudden appearance.

"What would you guess she had inside her, Lieutenant?"

"Ammonite, I expect."

"Surely, surely," said the old man. "Ammonite B or Ammonite D, would you say?"

"D, I expect."

"When was it dropped?"

"December, 1940—"

"Couldn't have been D, then. Wasn't in use till spring 1941."

"Nor was it, now," said the subaltern. He looked at the old man thoughtfully. "Well if it's B, so much the better. Less sensitive. One thing about these big fellows. They had to make the works on a large, simple scale. No funny jobs. It'll just be a case of taking the fuse out. The locking nut's rusted solid, of course. We'll have to cut that away."

He propped his torch on a ledge in the wall and took out of the haversack on his back an ordinary metal saw. "If you gentlemen are sure you want to watch . . ."

Now that it came to the point, Hazlerigg wasn't at all sure that he did. The size of the bomb in that confined space was overpowering. It was like sharing a bed with an elephant. The opposition, however, came from an unexpected quarter.

"Lieutenant," said Ticker, quietly, "you mustn't do it."

The subaltern said nothing. He raised his eyes from an adjustment he was making to the saw.

"I've been watching that bomb. I was alone with it more than an hour before you gentlemen came." The old man lowered his voice. "That bomb's angry," he said.

The subaltern still said nothing.

"You know what ammonite's like, sir. It hates heat and worse than heat it hates noise. Week after week they've been drilling and rattling up there, and now it's thoroughly upset. I know. I've been handling explosives all my life."

The subaltern looked at Hazlerigg.

"That last part's true, anyway," said the Inspector, absently. He was wondering whether he was going to be sick.

"I see," said the subaltern. "You think if I cut that bolt the friction of the sawblade may set her off?"

"No 'may' about it." The old man laid his hand almost affectionately on the plump flank of the bomb. "If you listen." he said, "you can almost hear it making up its mind."

"I'm afraid it's a chance I've got to take," said the subaltern.

He sounded neither convinced nor unconvinced.

"All right. You take your chances. But don't you bet against yourself. There's no sense in that, is there?"

"What do you suggest?"

It was one consultant to another.

"Ice," said the old man. "Dry ice, and plenty of it. That's the first thing."

"Where can we get ice at this time of night?"

"I'll have all you need here inside the hour," said Hazlerigg. "I'll get it from the refrigerators at Smithfield." He hoped he didn't sound too eager.

He was better than his word. It was fifty minutes later when the second big sack of ice had been lowered down the shaft. As he was about to follow a shout came up to him.

"Can you get a portable wireless set?"

"Certainly," said Hazlerigg. "You wouldn't like a cocktail cabinet as well?"

"No – just a wireless. Only hurry. We want to get going before the Light Programme finishes."

When Hazlerigg finally got back with the wireless – he had borrowed one from the nearest police canteen – he found that in his absence one or two changes had taken place.

A flex had been run into the shaft and a single bright, unshaded bulb illuminated every detail in the cavern.

The patient had been lowered very gently on to her back and wedged with huge wooden wedges against lateral rolling. She was covered from head to foot with ice packs.

The sapper was demonstrating something by means of a diagram he was drawing with chalk on the wall – but Hazlerigg got the impression that it was the old man who was really in charge of operations.

"I can't explain it," he was saying, "any more than I can explain about cows and milk. But they both like certain sorts of music. I *know*. I had to carry some gelignite half a mile once when it was in a very awkward frame of mind. I played to it all the way, on my mouth-organ."

Hazlerigg twiddled a knob and an educated voice said: "The String Quartets of Purcell—"

"For God's sake," said Ticker. "That's the Third Programme! Do you want to blow us all up? Try for Joe Loss."

As long as he lives, Hazlerigg will never forget the final scene. The bright light, the intent faces of the two experts. Ticker Batson's hand – long, muscular, and quietly controlled in its least movement – the hand of a brain specialist.

It was Ticker who did the cutting, and he used a long, oddly articulated saw with a thin blue blade which he had brought, furtively but lovingly, from an inner pocket.

"Whee-teedle-de-dee," said the saxophone, lovingly.

"Zi-hing, zi-hing." Ticker's saw went backwards and forwards as steadily and smoothly as the arm of a metronome.

Then the last blinding minute when the wrench was put on and both men heaved together.

Chief Inspector Hazlerigg's stomach turned right over as the big fuse came slowly off.

"That was Ticker's last job," said Hazlerigg. "He's living on an annuity now. The U.0.P. bought it for him. I don't know how much it cost them, but it was cheap at the price of what they'd have had to pay, in costs and damages, if that bomb had gone off.

"When I called on him the other day, I noticed a little gold cup on his mantelpiece. He tells me it was given him by the safe deposit people as a mark of their esteem for his efforts that night; which is quite funny, when you come to think of it."

Manchester *Sunday Chronicle,* May 7, 1950.

SOMETHING LIKE HARD WORK

FASHIONS CHANGE FASTER than human nature. Fifty years ago the Scotland Yard detective was a big blundering booby with no imagination, no luck and size twelve boots: you remember Lestrade.

Nowadays he gets rather more of his just desserts.

Even his severest critics recognise him as a worker: a professional, who gets his results like other professionals more by perspiration than by inspiration,

What isn't realised, even yet, though, is that in detection the hardest work can be the work that is done by the human brain. I cite the case of Miss Hatter.

Miss Hatter was a quiet old lady. She lived in Osbaldestone Road in Highbury and she occupied the floor of a house which had been built about the time of the Great Exhibition for an upper middle-class family and had been going slowly downhill ever since.

When it was first put up, Osbaldestone Road was a back street. Then, when they opened the new bypass and turned the northbound traffic into it, it became a highway overnight. And most of the front gardens were over-built with one storey shops and most of the quiet house-owners left, and the house got divided into flats, and people like Miss Hatter came in.

Miss Hatter didn't mind the traffic that roared past her window. She was a little deaf, and she found it companionable. Also, as transpired later, she has another reason for liking it.

It was never suggested that she was odd – not even that she was a recluse, in the proper sense of the word. She said good morning to her acquaintances when she met them in the queues, and she was quite sensible, and her rooms were reasonably clean. She didn't keep sixteen cats, or suffer from dangerous delusions, or anticipate the End of the World.

She just kept herself to herself.

One late afternoon, in early autumn, the ground-floor-front, not having heard Miss Hatter moving for nearly twenty-four hours, got alarmed and called the police. And the police said, oh dear, another of those, is it, and went back with the ground-floor-front and upstairs and opened the door – it wasn't locked, you just walked upstairs and straight in – and they found Miss Hatter.

Only it wasn't quite what they'd expected. It wasn't a stroke or heart failure or cumulative malnutrition.

Miss Hatter's head had been beaten in.

Quite early in the investigation Chief Inspector Hazlerigg – he was D.D.I at the time – put his finger on it when said to his Superintendent, "It's difficult, sir, to believe that anyone could have been so completely *alone*. She has no family. Her father and mother are dead. Her only sister lives in South Africa – they sent each other a card every Christmas. She's one or two acquaintances – shop and street acquaintances – nothing more."

"What did she live on?" said the Superintendent.

"Dividends," said Hazlerigg. He produced a thick, much folded bundle of multi-coloured script, and the Superintendent glanced through them.

"Good stuff," he said. "Quite a lot of it, too. Well, this is one of the things the murderer may have been looking for."

"He'd have had his work cut out to find them," said Hazlerigg. "Unless he'd known exactly where to look." He explained where his searchers had found them.

"Very ingenious," said the Superintendent. "Wonderful ideas these old ladies get. You'd think they'd never heard of banks. Was she killed for these—?"

"I don't think so," said Hazlerigg. "After all, share certificates aren't like bearer bonds. They're not a lot of use except to the owner. I think she was more likely killed for cash."

"Cash?"

Hazlerigg explained. "These shares would bring her in about five hundred a year. I've had her budget checked up as closely as I can. Her room cost her a pound a week – she spent about a pound a week on food. She never went out – except to shop and go to church on Sunday evenings. She didn't give to charities. She hated holidays. She *must have* saved something like £300 a year – probably more."

"How long had she been at Osbaldestone Road?"

"Ten years."

"Three thousand pounds, probably in bank notes," said the Superintendent thoughtfully. "Yes, I suppose that could be quite a motive. I suppose she kept it in an old stocking. Did she have any visitors."

"We've traced three, so far. Her landlady came up sometimes – to join her in a cup of tea—"

"It didn't look to me like a woman's crime," said the Superintendent.

"No, sir. Then the vicar visited her about once a month."

"Hmmm—"

"And a distant cousin, a Mr. Webb. He's almost her only relative in London. He says he saw her last sometime in early summer. And before that, about Christmas. A big, beery person. I think he's an insurance toot. Looked as if he could have done with the money, too."

"Sounds more hopeful than the vicar," agreed the Superintendent. "I suppose you—"

"Oh, yes. Nothing to go on at all. He lives in a basement flat at Muswell Hill. Keeps his own car. Comes and goes as he likes. He says he was in bed all that day and most of the next – with flu."

"Let me see now." The Superintendent ruffled through the files. "It was pretty certain that she was killed on the evening of Thursday, wasn't it? The day before we were called in?"

"Yes. Between four and six in the evening."

"About dusk – and there was a bit of fog."

"That's right."

"And there's no reason to suppose that the murderer was someone who had visited her before."

"Except that he seemed to know where the money was – if it was money he came for. There was no sign of a search having been made."

"It's a point. But he might be a visitor we haven't found out about."

"Yes."

"Or someone who knew where the money was but hadn't actually been there before."

"Yes."

"In fact, almost anyone could have walked in, in the dusk, knocked out Miss Hatter and helped himself."

"Yes."

"Then we haven't really got anywhere at all."

"Not yet, sir," said Hazlerigg.

That was when the work started.

Everything in the room was taken out for scrutiny. Everything was listed and docketed and tested for fingerprints, and scrutinised and, if it looked interesting, photographed in several positions.

The only fingerprints which came to light were Miss Hatter's and her landlady's, except for a broad and masculine looking set, which caused some excitement until they were proved to belong to the Superintendent, who had absent-mindedly placed one hand on the mantelpiece when viewing the scene of the crime.

Altogether a number of objects were unearthed which cast odd sidelights on the day by day existence of a solitary and religious minded old lady, but only one item proved in any way puzzling.

Inspector Hazlerigg sat in his office looking at it – or rather at them, for the exhibit was six thick exercise books. They were well thumbed but neat and legible. They contained about forty plain ruled foolscap sized pages, and five of the books were full (and the sixth almost full) of Miss Hatter's neat writing.

"Do you think it's some sort of code?" suggested Sergeant Pickup.

"If Miss Hatter was the emissary of a foreign power—" said

Hazlerigg slowly, "I'm—I'm Dick Turpin."

"What does it mean, then?"

"GR DAI WRG 9072 B WP 2436 BL CHE GG 909," said Hazlerigg. "I tried it on the cypher people, but they couldn't get anywhere with it – or they haven't done yet. They're still trying."

"Looks too logical to be a cypher," said Pickup. "I mean – it's mad but it sort of looks sensible at the same time."

"If you can make sense out of that—" said Hazlerigg irritably. He had missed his sleep for two nights and was beginning to feel it.

"RD TRI PBL 4208 TB GO 2323 BL FD 8 PR 9293."

"What's that you've got there," said the Superintendent.

Hazlerigg climbed wearily to his feet.

"It's those books, sir," he said. "We found one actually under Miss Hatter's chair and the others in a cupboard."

"My goodness," said the Superintendent. He was staring at the last five groups. "BL FD PR 9293. What a coincidence."

"What is it, sir?"

"It's me," said the Superintendent.

His subordinates looked at him blankly.

"My car, I mean. A blue Ford-8. Registration number PR 9293."

"A car watcher," said Hazlerigg and Pickup simultaneously.

"I always wondered how she spent all her spare time," said the Superintendent.

That was when they *really* got down to work.

"It's all we've got to go on," said Hazlerigg. "We'll do it systematically."

He had the whole of the detective staff of the division at it, and it wasn't long before the uniformed branch were called in as well. Anyone with a quarter of a moment to spare found themselves involved in Hazlerigg's motor car game.

He early discovered that there is a great division in the ranks of mankind. Some know about motor cars. Others don't.

Probationary Detective Constable Walkinshaw, for instance, immediately solved BL CHE. "Blue Chevrolet," he said. "That's the doctor's little job. I've seen it up and down the streets this last six months. He had a grey Riley coupe before and before that a black drop-head—"

"You're on," said Hazlerigg and enrolled him permanently.

There were two hundred and twenty-seven closely written pages to be sorted out and interpreted.

"I wish she'd dated 'em," said Sergeant Pickup.

"Well, we can place some of them from the doctor's visits," said Hazlerigg. "Get hold of his log book."

"And the bus schedules," suggested Pickup. They had soon spotted the difference between "B" and "TB." "You see what I mean. The trolley buses have to keep to the same order, they can't pass each other. But the petrol buses are sometimes ahead and sometimes behind—"

"Where's it all going to get you to when you have worked it out?" asked Inspector Martin, who had come over from a neighbouring division on other business and had already overstayed his intended visit by more than three hours, and incidentally had covered himself with glory by identifying SG TV as "small green tradesman's van" and a very mysterious entry H ? M 3 ? 24 as a motor hearse belonging to the local undertaker.

"I've no idea," said Hazlerigg cheerfully. His eyes were gritty from lack of sleep, but he was lit by the invisible flame which warms a policeman with the inner certainty that he is on to something good.

"I think I've got the hang of those odd little sections when none of the regulars seem to put in an appearance," said Pickup. "I think they were times when she couldn't sleep. There's a big overhead street light outside her house, and she could play this game just as well after dark—"

"Of course," said Hazlerigg softly. "They must be the all-night lorries coming into London. Check with the Road Transport people."

This proved unexpectedly to be the first fruits of their work, because Road Transport identified all the lorries very easily except for one, an "S BV RT ?? 55" (which in Miss Hatter's shorthand was a very small black van) and which proved to belong to an enterprising gentleman who ran stolen poultry into London for the early market, and was extremely upset when an accurate schedule of his movements was produced for him to explain.

"They can't say we're wasting our time," said Hazlerigg. "Press on."

They were getting good at it now. They could identify their "regulars" at a glance and dates, and even times of day were become increasingly certain.

The end came quite suddenly, as the end often does.

"Didn't that chap Webb say he'd visited Miss Hatter in midsummer? What's his car – an Austin-7 RHQ 3232? Here you are – June 15th – about tea time."

"And before that at Christmas," said Pickup. They found that one too without any difficulty.

"My God," said Hazlerigg. "What fools we've been."

In silence they turned back to the last book – the one they had found actually under Miss Hatter's chair. It was the last entry but one on the last page.

"A 7 RHQ 3232."

"And Webb," said Hazlerigg, "was in bed all day with a cold, was he?" He reached for the telephone.

London *Evening Standard July* 11, 1950.

BALLOONS WILL BE RELEASED

LUIGI DONATELLO, A NATIVE OF CREMONA, a temporary citizen of Great Britain and an inhabitant of Bury Gate – which is part of Q Division in the Metropolitan Police District of London – was the only man whom Hazlerigg had ever heard speak of "the British way" as if he understood what he was talking about. This may only be one more example of the well-known fact that it takes a foreigner to understand an Englishman.

Hazlerigg was Divisional Detective Inspector of Q Division at that time. He had held the post for nearly three days, and he was already beginning to experience the fascination of a first independent command; a command, moreover, of those peculiar streets and alleys, those blind courts and echoing railway yards, that ribbon of concrete which the embryo of the Great North Road, that grey, greasy serpent which the birthplace of the Grand Union Canal, and all the corners and pieces which make up one of the most difficult, most interesting, police districts in London.

Hazlerigg heard about Luigi on his first day in office. His temporary second-in-command, Inspector Hodges, appeared on duty with a yellow face and grey pockets under his eyes. In a less abstemious man these might have been the signs of a considerable hangover, but Hazlerigg knew Hodges well. He was a solid West Countryman, with a liking for draught cider and a head like iron.

"I can't understand it," he said, "but I'm never going to take a chance on Luigi again."

"Who's Luigi?"

"Italian. He runs a restaurant off Bury Market. The wife and I have been going there for months. At first I thought the food was a bit fussy – foreign, you know. Then I got to liking it."

"An Italian restaurant," said Hazlerigg incredulously. "In Bury Gate! Do they get any customers?"

"As a matter of fact," said Hodges, "they do. I thought just the same myself when I saw the board go up. It was the sort of place that might do well enough in Soho, but not up here. The wife and I looked in as a bit of a joke. The food was so damned good we've been going back ever since – and so have plenty of other people, characters who normally use the fish-and-chip emporiums."

"It doesn't seem to have been too good last night," said Hazlerigg. "By the way, how do you know it was Luigi's food? It might have been something you had somewhere else."

"It might," said Hodges, "but it doesn't seem—excuse me a moment, the ship's still rocking." He disappeared. When he came back ten minutes later, he was pale, but more composed. "I think that's the last of it," he said. "As I was saying, I don't see what else it can have been, barring Luigi's. I never had time for any tea yesterday, and my wife and I went straight there when I came off duty. She's got it, too, worse than I have."

"It certainly sounds like it," said Hazlerigg. "It might be food poisoning. Would you like me to get the town hall on to it?"

Hodges looked quite upset. "Oh, no," he said. "I wouldn't want that. He's a decent little man, really. I wouldn't trouble about it. Not unless there are other complaints."

There were no other complaints and Hazlerigg forgot the matter. It came back to his mind three days later when he found himself in one of the small streets behind Bury Market, and saw the name "Luigi Donatello" in gold on white, and underneath in smaller letters, "Cooking in the Italian manner." It was past seven o'clock and, as Hazlerigg's new landlady had no mind above Irish stew, he pushed in.

He found himself in a big, single, ground floor room, with a curtained staircase at the back leading to the upper parts of the house, a partitioned doorway to the kitchen in one corner, and a door leading to the manager's office in the other. There were bad oil paintings of Italian beauty spots on the panels round the walls, and everything was very new and clean and had that smell of chicory and garlic and fresh coffee which makes up most of the charm of Soho. It was certainly an unusual smell for Bury Market.

While he was waiting for his food to come, he tried to answer a question that had been puzzling him. If Luigi was the master chef that Hodges made out, why had he come to Bury Gate? It wasn't a slum, by any means, but its inhabitants were people whose normal idea of dining out was fish and chips. Perhaps Hodges was right. They had come to laugh and stayed to pay. Maybe Luigi had reasoned it out for himself that they would do just that. And certainly this way he would avoid the cut-throat competition (and mad overheads) of the West End.

It was an interesting speculation, interrupted by the arrival of Luigi himself. The restaurateur was an olive-skinned Italian of medium height, whose long nose, shrewd eyes and plumb, firm chin, combined to give him an appearance curiously like that of the young Bonaparte.

He brought the *ravioli-au-jus* and the river trout which followed it. He decanted the red wine from a wicker flask with a care and reverence which suggested a Chateau-bottled claret – which it certainly was not, though very drinkable – and he filled and refilled Hazlerigg's cup with strong, black coffee, all with a sort of dynamic cheerfulness. But somewhere behind his grey eyes there lurked an abstraction, something which, in a less composed person, might have been described as an anxiety.

Hazlerigg wondered at first if Luigi had identified him. He thought not. He had only a few days in the division and had never worked in that part of London before. He made up his mind that he would take the opportunity of introducing himself when he congratulated his host on the dinner, and he had raised his hand to call for his bill when he checked the movement. A group at a table in the corner caught his eye.

The big man with the sleek, shiny black hair and the big nose, he had met before. His name was Sparks; he was a minor racketeer. One of his companions, a thick, stupid-looking man, with a red face, was an ex-boxer called Coulan. The third, a smaller, quieter person, with the look of a lawyer gone to seed, was unknown to him.

Sparks said something in his loud voice, and Luigi hurried across to his table. Sparks had half risen to his feet and was about to repeat his words when, across the width of the room, his eye caught Hazlerigg's. He broke off the sentence and sat back in his chair. He said something to Coulan and they both looked in Hazlerigg's direction. Luigi backed away from the table, and hurried into his office. That was all.

Hazlerigg paid the waiter and went thoughtfully back to the station. Hodges was on late duty, and he put a question to him.

"Yes," said Hodges, "I know Sparks. It's difficult to say exactly what he does, but I should describe him as a troublemaker. He's got a finger in most of the dirt in this division. Coulan's his bodyguard. I can't place the little chap, but we can probably turn him up in Records."

"Do you think Luigi might be in with them?" asked Hazlerigg. "They seemed to know each other – the restaurant might be a rendez-vous – something of that sort."

Hodges looked surprised. "I never thought about it," he said. "We've never had any complaints about Luigi."

"Well, he hasn't been here very long, has he?" said Hazlerigg. "He might be worth keeping an eye on. I think I'll drop in from time to time myself."

Having formed this resolution, Hazlerigg found so much to do in his new job that he forgot all about it, and it was chance and hunger again, not design, which brought him to Luigi's restaurant two weeks later.

It was a visit he had every reason to remember. It started with an excellent minestrone and it ended in a shower bath.

He had a table at the far end of the room, beside the rise of the staircase. He had finished the first course and was studying the long, handwritten menu in purple pencil when something dropped on the back of his head. It felt like a fly and he was about to put a hand up to brush it away when a steady jet of cold water hit him on the nape of his neck, just above his collar.

He jumped to his feet, knocking the chair sideways into the married couple sitting on his left, and looked round him for an explanation. He saw at once that the water was coming through the ceiling directly above his head.

Next moment he was overwhelmed in a flurry of management. Luigi arrived at a trot, spat something at the waiter, muttered something incomprehensible, but clearly placatory, to Hazlerigg, and disappeared up the stairs. The waiter seized a napkin with one hand and started to mop Hazlerigg's head, and with the other hand swept an empty soup bowl under the downpour, which was increasing.

In the excitement, a carafe of wine got knocked on to the floor and the married couple removed themselves to an empty table on the other side of the room. As they went, the man remarked to the woman: "Never a dull moment here." He didn't sound amused, all the same.

The next thing that happened was that a woman appeared from the kitchen, grabbed Hazlerigg by the arm and led him out into the office. She didn't seem to speak much English, but she produced a towel. Hazlerigg took it from her and assured her that he was quite all right. This was not strictly true, because his collar was a damp rag and he had a feeling that some water had got down into the small of his back, but the woman was so obviously distressed that most of his irritation vanished.

At this moment, Luigi reappeared. "It was the bullcock," he said.

"I beg your pardon?" said Hazlerigg.

"The bullcock in the cistern."

"Oh – the ballcock. Yes. Very tricky things, ballcocks." Hazlerigg was combing his tousled hair and looking into a mirror over the mantelpiece. Without turning his head he added: "Someone wedge it down?"

He saw all the answer reflected on Luigi's expressive Latin face, and he turned slowly. "Hadn't you better let me in on this?" he said.

"I do not understand."

"You know who I am, don't you?"

"Si – you are the head of the detectives."

"Well, not yet," said Hazlerigg. "But I'm head of them in this district. If you were having any trouble"—he chose his words carefully—"I should be the person you would come to first."

"Trouble?" said Luigi. "Now what sort of trouble would you mean?" His eyes looked sick.

"Brawls in your restaurant, foreign matter in your food, water all over your customers. That sort of trouble." Still Luigi said nothing.

"Trouble," Hazlerigg went on, "caused by people who have warned you that if you report it to the police you will get it twice as hot – and have suggested, too, I dare say, that the only result of your dealings with the police will be that they will oppose your licence and have you shut down."

He saw that this one was right on the mark.

"We won't mention any names," he said, striking while the iron was hot, "but if you'd like to tell me exactly what Mr. S—shall we call him?—is up to, I'll see what we can do."

"Clearly you know everything," said Luigi. "I was a fool not to come to you sooner. These men terrify me."

"What do they actually do?"

"All that they can possibly do to drive me out of business. This evening you saw – you felt—"

"This evening I felt," agreed Hazlerigg.

"Someone must have broken in upstairs. It would not be difficult. During dinner we are all busy. A wedge was pushed in under the arm of the float. The overflow pipe had been blocked, also."

"Have they played any more tricks like that on you?"

"Many. Some weeks ago they ruined my wine. I buy the ordinary white and red wine in six-gallon flasks. They ruined a whole flask."

"What did they put in it?"

Luigi told him, and Hazlerigg wrinkled his lip in disgust. "Yes," he said. "Not pretty. That must have been the night Inspector Hodges and his wife were so ill. I wonder why no one else complained."

"Inspector Hodges was the first I served from the new flask. When I was clearing the table, I smelt the wine that was left in the glasses. I knew something was wrong. I threw away all that was left – nearly six gallons. It broke my heart."

"It won't only be your heart that will be broken if you go on at that rate," said Hazlerigg. "Has anything else happened?"

"Yes, much else. Often much worse. One night those three men came in. They complained of the food and one of them sicked."

"Sicked?"

"Yes. He vomited." Luigi sounded so comically distressed when he said this that Hazlerigg almost laughed, but a look at the little man's face stopped him.

"You're sure it was nothing in the food?"

"The food was of the best. Also, they told me afterwards that it had all been arranged. The red-faced man told me that he could vomit when he wished. It was an accomplishment, you understand?"

"Did they say why they were doing it? Have they asked for money?"

"They do not ask me for money."

"Pity," said Hazlerigg. "It might make it easier if they did – easier from my point of view, I mean. What are they after?"

"They wish to drive me out of business."

Hazlerigg nodded slowly. It was much as he had thought. A foreigner, coming newly into the district and opening a highly successful restaurant, was bound to make enemies. Other restaurant owners, less successful or less scrupulous, might think it worth their while to hire Sparks and his circus. It tied in, too, with his previous idea that the North London fish-and-chip brigade represented fairly solid money to the man capable of exploiting them.

Nevertheless, it was difficult. A Divisional Detective Inspector in his division is like a headmaster in a school. He must keep order, but he must draw that firm, invisible line that runs between discipline and interference. He must put down flagrant bullying, but he must not seem to go out of his way to protect the person who is being bullied. Too much protection may, in the long run, hurt the victim more than too little. And apart from all that, what offence does a man commit if he is deliberately sick in a restaurant?

Hazlerigg tried to convey some of this to Luigi. "One of the difficulties is," he concluded, "that even if you asked for protection, it couldn't go on forever. All they've got to do is to bide their time. The difficulty is to get them to fight on *your ground* and in *your time.*" Luigi listened with exaggerated deference as the Inspector spoke. At the end of it his face lit up. *"Bemissimo,"* he said. "I understand exactly."

"Well, I only wish *I* did," said Hazlerigg.

"It is as you say. We must not tell tales. We must be sportsmen. That is the British way. And we must choose our own time and our own ground. That is right?"

"That's right," said Hazlerigg. He wondered exactly what ideas might be moving in Luigi's Napoleonic head.

Two months later he found out. He received a card. It was a handsome card, with a gilt-deckled edge, and it announced that Luigi Donatello, proprietor of Luigi's Italian Restaurant, intended to have a gala dinner on the Wednesday following, to celebrate the successful conclusion of his first six months in business. "Good Will and Good Cheer to all our Regular Patrons," it concluded. "Balloons will be Released."

"Balloons will be released," Hazlerigg repeated thoughtfully to himself. It seemed to be Luigi's idea of a gala occasion. And in Luigi's situation, a gala was plainly asking for trouble. He looked at the invitation again. There was an unmistakable air of cockiness about it.

He said to Hodges: "I don't see the boys resisting an invitation like that. I should imagine the balloon will go up and no mistake."

Then he noticed some writing on the back. "You will see, Inspector, that I am choosing my own place and time. It would cause me much pleasure if you would consent to be present – unofficially. Please arrive at eight o'clock – and might I ask you to come by the back entrance?"

At eight o'clock, on Wednesday evening, Hazlerigg made his way, unobtrusively, to Luigi's restaurant. He was admitted through the service door at the back by Luigi's wife. He took a quick look over his shoulder as he entered. He had been careful to use the back streets and was reasonably certain he hadn't been observed. But he couldn't be too sure.

Luigi's wife led the way into the office, where Hazlerigg saw that a table had been laid out for him. It was so placed that, without moving, he could see, through a crack in the door, the whole of the left side of the restaurant and, by means of a well-placed mirror, most of the right side, too.

Already, the party in the restaurant was beginning to warm up. Without any notable extravagance, Luigi had created a scene full of light and colour. The new, white tablecloths shone against the dark gold and red of the walls. There were chrysanthemums in vases, and high up, in the middle, hung the promised cluster of balloons. A wireless was playing softly and the room was already quite full.

Then it struck Hazlerigg that there was a curious waste of good floor space. The middle of the room, from the swing door which opened on the street to the stairs at the back, was clear of tables, which were crowded into the remaining space round the outside. It was too small a space for a dance floor. It almost looked as if Luigi was planning some very intimate cabaret turn.

The next thing he noticed was that Luigi had hired a new waiter for the occasion. He was above normal height and carried a good pair of shoulders under his evening coat. Hazlerigg was certain he had seen his face before.

His thoughts were interrupted by the entrance of Sparks and Coulan. Neither was drunk, though clearly both of them had been drinking.

Luigi hurried affably out of the shadows and, somewhat to Hazlerigg's surprise, offered them one of the most prominent tables in the room on the edge of the cleared space.

It was not difficult to see that both men were in for trouble. They laughed too loudly and too often, and some of their remarks had already caused offence to their neighbours. The climax came when the new waiter placed in front of them the dish they had just ordered.

"What do you call this?" said Coulan.

"Goulash, sir." At this moment, someone turned off the wireless, and in the sudden silence the waiter's voice sounded loud.

"Messed-up horse's guts," said Coulan. "Take it away and give me a steak."

"You do not like our food?"

"I hate the food, and I hate the place, and I hate to see a pretty boy dressed up like a performing monkey," said Coulan, and moving in his chair, he took a swipe at the waiter's face with his open hand. Only, by the time it arrived, the waiter was somewhere quite different.

He moved back a couple of yards, took off his tailcoat and hung it carefully over an empty chair.

Some of the diners were already edging towards the door, and Hazlerigg wondered if there was going to be a stampede. Suddenly, Luigi spoke from the service door. One of the overhead lights shone directly on him, and, in his evening dress, he looked like some stage manager coming forward to collect the applause.

"Please do not move," he said, pleasantly. "There will be no trouble. I, myself, guarantee it."

It was a remarkable feat of personality. People sank back in their chairs. There was a scattered and uncertain laugh.

As the waiter moved forward again towards Coulan, who was now on his feet, Hazlerigg heard a name going round the now silent room like a whisper in a field of corn. Morelli.

"Of course it's Morelli," said a stout man who was dining with two friends. "I've paid half a nicker often enough at the Hoxton Baths to watch him fight. This ought to be good."

The waiter had started by manoeuvring his opponent deftly out into the open space in the middle of the floor. Then he really got to work on him. Coulan had been a boxer once, and he was still an Irishman, and he had plenty of fight in him.

In the opening minutes, the waiter contented himself with hitting Coulan on the body and avoiding his returns by neat footwork. This sort of fighting is apt to be exhausting for a man who is not as fit as he used to be. Coulan began to show signs of distress. The waiter then started to hit him on the face.

After a little of this, Coulan lost his temper and did a thing he would never normally have done. He put his head down and charged.

The waiter sidestepped to the left and put all his heart and soul into one right handed uppercut. Propelled equally by the weight of the blow and the momentum of his own rush, Coulan performed a short, flat dive and landed on the staircase. His head and body went through the curtains. His feet twitched.

The waiter turned, still polite, still unruffled, to Sparks, who sat apparently nailed to his chair. "You had a complaint about the food?"

"No," said Sparks. "No. The food is quite all right."

"Eat it then," said the waiter.

Sparks took one look at the lukewarm goulash on the plate in front of him. Then he looked at Coulan's feet, which were still twitching.

"Thank you," he said. "I—I've got a date." He seized his hat and made for the door. The waiter stood politely aside.

At that moment, Luigi, with superb showmanship, released the balloons.

They floated down from the ceiling in a shining cascade of red and green and silver, and a yellow balloon bounced off Sparks's head as he shot out of the front door, blasted on his way by the gust of laughter behind him.

It was very late when Hazlerigg finished his dinner. Luigi had found some old brandy and it was a celebration.

"Morelli is a good boy," said Luigi. "He is my cousin's son. One day he will be lightweight champion of the British Isles."

"You can't keep a man like that permanently on hand to deal with things," said Hazlerigg, sleepily.

"It will not be necessary," said Luigi. "You heard how they laughed. Sparks will not come here again."

Hazlerigg looked up at the plump, smiling, Napoleonic face. There was a gay determination about it.

"I've got a feeling you might be right, Luigi."

John Bull, May 12, 1951.

THE AWKWARD CUSTOMER

WHEN CHIEF INSPECTOR HAZLERIGG was a young constable, his duty took him to most of the magistrates' courts in London. Later, as a Divisional Detective Inspector, his official appearances became rarer, but he made a point of visiting them when he could.

The greater part of London's criminal population passes through these courts. An inspector can learn a lot by sitting quietly in the back and observing the faces and listening to the voices of the men in the dock.

On that particular morning it was largely sentiment that brought him to the Marsham Street Police Court. In that court, thirty-five years before, his first evidence, given in a voice that had not long broken, had led to the imposition of a five shilling fine on a drunken cab driver. Mordaunt had been magistrate in those days. The bearded bullfrog, as the junior members of the police force had called him. Now it was the gentle and experienced Sharpe.

Hazlerigg pushed open the swing door and looked in.

"I said to him," said a large man with a brown face and a craggy nose, "if you don't like my roses, you can go chase yourself up the Nelson Column."

Hazlerigg deduced that it was the prisoner who was giving evidence.

"Roses?" said Mr. Sharpe patiently. "In March?"

"On the wallpaper."

"Oh, he objected to your wallpaper?"

"That's right. This joker comes bustling into my office and starts talking about my wallpaper."

From his voice, Hazlerigg guessed a New Zealander. "And then what happened, Mr. Cooper?"

"What happened?" said Mr. Cooper. "Why I busted him right on the nose."

"That seems rather drastic," said Mr. Sharpe.

"He'd got no right to go calling down my wallpaper. I chose it myself."

"I see."

Mr. Sharpe glanced at the witness who had suffered the assault. He was a big, red-faced man, and from the way in which he had given his evidence Mr. Sharpe judged that he might be an irritating customer.

However, it wouldn't do to allow art criticism to develop into a vulgar brawl.

He imposed a fine of forty shillings and bound Mr. Cooper over.

Hazlerigg attached himself to the New Zealander as he left the court. A man who feels himself to be in the right, and has had to fork out £2 is usually ready for a drink. Mr. Cooper was no exception.

Presently he was steaming gently over a pint of beer.

"It was just a lot of hooey about nothing," he said. "Way back in Auckland we don't set all that store by a punch on the nose. I keep this hotel, see – the Commodore in Endell Street. I've had it since the war, and it's doing all right. Then one evening this joker comes along. We give him the best room. I chose those roses myself, and roses are something I know about, and the man who says the contrary—"

Hazlerigg hastily ordered more beer.

"Then, about nine o'clock, he comes along and wants to change his room. If he'd had a reason, I wouldn't have minded, see. But picking on my roses—"

When he got back to his office at Scotland Yard Hazlerigg sat and reflected for a bit.

There was nothing in the story at all. Absolutely nothing. It was wasting time to think further about it.

All the same, he rang his bell and said to Sergeant Crabbe, when that mournful man appeared, "At Marsham Street Police Court this morning a gentleman with a red face gave evidence against the proprietor of the Commodore Hotel in Endell Street, who had hit him on the nose for objecting to his roses."

"Roses, sir?"

"Yes, yes. I can't explain it all now. I just want to know the name and address of the man who made the complaint. And see if we've got anything on him."

Sergeant Crabbe reported back an hour later. "The gentleman's name is Mitcham. Leslie James Mitcham. He's an ironmonger. Lives in Streatham."

"Mr. Mitcham of Streatham."

"That's right, sir. And nothing known."

"Did he register at the Commodore under that name?"

Crabbe didn't know. He said he'd find out. This time he used the telephone to save his feet and was back in five minutes.

"That's right," he said. "Registered as Mitcham of Streatham. English subject. Intended duration of stay, one night. Actual stay, three hours."

"Oh I see. He cleared out when the proprietor hit him. Can't blame him really. But if he's got a home at Streatham, why trouble to put up for the night in Endell Street? He could get home in half an hour."

"I couldn't say," said Sergeant Crabbe.

"All these hotel registrations are checked from time to time, aren't they?"

"They're supposed to be."

"Well, chase it up."

"Chase what up, sir?"

"I want to find if Mr. Mitcham has registered in a London hotel anywhere during the last three years."

"Yes, sir. Would there be anything else, sir?" inquired Sergeant Crabbe sounding as insubordinate as he dared.

"On second thoughts," said Hazlerigg, "I'll make if five years."

It was nearly a week before Sergeant Crabbe reported.

"Shocking state these hotel registrations have got into," he said.

"I've had to do most of it on my feet."

Hazlerigg made a sympathetic noise.

"Any luck?" he said.

"It depends," said Sergeant Crabbe, "what you mean by luck." He pulled out his note book. "Twelve months ago Mitcham stayed at the Enderby Hotel – that's off Bedford Square. Six months before that at the New Berkley, in Albany Street. And that isn't all."

"Ah," said Hazlerigg.

"Three days after he'd been at the Enderby they had a big robbery. Chap cleared the valuables out of about a dozen bedrooms."

"I see," said Hazlerigg. "Same story at the others, too?"

"Not quite. The day after he left the Collingridge it was burned down. It's been rebuilt now. The New Berkley went bust and sold up."

"He doesn't seem to have brought much luck with him, our Mr. Mitcham," said Hazlerigg softly. "What do you make of it?"

"Coincidence," said Sergeant Crabbe promptly.

"Two may be a coincidence," said Hazlerigg. "Three's too many." He rang up Mr. Cooper at the Commodore and reintroduced himself. "I just wanted to find out," he enquired, "if anything has happened to you in the last week."

"What sort of thing," said Mr. Cooper, suspiciously.

"Fire – burglary—"

"Not yet, it hasn't."

"Keep your fingers crossed," said Hazlerigg, and went off to see the proprietors of the Enderby and the Collingridge, and the ex-proprietor of the New Berkley.

When he came back he found Sergeant Crabbe waiting for him.

"One more," said the sergeant, "Mitcham stayed three years ago at the Family Hotel in Euston Lane. And it's a funny thing. Three days after he left—"

"They had a big burglary. Cleared out all the bedrooms."

"Someone told you," said Sergeant Crabbe resentfully.

"I guessed. You told me the Enderby had a burglary. Well so did the New Berkley. They were under-insured. That's one of the reasons they went bust."

"No one burgled the Collingridge," said Crabbe.

"Have a heart," said Hazlerigg. "It burned down the day after Mitcham left. Fault in the electric wiring. You can't burgle a heap of charred cinders. In both the other cases our Mr. Mitcham had been staying in the hotel two or three days before the burglary. In both cases he objected to the wallpaper in his room."

"Wallpaper?"

"In one case he didn't like the stripes. In the other case it was the dots that put him off. In both cases the proprietors being effete Englishmen, not trained in the rougher school of Auckland, New Zealand, didn't give him a punch on the snoot. They merely gave him a new room."

"That's right," said Crabbe. "He changed his room at the Family Hotel, too. It wasn't the wallpaper. He didn't like his bed running north to south."

"Well, that's quite plain now."

"It isn't plain to me," said Sergeant Crabbe.

"Use your head. Why does a man stay at different hotels at regular intervals, and always makes a point of changing his room? Ironmonger."

"Oh, that lark," said Sergeant Crabbe. "What are you going to do about it?"

"Warn all hotels. He failed at the Commodore. He may try again quite soon."

Three months later a Mr. Mitcham duly turned up at the Blackwater Hotel in Dorset Square. He booked a room on the second floor, and seemed quite satisfied with it, but before the evening was out he had changed his mind.

He wanted one with running water, he explained. The proprietor was quite agreeable. He allotted Mr. Mitcham a room on the first floor. He also got busy on the telephone.

The next morning, Mr. Mitcham left, and Chief Inspector Hazlerigg arrived. He made a tour of the premises, seeming to be particularly interested in service doors and backstairs. He left a man behind.

Two days later, at about three o'clock in the afternoon, the door into the court at the back of the premises opened quietly and a nondescript man came through. He had a small laundry basket under his arm.

He made his way confidently up the servants' stairs, and out into the corridor where he knocked at a bedroom door. Receiving no reply he took a key from his pocket, unlocked the door and went in.

When he came out, the basket seemed heavier. He moved along to the next door and repeated the performance.

When he came out this time he was quite upset to find three men waiting for him. One was the manager. The other two were policeman.

"What beats me," said the manager, "is where he got that key. Do you realise it's a master key, and will open any bedroom in the hotel?"

"Of course it's a master key," said Hazlerigg soothingly. "I should have been very disappointed if it hadn't been. Why do you suppose Mr. Mitcham changed his room?"

"Even so—"

"A master key is a combination of all the other keys, with the unnecessary bits left out. Anyone who knows about keys can construct it if he get hold of any two keys in the set. Simple, isn't it. Practically infallible."

"Not quite," said Sergeant Crabbe. "God bless New Zealand."

London *Evening Standard,* April 9, 1953.

FOLLOW THE LEADER

NIGHT DRIVING WAS TOFFEE. Sam did fifty hours of it every winter week of his life. Fog was a minor nuisance. Ice could be bad. Ice made his ten-ton lorry wag her tail like a dog.

Night, fog and ice together were unprintable. And now he had them all. The fog had come up with the dusk. The ice was a fixture.

If anyone could get along in bad conditions, Sam could do it. Perched high in his cab astride the powerful foglight slung between his front wheels, he was a lot better equipped than any private motorist.

Now even Sam was beginning to wonder. It hadn't escaped his notice that not a single vehicle of any sort had passed him in the last quarter of an hour, which could mean that bad though things were, they were a lot worse ahead.

A dim shape on his left – the piston ring factory. Sam sucked at his teeth. Half a mile to Grandpa's. He'd got to stop there anyway. Maybe he'd knock off for three or four hours and give the fog a chance. When it was foggy at dusk, it often cleared, he had noticed, before midnight.

Grandpa's place was a pull-in well known to all lorry drivers and not unknown to the snob traffic. Grandpa had a way with ham and eggs that would have made him a small fortune in London's Soho. He didn't seem to be doing too badly in his lonely outpost beside the Great North Road. Grandpa was a warm man.

The lights of the diner were suddenly ahead, very dim, to the right just off the road. The run-in was half left down a slight incline into an open, gravelled yard. Sam could have done it with his eyes shut. He slowed for the entrance, touched his wheel, and felt his lorry slithering down the slope which the ice had turned into a slide.

He levelled off, ran to the far end, and stopped. As he stopped he felt something bump gently but firmly into him from behind. Then another bump, more distant. Then another.

It was like a freight train coming to a halt. Clank, clank, clank.

Sam climbed out to investigate.

"Blow me down," he said. "I've brought 'em all in with me."

Touching his tailboard was a shiny saloon car. Behind the saloon, a little two-seater. Behind the two-seater stood an old family model.

Sam had been vaguely aware for some time that he had picked up a "tail." Driving in fog he sometimes had a couple of dozen followers, and accepted their presence as a tribute to his skill.

It hadn't occurred to him that they would all follow him into Grandpa's for a cup of tea. As he stood, disconcerted more than amused, car doors begin to open. First a man and then a girl stepped out of the two-seater. They were stiff with cold. A fat, red-faced commercial traveller type climbed out of the saloon. He looked cheerful. Probably his car had heating. Finally the door of the family model opened and a third man joined the party. He was on the young side of middle age, and, as far as he looked like anything, he looked like a farmer.

"Here we are," said the red-faced man. As soon as he opened his mouth, a further cause of his cheerfulness became apparent.

"Where exactly are we?" asked the man from the two-seater. He and the girl both looked cold and nervous.

"It's a pull-in," said Sam. "Known to the trade as Grandpa's. Does a good cup of coffee."

"W-what are we w-waiting for, then?" asked the girl, through chattering teeth.

"What indeed?" said the farming type. They surged indoors.

Grandpa and his assistant, a lout of twenty addressed as "boy," were sitting in front of the fire. They rose to greet the company. Sam they knew.

"Just followed me in," said Sam, helplessly.

"Did they, though?" said Grandpa. He, too, seemed a little

disconcerted. "What'll it be?"

"Coffee," said Sam.

The man and the girl nodded. The Commercial said, "And I'll have a drop of rum in mine."

Grandpa looked at him under his grey eyebrows and said, "You'll lose me the licence I haven't got, sir. I might have a drop in the medicine chest. I'll go and see."

"Never known a time when you hadn't," said the Commercial.

"Come out and give us a hand with the lashings," said Sam to the boy. "They started slipping at Baldock but I couldn't stop."

They went out. The man and the girl sat in front of the fire.

"Sugar?" asked the man. The girl shook her head. She was very young, the farmer decided. Under twenty, he'd have guessed. The man was in his middle thirties, a powerful-looking brute.

"Smashing place this," said the Commercial. "Get anything you like. Drink. Smoke. Eat. When rationing was on, I always stopped here. Rationing!" His face grew redder. "Never knew the meaning of the word, did you, Grandpa?"

Grandpa, who had come back with a medicine bottle full of dark brown liquid, poured some into the Commercial's coffee and said: "I'm sure I don't know what you mean."

The man and the girl had finished their coffee. The man took out a cigarette case and they both helped themselves to a cigarette. There was a box of spills on the mantelpiece. The girl stood up to get one, but before she had lit it the man had taken out a handsome solid silver lighter and snapped it.

Sam and the boy came back, and Sam got on with his coffee. Grandpa tipped a dose out of the medicine bottle into his cup, too.

"What's that? Cough mixture?" said Sam, innocently.

"That's right," said Grandpa. "I keep it for the boy."

The warmth and the light were thawing people out. The thought of facing the road outside seemed doubly distasteful.

"Doesn't run to a bed, I suppose?" said the Commercial, hopefully.

"We've got one," said Grandpa, "but it's full of me most nights. What about a nice shakedown on the divan?" He indicated a couch in the corner.

"I wouldn't say no to that," said the Commercial. "I could get in touch with my old lady. Are you on the phone?"

"We've got a telephone." said Grandpa. "But it's not working," he added sharply, as though someone had nudged him.

"There's one back down the road," said the girl. "How far would you say?" She seemed to be addressing this remark to the farming type, who had been sitting very quietly in the corner.

"I—well – I don't think that I noticed it," he said.

"*Noticed* it!" said the girl. "But you were using it. We were behind you. That's when we passed you."

"Ah, yes," said the farmer. "So I was. I'd forgotten."

The spotlight of popular interest focused on him. Remarkable man. Stopped to telephone. Forgot about it ten minutes later.

"Odd sort of memory you've got," said the Commercial jovially.

"Don't I know your face?" said Grandpa. "Strike a light, but it's my old friend Chief Inspector—what's the name?—Horsebox? Has been? Hazlerigg. That's it. The racket-buster. The man who's put more food-and-drink thieves behind bars than the rest of the Flying Squad put together."

The high old voice had a venomous edge to it.

Sam looked shocked almost out of his wits. The Commercial had his mouth wide open. The girl had gone white, her companion red. The boy sidled unobtrusively towards the door.

"And what brings you to these parts?" said Grandpa.

"Murder," said the Chief Inspector.

The word stilled all movement.

"There now!" said Sam at last. "And who's gone and murdered who?"

Curiously enough, he seemed relieved, as did Grandpa and the boy.

"Murder, eh?" said Grandpa. "That's a new lay for you, Inspector."

"It's the oldest lay in the world," said Hazlerigg mildly. "Elderly husband, found dead. Young wife disappeared. Lover with her. Certain indications that they've gone north. Nothing more at the moment, but I expect we shall hear of them before morning."

"Travelling as husband and wife, I expect?" said the Commercial, bringing himself back into the picture.

"That's it," said Hazlerigg. He gave a short laugh. "I've no doubt they'll make all the usual mistakes."

"Mistakes?" said the Commercial.

"Oh," said Hazlerigg, "you know the sort of thing I mean. Posing as man and wife, but he asks her if she takes sugar in her coffee. Or perhaps she takes out a cigarette and looks round for matches, not realising that he's handy with a lighter. A hundred and one little things like that, if you keep your eyes open."

The man and the girl seemed to become aware that the centre of interest had shifted to them.

"Perhaps we ought to be getting along," said the man defiantly, rising to his feet.

"Well," said Hazlerigg. He had his head on one side and seemed to be listening.

They all heard it.

A slithering noise of tyres trying to grip on the ice. Then, twice, the gentle thud of bumper on bumper.

Two other cars had joined the queue.

"Now I want you all to stand quite still," said Hazlerigg. "That's my reinforcements arriving. The ones I phoned for. Oh, come in, Inspector. These are your birds."

He indicated Sam, Grandpa and the boy. "Something a little more serious than rationing offences this time. Fifty thousand cigarettes stolen in Hounslow last night. Sam brought them up in the back of his lorry. And he was expected. The boy helped him unload them as soon as he arrived. A planned job, and they're all in it."

"Do you mean to say," said Grandpa furiously, "that all the skite about murder was just to keep us quiet while the troops turned up?"

"That's right," said Hazlerigg. "Easy now. There's room for all of you in the cars. You'll probably have to manhandle them up the slope." A policeman appeared from the rear parts, staggering under a carton.

"That looks like some of it," said Hazlerigg. "The rest's probably still on the lorry. Get moving."

"I think," said the man to the girl, "that perhaps *we'll* get moving too."

Nobody said no. They went out. Hazlerigg finished his coffee. It was still hot. The Commercial was almost beyond speech.

"What about that couple?" he said at last. "Were they—did they—I mean, do you think—?"

"Not thinking about them at all," said Hazlerigg. "One thing at a time. Not my job. Goodnight."

Reveille, March 1, 1955.

AFTER ALL THESE YEARS

"IT HAPPENED A LONG TIME AGO when I was only a girl," said Great Aunt Emily.

"In fact, it was the year I came out, because I remember I was staying with my sister Alice and her husband, Bill, in their house in Stanford Gate."

"Bill?" said Bohun casting his mind through the ranks of his great uncles. "That was the one in phosphates who had a weakness for Gaiety Girls."

"*Any* girls," said Emily. "However *de mortuis*—"

"Alice must have been a good deal older than you, though," said Bohun. "She had quite a family by then, hadn't she?"

"Only four then. Bertha, Tom, Augusta, and Brian. It all happened on June tenth."

"You've a remarkably accurate memory," said Bohun approvingly. He was an accurate man himself.

"There's no question of accuracy. I remember it *because* it happened on June tenth. It was Bertha's birthday. She was five. Alice always had a tea party on her children's birthdays. And a big cake – she used to ice it herself – and animal biscuits for the children and sandwiches for the grownups."

"Grownups were invited, too?"

"Oh, certainly. Miss Twomey was one of them."

"She was the one who—?"

"That's right. She died – the next morning. In terrible agony. Poor woman." Emily pursed her lips. The horror of it was still with her after all those years. She added. "She was a harpist, you know. Quite famous in her way."

Bohun refrained from a facetious comment. Indeed, he looked unusually serious. "Who else was at the party?" he said. "Tell it all to me."

"I remember it," said Emily, "as if it were yesterday. There were six of us grownups – Alice, myself, poor Miss Twomey, the Vicar of All Souls Lavender Hill and a splendid man, though he afterwards became an agnostic and sold sewing machines in America – and his wife, rather a dull little woman – and Mrs. Armstrong."

"And she was *not a* dull little woman."

"Far from it," said Emily. Her voice had acquired the detached coldness which the older generation reserved for Certain Topics and Certain People.

"A merry widow?" suggested Bohun.

"Well," said Aunt Emily. "We must speak no evil of her either. She's dead. In fact she died soon after the party I was telling you about. She slipped, on a very wet night, and fell under a horse-bus. Alice was walking with her at the time and it was a great shock to her."

Bohun preserved in his own mind a picture of his great Aunt Alice. She had been very old, and he had been very young. But he had not been deceived. An amiable-looking woman of mild disposition and gentle manners, but under it all a character and determination beside which concrete was soft and steel yielding.

"Tell me more about the birthday party," he said. "A lot more."

"Let me see, then," said Emily.

"I've told you who were there – the six of us grownups and the four children. I think I can even remember how we sat. The vicar on my right. His wife on his right. Mrs. Armstrong on my left. Then Miss Twomey.

"Where was Alice?"

"She hardly had time to sit down. At the moment I visualise her"— Emily screwed up her birdlike eyes—"she is cutting the cake. A lovely birthday cake. I don't think she made it herself – one didn't in those days, you know. But she'd certainly iced it, and very pretty it was. In the middle was the name *Bertha* in green icing – green was the child's favourite colour. Then on the bottom edge *Five Years Old* in blue – and on the top edge the year, in red figures."

"Remarkable," said Bohun. "Remarkable."

Emily accepted this is a tribute to her memory. "But of course," she explained, "we all talked about that tea a good deal afterwards. The inquest, you know."

"Tell me about that."

"Poor Miss Twomey. Three hours later – while she was changing for dinner. The most agonising cramps and—er—other things. Acute arsenic poisoning. She died at dawn."

"And the tea party naturally came under suspicion."

"Well, it couldn't have had anything to do with it," said Emily. "How could it? That was the whole point. Cook was furious. She had made all the sandwiches herself. And the cake. Everyone ate the sandwiches and the cake. And they ate nothing else."

"I see," said Bohun. "That did make it awkward. Had Miss Twomey had anything else to eat recently?"

"She had luncheon alone, in a Station Restaurant." Emily's tone expressed very clearly what she thought of people who ate in Station Restaurants. "It was impossible to prove anything, but it was just when Home Rule was becoming troublesome again and one of the waiters was an Irishman."

"Did Mrs. Armstrong take sugar in her tea?" asked Bohun.

"Mrs. Armstrong?" Emily brought her mind back with some difficulty to the gay widow. "No. I don't think she did. Nor milk either. Why do you ask?"

"Fascinating," said Bohun. "Fascinating. After all these years. By the way, I don't think you told me. Was it 1896 or 1906? No. Come to think of it, it could hardly have been as late as 1906. Bertha must be well over sixty."

"As a matter of fact," said Emily, "it *was* 1896. What horrible ideas are you turning over in that head of yours?"

"I was thinking," said Bohun, "that you never know when you stand in the greatest danger. The Mafeking Celebrations? Zeppelins?

Buzz bombs? Traffic? Don't let them kid you. You'll never be nearer death than you were at tea that afternoon in 1896."

"Now you must explain what you mean – at once!"

"It's very simple," said Bohun. "Dear Aunt Alice. A tigress in defence of her mate. She must have known or suspected – more than you thought about Bill and Mrs. Armstrong."

"Yes, there was something in it, I believe. But when Mrs. Armstrong had her accident—"

"Accident my foot," said Bohun. "Alice pushed her good and hard. It was her second attempt – after the first had misfired, don't you see, and carried off poor Miss Twomey."

"Really," said Emily. Curiosity struggled with repugnance. "How did she manage it?"

"The only way she could pick on one individual – particularly if that individual was awkward enough not to take sugar in her tea. That would have been simple, of course, because she could have impregnated a lump and popped it into her cup when she served her. However, she didn't do too badly."

"You are being irritating and obscure," said Emily. "How?"

"The icing. It must have been. First, she'd spread the white icing over the whole cake. Then she'd get one of those nice little icing-gun gadgets and put on the words and letters. Only right at the end, when she was putting on the last letter of the year 1896, she recharged the gun, with a special dollop of red icing plus arsenic. That was the only poisonous part of the whole cake, you *see – the final letter in the date – the letter 6.*"

"Then when—oh, yes, I see."

Even after the years Emily turned pale.

"That's right," said Bohun. "You've spotted it. After she'd cut the slices she got them turned round. Mrs. Armstrong got the 9. Miss Twomey got the 6 . . . You know, it might have been any of you."

"It might, indeed," said Aunt Emily.

She recovered herself.

"Anyway," she said, "Alice is dead now. And you've no proof. And it all happened a very long time ago."

Finally, firmly, she buried it after all these years.

London *Evening Standard,* July 10, 1954.

EVERY MONDAY, A NEW LETTER

CURIOUSLY ENOUGH, CONSIDERING the tortuous ramifications of his own mind, Bohun had never been attracted to mathematics. The routine of his schooldays had carried him to the fringe of statistics but a merciful twist of fate had then diverted him into the byways of history and literature.

A knowledge of quite elementary mathematics had, however, once enabled him to solve an unpleasant problem without moving from his desk in his Lincoln's Inn office.

Mr. Taylor was a new client introduced by the country firm for whom they did agency work. He was a pleasant-looking, rather pale-faced man of about thirty, with indeterminate-coloured hair, a modest smile, and a tie which proclaimed that he had been to the same public school as Bohun himself.

"It's the terrible regularity of it," he said. "Wasn't there a Chinese torture – drops of water – well, that's the effect it has had on me. Every Monday morning, a new letter. It's been going on for nearly three months now.

Bohun examined the letters spread out on the top of his desk. There were eleven of them, all put together in the same way, with words and letters cut from newspapers and pasted onto paper.

None of the letters was pleasant, but it was difficult to put a finger on their exact unpleasantness. They jeered. They probed. They twisted. They did not threaten – at least, not directly.

You always were a coward, said one, *who would rather cry, than sing for his supper.*

Afraid of the dark? said another; *have you ever thought that, for the blind, darkness goes on forever?*

Bohun turned the pieces of paper over thoughtfully. He could sympathise with Mr. Taylor. One of them might be laughed off. A weekly dose for nearly three months was a good deal less than funny.

"Have you told the police about them?" he said.

"They hardly seemed to be a police matter," said Mr. Taylor. "They're sort of intimate family things. Not really criminal."

"Crime often flourishes inside the family circle," said Bohun. Nevertheless, he was inclined to agree – it was not a police matter. *The dogs of war,* said a third message; *by the way, you never liked dogs did you? War was more fun. Are you still wearing your wound stripe for that Mess party at Catterick?*

There were others in the same strain.

"What's all this about dogs?" said Bohun.

Mr. Taylor turned a little pink. "I was bitten in the ankle by a dog when I was four years old," he said. "I've always had a—a thing about them. I can usually control it now – but if it happens unexpectedly – if a dog comes running out of a garden and starts yapping at me – I'm quite likely to take to my heels."

"Elephants react in exactly the same way," said Bohun. "Are the other things founded on truth as well?"

"Yes," said Mr. Taylor, uncomfortably but defiantly. "I suppose it is true that the only actual wound I did get was when I fell off the billiard table after a Mess night at Catterick and broke my ankle – I was in Signals."

"Lots of people didn't hurt themselves even that much," said Bohun. "And the fear of darkness – I suppose that's a childish inhibition, too."

"That was a long time ago," said Mr. Taylor. "I got over that before I went to school."

"You were at Slaughterhouse, I see."

"That's right – were you?"

"Before your time, I imagine. I happened to notice, in the first note I read, the reference to 'singing for your supper.' An old Slaughterhouse custom. Most unnerving."

"It unnerved me," said Mr. Taylor. He seemed to be easier now that he had actually started on the confessional. "I think I was the only one of the new boys who was actually reduced to tears."

"It's curious," said Bohun. "Very curious. Not your being reduced to tears – I remember feeling that way myself. But the selection of these particular events. In some ways they seem to hang together. In other ways, they're curiously unrelated. Perhaps you'd better tell me. We shall have to come to it sooner or later. *Is* there anyone you actually suspect? It must be someone who knows you pretty well."

"That's what makes it so disturbing," said Mr. Taylor. "And I most particularly don't want to be disturbed just now. I'm holding down a new job – which is ticklish enough – and – well, I'm getting married."

"Congratulations," said Bohun. He was a bachelor and had every intention of remaining so. "Do you live at home at the moment, then?"

"I share a flat with my elder sister, Constance. My mother and father are dead."

"Ah," said Bohun. He wrote down *Constance* on the blank piece of paper in front of him. "By the way, you didn't tell me your fiancée's name."

"Miss Holman – Valerie Holman."

Bohun wrote down *Valerie.*

"And you haven't told me yet whom you suspect," he said.

"It's all so indefinite," said Mr. Taylor. "However – yes – there is someone. It's Bill Bayes. I've known him, oh—a long time. He was at Slaughterhouse with me. And after that in the Army. Not the same crowd, but I keep running across him."

"Sounds promising," said Bohun. "Very promising, indeed. But is there any particular reason why Bill should feel that way about you?"

"There could be," said Mr. Taylor. "You see, this job I got – if I hadn't got it, he would have had it. I think he felt it."

Bohun added *Bill* to *Constance* and *Valerie* and stared thoughtfully at his little list.

"Is there anyone at all, outside these three, who would know enough about your affairs—"

"But look here," said Mr. Taylor, angrily, "I never said I suspected Connie. And as for Val – the idea's absurd."

Nevertheless, though he spoke explosively, there was something in his voice that gave Bohun the courage to persevere.

"I can't pretend," he said, "to understand people who are in love. They hurt themselves. They hurt each other. And as for your sister, has it ever occurred to you that she might be jealous? I don't mean of your fiancée, but of the idea of your getting married."

"It's a possibility," said Mr. Taylor.

"Then let's get back to my question. *Could* there be anyone else?"

Mr. Taylor considered the matter. "I don't really see that there could," he said at last.

"Well, then, we've got somewhere," said Bohun. "Now. Take these four incidents. I take it that your sister would certainly know about your fear of the dark and your fear of dogs. You might have told her, in the holidays, about your experiences at school. That makes three. But the fourth – I take it you never told her about Mess nights at Catterick."

"I don't think I ever told her about school either."

"All right," said Bohun. "That's clear enough." As he spoke he was making a series of marks after each of the names on the paper.

"Bill Bayes would know about your schooldays. And even if he wasn't in the same unit, he would almost certainly know about the Catterick episode. He might also have found out about the dogs. But you mentioned that you'd got over your fear of darkness *before* you went to school. He couldn't have known about that."

"No, I suppose not," said Mr. Taylor, unwillingly. He seemed to find Bohun's analytical method somewhat disconcerting.

"Finally," said Bohun, "there is your fiancée. Here there are no rules. I should imagine that a man might tell his fiancée almost anything. There's a certain sporting flavour about getting drunk and falling off a billiard table. And the fear of darkness, especially if conquered a long time ago. The matter of dogs – well – possibly it would be better to explain it than to have her find out for herself. I should have thought, however, that a schoolboy episode which reflected no credit – however,

I'm theorising unnecessarily. You can tell me yourself. Which of them *did* she know about?"

"Look here," said Mr. Taylor, uncomfortably. "I don't like this. I'm not at all sure I want to go on with it."

"Come along," said Bohun. "We're nearly finished. What was it? The first three and not the last?"

"I suppose so. I certainly never talked about school to her."

"In that case," said Bohun, cheerfully, "we have a most interesting equation." He drew a line under his calculations. "Of the three people who might have written the notes, no one of them has all the necessary knowledge. All three persons probably knew two facts out of four. Two of them might have known three. But none of them can have known all. And I think we call dismiss any idea that two of them collaborated. Unthinkable? I agree."

Mr. Taylor nodded miserably.

"'It's just like a problem in H.C.F. You remember H.C.F.? The highest common factor. You take three numbers – say 48, 24, and 18. Problem, to find the highest common factor of all of them. In that case 6. You see? In other cases it wasn't a matter of the highest common factor but of finding any common factor at all. That's the situation here in a nutshell, isn't it? Four totals. Three possible factors. Only no one of the factors will go into all the totals."

Mr. Taylor seemed to be beyond speech.

"However," said Bohun, "don't despair. Mathematics is a marvellous science. There *is* a number that will go into any other number."

He finished his calculations with flourish, and passed it across the table. Mr. Taylor stared at the paper blindly, grasped his hat, and stumbled, out of the room.

"I'm afraid I've lost us a client," said Bohun to his partner, Mr. Craine. He had been recounting the events of the morning.

"I don't see it yet," said Craine. "What number will go into any other number?"

"One, of course," said Bohun. "It's the universal common factor."

"You mean—?"

"He'd written all the notes to himself. Must have. Don't ask me why. Might have planned to get Bayes in trouble. Might have been an expression of hostility to his sister. Remember that lady client of yours who used to write herself love letters? Unaccountable thing, human nature. Give me mathematics every time."

London *Evening Standard,* November 1, 1954.

AN APPEALING PAIR OF LEGS

NORMALLY BOHUN HAD NO PROBLEM at all about getting home from work. His office was in New Square, Lincoln's Inn, and his flat was off Chancery Lane. That summer, however, he had been lent a pretty little bungalow near Farningham. It was undoubtedly nice to get away from the thrice-used air of central London, and to see roses growing on bushes instead of in barrows; but it did sometimes occur to him to wonder whether it was worth all the bother.

His terminus was Victoria. It offered him a choice of three trains home: the 6:16 which was a little early and invariably jampacked; the 7:16 which was a little late and carried only a moderate number of passengers; and the 8:16 which was almost empty but much too late.

For some weeks now he had been compromising haste with comfort by catching the 7:16. His first-class season ticket entitled him to a degree of elbow room and his normal travelling companions were three in number.

Number One: a middle-aged man with whitish hair and a bright red face – his name, Bohun gathered, was Conyers.

Number Two: a tall, depressed looking man, name unknown, who spoke little, invariably called Conyers "sir," and was in some way dependent on him. Not in the same office, Bohun guessed, but in the same general line of business.

Number Three: a hard, brisk, cheerful man who always smoked a pipe, talked constantly, and called Conyers "Mr. Conyers" and, Bohun was sure, disliked him heartily; and who, in turn, was called "Sam" by Number Two, the tall unhappy man. Number Three's second name was probably Blessingham – inferred by Bohun from having once spotted that name on the label of a suitcase Number Three was carrying. The inference was confirmed by the fact that the brisk, pipe-smoking man's brief case had the initials S. B. on it.

Bohun sometimes speculated about the three men – about their homes of which he knew little, except that they all got out at different stations along the line; about their businesses, of which a certain amount did seep out from their talk. Conyers was managing director of a large group of magazines; the tall man had something to do with advertising – which would account for his servility towards Conyers, since Conyers evidently placed considerable advertising for his magazines; and Sam, the pipe-smoker, was a senior executive on the printing side – whether directly under Conyers or not, it was hard to say.

More intriguing, perhaps, were Bohun's glimpses of their backgrounds, as revealed by their daily reading. Conyers: *The Financial Times.* Tall, dejected man: *Home Gardening* and – during the newspaper strike – *The Three Musketeers.* Sam: *Daily Mirror and Printing Trades Gazette.* In the evening they all read newspapers – the London *Evening Standard.*

It was a fact, however, that although Bohun could no more help observing than he could stop breathing, his interest in his fellow passengers was only casual until the day he saw Conyers die.

He was forced to recall the events of that particular evening for the benefit of his friend, Superintendent Hazlerigg, and Bohun's excellent visual memory supplied him, after a short period of concentration, with all the necessary details.

"I got to Victoria," he recalled, "just behind Conyers. I've done that before – in fact, we sometimes catch the same bus, a No. 11, which he picks up on Fleet Street and I catch at Temple Bar. Conyers bought his evening paper, as I've often seen him do, from the man with the pitch under the clock. We reached our first-class carriage at about the same time. The tall chap—what did you say his name was, Ruddock?—he was already there. Sam Blessingham came along almost immediately afterward. There were quite a few people on the train but we had the four corner seats and no one else butted in."

"Exactly where were the four of you sitting?"

"I was directly opposite Conyers. He had his back to the engine and I was facing it – on the outer side. Blessingham was on the same side as me, with Ruddock opposite him on the corridor side. The seats between us were empty."

"Any talk?"

"We don't talk much on the way home. Just four tired businessmen, browsing through their *Evening Standards*. Incidentally, my eye for detail told me we'd all got different editions. Ruddock had a midday one. Blessingham had the lunch edition – I could see the list of "Runners and Jockeys" on the back page. I had one that I'd bought earlier to read with my tea. It was like the one Conyers had bought in the station, labelled "Final Night Extra," but his, I noticed, was a later version than mine. His had the most tantalising pair of legs – I saw them sticking up in the air—"

"*Legs?*"

"A drawing of a very beautiful and appealing pair of feminine legs. Advertising, I suppose – Messrs. Somebody-or-Other's fully-fashioned nylon stockings. I couldn't see the top of it – the paper was folded. That's why I saw the legs upside down."

"They seem to have made quite an impression on you."

"You may sneer," said Bohun, "but they were works of art. I searched for them in my edition. But alas, I could find no sign of them."

"Suppose you get on with the story," said Hazlerigg, impatiently.

"Well, a few minutes later we ran into the tunnel. There's no lighting in those carriages, so we sat in darkness. It lasts about half a minute. By the time we came out again, poor old Conyers was either dying or dead. He sat rigid in his seat, face white, lips blue – the obvious symptoms of a violent heart attack. Luckily we were running up to a station. I pulled the emergency cord, and the rest you know."

"Yes," said Hazlerigg, "the rest, I know. You say you were sitting directly opposite Conyers?"

"Our knees were almost touching."

"If either of the others had moved up to him would you have felt them?"

Bohun considered.

"Yes, I am almost certain that I should," he said. "It's just possible – just barely possible – that Ruddock might have moved along their seat, in the darkness, and back again, without my knowing. But Blessingham couldn't possibly have done so. Why?"

"The autopsy," said Hazlerigg, "confirms that Conyers died of heart failure caused by violent shock. I've just been talking to Simcock, who performed the autopsy. He says that Conyers had a bad heart – hence, incidentally, his high colour. But it wasn't as bad as all that. Simcock swears that *something must* have happened to set him off – something, perhaps, almost physical. As if some practical joker had pulled his chair away from under him as he was about to sit down, or suddenly produced a luminous hand floating in the air, or touched off a firecracker just behind him – something like that."

"But," said Bohun, blankly, "it's impossible! Or are you implying that Ruddock might have slid along their seat and stuck a pin into him, or given him some kind of violent electric shock?"

"That might have done it. Only it didn't. A pin would have left a puncture. And any sort of violent electric shock would have burned him. Conyers's body was absolutely unmarked."

"It's crazy," said Bohun. "And anyway, why?"

"Both men had good reasons for wishing him dead. Conyers was on the point of taking the whole of his group's advertising away from Ruddock. He had formed the opinion that Ruddock was inefficient."

"If Ruddock was the murderer," said Bohun, "there was nothing inefficient about his performance."

"I agree. Blessingham was head of the group's printing works. He'd had a personal row with Conyers and was on his way out – and he knew it. On the other hand, if something happened to Conyers, he'd probably not lose his job. So his livelihood was at stake."

"There was a bit of personal hate there too," said Bohun. "It was concealed, but you couldn't mistake it . . . Which one was it? And how did he do it?"

"If we knew how, we'd know which one," said Hazlerigg.

Bohun took the mystery home with him that night. He travelled on the 8:16, and had the carriage entirely to himself. In his brief case he had seven different editions of the *Evening Standard,* which his secretary had rounded up for him throughout the day. He spread them all over the empty seats, and pored over them. The ticket collector looked in at Bromley and said, "Ar. A competition. They give big prizes for 'em."

"There's no prize for this one," said Bohun, gathering up the news-papers.

Since there was no time to waste, he rang Hazlerigg from the Station-master's Office.

"It was Conyers's newspaper," he said. "I knew there was something wrong with it. They change a good many things from edition to edition – *but they never change the advertisements!*"

"Good lord," said Hazlerigg, "I believe you're right."

"If you know how, you know who," said Bohun. "Blessingham is a printer – that makes it him. If you get round to his house quickly, you may still find some evidence."

He heard the end of the story two days later.

"It was Blessingham, all right," said Hazlerigg. "He faked up a copy of the *Standard* with a phony centre page – and persuaded the chap at Victoria to sell Conyers that copy. Said it was a joke on a friend. The newspaper vender has identified Blessingham – so we're in the clear."

"And I suppose he exchanged his own paper for the bogus one in the confusion after coming out of the tunnel."

"I guess so – and destroyed the phony. And broke up the form he'd printed it from, in a shed back of his house. Only he forgot that he'd taken a couple of trial pulls and we found one of them. Most of it was genuine – all but the stocking advertisement from an old edition, to fill space, and one news item which was entirely the product of Blessingham's malice. *Cashier Held by French Police,* it was headed. I'll let you see it some time – it's rather well done. And nicely timed too. The head cashier of Conyers's group is actually on holiday in France right now. This fake news item says that the French police are holding him and that he's already confessed to 'substantial defalcations which might involve other persons in the group.' Conyers must have reached that item just before the tunnel."

"Yes," said Bohun, thoughtfully. "Not good medicine for a dicky heart. Clever, too. If it came off, it seemed foolproof. If it didn't, it was just a joke in doubtful taste, in very doubtful taste."

Then Bohun added, "I have noticed that there are two sorts of people: those who talk on trains and those who listen. If Blessingham had listened more and talked less, he might have learned from Ruddock that it doesn't always pay to advertise."

London *Evening Standard,* September 22, 1955.

MONEY IS HONEY

"FOR THE DEAR LORD'S SAKE go down and deal with Mallet direct," said Mr. Craine, senior partner of Horniman, Birley and Craine, solicitors, of Lincoln's Inn, to his young partner Mr. Bohun. "He was on the telephone to me yesterday afternoon for two hours. My left ear still feels the size of a watermelon. You know as much about his blasted companies as I do. Ask yourself down to lunch. It's only ninety minutes out of Liverpool Street. You'll like Humble Bee House. It sounds a sort of stockbroker Gothic joke; actually it's early Victorian and rather nice—"

Further telephoning followed, and at half past twelve Henry Bohun stood at the wrought iron gates of Humble Bee House. He saw at once what Craine had meant. The place had been built as a gentleman's residence at a very bad period of English domestic architecture, but time and nature had dealt kindly with it. Myrtle, privet and laurustinus had lost planned formality and had run together to turn the driveway into a funnel of light and shade. Halfway along, on the left of the drive, a formal sunken garden had slipped back to the simple grassy glade from which it had been hewed; its ledges supported a colony of blue-and-white hives, eight or ten small ones clustered round a large one. In the September sunlight the bees were pottering about, making their last preparations for winter.

Next moment he was startled to see a fox look out at him. He stopped. The fox grinned, crossed the drive, and disappeared silently. Bohun wondered if he ought to do something about it. Would it be correct to shout View Halloo! He was too much of a Londoner to feel any certainty about the matter.

The door was opened by a middle-aged maid. He announced his business, and was shown into a large, dark room intersected with bookcases, and branching out into unexpected window seats and embrasures, so that it had the appearance of three or four separate rooms in one.

"By the way," said Bohun, as the maid was about to withdraw, "I don't know if you knew – but you've got a fox in your front garden."

"There's a badger, too," said the maid. "They belong to Master Norman. I'll ask if Mr. Mallet can see you."

Reflecting that he had come all the way from London at Mr. Mallet's express invitation, it seemed to Bohun conceivable that he might. However, he merely nodded and sat down. The maid withdrew and Bohun opened his briefcase and sorted out the papers dealing with the Mallet-Sobieski Trustee and Debenture Corporation.

Click-click-click-click. Clickety-click.

Bohun looked up from his papers.

Click-click. Clickety-click-click-click.

Too regular for a cricket. Too loud for a death-watch beetle.

After standing it for a few minutes he put down his papers and moved softly across the carpet. The noise seemed to come from behind a parapet of bookshelves in the far corner of the room.

When he rounded the corner he was surprised to find that he had not been alone in the room after all. A tall man with a thick moustache and one eye was sitting on the edge of the window-seat. He was rattling three dice in his large, brown right hand, and turning them out on to the table in front of him.

"Morning," he said. "You the lawyer?"

"That's right," said Bohun.

"Bloody house, isn't it? Poker dice. Fancy a game? My name's Rix – Major Rix."

"Mine's Bohun," said Bohun. "No, thank you. I'm just waiting to see Mr. Mallet."

"Doubt if you'll be able to," said Rix. "He's pretty ill, you know."

Bohun looked surprised.

"It must have been very sudden," he said. "He spent most of yesterday afternoon talking to my partner on the telephone. I gather he was in rather strong form."

It was Rix's turn to look surprised. "I wouldn't know about that," he said. "He's been in bed for a week. Had a stroke or something. Oh, there's that bloody man Morgan. Morgan, I say—"

"Sir?"

Although he had heard nothing the voice came from directly behind Bohun's right shoulder. A middle-aged man, in dark clothes, had come quietly into the room and added himself to the party.

"Oh, Morgan. Someone has locked the corner cupboard."

"Yes, sir. I locked it, on Mr. Mallet's orders."

"Then kindly unlock it."

"There was something you wanted?"

"You're damned right there's something I wanted," said Major Rix. "That's where the whisky lives."

Morgan moved across to the cupboard, selected a key from a ring of keys and opened the cupboard. He then went over to the sideboard, opened that, and took out a tumbler. Into the tumbler he poured a very reasonable quantity of whisky, replaced the bottle in the cupboard, relocked the cupboard, and handed the glass to Major Rix.

He did all this in the most serious manner possible.

"There is a syphon of soda in the sideboard – if you require it, sir," he said. "That is not locked."

Major Rix said nothing at all. He simply picked up the tumbler and swirled the whisky round in it.

"Perhaps you would care to come with me," said Morgan.

"Oh – certainly." Bohun recovered himself with an effort. As he looked back he saw that the major was still sitting in his chair. His single eye had a frosty, faraway look in it.

Bohun followed Morgan up the stairs. As they reached the top a door opened and a woman came out. Pre-war Oxford, thought Bohun at once. About thirty-five. Bluestocking, but overlaid now with a certain amount of country moss.

"Good morning?" she said, managing to turn it into a question.

"This is Mr. Bohun, Miss Rachel. He's here to see your father on business."

"Business." Miss Mallet sounded upset. "But – is Daddy well enough to see this gentleman?"

"I expect it will be important business," said Morgan. "Some matter which *has to* be attended to. You understand."

"Oh – yes, I expect that's it." Miss Mallet turned to Bohun, drawing him aside with her glance in a way which seemed to exclude Morgan from the whole conversation.

"You must be as quick as you can, Mr. Bohun. If you've brought something – something for him to sign, get it done as quickly as possible. He's a dying man."

"He's—"

"If you'd come this way," said Morgan loudly. Miss Mallet laid a hand on his arm. "I want you to promise me," she said.

"I'm afraid," said Bohun carefully, "that there may be some mistake. The business I have to discuss with your father – it isn't family business at all. It's to do with his work in London. We've got quite a few important decisions to make. However – I'll certainly be as quick as I can, I promise you that."

All the time that he had been speaking she had kept hold of his arm. Morgan had taken a step forward and seemed almost ready to grasp him by the other arm. Penelope and the Suitors, thought Bohun. He was inclined to let the scene develop but it was broken up by a noise from below.

Major Rix had come out into the hall.

The drink which Morgan had poured for him must have been stronger than it looked, for even from above it could be seen that he was swaying very slightly on his feet, and he fumbled with the door handle for a few moments as he closed the door.

Miss Mallet had dropped Bohun's arm and was looking down into the hall. The expression on her face reminded him of a visitor at the zoo, some adult, intellectual spinster, peering down into the trough of the Reptile House. Detached, intrigued, very faintly nauseated.

"If you'd come along now," said Morgan.

When they had turned the corner of the corridor he halted. It was too dark for Bohun to see his face.

"I expect you haven't met Miss Rachel before," he said.

"I haven't had the pleasure—"

"Nor Master Norman?"

"No, I've never met him."

"You don't want to pay too much attention to what either of them say. They're both a little bit – you know."

Before Bohun could say anything more he had turned, knocked at a big, double door and opened it without waiting for an answer.

The room was in half-darkness, and what light there was came from a reading lamp placed slightly behind the bed in such a way that it deepened the shadows on the face of the man who lay there.

Bohun was considerably startled at the picture. But he was even more startled when Mr. Mallet sat up vigorously from his supporting pillows. His voice, when he spoke, showed no trace of weakness.

"Where are the children, Morgan?"

"Miss Rachel has gone downstairs. Mr. Norman is out with his birds."

"Then draw the curtains back a bit. We must have some light. Fetch Mr. Bohun a chair. That's right, we can use this table. Now, Bohun – this holding company. I tried to explain it to Craine, but he seemed to find it very difficult to understand. Perhaps I oughtn't to say so, but he seems to be losing his grip a bit—"

Fortunately Bohun had met Mr. Mallet before; most people in a certain line of business in the City ran across him sooner or later. Rumour had it that he had been a sergeant major in one of the administrative branches during the First World War and had made a pile out of the barter of vehicle spare parts. Whatever truth there may have been in this was now buried in the drift of time. The early 'twenties had been spent in company flotation, as audacious as it was profitable. After this he had transferred his energies to the field of the Trust Corporation. At sixty he was rich and practically respectable.

"He's quite a character," Mr. Craine had warned him. "He shouts and bangs and swears and insults you and roars with laughter and sends you a dozen bottles of Scotch for Christmas. One year he sent me a box of exploding cigars. In some ways he's got a lot in common with the late Joe Stalin—"

At the end of two hours, although he had been sustained with a plate of sandwiches and a glass of milk, brought up by Morgan, Bohun felt limpish. The table was littered with papers, and Bohun was beginning to wonder whether it was he who was advising Mr. Mallet on the effect of the latest Finance Act, or vice versa. However, they had reached some sort of conclusion when steps sounded in the passage. Mr. Mallet swept the papers together, stuffed them under his pillow, turned off the second light, and sank back with a loud groan.

The door opened, and Morgan came in.

Mr. Mallet came to life at once.

"Thought it was Rachel," he said. "That's all right then. If anything further's needed, I'll telephone Craine tomorrow. I think you've got a good grasp of it, quite a good grasp."

"Thank you," said Bohun faintly.

"One other thing. If you happen to talk to either of my children before you go, would you mind remembering that I'm a dying man? I had a stroke at the beginning of the week which paralysed my left side. It hasn't affected my brain in any way, but if I should have another – which seems very possible – it may well finish me. You understand?"

"Oh, certainly," said Bohun. "I'm sorry to hear—"

"Not at all," said Mr. Mallet. "Stay to tea if you like. Morgan will drive you to the station in time for the five o'clock train."

It was two mornings later before Bohun got round to discussing the Mallet family with Mr. Craine.

"You've never seen such a crazy setup in your life. Either the father's mad, or the children are mad, or they're all mad—"

"I've never noticed anything actually mad about Mallet," said Craine. "You're certain he wasn't really ill?"

"I'm not a doctor," said Bohun. "Strokes are funny things. But in my view he was no more ill than—"

"Blast that telephone," said Mr. Craine. "Excuse me a moment.

Who? Mr. Mallet? Oh, young Mr. Mallet. Put him through please—"

The telephone squeaked and bumbled. Whoever was speaking at the other end had a lot to get off his mind, and was determined to unload it fast.

At last Mr. Craine succeeded in breaking in.

"I've got Mr. Bohun here with me," he said. "Yes – that's my partner. He came down to see you two days ago. He knows all about it. When? Oh, right away. If he gets the next train he should be with you before lunch."

He rang off.

"Look here," said Bohun, "I've got Lady Maidsmoreton coming—"

"Mallet's dead," said Craine. "He died this morning. The house is in an uproar. You'll have to go and cope. Take the will with you. I've got it here. I'm sole executor so you've got my full authority to spend any money and take any steps you like. I expect you may have to be down there a couple of days, so I'll get John Cove to look after your work. Miss Thwaites, would you mind getting hold of a taxi?"

"Oh dear," said Norman Mallet. "Oh dear. I'm so g-glad you've g-got here, Mr—Mr. Bohun. I'm sure it will make a great difference having you here. I'm sorry you had to walk up from the station. I couldn't find Morgan and I couldn't – I mean, he always k-keeps the keys of the car on him, so it was very awkward." He had a slight, rather pleasant stammer. "How did it happen?" said Bohun.

"Last night. Just as he always s-said it would. Quite suddenly. Like that—" Norman snapped his fingers, then seemed to find the gesture slightly indecorous and restored his hand to his trouser pocket.

"It was between n-nine and eleven. Rachel saw him at nine. She usually went in to see him last thing at night, to tuck him up and give him his – well to make him comfortable. When Morgan went up at eleven o'clock to settle him for the night, he found him d-dead. We sent for the doctor, of course. That's Dr. Runcorn. He's up there now. You'll be able to see him."

"Did Dr. Runcorn know that your father was ill?"

"Of course. He's been father's d-doctor for years."

"But he knew about the stroke?" persisted Bohun.

"Oh, yes, he knew about that."

"Was he attending him?"

"Well, there was nothing much he could do."

The elderly parlourmaid appeared. She had been crying.

"Will Mr. Bohun be staying?" she enquired.

"Why, yes – certainly. That is, I hope you'll be staying—"

"I'd like to stop to lunch, if it wouldn't be troubling you," said Bohun. "I've booked a room at the Black Goats."

"I expect you'll be more c-comfortable there," said Norman, without making a great deal of effort to conceal his relief. "Placket, would you show Mr. Bohun up – he'd like a word with the doctor."

"It's quite all right," said Bohun. "I know the way."

He was halfway up the stairs when the study door opened and Major Rix appeared. He snapped a finger at Bohun and said, "Come on down here a moment, there's something I want to tell you."

"I must—"

"It's important," said Rix. "You'd better hear it."

"Oh, all right," said Bohun.

"They'll tell you Mallet died of a stroke," said Rix, as soon as the library door was shut. "Nothing further from the truth. The doctor's an old fool. He wouldn't know a stroke from German measles."

"I—" said Bohun.

"Just let me tell you this," said Rix urgently. "Mallet was murdered. Morgan did it. I don't know how. Poison or something, I should think. There's enough poison in this house to finish off the French Navy. Herbal muck. Rachel brews it. Another thing. What did Morgan slip up to London for last Thursday? Mallet never sent him. But I saw him. I was up there on business. He was coming out of some place off the Gray's Inn Road. Lot of shady chemists shops in that district. Don't tell me he was up to nothing."

Bohun hardly liked to point out that if there was plenty of poison in the house it seemed a waste of time to go all the way up to London to buy more. But Rix was beyond such considerations. He was also more than a little drunk.

"Have you any idea," he said, "why Morgan should want to do that?"

"Of course," said Rix. "You know it as well as I do. Mallet had left him five thousand under his will. He was going to change it when Rachel married me. Morgan was afraid he'd get left out of the new one. I needn't tell you."

"Er—no," said Bohun. He had Mr. Mallet's will in his pocket and was reasonably familiar with its contents. "Well, I think perhaps you ought to be rather careful about saying things like that to anyone—"

"I wouldn't say them to anyone," agreed Rix handsomely. "After all, you're just a bloody lawyer. You're paid to have things said to you."

"Quite so," said Bohun. It was a view of his professional duties which had been expressed to him before, though never quite so bluntly. He went upstairs to find the doctor.

Dr. Runcorn was just finishing. He was a dignified little sheep with a respectable crown of smooth, white hair, and muddy grey eyes. He shook Bohun's hand and said, "I'm glad you've come. The lawyer takes on where the doctor leaves off. Very sad, a busy man like him. But businessmen often go that way."

"It was the stroke, then."

"A recurrence of the stroke, yes."

That seemed to be that.

Bohun said, "I know nothing about strokes, of course, but I saw him two days ago and he seemed so alert and vigorous."

"Vigorous enough in mind," said the doctor. "That's often the way. It attacks the body first."

"He seemed comparatively vigorous in body, too."

"I'm afraid I don't follow you," said Dr. Runcorn. "I saw him myself on – let me see – Monday morning, and he was completely paralysed. He could only move his head and neck."

"Then he'd made a remarkable recovery," said Bohun. "When we were discussing business on Tuesday afternoon he sat up without apparent effort, handled the various papers extremely vigorously and generally behaved like a man who was perfectly well, but happened to be taking a day's rest in bed."

"Did you see him out of bed?"

"Well – no."

"You're quite sure you're not exaggerating his other movements?"

"I'm not in the habit of exaggerating," said Bohun.

"Well, it's very remarkable. But, then, nature is remarkable. It is of academic interest now, poor fellow."

"There was more to it than that," said Bohun steadily. "Once or twice in the course of our conversation he suggested that the whole of his illness was a sham. Something intended to deceive his children."

Dr. Runcorn went very red and his mouth tightened disagreeably.

"Am I to understand that you are suggesting that he deceived his medical adviser, too?"

"Well, it would be possible, wouldn't it? Who's to know? A man says to you, 'I've had a stroke. My mind is quite clear but my body won't move.' There's nothing to show, is there? Or is there?"

"There can be certain secondary symptoms—"

"Were these present in Mallet's case?"

"To a limited degree. But I'm afraid I cannot see where this is taking us. Are you suggesting that he is not dead now?"

"No," said Bohun softly, looking at the sheeted figure on the bed. "No. That is a fact that I think we will have to accept."

"Then what do you suggest, pray?"

"Perhaps a further examination into the cause of death."

"I have made my examination."

"Then I suggest a second opinion."

"And your authority for making the suggestion?"

"The lawyer," said Bohun unkindly, "takes on where the doctor leaves off. I act for the sole executor – who happens to be my partner. I will obtain his written directions if you insist."

Dr. Runcorn went white. "Really," he said. "I think you are making a mountain out of a molehill. You realise, I hope, what you are doing. Perhaps you would like the police in the house as well—"

The door crashed open. The noise and urgency of it made both men jump. It was Major Rix. He looked almost sober.

"Morgan's been shot," he said. "I just found him in the spinney at the back of the house."

"Well, now," said Inspector Franks patiently, "and where do you come into this?"

Bohun told him where he came in.

Inspector Franks spelled his name out carefully, and said, "It's a long shot, but you wouldn't by any chance happen to know a Superintendent Hazlerigg?"

"Yes. He was a Chief Inspector when I knew him."

"Then you're the chap who doesn't go to sleep?"

"The eye that never closes," agreed Bohun.

"Ah," said Inspector Franks. He thought for a minute, and then said, "I expect it'll be a help to me, having an independent inside view, as you might say. If you've no objection."

"None at all," said Bohun. "But don't expect too much. I've known Mallet for some time, but I only met Rachel when I came down on Tuesday – and I actually saw Norman for the first time this morning."

"Norman and Rachel," said Franks. "Those would be the only children?" He turned back the pages of his book. "I've seen both of them, but I couldn't make much out of them. Both a bit young for their age, I thought."

"Retarded adolescence," agreed Bohun. "Stern parent. Not much contact with the outside world. Norman keeps foxes and badgers. Rachel brews herbs."

"Well now," said Franks. "Herbs?"

"Just before we go on with this," said Bohun, "there's a point I'd like to be quite clear on. Which death are you investigating?"

"Both, at the moment," said Franks. "Morgan could be suicide – but I don't think it is. Mallet could be natural causes. I'm keeping an open mind about that."

"Have you got someone doing the necessary?"

"Police surgeon. Yes. He won't miss much."

"Good," said Bohun. "As long as that's settled."

"I've got one or two other people to see. Perhaps you'd like to listen in. Representing the next of kin."

"That's very good of you," said Bohun, trying to conceal his surprise. It occurred to him that Hazlerigg must have given him an exceptionally good ticket.

The middle-aged maid came. Her name was Placket.

"Such a good master," she said, "and such a kind father."

"Really, now," said Franks. "No trouble at all?"

"A happy, united family," said Placket. "The children stopping at home, and not rushing off the very moment they were out of the schoolroom."

"Let me see. Mr. Norman is just forty and Miss Rachel is thirty-five?"

"She was thirty-five last month. I still make them each a cake on their birthday. Thirty-five candles. It has to be a big cake."

"So I should think," said the Inspector, impassively.

"You say they were a happy, cheerful family? I suppose Mr. Mallet spent a lot of time up in town. What did the children do all day?"

"Employed themselves as country people should," said Placket, rather tartly. "Master Norman had his studies. He's a great naturalist. What he doesn't know about birds and beasts – but there! You'll have seen for yourself. And Miss Rachel, she collects herbs. She's published a book—"

She went over to the shelf and pulled out a volume. It was a solid-looking book and published, Bohun saw, by a well-known firm. *The Herbs and Plants of East Anglia. Their Uses in Medicine and Cookery* by Rachel Mallet.

The Inspector looked happier. "I'd like to keep that for a bit."

"I expect Miss Rachel would sign it for you if you asked her," said Placket.

"Happy family," said Major Rix. "Don't you believe it. I've never seen such a little hell-kitchen in my life. Wogs, Wops and Wuzzies – I've seen them all. Believe me, for real hating you want to come to the English Shires."

"Well, now; that's very interesting—"

"Old Mallet was a pirate, you see. He'd got the pirate mentality.

When he'd made his haul, he liked to put it in a chest and sit on it. He liked his bits and pieces all round him, where he could see 'em. Rachel and Norman were bits and pieces. If he'd had his own way, he'd just like to have had them sitting round, quietly, as if they'd been carefully preserved and put under glass. Only human nature doesn't work out like that. All it did was to make 'em branch out in other ways. Norman and his birds and bees, and Rachel and her herbs. That sort of thing. The more they tried to lead lives of their own, the more he tried to stop them. First he tried to argue them out of it – no good. Then he tried to laugh them out of it. Do you know, he got a chap to write a sort of skit of Rachel's herb book – not very funny really. I read some of it. I reckon he had to pay through the nose to get *that* published—"

"Rather an elaborate joke," said Franks.

"Oh, he was like that. Go to any lengths for a laugh. As long as it made someone else uncomfortable. Very like a man I once knew in Jamaica – trained a tortoise to drink rum. However, that's another story. Lately it's been leg-pulling. Country superstitions and that sort of thing. Norman knows 'em all. Swallows go up at night, good weather coming. Rooks fly round the trees, it's going to rain. Norman believes in 'em all."

"There are certain scientific explanations—" began Bohun, but he caught a look from Inspector Franks and subsided.

"Well, I don't know about that," said Rix. "Prefer a barometer myself. However, Mallet used to pull his leg about it properly. When they had visitors. Particularly when they had visitors. I've heard Mallet say, 'Oh, Morgan, when I was out in the garden this morning, I saw the bees flying backwards round the hive. What do you suppose that means?' And Morgan would say, solemn as a judge, 'I am given to understand, sir, that it signifies that Consols will rise two points before the next account.' And so on. The more he bullied 'em the quieter they hated him."

"Not a very happy family," said Franks.

"You're telling me."

"But you were proposing to marry into it?"

"Yes. But I wasn't going to live with them afterwards."

"You didn't anticipate any trouble, then."

"Marriage always leads to trouble," said Major Rix frankly. "It's just one of those things you've got to put up with. My last wife used to shoot at me with an air gun."

"Hmph," said Inspector Franks. "Now, about the evening of Mr. Mallet's death."

"I know just what you're going to say," said Major Rix, "and I know it didn't sound good, all that stuff I was telling you about Rachel and Norman hating their father. But it doesn't mean they killed him. It wasn't them at all. That sort of hating doesn't lead to killing. You can take my word for that. It was Morgan. I never trusted him an inch myself. Then, after he'd done it he got cold feet and went out and shot himself. I've seen that happen before."

"Yes," said Franks. "No doubt it's one of the solutions we shall have to investigate. Thank you very much for what you have told us. Meanwhile—"

"There was one thing," said Bohun. "When you found Morgan this morning – were you certain he was dead?"

"Of course I knew he was dead. I've seen lots of dead men before."

"Did you disturb the body in any way?"

"Did I—certainly not."

"To be quite specific," said Bohun. "Did you take a key from the ring of keys in his hip pocket?"

Involuntarily the Major turned to look over his shoulder at the corner cupboard. It was ajar.

"All right," he said. "Very smart of you. I borrowed the key of the drink cupboard."

"Why did you do that?" said Franks sharply.

"Well, really," said Rix. "Just because the bloody man had shot himself, I saw no reason to put all the whisky into pawn."

"Well, now," said Franks. "You'll be doing me a service if you tell me what you make of all that?"

It was evening, the oil lamp had been trimmed and lit, and they were alone in the coffee-room of the Black Goats, an ancient apartment approached by so many twisted stairs and winding corridors that it seemed improbable that anyone else should ever find his way to it.

"I don't mean the routine bits," he went on. "I shall have to wait for the reports to come in tomorrow. There's the doctor's report on Mallet and on Morgan and I've had an expert look at the gun which killed Morgan – it's an ordinary twelve-bore sporting gun from the case in the gun room, but it might tell us something. And there's the fingerprints and photographs and so on. They might be useful." He spoke as a man who has not got a great deal of faith in fingerprints and photographs, but Bohun was not deceived.

He did not know much about police routine, but he did know that most cases were solved by simple hard work on matters of detail by a great number of policemen.

"It's the shape of the thing that rattles me. Usually you can see which way a thing goes, right at the start. Man or woman gets killed – in nine cases out of ten it's the husband or wife who did it. That's one of the things about marriage. You do know where you are. Or else perhaps it's a professional – breaking and entering and so on. You just look up the list. But this—" He spread his hands despairingly.

"It is a bit confusing," agreed Bohun. He got up, trimmed the lamp, and sat down again sympathetically.

"First of all you've got Mallet, if that *was* murder. Even allowing for it being an inside job, you've got plenty of candidates. Norman and Rachel who hated him – according to Rix. Morgan who wanted his money—"

"Oh, there's nothing in that one," said Bohun. "I've got the will here. So far as I know it's the only will Mallet made, and he never had the slightest intention of changing it. Morgan got five hundred pounds in either case – not five thousand."

"It's not always what's in a will that causes the trouble," said Franks. "It's what people think may be in it. Can you tell me what happened to the rest?"

"Oh yes, I think I can do that. There are a few other little gifts – five hundred pounds to Placket – the others are people in his London office. Then the rest goes into two parts. One half to Norman and one half to Rachel. Only she can't touch her capital. It's tied up in the usual way to prevent a husband getting hold of any of it."

"Do you suppose Rix knew that?"

"Even if he did, he was on to quite a good thing when Mallet died. They couldn't touch the capital, but Rachel's income would have been about six thousand a year. That would have done very nicely to pay the bills – he'd have had free board and lodging, food and drink for the rest of his life. Particularly drink."

"So far as money goes then, Rix and Morgan both had motives. Only Morgan's may have been smaller than he imagined."

"That's about it," said Bohun.

"When you look at the means," said Franks, "there's nothing to choose between them. We make it as difficult as we can for people to buy poison, but the law hasn't yet got round to stopping them making it for themselves. Mallet used to have a hot whisky at nine o'clock. Almost anyone got it ready and took it up. There was no rule about it. Norman and Rachel say Morgan took it up that night. Placket says she thinks Norman did. Rachel certainly went up to see him at nine o'clock."

"And what about Morgan's death?"

"There's even less there. The gun was in a cupboard with the cartridges – not locked. Anyone could pick it up, follow Morgan into the spinney – and shoot him. No one would take any notice. The fields are full of those automatic bird-scarers. They go off about once an hour."

"Then perhaps Morgan did shoot himself."

"If he did," said Franks. "All right. He's the obvious candidate for Mallet. Then the thing's reasonably straight. But if he didn't – it doesn't seem to have any shape at all. There's a piece missing somewhere."

"I'm only here to make suggestions," said Bohun. "You do the work. I'm under no delusions about that. I quite agree with what you said – the middle piece is missing, and the other pieces won't match up till you find it. All I've got at the moment is three questions in my head. The first's a tiny matter of fact. What was Morgan doing up in London last Thursday?"

"I've got an enquiry going," said Franks. "I circulated a photograph. Unfortunately it's not a very good one – and there are quite a lot of shops in and around the Gray's Inn Road."

"All right," said Bohun. "It may be nothing."

The lamp was smoking again, and he got up to adjust it, first turning the flame right down, then carefully up again, talking as he worked. "The second question is, were the two deaths connected? I don't necessarily mean, did the same person do both. But were they logically connected? And, if so, how? The third point seems to me to be the oddest of the lot. Suppose that the postmortem on Mallet shows that his stroke was a fake. Then what was the point of it? Mallet was a notorious joker, but his jokes always seemed to end with a big belly laugh for Mallet and someone else feeling all kinds of a fool. This one doesn't seem to have worked out quite like that. *What went wrong?*"

"First report," said Franks next morning, "from the doctor, on Mallet. No sign of any cerebral congestion or haemorrhage. In plain English. No stroke."

"So much for old Uncle Runcorn."

"Yes. Not very good. But there's more to it than that. Equivalent of three grains of hyoscine or hyosciamine in the stomach and digestive organs. Not *materia medicastuit*. Vegetable origin. Derived from distillation of the seeds of henbane, alias hogsbean, alias stinking nightshade. Probable that the dose was taken after Mallet had his evening meal but before midnight. To be continued."

"Quite enough to go on with," said Bohun.

"I thought you'd like it. Second report. Doctor on Morgan. Suicide barely possible, but most unlikely. Position of wounds – direction of wounds – powder burns, etc., etc. You can read it for yourself."

Bohun did so. "It certainly sounds acrobatic," he agreed. "Muzzle at least twenty-four inches away from the head, but pointing practically straight at it. I really think you can rule out suicide."

"I had already done so," agreed Franks. "Listen to this. Report number three. Absolutely *no fingerprints* on the gun of any sort. Morgan wasn't wearing gloves. Tell me how he could shoot himself without leaving any prints on the gun."

"All right," said Bohun. "That's that. Anything else on Morgan?"

"General state of health. State of clothing. Contents of pockets—"

"Let's have that one."

"Wallet, money, old letters, bills. Nothing recent. Handkerchief, packet of fags. Lighter. Large pocketknife. Key ring—"

"Key ring?"

"That checks up with Rix's story. The key of the drink cupboard was missing – and we picked up half a possible Rix fingerprint on one of the other keys. He probably touched it when he was removing the first key."

"A cool customer," said Bohun. "What other keys?"

"Two house doors, cellar and two safe keys."

"Hmph," said Bohun. "House. Cellar. Safe. Hmph?"

"One other small point. He'd got three recent bee stings. Two on his right arm, one on his left wrist."

"Had he though?" said Bohun.

He went off to telephone Craine.

"You'd better stay down there," said Craine. "I suppose there's bound to be an inquest. When they've finished cutting him up perhaps you can get him buried. The instructions are in the envelope with the will."

After lunch Franks reappeared. He had a look in his eye which meant more news.

"I've got a good identification of Morgan on his shopping expedition," he said. "The shop assistant picked the photograph straight out of a dozen without even stopping to think, bless him. I'll give you three guesses what he went up to London to buy."

"I'm not that good," said Bohun. "You tell me."

"A dictaphone. The sort of thing a businessman keeps on his desk to breathe his secret thoughts into. Not very big"—Franks demonstrated with his hands—"A small dispatch-case would hold it. But powerful, and up to date. Records on a roll and the typist plays it back later into earphones."

Bohun digested this.

"Have you found it yet?"

"I've got every man I can lay hands on, busy now taking the house apart. If it's there I'll find it before dusk." Dusk came. And dark. But no dictaphone.

At one o'clock in the morning Bohun was sitting by himself in the wheel-back rocking chair in the coffee-room. He had got the wick of the lamp adjusted to a nicety now and the oil flame spread its low, warm, kind light over the dingy old room.

He was not asleep, nor even sleepy, because he suffered from para-insomnia and rarely slept more than an hour in any night. None of the doctors who had examined him had agreed about any point in his rare complaint except that one day he would drop down dead.

He knew, by experience, when he was due to sleep and until that moment it was a waste of time even to go near his bedroom. He found the night hours useful. Sometimes he wrote, sometimes he read, sometimes he thought – a luxury which few normal people can fit into their crowded waking lives.

He was thinking at that moment and he was making quite reasonable progress. For example, he was certain, now, that the double murderer was Norman Mallet. He was the only man with a real motive. As Major Rix had pointed out, people often got angry over their family's idiosyncrasies, but they very rarely killed each other on account of them. With Norman it was different. If he believed that his father was using his money to coerce Rachel into a loveless marriage with Rix, then he might well think it his duty to stop it. More particularly if he was convinced that his father was dying already. And most particularly if he saw a lawyer coming to the house. Lawyers meant settlements and new wills or codicils. From that point of view his own visit had probably timed the murder. It had set it off. And this despite the fact that both Norman's assumptions were false. His father had *not* been dying, and Bohun's visit had been *nothing* to do with his will.

Where motives were concerned, as the Inspector had so truly remarked, it wasn't what actually happened, but what people thought was going to happen that produced results.

As for the killing of Morgan, Norman had given himself away at his very first meeting. Bohun had not observed the fact at the time, but had remembered it afterwards. Apologising for not coming to the station to fetch him, he had said, "Morgan always keeps the keys of the car on him." Now that was not true. Search of Morgan's body had shown a number of keys, but they were house keys, not the garage key, and not the car key. It seemed logical to suppose that the reason Norman had been unable to meet him was that he had been too busy murdering Morgan.

Why he had done so, and what sort of connection it could have with the death of Mr. Mallet, was the final step in this tangled business.

Franks had been right about that. There was a piece missing. It was the middle piece of the jigsaw puzzle, and when he saw it, all the other little edges and twists would fall into position, and a recognisable whole would appear.

What had been the point of Mallet's last great pointless practical joke?

What connection had it, if any, with his previous jokes? His ridiculing of his children's love of birds and animals and country life and country superstitions?

What use had he for a dictaphone? Why had it to be obtained secretly? And where was it now if it wasn't in Humble Bee House?

How had Morgan managed to get his wrists and arms stung three times?

There is enormous virtue in sequence. It is conceivable that if Bohun had asked himself these questions in any other order he might not have spotted the truth which, by now, was staring him in the face.

Feeling a little shaken in spite of himself he got to his feet and made his way to his bedroom. From his suitcase he took a torch and from the pocket of his coat a pair of gloves. It would be dark but there would be light enough for his purpose. And in any event, night was the best time, as Morgan had no doubt discovered. As he was leaving the inn he saw, in the corner of the hall, a heavy stick, and after a moment's hesitation he added this to his equipment.

Half an hour later he was standing once more at the gate of Humble Bee House. The driveway was a tunnel of darkness. It was the hour of false dawn, and, standing quite still, he could hear life moving in the thickets which bordered the drive. He opened the gate as quietly as he could, and the ghost of a wind set the leaves whispering, so that the news of his arrival seemed to run ahead of him up the drive.

He went silently, on the turf edge, and presently he found himself by the glade of beehives. The large one in the middle was clearly the place. He could have wished that he knew more about bees.

Putting down his torch and stick he grasped the roof very gently with both hands. It came up, in one piece, together with the top section of the hive. Underneath was nothing more alarming than a folded blanket.

He listened very carefully, and in the stillness he sensed rather than saw the legion of sleeping bees. Very gently he raised the blanket and, sure enough, there was the dictaphone, a box-like affair above the first comb-section, with its receiver immediately behind the ventilation grille in front of the hive. Carefully he lifted it, carefully replaced the blanket and hive-top. Then he tiptoed away with his spoil into the thickest part of the shrubbery.

A quarter of an hour later he was back in the bee glade. He lifted the top and replaced the dictaphone exactly where he had found it. He stood for a moment as if undecided. Then, with a quick, almost abrupt gesture, he pulled a pencil and notebook from his pocket and, using his torch guardedly, scribbled a note. When he had finished it, he tore out the page, folded it in four, and wrote a name on the outside. Then, with the paper in his hand, he made his way up the drive, towards the sleeping front of Humble Bee House.

It was eleven o'clock on the following morning when Bohun reached Humble Bee House once again, and rang the front door bell. The door was opened by Placket, who had no word to say to him. The Inspector was behind her in the hall.

"It's all over," he said. "Perhaps you'd better come up."

Norman and Rachel Mallet were sitting, upright, in chairs on either side of the empty hearth in their father's room. It was difficult, in the shadows, to realise that they were dead, so quietly and calmly they sat. Almost as if they had been carefully preserved, thought Bohun, and put under glass. The words formed an echo in his head.

"They took the same stuff as they gave the old man," said Franks. "Norman left a note – just to say that he was responsible for both his father and Morgan. Not much explanation. He says it was him, not his sister, but she knew about it – afterwards. I don't suppose we shall ever understand the whole of it now."

"On the contrary," said Bohun. "If you'll come out in the garden I'll do my level best to explain it to you."

"I wouldn't try to open it now, not unless you happen to be a skilled apiarist," said Bohun. "But inside that large central hive you'll find the dictaphone Mallet and Morgan bought for the consummation of their final stupendous joke."

"Joke?"

"So elaborate. So funny. So much in character. What's the best-known and oldest superstition about bees? That if there's a death in the house, they must be the first to be told about it. Can't you imagine it? After a week or ten days of preparation and preliminary fun, getting everyone in the mood for it, Morgan suddenly comes down last thing at night with the news that the master has had a second stroke and passed away. Chaos and confusion and the doctor to be sent for, and the lawyers to be telephoned. And in the middle of it all, Norman creeps down to the hive and whispers the news to the bees."

"I see," said Franks. "And the message is picked up on the dictaphone."

"That's right. To be preserved, forever and ever as the joke of a lifetime. I think it must have been due to take place that very evening. You can imagine Morgan's feelings when he went along to arrange for the culmination of the jest – *and found his master really dead.*"

Franks thought this out. He brushed off a bee which had settled on his coat.

"Later," said Bohun, "I don't suppose he thought of it at once, but later. Perhaps in the early hours of next morning, when things had settled down, it did just occur to him to wonder. So he went off to the hive. The dictaphone had run down by that time, but he wound it back and listened in – and heard what I venture to think was one of the plainest and most singular confessions of murder which has ever been made – a *confession unmistakably identified by a slight stutter.*"

"You mean to say," said Franks, "that after he'd done the job Norman went off and told the bees all about it."

"Certainly," said Bohun. "You must never keep anything from the bees."

Another bee came past, and settled on Franks' sleeve. The Inspector looked at it in silence. The bee looked back, for a moment, impassively, then flew off.

"After that," went on Bohun, "Morgan re-hid the dictaphone in the safest place – back in the hive. The bees must have been a bit more active by then. I think that's when he got stung."

"He got stung a lot harder when he tried to blackmail Norman next morning," said Franks thoughtfully.

"Yes. Bad tactics to blackmail a desperate man."

"That's not entirely guesswork, I take it." Franks nodded towards the hive.

"I'm afraid not. I thought it all out last night. I've listened to the confession. You won't find *my* fingerprints on the dictaphone, because I wore gloves. But I'm prepared to bet you'll find Morgan's—"

"I see." The Inspector sat, swinging his legs. He seemed to be in difficulties over something. At last he said, without looking up, "I take it you told him. Sent him a note or something."

"Without prejudice to my having to deny it later," said Bohun, "and since you haven't found it, I gather he must have destroyed it – yes, I did."

"I see," said Franks. "Best way out, really. I don't see much of this coming to light now. What exactly did you say to him?"

Bohun got to his feet, and started down the drive with Inspector Franks beside him. They had reached the gate before he spoke.

"It is a couple of lines of verse. I've known them all my life – though I couldn't tell you, even now, who wrote them. They go like this:

'Money is honey, my little sonny
And a rich man's joke is always funny.'"

Behind them, Humble Bee House dozed in the morning sun.

Butcher's Dozen, 1956.

THE CRAVEN CASE

"SPEAKING AS YOUR SOLICITOR," said Bohun, "it sounds an impossible assignment. But speaking as a man, it needs no argument to get me down to Vambrill Court for Christmas. Sir Hubert's reputation as a host has reached even my ears. Wasn't he the man who said, 'Turkeys are old-fashioned, but there's nothing wrong with a well-boiled peacock?'"

"That's just newspaper talk," said John Craven. "But why do you call it an impossible assignment?" He leant forward to say, through the communicating panel, "Better stick to the Great North Road, Peters. The A.A. say there's snow north of Hitchin." Then he shut the panel carefully.

"Well," said Bohun, "admitted that Captain Miller will be a member of the Christmas party. And therefore, in a sense, under our observation. I shouldn't have thought that a social weekend was the time or place to investigate financial dishonesty. Alleged financial dishonesty," he added, carefully, being himself a solicitor.

"Maybe not." Craven sat back and pulled the rug over both of them. "I'd like you to meet him, all the same. He's an odd mixture. When I took up this politics game, I thought it was a fairly straightforward sort of business. Once you were lucky enough to get elected. You sat up at Westminster, and spoke when you could, and voted the right way—"

Bohun grinned. "It's no use your coming the simple soldier man with me, John," he said. "I've checked up on you. If you don't look out you're going to get a job when they have their semi-annual stocktaking in the new year."

"A Parliamentary Secretaryship, maybe," said Craven. But he couldn't quite conceal his satisfaction. For a man who had been in Parliament only five years he had undoubtedly done well.

A first-class war record had helped. Perhaps an inherited income had helped even more. But undoubtedly there was ability under that thatch of smooth light hair. The ability to plan and to persevere. Possibly even to accomplish. Time would show.

"What I hadn't visualised," he said, "is the constituency end of it. Hamboro West is a good constituency, I think. For me, certainly. It's full of ex-Army types ruining themselves on farms and that sort of thing and I get on with 'em. But you can't let up. You've got to think about them the whole time. Every time you open your blessed mouth there are all those thousands of householders sitting in judgment and all of 'em ready to take offence."

"I quite see why it's important to have a good agent," said Bohun, thoughtfully.

"He's not just got to be good. He's got to be a miracle of tact and ability and organisation and probity. And the Constituency Association pay him – what? £500 a year, if he's lucky. A bit more in the big constituencies. But not much. You can't buy miracles today for £500 a year."

"I take it," said Bohun, "that that's why you so often get a man who's retired from some other job with a pension. Like Miller."

"Miller seemed all right. A nice little man. Obviously as tough as nails. The M.C. he got in Holland wasn't something that came up with the rations. I took the trouble to read the citation. And that was the piece of the war I was in – hard, cold, dirty, damp fighting."

He seemed to be looking out again across the steel grey dykes, their surface whipped alternately by hail and bullets.

"You were saying," said Bohun, "that he seemed all right."

John Craven gave an involuntary shiver, and pulled himself back into the comfortable warmth of the car. "You can imagine," he said, "that I was prepared to give a man like that every latitude. Anyway, I was in the constituency so little that I wasn't in a position to notice things. But a week ago Priday – Alan Priday, he's Chairman of the Constituency Association – came to see me. Alan's a very able man. If he says something, you listen to it. And when he said he wasn't quite happy about the finances of our organisation, I sat up."

Bohun said, "Priday? What is he besides being your Chairman?"

"He was an accountant of some sort. Now he gives his whole time to politics. You'll meet him tonight. He's a bachelor, like me. And Sir Hubert always asks us both down for Christmas. It gives us a real opportunity to talk. Also I think he hopes one of us will marry his daughter, Vanessa."

"Miller," said Bohun, firmly.

"Yes," said Craven. "Well, Priday told me that he'd been looking into the Association accounts – we're not a business, you understand that. But we handle quite a lot of money and have to keep things pretty straight. The first thing that struck Priday was that Miller seemed to pay almost all his bills in cash. Even things you'd always expect to pay by cheque, like the rent of the headquarters office."

"I know people like that," said Bohun.

"It's a form of phobia."

"All right. Suppose it was just a habit he'd got into. It meant that he was constantly drawing large cheques to 'Self or 'Cash.' Nothing actually wrong with that. But he seemed a bit vague when Priday questioned him about where it had all gone."

"Did he like Priday questioning him?"

"Not a bit. He's got a temper like a Mills bomb."

"Then his evasiveness might have been annoyance more than guilt."

"It could have been. Yes." Craven was obviously trying hard to be fair. "There was one other thing. It was Sir Hubert who pointed it out to me last time I was down there – quite innocently. He said, 'Miller seems to be smartening up a bit. Got himself a nice new car, and stopped dressing like a tramp.' It was true, too. During the last two years he's been showing distinct signs of prosperity."

"Which wouldn't be accounted for by an agent's salary."

"We pay him as well as most. But I don't think he could do it on his salary. Might have come into money, but I never heard of it. These things usually get out."

"Yes," said Bohun. "I think you've made out a *prima facie* case. The real proof will be in Miller's bank account. If that has got a lot of fairly large, fairly regular unexplained payments in of cash, I'd say that would clinch it."

"Can one look at his bank account?"

"With a judge's order," said Bohun. "Which you won't get without something a lot more definite than what you've told me. However, I'll keep my eyes open."

Sir Hubert Vambrill was an excellent host. A very tall, very thin, outwardly serious man, who had started life as an office boy in Liverpool and made a fortune in cotton before he was forty. He had, for the past twenty-five years, been living the life of a country gentleman and fighting to preserve what he had won.

The success of his fight was evidenced by the fact that he was still able to maintain a large house and an adequate staff of servants.

Clare, Lady Vambrill, a square, leathery woman, had hunted until she was fifty and then relapsed into almost complete insensibility. The daughter of this curious couple, Vanessa, was a strikingly pretty girl with characteristics derived, in unexpected proportions, from both sides of the family.

"What does it mean," she said confidingly to John Craven, at dinner that Christmas Eve, "when it says that outside calling was normal, but the clearing banks were active as buyers of bills?"

"Well, it's a bit difficult to explain."

"I read that in the *Financial Times* this morning. Daddy couldn't explain it either."

"I dare say I understood it once," said Sir Hubert. "Curious girl. Only papers she ever reads are the *Financial Times* and *Horse and Hounds*"

"The other papers are so impossible," said Vanessa. "*The Times* is so stodgy you can't even light the fire with it – or that's what Jane says. The others are just impertinent. Why should they always be trying to run people's lives for them?"

Craven thought rapidly of those organs of the Press which his calling forced him to read every morning, and was inclined to agree with her. He was not certain whether he disliked more the papers which normally supported his party or those which openly attacked it.

"Did you have a good run today?"

"Not bad," said Vanessa. "Two-mile point. The ground's still a bit soggy."

"It's freezing now," said Priday.

"It's going to be a real old-fashioned Christmas Eve," said Sir Hubert. "At least, I hope it is, because I've got a surprise for you all."

"Daddy. Not carols."

"Wait and see," said Sir Hubert.

"At the fourth tee," said Captain Miller to Lady Vambrill, "I hit a humdinger. Right down the middle."

"I hope you didn't hurt him," said Lady Vambrill.

Bohun on her right, choked on a walnut, and said, "Do you play golf, Lady Vambrill?"

"Waste of time," said her ladyship, briefly. "Come Vanessa."

The departure of the only two ladies left the five men to their devices. Sir Hubert tipped the remains of the port into his own glass, fetched a full decanter from the sideboard and circulated it to Captain Miller, who filled his glass gratefully. His chances of drinking a 1924 vintage port were few and far between, and the fact that he was adding it to the Burgundy drunk at dinner and the gin drunk before dinner seemed to cause his seasoned stomach no qualms. In fact, however, he was getting very slightly drunk.

Craven filled his own glass. Priday said "no." Bohun topped his own up.

"Another Christmas," said Craven. "A barbaric and outdated ceremony, but useful as a sort of milestone."

"That's the trouble with milestones," said Sir Hubert. "At the start of your journey they show you how far you have gone. After a certain point they get turned round and only show you how far you have to go."

"In my opinion," said Priday precisely, "the traditions of Christmas are mainly kept up by shopkeepers for the good of their profit and loss accounts. It carries them nicely over the dead season at the end of autumn, and anything that's over can be 'marked down' for the January sales."

"Thank God we're not all accountants," said Miller.

Priday said acidly, "A little accountancy isn't out of place sometimes." And Bohun looked at him sharply.

Captain Miller seemed to be debating whether to accept the challenge. His face was normally the colour of a south wall, so it was difficult to see whether he was flushing. Before he could reply—

"I sincerely hope," said Sir Hubert mildly, "that none of you are actively opposed to a little entertainment at Christmas."

"You mustn't take any notice of them," said Craven, "they're just trying to shock you."

"I must admit," said Bohun, "that I rarely let Christmas go past without casting my eye back to other Christmasses. Last year I spent it in Germany. Never again. The Germans may have invented Christmas, but they've forgotten the secret."

"Past Christmasses," said Sir Hubert, with a sigh.

He walked across to the window and pulled back the heavy, swinging curtain. Outside the moon was riding in glory. The snow had stopped falling and the frost had laid its iron fingers on the world.

"When I was a boy," he said, "I could remember each Christmas on its own. Each one was distinct and separate and each had its own glories. Now, I'm afraid they seem to blur and run together. I wonder if I shall remember this one."

Three of the others had joined him at the window as he was speaking and stood, looking out at the glittering snowscape. The silence was broken by an almost hysterical laugh. It came from Captain Miller, seated alone at the table. He had recharged his glass and was gazing into the red heart of the thirty-two-year-old wine.

"There's one Christmas," he said, "that *I'm* not going to forget in a hurry."

"And which was that?" enquired Sir Hubert, politely.

"Just a wartime reminiscence," said Miller. "I won't bore you with it now."

Bohun was not unduly sensitive but he could feel, almost as if it was something physical, the shock waves of emotion loosed by that innocent remark. Priday was staring fixedly into his empty glass. Craven had his back turned and was looking out of the window.

"In that case," said Sir Hubert, "I suggest we join the ladies."

One of the delights of Sir Hubert's hospitality was its unexpectedness. Vanessa's "Daddy, not carols" was based on experience. Sir Hubert was capable of asking his guests not only to listen to carols, but to sing them too.

This time the ordeal in front of them was of a milder nature. Just after eleven o'clock he looked over his glasses. Bohun was doing his best with Lady Vambrill. Craven and Priday were deep in political shop. Captain Miller was gazing lovingly with one eye into a full glass of whisky and with the other at Vanessa. He seemed to be telling her a story.

"Now," said Sir Hubert. "I don't want to disturb any of you—"

"A sinister gambit," observed Vanessa.

"But if you'd like to come along with my wife and me, we're just going down to the stables. You'll need coats."

"A midnight steeplechase," said Captain Miller. "I remember once in Ireland—"

Sir Hubert cut him short with a charm and a ruthlessness which he must have learned from Balfour (who was, indeed, his ideal statesman). "Another time, Captain. We mustn't keep our mummers waiting."

In the stables which were large, well appointed and, fortunately, adequately heated, they found the servants and quite a number of friends and neighbours. And there the mummers (whom Bohun found fascinating) performed their age-old ritual to the snorts of the horses, the lowing of the cattle and, more distantly, the outraged clucking of the hens.

Bohun, finding himself next to Sir Hubert in an interval when the Dragon was removing his head in order to become St. George's old mother in the final scene said, "I think I've guessed your secret, sir."

"Indeed," said Sir Hubert, "then tell it to me."

"Isn't there a tradition that on Christmas Eve the cattle all talk together in the stable? I believe you're doing this to give them something to talk about."

Sir Hubert laughed immoderately; but Bohun saw him making a mental note and realised that he might have let some future house party in for a truly terrifying ordeal.

Half an hour after midnight he was standing at the open window of his bedroom, drinking in the sharp air. Outside the white countryside was asleep. His bed looked most inviting. He hopped into it and turned out the lights.

At first sleep seemed just round the corner, but the harder he wooed it the more firmly did it retreat. Something was worrying him. Some remark which had been made. The curious strain he had sensed earlier in the evening. After what Craven had told him, he had indeed expected a strain, but this, surely, had been of the wrong sort?

One o'clock struck from the clock over the stable, and, as if echoing the note, a cock crowed, once, twice, three times, angrily. Later Bohun woke again. He was far from certain what had disturbed him. He looked at his watch. It was a minute after two. Then he heard it again, sharp and clear. The crowing of the cock.

Into his sleep-drugged mind crept a line or two of Shakespeare, long known and loved.

Some say that ever 'gainst that season comes
Wherein our Saviour's birth is celebrated,
The bird of dawning singeth all night long,
And then they say . . .

Sleep was crowding out thought.

And then they say, no spirit dare stir abroad.

No spirit. No angry spirit. None of the evil dangerous spirits released by the drunken Captain.

He woke to broad daylight and someone shaking his arm. It was

Priday, and he was white as paper.

"Come quickly, Bohun," he said. "Sir Hubert wants you. Better get some clothes on."

"If this is one of his bright ideas—"

"It's not a joke," said Priday. "They've just found Miller. Hanging in the stable. He's been dead for hours."

One of the things which normal people faced with murder tended to do, Bohun reflected, was to behave as if they were characters in a book. Reasonably so, since very few people had any real life experience to guide them. Bohun himself, fortuitously, had been concerned in more than one such episode, and Superintendent Monks soon realised that he had found in him an admirable, disinterested and observant witness. He therefore questioned him twice. Once at the beginning, and once at the end.

It was at this second interrogation that Bohun was able to make a helpful suggestion.

"I gather," said Monks, in his slow, Midland voice, "from what you've told me and what Mr. Craven says, that you were brought down here with an object, as it were."

"I hope they welcomed me for my company too," said Bohun. "But yes. There was the idea of keeping an eye on Miller."

"The idea being that he was playing fast and loose with the constituency funds."

It was clearly no time for reticence, and Bohun repeated all that Craven had said to him in the car on the way down.

"Yes," said Monks. "You see, it makes a sort of motive, if it's true."

"Then you do think it was suicide?"

"It's possible. In fact, I'd say it's very possible. Putting all the stories together, it's clear that no one saw Captain Miller come back to the house at all. And he'd been drinking. If you add up all the drinks everyone said they saw him drinking it comes to quite a lot."

"You think he subsided gently into one of the mangers to sleep it off. Got overlooked, woke in that terrible, thin, time between midnight and dawn, when nothing looks worth it any more. Realised he was in an inescapable spot and hanged himself."

"Something like that," said Monks. "It was a bit of rope out of the stable," he added. "No doubt about that."

"There *was* one thing – it might have precipitated it – at dinner that night, Miller said something rather rude about accountants to Priday. And before Priday could stop himself he cracked back at him. To the effect that accountants had their uses. If Miller had a guilty conscience, don't you see, that would be a pretty plain hint."

"Yes," said Monks. "Well, we'll know more when we get the pathologist's report. I gather you're all staying on over Boxing Day."

"That's right," said Bohun. "You'll be able to keep all your suspects together quite painlessly."

By common consent the festivities of Christmas Day were abandoned. Sir Hubert retired to his study, and left his enforced guests to themselves. Lady Vambrill remained doggedly in the drawing room. She was unable to understand the fuss. Captain Miller was a tiresome little man, tolerated at Vambrill Court only on account of the office he held. She could not see that his taking his own life (a typical lower-middle-class piece of self-importance) should have caused such an upset.

Bohun wandered down to the stables. A constable forbade him entrance sourly, but he was allowed to prowl around the outside. It was a well thought-out, composite block, with a range of stables and stalls all open to a first-storey hay loft, which, in its turn, gave on to a run of chicken houses at the back; and enabled one man to feed, water and look after all the livestock.

As Bohun examined it, a first, uncomfortable, premonition formed at the back of his mind.

It was late that afternoon that Priday sought him out. He was not a man who gave his confidence easily, and Bohun could see that he was making a considerable effort.

"You've had experience of these—these sort of things," he said. "So I wanted to ask you a question. If you knew something – or had done something – nothing to do with the 'crime' itself only it might lead to questions being asked – would you tell anyone about it, or would you keep quiet?"

"There are rather a lot of if s about that," said Bohun, "but I know enough about criminal investigation to have learned the First Rule. And that is, not to try and keep things back from the police. Unless you're the murderer, of course. Then, I suppose you've got to do your best."

"This isn't a joke," said Priday, stiffly.

"No, of course not," said Bohun. "I'm sorry. What was it you wanted to tell me?"

Priday said slowly, "I went down to the stables last night at about two o'clock. And I found Miller. He was quite dead. There was nothing I could do."

"Good God," said Bohun, really startled and upset. "Do you mean you just left him?"

"There was nothing I could do," said Priday miserably.

"How could you be sure—good heavens man!—artificial respiration—"

"There was no question of that. He was cold. I can see now that it was silly. But I was sure it was suicide. And really, in a way, it seemed the best way out. Miller was facing a criminal prosecution. And there was the scandal—"

Typical accountant's outlook, thought Bohun. Balance against each other one political scandal, one criminal prosecution and one human life. And draw a firm red line.

"Why did you go down?" he asked.

"I noticed he hadn't come back," said Priday. "I think I was the only person who did notice. I thought he was drunk and a night in the hay wouldn't do him any harm. Then I couldn't get to sleep myself and started worrying. I mean, if he'd fallen down outside he might have died of cold—"

Bohun remembered the strange, hard, white world he had seen from his window and nodded. "Well," he said, "it was a Christian act. But I think, all the same, I should have cut him down and called for help. I don't know. It's easy to be wise after the event. One thing's plain. You'll have to tell the Superintendent all about this."

"I was just wondering," said Priday, "whether you'd handle it for me. You're a lawyer and used to telling stories."

"That might, perhaps, have been better put," said Bohun. "But all right. He's coming up after dinner this evening."

Monks took the story calmly. He almost looked as if he might have been expecting it. At the end he said, "I've got two new facts you might like to hear, sir. The first is that I've got the autopsy report. Miller died by hanging all right. No doubt of it. But the pathologist found enough sodium pentothal in the stomach to have put three men to sleep."

"Enough to kill?"

"No. But enough to make Miller unconscious. Particularly on top of the alcohol he'd had already."

"And your idea from that," said Bohun, "is that someone offered the Captain a nip — say from a flask — of brandy and pentothal, and then waited to see if anyone was going to notice his absence. If they did, no harm done. Captain Miller drunk again. But if they *didn't* — how easy to slip down later and fake a hanging."

"Not easy," said Monks. "Damned difficult to do. But possible, if the man was bigger than Miller."

"That hardly narrows the field," said Bohun. "Priday, Craven, Sir Hubert and I are all tall men, and Miller was jockey-size."

"Agreed," said Monks. "But only one of you left fingerprints all over the stall where he was hanging."

"And that, no doubt, was Priday, when he made his two o'clock visit."

"No doubt," said Monks drily. "You don't believe him then?"

"I haven't got as far as believing or disbelieving. I'll just say I'm not very happy about it."

"Time of death?"

"You know what doctors are like," said Monks. "Any time between midnight and three."

"Motive?"

"That's where I was hoping you could help me, sir."

"I'm not sure," said Bohun. "I was brought down here on the

assumption that Miller was the villain of the piece. That he was embezzling money. Now that he's turned out to be the victim, I've had to re-orientate my ideas. I think I see how it might work. But it's only supposition. And I'm not sure how far it's a breach of confidence. Would you mind if we had Craven in on it?"

The Superintendent tilted his head on one side, and considered the idea. Then he said, "If you like, sir."

When he had been brought up to date, John Craven said, "The whole idea is mad. Mad and bad. Of course it was suicide. Why should Priday do such a thing?"

Bohun said, so slowly that he might have been measuring and weighing each word, "You told me that Miller had been showing signs of affluence. I suggested that we should try somehow to get a sight of his bank passbook. And that if we found frequent credits to cash it would be proof that he had been fiddling the funds. *But it could prove something different.* Suppose Miller was blackmailing someone. Some-one connected with the Constituency Association. Someone who knew of his unbusinesslike habit of drawing frequent large cheques to cash. And suppose that someone said to Miller, 'All right. I'll pay you,' and took the precaution of paying the hush money in cash, each time at a different branch, into Miller's account. Do you see?"

Neither man said anything.

Bohun went on. "It would be perfect cover, wouldn't it. A fake suicide. That leads to an examination of Miller's own bank book. We find all these sums being paid in all over the place. Clearly Miller's a crook. He's faced with exposure. He takes his own life."

Craven's face took on an obstinate look that Bohun recognised of old.

"Can you prove this?" he said.

"I should think so," said Bohun. "Bank clerks are trained observers. If I'm right, and the money was paid in in this way, and the police go round the various branches with a photograph, someone will be bound to pick Priday out."

Craven looked at the Superintendent, who nodded his head. "I'd say it was likely," he agreed.

"There is one other thing," said Bohun. "It's only a trifle, but if I can borrow a torch and get down to the stable I can probably prove it."

"Prove it and be damned," said Craven, and slammed out of the room.

Bohun sought out Lady Vambrill. She evinced no interest in his request but said she thought there was a torch in the cupboard in the gun room. There was; a large, nickel-plated affair. Bohun armed himself with it and he and the Superintendent stepped down the path towards the dark stable block. In the frosty distance church bells were ringing out a Christmas night peal.

"I don't know what you want the torch for," said the Superintendent. "There's electric light in all the outbuildings."

"The murderer wouldn't turn the lights on," said Bohun.

After that no more was said. The police guard had gone, and they opened the big end door with difficulty. In the warm, hay-smelling interior, the animals snuffled and snorted and stamped. The two men made their way between the stalls to a ladder at the end, and Bohun motioned the Superintendent to climb first. A few minutes later they were kneeling in the darkness, a few feet from the beam from which Captain Miller had swung and jerked.

"I think," said Bohun quietly, "that the murderer would have to use his torch a little for this bit."

"Bound to," grunted the Superintendent.

Bohun pressed the switch and a white swathe of light cut the darkness. It revealed nothing but the dancing dust motes. The Superintendent was about to speak when Bohun laid his hand on his arm.

Beyond the open-topped partition they heard a rustling. Then a muted clucking. Then suddenly, so loud that Bohun almost dropped the torch, the strident crowing of a cock. Once, twice, three times. Then almost as if it had been an echo, from the direction of the house, came the crack of a gun.

"What the devil's that?" said Monks, jumping to his feet.

"I think," said Bohun, steadily, "that the murderer has taken a very plain hint which I just gave him."

"Do you mean to say," said Vanessa very much later that night, "that John Craven was a murderer. And took his own life? I, for one, refuse to believe it."

"I'm passing no judgments," said Bohun. "In fact, I'm sorry for him. But you can't avoid the facts."

He was sitting in the library with Sir Hubert and his wife and daughter.

"What facts?" said Sir Hubert. "Why should he do such a thing?"

"I'm not sure," said Bohun. "I know exactly what sort of motive it was, but I don't know the details yet. Craven was a politician. And a part of his reputation was his war record. I'm as certain as I can be that Miller – they'd soldiered together remember – knew of some disgraceful secret – it may only have been a ludicrous secret. Some time when Craven, for once, didn't behave quite as a soldier should."

"Then I'd guess," said Sir Hubert, "that it was something that happened on a Christmas Day. Christmas 1944, I suppose, in Holland. That would account for his extraordinary remark at dinner last night."

"I think you're right," said Bohun. "Craven had been paying blackmail for two years. Ever since Miller demanded part of the price of his silence, the vacant job of agent. Craven had also made up his mind, in a general way, to kill him. As I explained to the Superintendent. But what he did was, I think, largely impromptu. I mean, the actual timing and staging of it. Possibly Miller's drunken remark finally convinced him that he couldn't afford to let him stay alive."

"Look here," said Vanessa. "You're saying all this just as if you were certain of it. Priday says he went down to the stable at two o'clock. He admits it. He left fingerprints. How do you *know* that any one else was there at all?"

"I heard it happening," said Bohun. "I heard the cock crowing. On two occasions. First at one o'clock when the murder was committed. Again at two o'clock when Priday went down. At the time I vaguely assumed that the chiming of the stable clock had woken up the cock and made him crow. But that was nonsense, of course. He heard the chimes every night. He wouldn't take any notice of them. There was one thing, and one thing only that would make him open his beak. He saw the glow of the torch over the partition and sang out the news to the sleepy world that the sun was getting up once more in the east."

Lady Vambrill said suddenly and decisively, "Fiddlesticks!"

"What is fiddlesticks, my dear?" said Sir Hubert. "It sounds unhappily convincing to me."

"I don't believe what this young man said. That Craven did it on the spur of the moment. It's plain to me that he'd been planning it for at least six months."

"How can you possibly know that, my dear?"

"Didn't he vote for the Abolition of the Death Penalty?" said Lady Vambrill. "Don't tell me he hadn't got some good reason for that."

National and English Review, December 1956.

THE MAN AT THE BOTTOM

MERCER ROLLED OVER IN BED, yawned, pulled himself up onto his elbows, and said, "I could do with a cup of char. Strong with sugar and no milk."

The girl who was lying beside him sat up. She wore a watch on a plaited gold strap on her left wrist and a small gold cross on a chain around her neck.

She looked down at the watch and said, "See, sluggard, it is eleven o'clock. That is not the right hour for getting up in the morning."

"I always have a lie-in on Sundays."

"It is not Sunday. It is Thursday."

"To me all days are Sundays."

"You are a great lazy hog! Also you are covered with bristles like a hog. You shall shave off your bristles and I will make tea for both of us."

"Okay. That's a bargain," said Mercer. He swung his legs over the side of the bed and stood up. "My God, I've got a head like a buzzsaw and a mouth like the bottom of a hen coop."

"That is because you drink too much."

"If I didn't drink, I'd die of boredom."

"Then you should get work. Real work."

Mercer said, "Ugh," and went into the tiny bathroom which opened off the bedroom. Over his shoulder he said, "Sometimes you talk sense, Shallini. But mostly you talk drivel."

The girl, busy with the electric kettle, said, "Pig," without rancour.

"Work," said Mercer, turning on the tap, "is something you do when you need money. People who work when they don't need money are wasting the one life God gave them. Or maybe work has become a drug which they can't leave alone."

He inspected his face in the glass. It was a relief map, seamed with the ravines and crevices dug by experience. The deep pits under his eyes were bruise-coloured. The highlands of his cheeks were a mottled red. He said, "You're an ugly buzzard."

"What did you say?"

"I was talking to myself. Get on with that tea."

Five minutes later he was back in bed.

The girl ran a finger down his cheek and said, "That is better. Now it is nice and smooth." Her finger checked for a moment. "You promised you would tell me how you got that scar."

"It's a long story. And not very interesting. This tea's too hot to drink."

"Of course it's hot. You do not make tea with lukewarm water."

"I saw Nahmal yesterday. She looked worried."

Shallini was used by now to Mercer's sudden switches of conversation. She said, "If you were Nahmal, you would be worried."

"Why? Tell me."

"Nahmal has a very complicated life."

"You mean she's running two men."

"She is not running two men. And that is a very coarse way of expressing it."

"Sorry. Go on."

"Why are you interested in Nahmal? You should be interested only in me."

"I'm capable of being interested in more than one thing at a time." He found the tea was cool enough for a cautious sip. "Tell me about her complicated life."

"Well, she is going with Mr. Parker. You know him?" Mercer shook his head. "He works now for the Arnold Rowe Company. You have heard of Mr. Rowe, surely."

"They are ships' chandlers. Right? With offices and a big yard and store in Lower Creek Street."

"That is right. Mr. Parker is in charge of Mr. Rowe's office. He used to be an officer on one of the ships. I think perhaps it was the *Tamar.*"

"If it's the *Tamar* it brings in timber from Scandinavia. Takes out electronic machinery, computers, adding machines. Things like that."

"When Mr. Parker was First Officer it did not only bring in timber. It brought in other things, hidden inside the timber."

"What sort of things?"

"Dirty things. Things like you keep in those parcels." She nodded at the cupboard in the far corner of the room. Mercer jerked upright in bed, spilling some of the tea as he did so. He put the cup down on the bedside table and looked at the girl who put down the cup she was holding and placed both her hands on Mercer's bare forearm.

"Have I said something which displeases you?"

"It's not what you bloody said. It's what you've been bloody doing. Who told you to search my belongings?"

"I did not search them. Please. I keep things of my own in that cupboard. One of the packets was open. I happened to look. Some of the pictures are so very peculiar. I did not like them at all."

Mercer relaxed slowly. He released his arm from her grip and slid it behind her shoulders. He said, "I like you, Shallini. I like you very much. But little girls who look at things they're not meant to see get their bottoms smacked. You understand?"

"I shall not look at them again, I promise you. I did not think they were at all attractive."

"Go on telling me about Parker. You say he used to bring in pictures and books like that."

"Yes. They were hidden right inside one of the big pieces."

"In one of the baulks of timber."

"Yes. It had been hollowed out. It was done very cleverly. No one could suspect. He made a number of trips and much money. Then someone – I think it would have been Mr. Rowe – I think he found out."

"Arnold Rowe. Fat man always smoking a big cigar. I guess he's on the fiddle himself. What did he do?"

"He gave Mr. Parker a post in his warehouse. Now Mr. Parker does not sail in the ships himself. He arranges for other people to do it."

"Sounds a cushy sort of job. Why did you say it was complicated?"

"It is not the job. It is Nahmal."

"Ah," said Mercer, "I guessed the complication would be female. What has Nahmal been up to?"

"I told you. She is going with Mr. Parker."

"Lucky Mr. Parker. A shore berth and an attractive girl. Where does the complication come in?"

"The complication is Ramesh Chatto Baba."

"And who the hell is he?"

"He is a steward. On that same ship. The *Tamar*. He was Nahmal's friend. Oh, for some time now. He had promised to marry her. It is Mr. Parker who arranges the cabin crews on the boats, you see. So he arranges for Ramesh to be much away. As soon as one trip is finished he finds him another job."

Mercer started to laugh. He said, "What a lovely setup! He sends the boy friend away on a trip so that he can be with the girl. What's he got to worry about? Surely he can handle a cabin steward."

"Ramesh is not an ordinary steward. Before he came here he was in a circus."

Mercer seemed to have lost interest in Nahmal and Ramesh. He said, "I'd like to meet this chap Parker. I fancy we might have something to talk about. Nahmal should be able to fix it for me. Shouldn't she?"

The prospect of something to do seemed to have put life into him.

"We'll do it now." He padded across to the window and looked out. "Only thing is, we'll have to shake off Weary Willie first."

"Who are you talking about?"

"That bald man in the car. He's been hanging round here on and off for days."

"You mean he is watching us?"

"I don't think he's just admiring the view," said Mercer.

When they had both dressed they went out – Shallini to find Nahmal at the hairdresser's where she worked, Mercer to annoy the bald man in the car. They came out of their front door at the same moment. The girl turned to the left, and Mercer, according to plan, switched to the right. The bald man got out of the car, lit a cigarette with elaborate casualness, and allowed Mercer to reach the corner of the street before he started after him. Mercer, as soon as he was round the corner, started to run with great lolloping strides which took him along surprisingly fast. Timing it to a nicety, he reached and slipped into the mouth of an alleyway as the bald man turned the corner.

Clearly he had expected to see Mercer twenty yards ahead of him. When he saw nothing but a Jamaican sweeping the pavement and an old lady being towed along by a small dog, he hesitated. Finally he made up his mind to advance. Mercer retreated down the alley which led, he knew, into a cross alley and so back by a circular route to the High Street.

Ten minutes later he was sitting in the café where he had arranged to meet Shallini. He was wondering about the bald man who made the elementary mistake of allowing his quarry to get too far ahead of him; but the bald man could not really be faulted for this. To keep trailing a suspicious quarry you needed an experienced team of three or four people.

Mercer was drinking his second cup of coffee when Shallini arrived. She said, "Nahmal will speak to Mr. Parker. He is not in his office this morning. She thinks he could see you this evening. The best time would be about six o'clock, just before the office closes. She wanted to know what you wished to talk to him about."

"But you didn't tell her."

"I did not tell her, stupid one, because I did not know."

"That's right," said Mercer. "You didn't know."

Lower Creek Street is a long winding thoroughfare which ends in a wall. An opening in the wall gives onto a flight of steps which in turn takes you down to the waters of the Lower Creek. Unless you have a boat you can then go no farther. All the buildings on the north side of the street are connected, in one way or another, with the river and its trade.

The last three buildings before the wall are a barge repair yard, once prosperous but now becoming derelict as the barge trade declined; the store yard and offices of Messrs. Arnold Rowe and Company (Ships' Chandlers and Marine Contractors); and the premises of the Marine and Waterside Employment Agency occupying the end house and overlooking the point where the Lower Creek ran out into the Thames.

At six o'clock Mercer was sitting in an office on the first floor of the middle of these three buildings, talking to Mr. Parker, a tall tough red-faced man of about Mercer's age, who looked more like a soldier than a sailor.

They had reached a degree of cautious understanding.

Parker said, "It's quite true. And since the girls seem to have been talking out of school"—Shallini and Nahmal looked at each other guiltily—"and since it's all over and done with long ago, I've no objection to telling you. It was a good little racket while it lasted. You buy the stuff wholesale in Copenhagen. Books, photographs, films, the lot. We had a very safe way of bringing it in – I expect you were told about that, too."

Mercer nodded. He was staring out of the window at the river and seemed to have only half of his mind on what was being said.

"There was five hundred percent profit in it at least. You had to spread it round a bit among the people who helped you. But it added up to a good tax-free bonus at the end of the year."

"Why did you drop it?"

Parker hesitated. Then he said, "Difficulties were beginning to crop up at the sales end. I thought it was time to get out."

Not the whole truth, thought Mercer; I wonder what really happened. He said, "The distribution was just the part I might have been able to help with. I've got a number of contacts in the Soho area. The Water Guard has been so bloody officious lately that their supplies are beginning to dry up."

"Terrible to think of their customers drooling with unspeakable fantasies and nothing to feed them on," said Parker. "Me, I never saw anything in that sort of stuff at all. What's the point of pictures when you've got the real thing?" He smiled at Nahmal who smiled back. "All the same, I have still got one or two contacts in the shipping business. They might be interested, particularly if you can guarantee the buying end. I'll ask round. Look in tomorrow night at the China Clipper. We've got a private room at the back that we use most evenings. Come about nine o'clock."

When Mercer got outside, a car was drawn up by the curb. The bald man was standing beside it. He came across and blocked Mercer's path.

Mercer said, "What's this? A mugging?" He seemed not at all alarmed.

The bald man said, "I'm Detective Sergeant Russ. I've been instructed to take you to Balfour Street Police Station."

"I'm quite sure Superintendent Browning didn't say that. He knows the ropes, even if you don't. What he said was, you were to ask me to accompany you to the Station. Right?"

"I'm prepared to show you my warrant card if you require to see it."

"That's much better. No, I won't ask to look at your warrant card. I guessed you were a policeman. You're so bloody bad at following people."

Russ opened the door of his car without another word.

Superintendent Browning was a hard man, in charge of a hard Division. His superiors, while disapproving of some of his methods, approved of the results. Chief Superintendent Morrissey had summed him up when he was in charge of Number 1 District. "If Bull Browning 'ad as much up top as he's got down bottom 'e'd end up Commissioner."

Browning came straight to the point. He said, "I know all about you, Mercer. I want you out of my manor and I want you out quick"

Mercer said, "Oh," in a tone which might have meant anything or nothing.

"Another thing. You've been greasing up to Parker. I don't know what your game is, but Parker's boss wouldn't be happy about you having anything to do with him."

"Parker's boss is Arnold Rowe. What's he got that lets him give orders to the police?"

"No one gives me orders." The Superintendent's face began to colour. "Mr. Rowe is a Councillor and a respected citizen. If he asks me to pass a request, I pass it on."

"All right," said Mercer equably. "You've passed it on. What next?"

"Are you going to be sensible? Or are you looking for trouble?"

Mercer said, "Twenty years ago, when you were on a beat, the boys used to call you Bull Browning. Because bull was the only thing you understood. Your badge was polished daily with Brasso and your toecaps shone."

"You—"

"And if you'll excuse me saying so, you don't seem to have learned much in the years between."

"I'll show you whether I've learned anything," roared Bull Browning, jumping up. His forehead and cheeks were engorged with blood. So loudly had he shouted that Russ, who must have been waiting outside, opened the door and came in. Mercer, who had been leaning back in his chair, had not moved an inch. There was something formidable in his immobility. For a long moment Browning, erect behind his desk, stared down at him. His face was gradually resuming its normal colour.

"All right," he said at last. "I've warned you. I won't warn you again. Take him away."

"If that man lays a hand on me, you'll both be in trouble," said Mercer, climbing to his feet. Russ held the door open and Mercer went out quietly.

The room which led off the half landing at the back of the China Clipper had nothing on the door to indicate it was available to the public. When Mercer was shown into it by the landlord shortly after nine o'clock that evening he found Nahmal, Parker, and another man there, with a bottle of whisky, a soda-water syphon, and three glasses on the table. There was a coal fire alight in the small grate. A framed notice over the fireplace said: *TRUST YOURSELF. IF YOU DON'T, WHO WILL?*

The second man looked like Winston Churchill, but inflated several pounds per square inch in every visible aspect. He was smoking one of the longest cigars Mercer had ever seen.

Parker filled the third glass half full with whisky and pushed it across the table. He said, "Add your own soda. It's all on our friend. Arnold Rowe. Bill Mercer."

"Pleased to meet you," said Rowe.

"Now that really does surprise me," said Mercer.

Rowe chuckled and said, "You've been talking to old Browning. I hear he bawled you out."

If he was wondering how this particular piece of news should have got out so quickly, Mercer showed no sign of it.

"You don't want to bother about him. All right. I did ask him to keep you out of Tim Parker's hair. That was some time ago, before I knew much about you. Except that you'd been a policeman yourself."

"A policeman of a sort. A long time ago."

"I've got nothing against the police. They're quite all right, mostly. Good fellows." Mr. Rowe accompanied this handsome tribute by a puff at his cigar. "Sometimes they take themselves too seriously, that's all. Live and let live, that's my philosophy. Make other people happy and you'll be happy yourself. Take all this National Front business. What *good,* does it do? Marching round the streets, shouting and screaming. What do they get out of it?"

"Sore throats and brickbats."

"Exactly. Now I'm just the opposite. I don't object to seeing a few of our colonials coming into the country. Why should I? And once they're in, I do my best to find jobs for them. You saw that building next door? The employment agency. I run that too. We can usually find a slot for a boy who's willing to work. Or a girl." He looked at Nahmal, who smiled. "Well, I mustn't stop here talking all night. I expect you and Parker will have a lot of things you want to discuss, now you've met up."

Mr. Rowe finished his whisky, patted Nahmal on the cheek, and departed in a cloud of benevolence and cigar smoke.

"You mustn't mind his manner," said Parker. "He really does do a lot of good work among the youngsters from India and Pakistan."

"Does it extend to helping them into this country?" said Mercer.

Parker said, "That's a question I've never asked. And if I did ask it, I wouldn't expect it to be answered." He refilled both their glasses. "About that matter we were discussing I've been making a few inquiries. There might be something in it for both of us. We'd have to give Arnold a cut, of course – he'd be organising the import."

The conversation became technical and commercial. It was around eleven o'clock and Mercer could hear, from downstairs, the sound of the landlord encouraging the last of the drinkers to leave when another sound obtruded itself. It was a tiny sound, but significant – a click as though someone was turning the handle of the door with caution. Parker did not seem to have noticed it; perhaps his attention was entirely devoted to Nahmal who had got bored with sitting on a hard chair and was now sitting on Parker's lap.

Mercer shifted his own chair very slightly, so that he commanded an uninterrupted view of the door.

Gently, gently, the handle completed its rotation; then the door blasted open and a big brown-faced man came into the room and made straight for Parker. He was carrying a long knife which might have come from a ship's galley.

The speed of Parker's reaction suggested that he too had been forewarned by the click of the door handle. With his left arm he swept Nahmal onto the floor. His right hand grabbed the table and jerked it directly between himself and the newcomer, who was unable to stop and fell across it, face downward, dropping the knife as he did so.

Nahmal screamed, "Ramesh!"

The knife slid across the floor. Mercer, without getting up, put one foot on it. He did not think Parker was going to need any help and observed his technique with interest.

His first move was to grab Ramesh by the hair and crash his head down twice onto the table top. As Ramesh twisted himself free, Parker, now standing, grabbed the table with both hands and drove it into Ramesh, hitting him just below the breastbone. Ramesh fell onto his knees. Parker abandoned the table, grabbed one of Ramesh's wrists, and twisted his arm behind his back. The leverage he exerted lifted the Pakistani onto his toes. Blood was running down his face from the cut on his forehead.

"What I ought to do," said Parker, "is feed your face into that fire."

Ramesh said nothing. He was gasping for breath and there was white froth on his lips. Parker jerked his captive arm savagely. Ramesh opened his mouth wide, but no sound came out of it.

"Try anything like that again and you'll end up with two broken arms."

He let Ramesh go. The Pakistani backed away. He had no eyes for anyone but Parker. He said, between gasps, "For that – you will be sorry – I promise you." Then he turned round and went out, pulling the door shut behind him.

"Now I wonder what he meant by that," said Mercer mildly.

Parker had resumed his seat. Nahmal climbed back onto his lap. She was shaking. Mercer thought he would leave him to comfort her. The landlord saw him off the premises, saying, "Mr. Parker having some trouble up there?"

"Nothing he couldn't handle," said Mercer.

In the weeks that followed, Mercer appeared to spend most of his daylight hours wandering round the docks and the streets that lay behind them, eating in small cafés and talking to the Indians and Pakistanis who used them. His friendship with Shallini gave him the entrée to this tight little circle.

Most evenings he ended up at the private room behind the China Clipper and drank with Arnold Rowe and Parker. On one occasion he asked whether Ramesh had given any further trouble.

"Ramesh," said Mr. Rowe. "He'll give no trouble. He's back at sea."

"A long trip," said Parker. "He won't be back until Guy Fawkes's day."

The two men looked at each other and laughed. Mercer could tell that there was something behind this exchange, but he did not pursue the matter. He did, however, raise it with Shallini later that evening.

She said, "But of course. Ramesh has to do what Mr. Henderson tells him."

"Mr. Henderson?"

"I mean, Mr. Rowe."

"You didn't say Mr. Rowe. You said Mr. Henderson."

"It was a mistake," said Shallini, "I did not mean to mention his name. Please do not ask me any more."

"I should like to meet him – Mr. Henderson, I mean."

"Naturally you cannot meet him. If he should wish to see you, he will send for you." She was standing beside the bed as she spoke, wearing a thin pair of cotton pyjamas, and it may have been because she was cold that she gave a little shiver.

Mercer said, "He sounds an interesting sort of man from the little I've heard about him. No one seems anxious to talk about him."

"No one talks about him," said Shallini.

Nothing more happened for a month. As far as Mercer could tell, he was not followed. Either Superintendent Browning had lost interest, or the observation was being more discreetly arranged.

It was an early November morning of bright sun and blue sky. Mercer was walking up Maze Hill, on his way to Blackheath when the long snout of an Aston-Martin drew level with him, passed him, and stopped. The driver was a boy in chauffeur's uniform with a snub nose and impertinent eyes. He rolled down the window of the driver's seat, leaned out, and said, "Mercer?"

Mercer looked at him coldly and said, "Mr. Mercer."

"Okay, okay," said the boy. "Be like that. Only hop in quick. We haven't got a lot of time."

"I've got all the time in the world," said Mercer.

"Well, I haven't. And Mr. Henderson doesn't like being kept waiting."

"Ah," said Mercer. It sounded like the full stop at the end of a long and complicated sentence. He opened the door and stood for a moment before getting in. "You seem to know my name," he said, "but I haven't the pleasure—"

"That's all right. My friends call me Bobby."

"You must let me know when I have the privilege of joining that exclusive circle," said Mercer.

Bobby said, "Sarky, eh?"

He drove in exactly the manner suggested by his name and appearance, impudently, cutting every corner and extracting himself adroitly from every tight squeeze. They kept to the small streets on the South Bank, crossed the Thames by Vauxhall Bridge, and drew up finally in front of a house at the corner of Wilfred Street and Buckingham Gate. Bobby used his own key on the front door and showed Mercer into a room on the ground floor at the back of the house.

It was one of the most perfectly conceived rooms that Mercer ever remembered being in. The floor consisted of narrow strips of wood with a reddish tinge. There was one large rug in the centre which his experience in the East told him was either an Isphahan or a Qum. The walls were papered in neutral grey which made a perfect background to the framed prints hung on them. They were mostly military subjects and the scarlet uniforms blazed from the dull gold of the frames. The large fireplace was built into a surround of grey slate into which had been set twelve tiles, painted to represent the twelve months of the year. On the mantel over the fire stood a set of small silver gilt cups with spindly legs.

Bobby, watching him from the doorway said, "Don't try putting one of them in your pocket. We've counted them" – and disappeared quickly. Mercer continued his inspection of the room. He decided that it was the deliberate creation of a fastidious, but masculine taste and had just reached this conclusion when the door opened and Mr. Henderson came in.

Mercer saw a tall thin man, with the look about him of an Army officer in plain clothes or maybe the headmaster of a very exclusive preparatory school. The only sign of his age was that his neatly clipped moustache was grey. He said, "Sit down," and walked across and sat in an upright chair behind the table. Something that Mercer noticed about him was the way he controlled his body. When he moved it was with conscious elegance. He sat like a coiled spring.

Mercer slouched across to one of the easy chairs and fell back into it – a piece of defensive counterpropaganda which Mr. Henderson noted without apparent resentment. He said, "You do not seem to have made a great success of the last two years of your life."

"It depends what you mean by success," said Mercer.

"After being dismissed from the Metropolitan Police for an assault on a prisoner who was in your custody, you were given a fresh chance by being allowed to join the Police Force of the Ruler of Bahrain. You were dismissed six months later after charges of bribery and extortion were preferred."

"But not pursued."

"No. You were allowed the alternative of dishonourable dismissal. You then came back to England and worked for a time as a labourer. You were dismissed from that job for assaulting a foreman."

"He was a real swine."

"Your reputation by now was such that you found it impossible to get any legitimate work, so you turned to crime – in particular to trading in hard pornography. You took no direct part in this yourself, but acted as protector to men like Leo Chance and Victor Amesbury."

"And boy, did they need protection."

"I would rather you didn't interrupt me."

The words were spoken quietly but Mercer was conscious of the authority and the threat behind them. He had known, from the moment he came into the house, that its owner was no ordinary man.

"I happen to be a friend of Leo Chance. I have been able to do him a number of good turns in the past, for which he felt he owed me favours. One of these favours was to give me a very full account of the events which took place one evening last winter in Barkhurts Mansions. A full account, with the names of the two relevant witnesses, who have not, of course, seen fit to open their mouths, but could easily be induced to do so if necessary. You understand me?"

Mercer said nothing.

"I am telling you this so that there will be no possible misunderstanding about our relative positions. It might otherwise be thought that what I am now doing is to offer you a job. I am doing nothing of the sort. I am enrolling you to fill a necessary position in my organisation. Arnold Rowe, who has charge of my operations in the Dockland district, is forced to work with somewhat volatile material."

For the first time a very faint smile touched Mr. Henderson's thin lips.

"You have met Arnold and will appreciate that although he has many excellent qualities, he is not a pugilist. That was the reason we gave Parker a fairly nominal job in his office – to look after the welfare of Arnold Rowe."

"Where is Parker?"

Mr. Henderson considered the matter. He said, "It is a difficult question to answer without a precise knowledge of tides and the current in the Thames. But I should surmise that he will have reached Tilbury by now."

Mercer received this news without obvious signs of interest. He was seated at such an angle that the right side of his face was away from Mr. Henderson, who was thus in no position to notice that the white scar down that side of his face had changed colour.

He said, "Oh? Why did you kill him?"

"Kill is the wrong word. It suggests something accidental. I had him executed. He made the mistake of antagonising Ramesh. These people have their own methods of ferreting out secrets which people wish to keep hidden. He was able to confirm, without any possibility of mistake, that Parker was working for Customs and Excise. He was like yourself, an ex-policeman. It had sometimes occurred to me that we were allowed, rather easily, to discover the trivial smuggling offences Parker was said to have committed. That was why he was only taken into our organisation on probation."

Mercer said, "The one time I saw him in action I thought he might be a pro."

"We have a number of professionals working for us too. They had no difficulty in overpowering Parker. We then thought it appropriate that Ramesh should be allowed to execute him."

"And how did he do that?"

"He shot him six times at fairly close range. The first two or three bullets went into his stomach. Ramesh enjoyed that, I am told. It was only the last of the six that killed him."

"I imagine you're telling me all this as a sort of cautionary tale," said Mercer easily. "There's no need. I'm not working for Customs or the police or anyone else. I'm working for myself."

"You are wrong," said Mr. Henderson gently. "You are working for me. Arnold will give you your instructions. There is a Ford Consul motor car outside. It was used by Parker. You can consider it our property. Bobby will give you the keys and the logbook. He will also show you the catch of an ingenious locker, built into the thickness of the offside door. It is useful for a number of purposes. I doubt if we shall see each other again, so I will wish you good day."

In the course of the next few weeks Mercer discovered two things. The first was that "volatile" was an inadequate description of the employees of Arnold Rowe and Company and the clients of the employment agency. They were Pakistanis or Indians of both sexes and were found working either in Arnold Rowe's office or in and round the ships that he serviced. Mercer confirmed his suspicion that their entry into the country had been illegally organised and that this fact was used as a threat to bind them to the service of the organisation.

Beyond that he could come to no definite conclusion, since his second discovery was that certain rooms in the Office and the Agency were barred to him. It was in these rooms that the real work of the organisation was carried out. He guessed that the stewards and deck-hands might be being used to carry abroad gold and precious stones and to bring back the money realised by their sale on the Continent.

None of this worried him. He kept the simple record of jobs he was given, stood by when Arnold Rowe's clients or servants threatened to be difficult, and dealt with the difficulty appropriately. It took one broken arm and one fractured jaw to convince people that he was not a man to argue with. After that he had little trouble.

The year had turned the corner and it was early in March when he made a request which Shallini found curious. He said, "I saw an odd-looking knife in a shop in Charlton. It had a very thin wavy blade and the handle, I guess, was sharkskin or something of the sort. There were letters engraved in the blade, or it may have been pictures."

Shallini said, "From your description it sounds like a *kotah-chil* – that is, a girl's knife. There are certain circumstances, you understand, when a girl has to defend her honour."

"So that if I was found with one of those sticking into me, it would be assumed that I had assaulted a girl and that she, or perhaps her lover, had used it on me."

"That would be the assumption. Do you wish me to get it for you?"

Mercer considered the matter. Then he said, "Yes. But only if you can do it so cleverly that it will never be traced to you or me."

"It will take a little time then."

"Time is unimportant."

It was perhaps three weeks after this conversation that Ramesh came out of the Duke of Cumberland public house at closing time and started, alone, to walk back to his lodgings. It was a dark night with the wind driving the clouds steadily in from the east and bringing an occasional spatter of rain. He turned up the collar of his jacket and trudged on, unaware that he was being followed.

His body was found by a patrolling policeman at three o'clock on the following morning The pathologist who examined him reported one curious fact. The dagger which was driven into his back was not the cause of death. His neck had been broken by a single savage blow from behind. The dagger had been driven in after the man was dead.

"Indian dagger," said Superintendent Browning. "Some sort of symbolism. A feud perhaps."

"I have no doubt it has a message for us," agreed the pathologist. "If we were able to read it."

In spite of the thick carapace of his self-satisfaction, Arnold Rowe always went into the house in Wilfred Street with a sense of unease and breathed more easily when he got away from it again. He found Mr. Henderson in a thoughtful mood. He said, "Have the police made anything of the killing of Ramesh?"

"According to our contact, no."

"Then I suggest we help them. Allow our man to find the gun with which Parker was shot. It is untraceable, I am sure."

"Certainly. But how will it help them?"

"If you have preserved it in the careful manner I suggested, it will still have Ramesh's fingerprints on it. They will be matched with the prints of the body and the solution will be clear even to the uninspired mind of Superintendent Browning. Ramesh killed Parker. One of Parker's Indian friends killed Ramesh. Everyone will be happy. Our friend will gain kudos for discovering the gun. No one will bother further about the case. A grudge killing in an immigrant community."

"It might be the truth at that," said Rowe.

"It might be. But I am sure it is not. Ramesh was killed by Mercer. The leaving of the dagger was a diversionary tactic. It may have convinced the police. It did not convince me."

"How can you be sure?"

"Mercer is a man who is capable of killing in cold blood. His record shows it. Such men are not common. Why he should have killed Ramesh is not clear. Possibly he had private reasons for doing so. Possibly he considered that Parker had been made to suffer unduly."

"If that's true, do you think he himself might be—"

"Working for the police?"

"I must say, the thought had never entered my head."

"It entered mine," said Mr. Henderson, "the first moment he appeared on the scene. It is right to be suspicious, but we must not let our suspicions run away with our common sense. I have checked and cross-checked every move he has made since he was thrown out of the Metropolitan Police two years ago. The accounts all agree. No, I do not think he is a policeman, but I think he is a very dangerous man. He will have to go."

"He's been doing his work admirably. I hardly know who to put in his place."

"Loveridge? Manton? Banks? Straightforward hitmen, but hardly up to Mercer's weight, I agree."

"Are you sure it's necessary to get rid of him?"

Mr. Henderson rubbed a long finger down the side of his face. "I agree with you that we may be wasting a good man. But I have made it a rule in life that when I am in doubt I always take the safer course."

"When you say, get rid of him—"

"Set your mind at rest. I was not contemplating violence. We will, as so often, allow the law to assist us. I was recently asked to handle a set of eight cameos in their original frames. The frames are, as I think you will agree"—Mr. Henderson got up and went across to his wall safe—"almost more beautiful than the paintings. They are said to be the work of Cellini, the Florentine goldsmith. They are far too well-known to be disposed of either here or in the European markets. I convinced the gentleman who stole them on that point and he finally sold them to me for a very modest sum. They will have to be sacrificed for the general good."

Arnold Rowe said, "I don't quite follow you—"

"Take them and have them placed in the concealed pocket of Mercer's car. Bobby has the spare set of keys, so it should not be difficult. Then inform Superintendent Browning, who will be delighted to pursue the matter."

It was three days later, when Mercer was driving down to the Surrey Docks, that he was stopped. He drove up to the dock gates and sounded his horn for the pole to be raised. The gateman came out, examined the number on Mercer's car, and went back into his hut. The pole remained in place. Mercer got out of his car. A police car had driven up behind him, blocking the exit. Superintendent Browning got out, accompanied by a sergeant in uniform and Detective Sergeant Russ.

Browning said, "I have no search warrant, but I take it you have no objection to my making a search of your car."

"You don't need a warrant to search a car," said Mercer coldly. "All you need is reasonable suspicion that it is being used for some illegal purpose."

"I'd forgotten you were once a policeman yourself," said Browning equally coldly. "Well, what about it?"

"No objection," said Mercer. "Should we move it to somewhere where it's not blocking the traffic?" Mercer got back into the car. The sergeant climbed in beside him. The pole was lifted and Mercer drove on a few yards, pulled into the side, and stopped.

"Would you like me to open the door locker for you?" said Mercer. "The catch is a bit tricky until you get the hang of it."

"We can manage," said Browning. "You get out."

They spent an hour over their search while Mercer sat on an up-turned crate smoking and watching them.

But the secret locker and the rest of the car were empty of anything except the sort of things which should have been there.

It was six o'clock that evening when Mercer rang the bell of the house in Wilfred Street. He realised that he was being studied through the tiny glass optic which was set in the centre of the door. He seemed to be relaxed and at ease and was whistling gently between two broken front teeth.

After a full minute the door was opened by Bobby, who said, "Hullo," with an emphasis on the second syllable which turned it into a question.

"Hullo, Bobby," said Mercer. "Mr. Henderson here?"

"He's here, but I don't know whether he's free to talk to you."

"Ask him nicely and I'm sure he will," said Mercer. "He'd do anything for *you,* I'm certain."

Bobby grinned, showing a set of sharp white teeth. "You've got a nerve. I'll say that for you. Come in and wait."

Mercer sat on one of the four chairs which were positioned, two on either side, in the hall. They looked as if they might have come from a museum.

There was a murmur of voices from the room at the back and then Bobby reappeared, still with a smile on his face, and said, "In you go, Daniel. The lions are ready."

Mr. Henderson was sitting in his chair behind the table. There were two men with him, both standing. Mercer recognised them. One was called Banks. He had a heavy white face, scarred with the relics of youthful acne, and the shoulders of a weight lifter. The other was Manton, thinner, longer, and with a darkness of hair and complexion which suggested a native strain not far back in his pedigree. Mercer knew him as the more dangerous man.

Mr. Henderson said, "You wanted to speak to me?"

Mercer said, "Yes. I could talk more freely if we were alone."

Mr. Henderson looked at him thoughtfully, came to some conclusion, and made a gesture with one of his hands. Banks and Manton went out of a door in the far side of the room. Mercer made two guesses, both of which were probably correct. The first was that they had not gone very far from the door. The second was that Mr. Henderson's hand was not far from the bell which would recall them.

He moved away from the table and slouched down in the chair he had occupied when he had visited the house before. He said, "I had a turnup with the police. They seemed to think I might be carrying stolen goods in my car."

"Yes?"

"They didn't find anything. Being cautious by nature, I'd put a marker on the door locker, so I knew it had been opened. I found a very fine set of eight framed cameos inside. I recognised them, of course. It was headline news some months ago when they were lifted from Apsley House."

Again Mr. Henderson said, "Yes?" There was no more than polite interest in his voice.

"My first idea was to throw them into the river. But, really, I hadn't the heart to waste them. So I had a better idea. I got in touch with the small private insurance company which had covered them."

Again Mr. Henderson said, "Yes?" For the first time there was an undercurrent of real interest in his voice.

"You didn't know, perhaps, that they had been insured for £80,000. For some reason the fact was not publicised. I was working at third hand, through the friend of a friend. He found out that the insurers were prepared to pay £10,000 to get them back, no questions asked."

Mercer put one hand into his inside pocket. Mr. Henderson's hand shifted slightly behind the desk. Mercer pulled out a thick envelope.

"I thought, seeing the goods had come from you, we ought to split the proceeds. Even-steven. There's five thousand in there, all in nice old tens. No history to any of them." Without moving from his chair he tossed the envelope onto the table.

Mr. Henderson made no move to touch it. He said, "What exactly did you mean, seeing that the goods had come from me?"

"It was a fair guess," said Mercer mildly. "In view of the fact that the police seemed to know all about the locker. Also, I imagined that you would have kept a spare set of the car keys."

Mr. Henderson stretched out one hand, drew the envelope towards him, opened it, and examined the contents.

Then he said, "Perhaps I was wrong about you."

"Wrong?"

"I thought you had plenty of muscle, but no brains. I've been looking for someone like you for a long time. I think we might deal very well together."

"Do you know," said Mercer, "the same thought had occurred to me."

Ellery Queen's Mystery Magazine, April 1979.

THE MAN IN THE MIDDLE

"IF YOU TRY THAT AGAIN," said Mercer, "I'll break your arm."

"I tell you, I wish to speak to Mr. Rowe."

"And I tell you that he does not wish to speak to you."

"You treat us like children," said Bapu Ram. He was a tall Pakistani with a Groucho Marx moustache.

"If you behave like children," said Mercer reasonably, "you must expect to be treated like children."

Bapu Ram paused at the doorway of Mercer's office and said, "You may discover, Mr. Mercer, that children possess sometimes the facility to surprise those who consider themselves to be their elders and betters."

Mercer grinned and said, "You ought to set that to music. Don't slam the door, I've got a nasty headache."

He set to work again on a chart which he was compiling. It had the names of six ships written down the left-hand side – the *Tamar*, the *Dart*, the *Exe*, the *Teign*, the *Taw*, and the *Torridge*. Vertical columns to the right were headed: Cabin Stores, Crew Stores, Engine Room, and General Stores. Mercer was using four different coloured pencils and was achieving rather an agreeable colour scheme.

The inner door opened and Arnold Rowe came out. Although it was only ten o'clock in the morning he was halfway through his second cigar of the day.

He said, "You having some trouble?"

"It was Bapu Ram."

"That bolshy blighter. What did he want?"

"He wanted to know why we were switching him from the *Tamar* to the *Dart*. He said all his friends were on the *Tamar*."

"And what did you tell him?"

"Since I didn't know myself, the only thing I could tell him was to do what he was told and be thankful he had a job at all, with one and a half million unemployed. As a matter of fact, it did seem a bit odd."

"Ours not to reason why," said Rowe. "I have my instructions from Mr. Henderson, just as you have yours from me. You're doing an excellent job, my boy." He seemed to be about to pat Mercer on the shoulder, then thought better of it.

"All the same," said Mercer, "we might be in for trouble."

"Trouble?" Rowe looked up sharply. His large and generously con-toured face had lost some of its colour. "What sort of trouble?"

"Union trouble," said Mercer. "And if anyone does start anything in that line I don't mind betting it'll be Bapu Ram. He's a born shop steward, that boy."

"Oh. Union trouble," said Rowe. "We can deal with that." The colour had come back into his face. "We have so many staunch friends to help us inside and outside our organisation."

"I've got to see a solicitor."

Rowe looked at him in some surprise.

"You reminded me. Talking about trouble and friends who could help us. I'm having trouble. With my landlady."

Rowe laughed, swallowed some cigar smoke, coughed, and laughed again.

"You are an extraordinary chap," he said. "I've noticed it before. When you seem to be talking about one thing, I find you are talking about something quite different."

"I've got a devious mind," agreed Mercer. "I noticed a board up in the High Street. S. Klerk and Company. They're solicitors, aren't they?"

"They are indeed. And if Syd Klerk can't find a way through the law, he'll find a way round it. What sort of trouble are you having?"

"Our landlady is trying to turn us out. She's a highly moral woman. She suspects that Shallini and I are not man and wife."

"That's surely no reason for terminating your tenancy?"

"Ah," said Mercer, "you say that because you live north of the river. Up there anything goes. The permissive society hasn't got down to these parts yet.

It was more than a mile from the offices and store of Arnold Rowe and Company (Ships' Chandlers & Marine Contractors) on Lower Creek Street to Mercer's flat in Lower Greenwich. He usually kept his car in a lean-to in the yard behind the store and made the journeys to and fro on foot. A cheerful June sun was warming the streets, with their summer smell of tar and exhaust fumes, mixed with a salty tang from the river. In the ten months he had been there, Mercer had become an accepted figure in the community. He did his evening drinking at the China Clipper or the Duke of Albemarle and took his midday meal at the café at the corner of Lower Creek Street, where he was on nodding terms with most of the Indians and Pakistanis who had turned it into an unofficial club.

A sound obtruded itself. In the street ahead someone was playing, and playing well, on a cornet. As he turned the corner a big drum took up the rhythm and there was a scatter of applause.

Mercer saw a little group in Salvation Army uniforms clustered round the cornet player, a huge man with a long black beard. He wondered how he kept it from getting entangled with the stops. It was a meeting rather than a service. A young man in glasses was handing round leaflets and he was followed by a girl with a collecting box.

Most of the spectators put something in. As the girl came up to Mercer he felt in his pocket for a coin. He was aware of the work which the dedicated, cheerful men and women in their curious Victorian uniforms carried out among the dwellers in that part of London.

He put a 50p piece into the box and was rewarded with a smile. He thought that she was an unusually pretty girl. Hardly a girl. In the second half of her twenties, perhaps. And come to think of it, pretty was the wrong word. She had cool and unfussy good looks.

He smiled back at her.

When he got home he found Shallini setting out the supper things. He put one arm round her waist, lifted her an inch clear of the ground, and kissed her.

"Great brute," she said. "Leave me alone. I will drop this plate."

"Get another one," said Mercer, and kissed her again.

"What has made you so happy?"

"I've been listening to a concert. In the street."

"The Salvation Army, you mean? Yes, they are good people."

"Has the old battleaxe been at us again?"

"Mrs. Mainprice. Yes. She stopped me on the stairs this afternoon and asked me when we were leaving. I said we were not leaving and would have the law on her."

"That's the spirit," said Mercer,

Later, over supper, he said, "You have a lot of friends in these parts, Shallini. Quite a few of them work for Rowe, or have been found jobs by the employment agency next door which he operates. Have you heard any talk of trouble?"

"What sort of trouble?"

"A strike. Something like that."

Shallini thought about it. She said, "Mostly they are afraid of Mr. Rowe, but if someone would take the lead – yes, I think they might have trouble."

"Someone like Bapu Ram?"

"Someone of that sort. Or his brother Khalid."

Mercer looked at the calendar on the wall. June 6th. He said, "If trouble is coming, I hope it comes quickly."

His wish was granted. It arrived the very next morning, in the shape of Tom Hobhouse, a square pugnacious Yorkshire terrier. He was shown into Rowe's office and Mercer, who had rarely set foot in this inner sanctum since he joined the firm, was called in to help in what was clearly going to be an unpleasant encounter.

"Mr. Hobhouse," said Rowe, indicating him with a sweep of his cigar which left a fragrant trail of smoke behind it, "tells me that he is what is known as a Union Coordinator. I had no idea that such an office existed, but if he says it does, I suppose we must believe him."

"You'll find it exists all right," said Mr. Hobhouse.

"And might I be so bold as to inquire precisely which unions you—er—coordinate?"

"I chair a Joint Committee of the Local Representatives of the Dockers, the Stevedores, and Sailors Unions. We hold a watching brief for the Transport and General and Professional Staff."

"But since none of my employees, or the men and women for whom I find jobs, are dockers and stevedores or sailors, I fail to see what business they are of yours. You'll forgive me speaking bluntly, I'm sure."

"I don't mind blunt speaking," said Mr. Hobhouse. "If your people want to join a union I'll find one to suit 'em quick enough."

"But suppose they don't want to?"

"There's one way of finding out. Ask 'em."

"Oh, I have. Many times. Have I not, Mr. Mercer?"

Mercer nodded. He had been sitting quietly, withdrawn from the dispute, watching the disputants. Arnold Rowe, large, florid, and loquacious. Tom Hobhouse, chunky and taciturn. He knew which one would back down if it came to a fight.

"When I ask them and explain to them the advantages of unionisation, which seems to comprise paying away part of their salaries in order to support union officials – and coordinators – they do not appear to be very interested in the idea."

"It's not you who should talk to 'em. It's me."

"You mean summon a meeting of all my people for you to address?"

"Yes."

"I fear I could hardly countenance such an interruption of their working hours. They are all very busy people."

"Then let me have a list of their names and home addresses so that we can circularise them."

"It would be a total waste of time. Many of them speak very little English. They could hardly be expected to understand union dialectics."

"We've talked to one or two already. The impression we've got is that you're taking advantage of the fact that they're foreign to overwork 'em and underpay 'em."

"Perhaps you could let me know the names of the people you have talked to, who express this opinion?"

"Certainly not."

"I see. Then all we have to go on is the opinion of witnesses you are not prepared to produce. I don't think we can take the matter any further, do you?"

Tom Hobhouse said nothing.

"In two of the unions which you—er—coordinate, you have, I am aware, a closed shop; which you have obtained through the servility of a weak-kneed crowd of politicians who ought to be ashamed to call themselves a government. Fortunately, in our case, we have not yet come under that hammer, so—"

Tom Hobhouse rose and stomped out without another word.

"Dear me," said Rowe. "I seem to have annoyed the gentleman."

When he got home, Mercer reported this conversation to Shallini who said, "I have been speaking to some of our people. There will certainly be trouble. Bapu, Khalid, and three others are seeing Mr. Rowe this evening. They are demanding the right to join a union."

"What will Rowe say to that?"

"It is thought he will make it an excuse to dismiss them."

"He's stupid enough to do that," agreed Mercer. "Let's not worry about him, love. Let's worry about ourselves. I'm going to see that lawyer first thing tomorrow."

His appointment was for ten o'clock. S. Klerk & Co., Solicitors and Commissioners for Oaths, occupied modest premises on the first and second floors of a building in Deptford High Street. Sydney Klerk had grey hair, dressed down into sideburns, a superb set of false teeth, and glasses in rectangular frames.

He said, "Well, what's the trouble now?"

When Mercer was halfway through explaining what his troubles were, Mr. Klerk pressed the bell on his desk twice and a girl with a plain face and a very bad cold came into the room.

Mr. Klerk said, "My articled clerk. She knows much more about the law than I do. Start at the beginning again."

Mercer started at the beginning and was allowed, this time, to complete his story. The girl blew her nose and said, "Gidgin and bathroom?"

"I beg your pardon?"

Mr. Klerk interpreted. "Has the flat got its own kitchen and bathroom?"

"Oh, certainly."

"Unfurnished ledding?"

"All the furniture belongs to us, yes."

"Then your landlady is mad. She certainly can't durn you out."

"What do I do if she tries?"

"Dell her you are abblying to the Dribunal to fix a fair rent. I don't subbose you'll have any more drubble."

"And if I do have any more trouble?"

"Send for the Bolice."

The girl departed and Mercer said, "Well, that seems to wrap that up. How much do I owe you?"

Mr. Klerk looked at his watch and made a scribbled calculation. "Eleven minutes of my time, four of my articled clerk's. That's nine pounds sixty inclusive of VAT."

Mercer produced a ten pound note and was given four tenpenny pieces in return. Mr. Klerk said, "Is there anything more I can do for you?"

"Not just at this moment. But I may have some inquiries I want made. Can you undertake that sort of work?"

"If I can't do it myself, I can always find a reliable inquiry agent, or if it's a straightforward matter I can send my articled clerk."

"She certainly seemed to know her stuff," said Mercer.

"She's a good girl," said Mr. Klerk. He looked at his watch again and Mercer wondered whether he was going to be charged an additional fee for these closing exchanges. However, all Mr. Klerk said was, "Got to go now. Due in the Police Court at half past ten."

Mercer walked back to Lower Creek Street. As he turned into the end of the street he became aware that things were happening. A crowd was standing about round the main entrance to Arnold Rowe's office. He could see Bapu Ram and his brother Khalid and three or four others whom he recognised. They had a dozen supporters with them, mostly young. A girl was carrying a banner which had a well-executed picture on it. A fat man, smoking a cigar, was riding on the shoulders of a worker and flourishing a whip in the air. The legend, underneath in red letters said: *ROTTEN ROWE.*

When the crowd saw Mercer they embarked on an uncoordinated plain-song chant. The words, as far as he could make them out, were: "A fair wage for a fair day's work." Mercer grinned amiably and made his way through the crowd. No one made any effort to stop him.

He walked straight through into Rowe's office and found him finishing a telephone call. He said, "What are you going to do about that little lot?"

"I've been speaking to the police. I asked them to send a van and half a dozen policemen so that they could arrest the ringleaders. Do you know what they said?" His jowls were quivering with agitation and rage. "They said, as soon as they could spare him, they would send round a policeman to keep observation. And it's no laughing matter, Mercer."

"Sorry," said Mercer. "It was that picture of you. I thought it was lovely. If I was you I'd buy it off them and have it framed."

That morning a conference took place in Superintendent Browning's office. There were two other men present. One was Detective Chief Superintendent Whyman, the C. I. D. head of Number 1 District. The other was his predecessor in that particular job, Chief Superintendent Morrissey, now in charge of the six Special Crime Squads which operated in the Metropolitan area.

"What beats me," said Browning, "is why I'm supposed to use my men, who are overworked as it is, to provide protection for an outfit I'd give a good deal to see closed down altogether. It's not reasonable."

Whyman said, "When you talk about an outfit, do you mean Rowe and Company or the employment agency next door?"

"I mean both of them. They've got separate entrances, but I'm damn sure they're run by the same people."

"And why do you think they ought to be closed down? We haven't had any adverse reports on them from you until quite recently."

"That's correct. I used to think they were on the level. And they did a lot of good work, finding jobs for immigrant workers. And I like Arnold Rowe. He's a Councillor and a solid citizen."

"What made you change your mind?"

Browning thought for an unusually long time before he answered. He was an honest man, according to his lights, and he was being asked a difficult question. In the end he said, "It's Mercer. The new man there. I've an idea he's gradually taking the place over. And I happen to know he's a crook."

Morrissey grunted. He was leafing through a folder he had in front of him.

"I warned Rowe. And I warned his number two, a man called Parker, who was straight. Too straight for Mercer. He got rid of him."

"How?"

"We've no idea what happened to Parker. He just vanished."

"All right," said Whyman. "So Mercer's bent. He's taking over Arnold Rowe's setup. The idea, I gather from your last report, is that he's got some hold over these Paks and Indians and could be using them as couriers, to transport stolen items abroad for sale on the Continent."

"Your report went a lot further than that," said Morrissey. "It suggested that these people had been brought into this country illegally. If their employer knew about it, that would give him all the hold he needed, wouldn't it?"

"I've got no proof," said Browning. "Their papers seem to be in order."

"Which suggests," said Whyman, "that there's a larger organisation behind this one, able to produce forged papers."

"Let's get down to cases," said Morrissey. His nose was again in his file. "When you began to think these chaps might be couriers, you organised some snap checks, right?"

"We've run three very thorough checks covering the crew and cabin staff of a different boat each time. It didn't make us very popular with the unions."

"And the checks flopped?"

"That's right."

"Any reason why?"

"I suppose we picked the wrong ship or the wrong moment."

"There is another explanation, isn't there?" said Morrissey.

A slow flush spread across Browning's face. He said, without any attempt at politeness, "Meaning what?"

"Meaning a leak."

"If you're implying that any of my men here are capable of dirtying their fingers, I'd like names and definite accusations."

"Don't blow your top, Bull," said Morrissey calmly. Browning normally discouraged the use of the nickname which he had earned as a constable on the beat, but tolerated it from Morrissey, who was more than two hundred pounds of fighting policeman, still as formidable as when he had climbed into the ring to win the heavyweight championship of the Metropolitan Force.

"You've got six hundred coppers in this Division alone, so you can't be expected to know them all. What we want are the names of the ones, uniform or plainclothes, who were concerned in or knew about the three searches you just mentioned. That'll do for a start."

"Is that an order?"

"That's an order," said Whyman.

"Then I'll do it, under protest."

"That's right," said Morrissey. "You protest. But you know as well as I do that when A10 gets an idea into its noodle there's nothing anyone can do about it. They could investigate you, me, or the Commissioner himself."

"All right," said Browning. "But can I say this? What we need down here is help, not criticism and investigation. If this racket is as big as you make it out to be, all we've got down here is the tail. The head's somewhere up West – the people who actually receive the stolen goods and arrange the sales abroad. People who can organise forged papers. *They're* the ones you ought to be going after. In fact, I thought that was just the sort of job your Squads were organised to do."

He did not bother to keep out of his voice the hostility which the regular police force felt for the Special Squads, with their special facilities and privileges.

Morrissey said good-naturedly, "I'll keep it in mind, Bull."

The Public Bar of the Duke of Albemarle was always crowded on Saturday nights. It was a favourite drinking place for dockers, sailors on shore leave, and the miscellaneous types who picked up a living along the waterfront. The police regarded it as a rough house, but had never had any definite cause for complaint. This may have been due to the fact that the landlord had once been a professional wrestler and had two sons nearly as large as himself.

From his position behind the bar the landlord regarded, with some misgiving, the appearance of a girl in Salvation Army uniform carrying copies of their official publication, *The War Cry*. He need not have worried.

The drinkers were in a state of alcoholic good humour and many of them paid for copies which they had clearly no intention of reading.

There was one group in the corner who had been sitting by themselves. The landlord knew them by name – Loveridge, Manson, and Banks. They were members of a nasty crowd from farther west, in the Southwark area, and he wondered what they were doing in this district.

He was glad to see that the girl intended to bypass them; but they must have noticed her. She was a remarkably good-looking girl. As she went past the corner table, Banks gave a wolf whistle and stretched out a hand as if asking for a copy of the paper. She ignored him and continued on her way round the room.

When she reached the door and went out, the landlord saw Banks rise to his feet, say something to his companions, who laughed, then make his way towards the door. He was a heavy man, his white face pocked with scars, long arms swinging from a pair of hefty shoulders. As he plowed through the crowd of drinkers he trod on a few toes, but no one seemed inclined to object. The landlord wondered if he ought to do something about it, but decided that it was none of his business.

Outside in the street Banks spotted the girl walking briskly off down the pavement and started after her. When she heard him coming she stopped under a lamppost and looked round. She did not seem alarmed.

Banks, breathing heavily, said, "You like to help me win a bet?"

"It depends on the bet," said the girl.

"I got a bet with my friends there that for all your prissy uniform you were the sort of girl who wouldn't say no to giving me a kiss."

"Kiss you?" said the girl. "I'd as soon kiss the exhaust pipe on a lorry."

"Okay. If you want to play hard to get, that suits me too." He grabbed the front of her uniform jacket.

"It doesn't suit me," said Mercer.

Banks swung round. Mercer was standing just behind him. He said, "You can bug off."

Mercer said, "Surely you can't mean that. After all, we're old friends, aren't we? I'm *sure* you didn't mean it. Shake hands and we'll forget all about it."

He held out his right hand. Banks stared at it stupidly, Mercer straightened his arm so that the thumb and four fingers rested lightly on Banks' chest. Then the heel of his hand snapped down, with all the force and leverage of his fingers behind it. Banks uttered a sound which was halfway between a scream and a gasp, went down onto his knees, and folded slowly forward onto the pavement.

Mercer said to the girl, "The trouble with that little trick is that it can kill people. I wouldn't want to be responsible for finishing off even a creature like Banks. Lend a hand."

He had got hold of Banks by the coat collar. Together they lifted him until he was sitting, with his head forward. "Now we have to rock him," said Mercer. "Rather like starting a car when the starter's jammed."

On the last word Banks gave a strangled grunt and threw up with projectile force onto the pavement.

"That's fine," said Mercer. "He'll be all right now. I'd better take you home."

The girl looked for a moment as though she was going to be sick herself, then said, "No. I'll be all right now."

"They all say that," said Mercer. "And they never are. Come on."

"All right," said the girl. "Home's only a few streets away."

It turned out to be two rooms on the second floor of a small house in Batsford Gardens. Brushing aside her protests, Mercer marched up with her. He said, "I'm widely known as a trustworthy man, where girls are concerned. I'll put on the kettle. A cup of tea will do you good."

It was a typical bachelor-girl pad. One room for sleeping and eating and two large closets, one converted into a tiny bathroom, the other into an even tinier kitchen.

"I was certainly glad to see you just now," said the girl. She seemed to have recovered most of her self-possession. "It was rather a shock. Most of the men round here are terribly decent."

Public school education, thought Mercer.

He said, "First, Banks doesn't belong round here. Second, he's not a nice character at all. Professional bully. On sale to the man with the largest purse."

Over a cup of tea Mercer said, "I imagine I'm not the first person who's said this to you, so don't take it as the opening move in a seduction scene, but what is a girl with your looks and class, Miss Ford, doing in a job like this?"

"How did you—?"

"How did I know your name? No magic about it. I saw it on a card under the bell push downstairs. I'm Mercer. My friends call me Bill."

"I blush every time I admit it," said the girl. "But my name's Millicent. And I can't stop people from calling me Millie."

"It's a nice old-fashioned name. And you still haven't answered my question."

"It's a short, sad, simple story. Father, Rector of Christchurch. Died when I was eighteen. Mother paid for me to take a Teacher Training Course at Bristol. No grant, of course, because she had money of her own. My first job was at a posh school. I daren't tell you the name. I hated it. The girls were all like fat little pigs. Then Mummy died. That meant I had enough money to live on. I had a gorgeous row with the headmistress and came up to London to train to be a Probation Officer. The Salvation Army work was my idea. It's a useful way of getting to know people. Now it's your turn."

"Compared with you," said Mercer, "I've had a very uninspiring life. Mostly it's been a chase after money. Sometimes I catch up with it. Then it gets away again. And I'm afraid I'll have to go the moment I've finished this tea, or the old lady on the ground floor who spotted us coming in will be getting ideas."

Mercer walked back to the Duke of Albemarle. There was no sign of Banks, or his two friends. He had a final drink and went home to bed.

During the ensuing week the pickets at Arnold Rowe's establishment grew more numerous and noisier. They were joined by small contingents from other unions. Rowe himself never got through without booing and some jostling. Mercer the pickets seemed to ignore.

Rowe said, "I'm not standing for much more of this. They've even started sticking placards on my car. If the police won't control them, I'm going to have to do something about it myself."

"I don't see you can do a lot," said Mercer.

"Don't you?" said Rowe. "Just you wait." There were angry red patches in his pasty cheeks. A lot of the robust good humour had oozed out of him, leaving something uglier in its place.

Mercer thought, "He'll blow up soon."

After lunch Mercer called for a second time, by appointment, on Syd Klerk. As soon as they were alone together, Mercer said, "I mentioned a couple of inquiries I wanted you to make. The first might be a bit tricky."

"Not illegal, I hope."

"Not exactly illegal. You might have to cut a few corners. I've got my eye on a small house. Number 23 Swains Lane, Charlton."

"Swains Lane. At the bottom of the hill up to Blackheath. Quite a desirable residential quarter."

"I'm not buying it. All I want to know is whether there's a

mortgage on it. And whether part or all of the mortgage has been paid off in the last year or so."

Mr. Klerk said, "Hmmm." He took off and polished his rectangular glasses, then he said, "The first bit might not be too difficult. Swains Lane was part of the Bundy Estate. It was developed as a single unit after the war. That means that there's one title number for the whole area. At each sale off, the new title number would be noted on the main title – if you follow me."

"I think so," said Mercer. "And if you can find the title number of the house at Number 23 you can tell if there's a mortgage. And that would give you the name of the mortgagee."

"Yes. Probably a Building Society or Insurance Company. But the next part's a lot more difficult. The only person who would have access, in the normal way, to the record of repayments would be the borrower himself."

"If it's an Insurance Company," said Mercer, "I might be able to put you onto a man who's helped me before." He scribbled a name and telephone number on a piece of paper and pushed it across the desk. "Now, there's a second lot of inquiries. They're quite routine. Mostly a matter of looking up records. You'll probably have to employ an inquiry agent. I'd better give you something in advance. Would twenty-five be a good idea?"

"Twenty-five would be an excellent idea," said Mr. Klerk happily.

Mercer had one or two other jobs to do and it was nearly six o'clock by the time he got back to the office. Arnold Rowe was getting ready to leave.

"I've taken to wearing a bowler hat," he said. "It'll be some protection when they start throwing bottles."

It was bravely said, but as he adjusted the hat at a defiant angle, Mercer noticed his hand shaking slightly.

Mercer said, "I hope it won't come to that."

At seven o'clock the old age pensioner who locked up the office made his rounds. Mercer's room was empty. He collected a few late letters for the post, turned out the electricity at the main, and went out to lock up the front door. The pickets, who were themselves getting ready to pack up, greeted him with shouts of "Grandad," and sang a verse of Old Lang Syne. By half past seven the street was quiet.

Two hours later Mercer came out of the lavatory where he had been sitting and made his way back to his own room. From the locked drawer in his desk he extracted a number of items including a long coil of wire, several insulated two-pronged pins, and a telephonist's handset. He then attacked the lock on the inner door leading to Arnold Rowe's private office. He had a small shaded torch, but since there were no curtains on his window and the window gave directly onto the street, he had to use it with caution.

It took him ten minutes to open the inner door. Once it was shut behind him he was able to use his torch more freely. He set to work dismantling and reassembling the G.P.O. telephone on Rowe's desk. When he had finished there was no visible sign that the instrument had been tampered with. The only addition was a single thin black wire which ran from the telephone junction box down on the wainscoting and disappeared through a small hole at the far end. It would have needed close inspection to spot it.

After relocking the door. Mercer sat down at his own desk, propped up his torch so that it shone away from the window, and set to work on his own telephone. The light was so dim that he had to work largely by touch. It was eleven o'clock before he finished. He let himself quietly out the front door, using his own key to open and relock it.

Other people were busy that evening.

The offices of Tom Hobhouse, Union Coordinator, were on the first floor of a building in a quiet side street off Mears Road. The other floors were occupied by surveyors, accountants, and insurance agents, and the building boasted a resident caretaker, an old man named Salter, who lived in the basement with an imbecile granddaughter. At eight o'clock that evening the bell of the street door sounded. Salter ignored it, on principle, for the first two minutes. When it continued to sound he climbed the stairs grumbling and opened the door.

His first impression was that the three men outside had no faces.

Then he realised that they were wearing silk-stocking masks. His next impressions were uncomfortable. Two of the men picked him up and trundled him downstairs to the basement. The third had preceded them and was looking at the granddaughter, who was slobbering excitedly. Salter got enough breath back to say, "Don't you touch her. She's not all there. You'll be in dead trouble if you touch her."

"That's all right, Grandad," said the leader. "We've got nothing against you or her. Just you keep her quiet. Otherwise we'll have to tie you up and gag you."

The granddaughter was pointing at their masks and giggling.

"She thinks it's a game," said the second man. "That's all it is, lovely. Only we haven't got time to play with you tonight."

They went out and locked the door. Salter sat down to get his breath back. He heard occasional thuds and crashes from above, as though the occupants of one of the offices was dropping things on the floor. None of this worried him. He wasn't paid to be a guard. And, anyway, three to one! Let 'em get clear, then he'd ring up the police . . .

"You did *what*?" said Mercer incredulously.

"I wasn't going to let them have it all their own way," said Arnold Rowe. "Give 'em a taste of their own medicine."

"You sent round three men to wreck Hobhouse's office?"

"Right. And they made a thorough job of it."

Tom Hobhouse, who had been summoned to the building by the police at eleven o'clock the night before, would have agreed with him. Typewriters had been smashed, filing cabinets broken open, all his papers strewn about, with the contents of two or three ink bottles emptied onto them.

Hobhouse said, "Right. If that's the way they want to play it."

First thing next morning he telephoned the secretaries of three unions. By that evening they had massive support out in Lower Creek Street. When Rowe tried to leave he was manhandled and it took a heavy reinforcement of police to get him out safely. When he reached home, a service flat in an expensive block behind Theobald's Row, he poured out and drank half a tumbler of brandy. He was contemplating a refill when the telephone rang. With a sinking feeling he recognised the voice of Bobby, who was Mr. Henderson's chauffeur and performed a number of other duties as well.

Bobby said, "You're to come right over, Arnold. And I should advise you to wear your thickest pair of pants. Because you're in for a caning."

Mr. Henderson, tall, thin, grey-moustached, was standing rigidly upright in front of the fireplace in his beautiful drawing room. He looked not unlike a headmaster dealing with an erring schoolboy. He did not invite Rowe to sit down.

He said, "Do I understand that it was on your instructions that three of my men went round and wrecked that union man's office?"

Rowe managed to gulp, "Yes."

"I hope you realise what you've done. If you had gone out of your way to attract publicity you could not have done it more effectively. You have made it impossible for me to use the organisation, which I have been at great trouble and expense to establish, for several months at least. And that at a time when I had a number of extremely valuable cargoes which I was preparing to run."

"I didn't know. If I had known, perhaps—"

Mr. Henderson ignored him. He said, "I have, of course, been forced to buy those cargoes. The people I deal with don't give tick. The net result of your incredible stupidity is that I am out of pocket several thousand pounds. I don't like that. I look to you to clear up the mess you've made."

"How?"

"That I shall leave to you. I hope you will be successful." The impersonal coldness in his voice reminded Rowe of a judge pronouncing sentence.

Some evenings later, when Millicent Ford came home from a Salvation Army Concert at which she had been allowed to play a side drum, she found Mercer sitting in her room.

He got up as she came in and said, "I've got a lot to tell you and there isn't much time, so we'll consider you excused from all the usual opening remarks when you find a man in your bedroom. Sit down and take your coat off. It must be very heavy in this warm weather. That's better."

"What—?"

"Give me the floor for a few minutes. About a week ago, in a mood of reminiscence which you may later have regretted, you supplied me with a number of facts about your family and yourself. They were none of them true. Neither of the last two Rectors of Christchurch was named Ford and in any event one of them was unmarried and the other was a widower. The records of the Teacher Training College at Bristol contains no Millicent Ford. Inquiries were made for you, by an anxious relative, with the Probationary Service Training Department. They were equally unfruitful. I deduced from all this that you were not quite what you seem."

"So?" said Millicent. She seemed to have recovered her composure.

"So, after rejecting a number of other unlikely solutions, I came to the conclusion that you'd been put in by A10 to make a preliminary assessment of the position. That's the way they usually work, although the idea of using a woman officer is a novel one. Three days ago you got an anonymous letter advising you that a certain Detective Sergeant Russ, attached to Superintendent Browning's Divisional Headquarters Station, was receiving bribes to give advance information of intended police raids. It's no use denying it, because I sent the letter myself. Russ was a fairly obvious candidate anyway. Old and soured by lack of promotion, with an expensive wife, two children, and a heavily mortgaged house, Number 23 Swains Lane, Charlton. When I say heavily mortgaged, it *was* heavily mortgaged. Not any longer. Most of the mortgage has been paid off in lump sums of £250 over the past two years. £3,000 altogether. Significant, don't you agree?"

The girl nodded. She had started scribbling notes.

"As soon as you got the tipoff I take it you had him followed?"

"Naturally."

"Then you can tell me from your records whether he made calls from a public phone box at two thirty on Tuesday and at five thirty on Wednesday."

"I believe that's correct. I'll have to check."

"I hope it is. Because I can give you tape recordings taken at the receiving end, in Arnold Rowe's office. If the times coincide, I think that should tie the case up, shouldn't it?"

"Why are you doing this?"

"I told you the answer once, but you didn't seem to believe it. I do nothing unless I can see some cash at the end of the corridor. I'm going to give you these tapes on one condition."

"I don't know that I can bargain—"

"It's a very simple condition. You're to let it be known – I don't care how you do it as long as it gets known – that you got onto Russ *through some indiscretion by Arnold Rowe*. Something he said to someone who passed it on to someone else. Can you do that?"

"I expect so. Yes. But what—?"

"A word of advice. Tie the whole thing up and get out quick. There's going to be trouble in this part of the world quite soon – not the sort of trouble I'd care to see a nice girl like you getting involved in, police training or no police training."

When Mercer got to the office on the following morning, the number of people on picket duty seemed to have doubled; the number of policemen also. He found the rest of the staff still in reasonably good spirits. This was probably because the fury of the pickets seemed to be directed, with personal venom, against Rowe himself. He listened to the chants of "Rotten Rowe – Rotten Rowe – Rotten Rowe," and thought, "He'll break soon; I wonder he's stood it so long."

At that moment the click of his own telephone told him that Rowe was putting through a call on his outside line. Mercer lifted the receiver of his own instrument and listened. He waited until Rowe had finished speaking before replacing his own receiver. Then he lay back in his chair and gave himself over to contemplation of a patch of blue sky which was visible over the roof of the building opposite. He remained so without moving for some minutes. A close observer might have been disturbed by the look on his face.

Finally he heaved himself up onto his feet and made his way out of the building, through the crowd – the pickets seemed more pleased to see him than the policemen – and round the corner at the end of the street. Thereafter he walked fast, doubling back more than once on his tracks, ending up at a telephone booth about half a mile from the office. From there he put through a call to a number in the Victoria district.

Arnold Rowe left the office at half past four. This unusual manoeuvre caught the pickets unaware and he got through the crowd almost unscathed. At the very last moment a burly docker recognised him, swung his fist, and shouted, "We'll get you!" A camera clicked.

Rowe dodged the blow and got away escorted by two bored looking policemen. At the corner of the street he thanked them with unusual warmth and was lucky enough to pick up a cruising taxi which took him back to Theobald's Row.

He had a lot to do and not much time to do it in.

The aeroplane tickets which he had ordered by telephone that morning had arrived. He checked them and stowed them away in his wallet together with the money and travellers cheques. He tried to make a telephone call to a bank in Lausanne and learned that there would be a thirty-minute delay. Then he sent for the manager of the service flats, who arrived promptly. Arnold Rowe was a long-standing and favoured tenant.

Rowe said, "It's an awful nuisance. I have to go to the Continent on business. Almost at a moment's notice."

The manager smiled sympathetically.

"Since I've no idea how long I'll be away, I'd better give you a cheque for next month's rent and service charge. Perhaps you could take this opportunity of having the curtains and carpets cleaned. They're getting a bit dusty."

The manager agreed that this would be a good idea. "And could you order me a car for nine o'clock? I have to be at Heathrow by ten."

This would be arranged. The manager hoped that Mr. Rowe would not find the journey too fatiguing.

The call from Lausanne came through at six o'clock and seemed to be satisfactory. Since he did much of his important work at home, one of the rooms in the flat had been equipped as an office. Rowe spent a busy hour in it, sorting out and destroying papers using a shredder. Then he completed the packing of two suitcases and one large air bag and went down to have dinner in the restaurant which served the apartments.

At five to nine the manager rang up to say that the hired car was on its way. Rowe gave a last look round, slammed the door behind him, and took the elevator down to the front hall. The commissionaire was absent, probably having his own evening meal. Rowe carried the suitcases to the front door and went out onto the pavement.

It was a beautiful evening, dusk but not dark. He was a perfect target for Bobby, sitting in a parked car on the other side of the road. It is likely that Rowe never even heard the shot that killed him.

Mercer had often marvelled at the skill with which newspapers used the delicate weapon of innuendo. When he heard the news at eight o'clock next morning, he made Shallini go out and buy every paper she could lay her hands on.

Most of them had the picture, which had been taken by a News Agency man, of the docker striking at Rowe, with the words underneath it: "We'll get you!" This was followed by a factual account of the discovery of Rowe, shot through the heart, lying in the gutter outside the block of apartments.

When he had read them all he made a telephone call and by half past nine was in the hastily patched-up office of Tom Hobhouse. Here he spent an hour, before walking unhurriedly to the offices in Lower Creek Street. He noticed that the number of picketers had shrunk and the ones who were there seemed subdued.

When he reached his room the telephone was ringing. It was Bobby. He seemed to be in high spirits. "Naughty, naughty," he said. "That's the third time I've rung you. Where is Mr. Mercer? Not in yet, they said. When the cat's away, eh?"

"Well," said Mercer, "now you've found me. What do you want?"

"It's not me. It's the Great White Chief. You're to come right over. *Aussi vite que possible. Schnell, schnell!*"

"All right," said Mercer.

When he had put down the telephone he sat for a long time undecided. He was under no illusion as to the dangers of his position. There were alternatives, which he considered cold-bloodedly, and rejected. In the end he got into his car and drove slowly towards Victoria, parking it on the Old Stag Brewery site among a forest of No Parking signs.

The door of the house in Wilfred Street was opened for him before he had even touched the bell, Bobby showed him into the room at the back, where Mr. Henderson was waiting for him.

He was sitting in one of the armchairs in front of the fireplace. He did not get up, but indicated by a gesture that Mercer could take the other chair. Mercer ignored the invitation, pulled out one of the hard chairs from beside the table, and sat on it, his right hand in his pocket, his left-hand swinging freely to one side.

"You saw the papers?" said Mr. Henderson.

"Yes. A remarkably slanted piece of reporting. Some of them did mention the packed suitcases. It was assumed that Rowe was going abroad on business."

"Assumed?"

"He was running away."

"Why should he do that?"

"He'd made a mess of things and he knew that people in your organisation who make a mess of things are bad insurance risks."

"You infer that I knew he was running away."

"Of course you knew it," said Mercer. The predominant note in his voice was irritation. "I passed the information to a friend of yours yesterday morning. I don't suppose he sat on it." There was a long silence. Mr. Henderson seemed disinclined to break it. Mercer said, "Actually, it may have turned out rather well. I saw the union man this morning. He was glad of the chance of making a deal. The one thing unions can't stand is any suggestion that they use criminal methods to achieve their ends. People start confusing them with the Mob, with organised crime."

"What sort of deal did you propose?"

"The obvious one. I said I'd give them what they wanted. They can have every facility for trying to recruit our staff. And a lot of good may it do them. Hobhouse seemed to think that my influence would insure the deal being carried through peacefully."

"That would mean that you would have to take Rowe's place."

"It seems the logical solution, doesn't it?"

"Yes," said Mr. Henderson. "Yes, I suppose it is."

He spent the next half hour giving Mercer instructions and a limited amount of information. Mercer listened impassively.

After Mercer left, Mr. Henderson sat for a time contemplating the line of exquisite silver cups on the ledge above the fireplace. A technician himself, he admired technique in others.

"The logical solution," he said. "First move, to replace Parker. Second move, to dispose of Rowe. Now I wonder what he is planning as his third move. To dispose of me, perhaps?"

Mr. Henderson smiled gently and stroked his moustache with the tip of one well-manicured finger.

Ellery Queen's Mystery Magazine, May 1979.

THE MAN AT THE TOP

"THIS MAN," SAID SHALLINI, "has taken a room. It is the room inside the front door, on the left."

"Why shouldn't he?" said Mercer.

"But you remember, when we came. The landlady told us it was a room she never let. Never. It was her own spare room."

"Maybe she's hard up."

"She is not hard up. She has a great deal of money. I think she keeps it under her mattress."

"She's stupid enough to do just that," agreed Mercer. "But why does it worry you?"

"I do not like these strange men. First they watch the house. Now they come and live here."

"What's strange about this one?"

Shallini considered the matter, then said, "He wears glasses."

"Don't bother your sweet head about him," said Mercer. "If he wears glasses and looks strange he's a tax inspector. And bustle along with those scrambled eggs. I've got a feeling it's going to be a busy day at the office."

Unless the weather was foul, Mercer liked to walk to work. It gave both him and the people who followed him some exercise. An expert himself in the art of maintaining observation, he was interested in the careful network which enfolded him. It was ably done and unless he had been watching out for it, he would probably have missed the links in the chain. A youth on a bicycle. A girl on a moped. A small closed van. A one-legged newspaper vendor. A number of less easily identifiable men and women on foot. The permutations and combinations were made skilfully and unobtrusively.

Nothing unexpected in that. When he had taken on the number two job, Mr. Henderson had told him, "You're on probation." If being on probation included being under observation, that was understandable too. In this game no player trusted any other player farther than he could see him. If he ever took Mr. Henderson's place at the top, he would watch his number two just as carefully – well, to start with, anyway.

Mr. Henderson had defined the scope of his job with equal succinctness. "You're a middle man. You'll get instructions. You pass them on. And you see that they're carried out."

A beautifully watertight system, with half a dozen cutouts, everything operating downward and no leads back to the man at the top.

When Mercer got to his office in the building occupied by Arnold Rowe and Company (Ships' Chandlers and General Marine Suppliers) in Lower Creek Street, he examined the dozen letters which had arrived with the morning post. One of them seemed to interest him. It was in a dark-blue good-quality envelope and was addressed to him by name. The word CONFIDENTIAL had been stamped in red on the top left-hand side of the envelope. The word was enclosed in a rectangular frame, which was tilted very slightly to the left.

Before opening the envelope, Mercer took out a ruler and measured the distance between the top left-hand corner of the frame and the corner of the envelope. He seemed satisfied with the result and slit open the envelope. It contained a single sheet of dark-blue paper and a cloakroom ticket from the Main Line baggage room at Victoria. On the paper was typed the name Van der Hoek, followed by an Amsterdam telephone number. Underneath, also typed, were the words: "Bapu Ram – 5.5. *Torridge* – two percent additional."

Mercer pocketed the cloakroom ticket, memorised the telephone number, and fed both paper and envelope into an APC shredder. Then he left his office and walked along the corridor until he reached a door in the blank wall at the end, which he opened with a key on his own ring. This was a communicating door which led at first-storey level into the adjoining premises of the Maritime Employment Agency. He found Bapu Ram, a tall serious-looking Pakistani with an incongruous Groucho Marx moustache, interviewing a girl applicant for a job.

Mercer said, "As soon as you've finished, would you step along for a moment to the conference room?"

Under the previous management, a management which had terminated abruptly when its nominal head Arnold Rowe had been shot down outside his own flat, Bapu Ram had been a difficult employee and had even headed a successful strike. Mercer had managed to keep on reasonably good terms with him. He knew him to be resourceful.

Mercer said, "We've got a ferrying job in hand. Amsterdam. Okay?"

"The usual terms?"

"Plus two percent."

"Very well." Bapu Ram held out his hand and Mercer gave him the cloakroom ticket, repeating the name and telephone number and going on until he was certain Bapu had them correctly. That, for the moment, was all that he had to do.

What would happen next he had learned at second and third hand – from Shallini's friend, from casual remarks overheard, from occasional drunken indiscretions. He guessed that Bapu would collect a suitcase full of innocent truck and would find the real contents concealed in the lining or handle of the case. On this occasion, since the destination was Amsterdam, it would probably be precious stones. These he would conceal either on his person or more probably in the cabin stores which would be sent aboard the 5.5. *Torridge* and which would be under his control as steward.

In Amsterdam, Bapu would complete the sale to Van der Hoek, the terms of which would already have been agreed upon. His normal take was five percent of the proceeds. In this case he would get an extra two percent. The balance he would bring back in notes, similarly hidden, which would be stowed away in Mercer's office safe. Later, sometimes after a considerable interval, he would be given a rendezvous on the outskirts of London, would drive out, and hand the notes to a third party who would arrive in a car which had been stolen for that one trip and would then be abandoned.

Mercer gave high marks to the planning which had gone into the scheme. The profits were represented by the difference between the paltry price an English thief would get from a receiver in this country and the much larger price which a safer foreign buyer would pay for the same goods. Even allowing for the incidental expenses and commissions, the margin must be very handsome. And suppose he had wanted to give Mr. Henderson away to the police? What evidence had he got to connect him with the operation? "Not a sausage," said Mercer. "Clever as they come."

He said this to Shallini, who was busy setting the supper table. Shallini said, "He is very clever. No one sees him. We are not even supposed to know his name. It is even dangerous to mention it. Purunmal was punished for doing so."

"Is that the chap I saw hobbling round on crutches? I heard he'd fallen off a mobile crane when he was drunk."

"No. But when he was drunk, he could not control his tongue."

"There are people like that," agreed Mercer.

After supper he said, "I'm going out now. If anyone should want me, tell them I'll be back in about an hour.

The flat which he and Shallini were using was on the second floor. Mercer walked down the two flights of stairs, taking no particular precautions against noise. When he reached the hall he noticed that the doorway of the room Shallini had mentioned was ajar. He noticed also that the telephone, which was the only one in the building, had been moved. It now stood on a table outside that door.

They were giving him the full treatment, Mercer thought. He wondered how much of it was psychological, intended to warn him that he was under surveillance. They could not really hope to keep tabs on him every minute; nor could they keep it up indefinitely.

He went out into the street banging the front door behind him and proceeded at a moderate pace towards the High Street. When he reached the China Clipper he went into the saloon bar, nodded to the landlord, walked straight through and out by the door at the back, which gave onto an alley. This led, in turn, to a maze of little dockside streets. Mercer made his way through them, unhurriedly but quietly, and finally came out into the High Street 200 yards farther along.

As he did so a west-going bus was moving away from the stop. Mercer hopped on board and took a seat which allowed him to watch the passengers getting on and off. After a while he seemed satisfied, left the bus, and immediately dived down a side street.

Five minutes later he was ringing the bell of a flat in the Southwark area. The girl who opened the door did not seem surprised to see him. She was wearing a housecoat, had a scarf covering her hair, and a blob of whitewash on her nose. Mercer thought she looked very attractive.

"I'm just getting things straight," she said.

"So I can see," said Mercer.

"It was good of you to find me this place so quickly."

"It had to be quick. I gather from my friends that you'd been blown. If you hadn't moved smartly you'd have been in for a pack of trouble. What I can't see is why A10 didn't pull you out altogether."

"I suppose they thought there was still something for me to do."

"You've done your job. You've given them Detective Sergeant Russ nicely tied up with a label round his neck. What more do they want?"

"Actually, I understand Russ is to be left where he is. For the time being."

"For God's sake," said Mercer, his face going red. "What are they playing at? Russ is a bent copper. All they have to do is collect him and put him away somewhere, where he won't do any more harm."

"They were very grateful for the tip you gave us."

"I don't want gratitude. I want Russ out of the way. Why do they think I went to all that trouble to collect enough evidence for you to nail him?"

"It's a question a lot of people have been asking," said the girl calmly.

For a moment it looked as though Mercer was going to do or say something violent. Then, quite suddenly, the anger left him. The girl, who was watching him closely, had noticed the same thing before. His changes of mood were as sudden and unpredictable as changes in autumn weather.

He had sat down on the end of the bed, which was almost the only piece of furniture in the small room, and stayed there unmoving. The only sign of life in him was when the tip of his tongue came out, moved over his upper lip from left to right, and over his lower lip from right to left, and went in again.

Then he said, "I wonder."

Mr. Henderson sat in the beautiful drawing room of his house in Wilfred Street. The windows were wide open and brought in the scent of the carnations and stocks from the hidden garden at the back. He looked up from the handwritten report he was studying as the boy came in. He was wearing a white housecoat and carried a tray of drinks.

Mr. Henderson said, "Put it down, Bobby. I want to hear about Mercer. You can sit down."

The boy said, "Well, thanks very much," managing to make it sound grateful and impertinent at the same time.

"According to this report, he seems to be playing it straight down the middle."

"He hasn't stepped out of line yet."

"There was some question about a girl."

"You mean Shallini?"

"No. We know about Shallini. He's been living with her for a long time – she came back with him when he had to leave the Middle East. There's another one."

"There was a bint in the Salvation Army. Quite a good looker. Name said to be Millicent Ford."

"Said to be?"

"There was a buzz that she wasn't all she pretended to be."

"You'll have to be rather more explicit," said Mr. Henderson. "Do you mean that, although attached to that excellent institution, the Salvation Army, her morals were not all they would have wished?"

"The buzz was that she was a copper."

"Really?" said Mr. Henderson. "I should have thought it was a rough part of London for a female policeman to be operating in alone."

"Someone else must have come to the same conclusion. She's pulled out."

"And Mercer was familiar with her?"

"It depends what you mean by familiar," said Bobby with a grin which showed all his sharp white teeth. "If you mean, was he living with her, I couldn't say. I wouldn't have blamed him. The only time I saw her, I thought she was a roly-poly pudding. I could have gone for her myself."

"Get up."

At the change in Mr. Henderson's voice the boy jerked onto his feet.

"I have told you before, Bobby, that I don't like that sort of talk. I should hate to have to whip you."

"You wouldn't hate it as much as I should," said Bobby earnestly. "Is that all for now, sir?"

"That is all for the moment."

On the following morning Mercer said to Shallini, "If we had to clear out quick, is there anywhere you could go?"

"I have a sister at Portsmouth. I could perhaps go to her. Why?"

"I've got a feeling things may be getting a bit uncomfortable round here soon."

Shallini said, "You are thinking of something evil?"

"That's right, love," said Mercer. "I'm having very evil thoughts indeed."

In fact, he was waiting for a telephone call which he knew must come sooner or later. It came at the end of three days of exceptional heat, when men worked stripped to the waist and women spent the evening gossiping outside their doorways, as an alternative to going into their oven-like houses.

Mercer was on the point of going home when the telephone on his desk rang. A man's voice said, "You know who I am and you know why I want a word with you."

"I can guess," said Mercer.

"Okay. Do you know a café called Ron-and-Lon? About seven miles out on the Dartford Road. It's a pull-up for lorries. There won't be many people there at this time of night."

"I can find it."

"I'll be waiting for you."

Mercer got his car out of the yard next door and drove out into the sunbaked Kentish countryside. If there were people watching him he took no apparent notice of it, but drove slowly, tucked into the stream of home-going commuter traffic.

Ron-and-Lon's café was a construction of cement blocks, set back from the road behind a big lorry park which was empty except for two lorries and a single private car. Mercer parked alongside the car, but facing outward. He locked the car door and stood for a moment looking back at the way he had come. Behind him the sky was deep red, almost like a new Fire of London.

He stalked into the café, jerked the door open, and banged it shut behind him. A group of four lorry drivers looked up and then went on with their game of nap. The only other occupant of the room, sitting at a table in the far corner, was Detective Sergeant Russ.

Mercer stopped at the counter to pick up and pay for a cup of tea, carried it across to the far table, and set it down with a thump which spilled a lot of the tea into the saucer. Then he said, "Well? What is it? What do you want?"

Russ looked at Mercer in surprise. He had never seen him in this mood before. He said, forcing some truculence into his own voice, "I don't know what you've got to beef about. I'm the one who's complaining."

Mercer said, "And what the hell have you got to complain about?"

He hadn't troubled to lower his voice. Russ looked at the lorry drivers and then said, speaking quietly, "You know damn well what it's about, Mercer. I had an arrangement with your old boss, Arnold Rowe. He made a payment every quarter to the company that's got a mortgage on my house. Right?"

Mercer said nothing.

"The payment was due last week. It hasn't been made. I want to know why."

"Then I'll tell you why." Mercer was smiling, but there was nothing pleasant in the smile. "When you're dealing with a bent copper, you like him to be bent in one direction only."

"What the hell do you mean?"

"You've been blown, boyo. A10 uncovered your mortgage fiddle and one or two other little fiddles as well. They had you on the end of a string, Russ. But they didn't pull it tight. I wondered why. And now I've found out. They thought they could use a little fish like you to catch a bigger fish. Two nights ago you saw old man Morrissey and don't pretend you don't know who I mean. You're so bloody stupid you didn't even know you were being followed. You were chatting to him for half an hour, I heard, in his car in a layby in the Lewisham Bypass. What sort of bargain did he make with you?"

Russ had climbed slowly to his feet. His face was white and he was breathing through his nose.

He said, "I went because Morrissey's one of the top brass, and he sent for me. He chose the spot, not me. As for the rest of it, it's just a load of bull."

"You calling me a liar?" Mercer picked up his cup and jerked the hot tea at Russ. Most of it went down the front of his shirt. Russ grunted, pushed the table aside, and came for Mercer, who kicked him, without fuss, on the left kneecap. As Russ heeled over, Mercer picked a plate off the table and broke it over Russ's head.

He said, "That's just for starters. It'll seem like soft music to what Mr. Henderson's going to do to you when he hears."

He made for the door. The proprietor said, "Hey! What's all this about?"

Mercer pointed to Russ, who was squatting on the floor, nursing his knee. There were splinters of china on his bald scalp and blood was running down his face. Mercer said, "He'll pay for the damage."

The proprietor was about to say something, but saw the expression on Mercer's face and refrained. The lorry drivers seemed to be concentrating on their card game. Mercer went out and drove slowly back towards London. When he reached home he sat down at the telephone table in the hall and started to dial a number. The door of the room next to the telephone was shut, but he had no doubt that an extension had been led through into the room. When he had finished dialling, the telephone at the other end went on ringing for some time. Mercer waited patiently. There was a click and a tired voice said, "Oo is it?"

"Mercer here. Would you pass a message, please. I want a contact and I want it quick. I'll wait here till you ring back."

The voice said, "Okay," and the telephone went dead.

Mercer sat on, unmoving. An occasional car went past in the street outside. Ten minutes later the telephone rang. Mercer lifted the receiver.

The same voice said, "Westcomb Park Road. The Maze Hill end. An hour from now."

Mercer reached the rendezvous with time to spare and sat in his car smoking. A big car, using side lights only, drew up behind him. Bobby got out, climbed into Mercer's car. and wriggled down into the seat beside him. He looked very smart in his chauffeur's uniform of dark-blue with silver buttons. He said, "What's the crisis, daddy? Someone been horrid to you? Tell Bobby all about it."

At the end of it Bobby said, "Well, well, well – that's not good, is it? Quite contrary to Scout Law. Did you say you clobbered him. With a plate?"

"I lost my temper. It was a stupid thing to do."

"Excusable, in the circumstances. We shall have to do something about this. Won't we?"

"The sooner the better," said Mercer.

"Just you leave it to me," said Bobby. He sounded excited.

When he got back to Wilfred Street, Mr. Henderson was waiting for him. He was sitting in a big chair in front of the open window smoking a cigar. The only light in the room was reflected from a lamp on the patio outside the window. He listened to what Bobby had to say. When he had finished, he asked, "Has it all been cross-checked?"

"It certainly has. When Mercer heard this meeting might be taking place he had Banks follow him. And in case there was any slip-up, Loveridge followed Banks."

"And they both say that Russ met Morrissey and sat in the car with him for half an hour?"

"Right."

The tip of the cigar glowed red in the half-darkness as Mr. Henderson drew on it. He said, "A dangerous man."

"A stupid little two-timer really," said Bobby.

"I wasn't referring to Detective Sergeant Russ. I was speaking about Morrissey. He used to be the C.I.D. head of Number 1 District. Now I hear he's in charge of the Metropolitan section of the Special Crimes Squads. Ten years ago I watched him boxing in the police heavyweight finals. He didn't just knock his man down." Mr. Henderson smiled at the thought. "He knocked him clean out of the ring."

"Oh, he's a tough character," said Bobby. "No question."

"So now we must think what to do about stupid little Sergeant Russ."

"Yes," said Bobby. He sounded like a boy who is hoping he might be offered a bar of chocolate.

"You'd enjoy dealing with him yourself?"

"I most certainly would."

"Have you got any ideas?"

Bobby hesitated, but was encouraged by the benevolent look on Mr. Henderson's face. He said, "There was a thing. I read it in one of my – well – it was in one of those comics you got me from America. These gangsters took one of the gang. They found out he'd been betraying them. They took his clothes off and fastened him by the heels to the back bumper of their car and dragged him along the road, face downwards. What was left of him at the end, they threw into the river."

Mr. Henderson was watching Bobby's face while the words tumbled out. He seemed to be sharing the enjoyment which he saw there.

He said, "No. I'm afraid not, Bobby. It'll have to be something a lot simpler than that. Have a word with Mercer. He'll help you set it up."

"I don't need Mercer to help me," said Bobby, pouting.

"All the same, you will use him," said Mr. Henderson gently. "That is an order. And you know what happens to you if you are disobedient."

"I'm not being disobedient." Mr. Henderson could tell that tears were not far away. "It's just that I wanted to do this all by myself, to help you."

Mr. Henderson slid one arm round the boy and drew him up to him. He said, "That was very nice of you, Bobby. But you've got to be careful. We're dealing with dangerous people. Use Mercer. He's a professional. He'll set it up for you."

"As long as I can do the actual killing."

"Yes. You can do it. And I expect you can manage to hurt him a bit while you're doing it. But nothing too elaborate. You're not cross with me?"

"Not any longer," said Bobby. He sounded happy again. The chocolate had been given back.

"Of course I'll help," said Mercer. "I loathe the guy. The only thing is, I'd better not chop him myself. Seeing I've already busted a plate on his head. If something happens to him in the near future, I'm likely to be the number one suspect."

"That's right," said Bobby. "I'm going to kill him myself. Mr. Henderson promised me I should."

"Okay. Had you got any ideas?"

"I was thinking perhaps we could trap him in his house. We'd tie him to a chair and I could use this gun. I'm a good shot."

"You lowered Arnold Rowe in two, from across the road," agreed Mercer.

Bobby looked up and said sharply, "Who told you that?"

"These things get about. The boys respected you for it, you know."

"I suppose there's no harm in people knowing. This gun's a German Army P.38. It carries eight bullets. What I was thinking was, I could put one shot in each of his legs, one in each arm, two in the stomach, then two in the heart. Of course, I'd wait some time before firing the last two shots. I like seeing people squirm, you know."

Mercer looked curiously at the boy. His eyes were bright, his lips slightly open. He said, "He'd certainly be squirming by that time. But I don't think we can do it quite like that."

"Why not? The gun's got a silencer. No one's going to hear."

"The trouble is, he doesn't live by himself. He's got a wife. And a daughter."

"We could tie them up too and let them watch."

Mercer nearly said, "You've been reading too many horror comics, sonny." Instead he affected to consider the matter, then shook his head.

"Too complicated," he said. "Too many things might go wrong. No. Keep it simple. Here's how we must do it. Tomorrow evening I'll get Banks to watch the police station. That's the Divisional Headquarters Station which Russ operates from. We shall have to know the moment he comes off duty. Unless there's something special on hand it's normally around seven o'clock. As soon as he starts for home, Banks telephones me. I'll be waiting for the call at the café near the end of Swains Lane. You'll be in a car, which you'll have to steal for the job, parked opposite the corner of the street. Okay so far?"

"It doesn't sound very exciting."

"It gets better as it goes along. When Russ turns the corner I shall be coming from the other direction. I'll time it so that I'm opposite to him, but on the other side. I'll call out something which will stop him in his tracks. He may even start to cross the road to take a poke at me. That's when you fire. Aim for his legs first. When he's down on the ground you can empty the gun into him if you like, only for God's sake don't waste too much time."

"That sounds more like it," agreed Bobby.

"The only thing is, I hope you really can shoot. I don't want you to hit me in the leg."

"Don't you worry," said Bobby. The thought of stealing a car seemed to have cheered him up a lot.

At six o'clock on the following evening Mercer finished packing the second of two large suitcases. A smaller case with Shallini's personal belongings in it had already been packed.

He said, "When you wrote to your sister in Portsmouth telling her to expect you tonight, you did warn her not to write back or try to telephone you?"

"I did. She must have thought it most peculiar."

"Blame it on me. I've ordered a car. It will be here in five minutes. The driver has been told that he has to take you to Waterloo. *There's no need to say anything to him.* When you get there, the driver will help you with the suitcases."

"What about the furniture?"

"Are you very attached to it?"

Shallini looked at it and shuddered. "Not very. No."

"Then you won't be sorry to hear that I've sold it to our landlady. She was so glad to get rid of us, she paid what I asked, without arguing."

Shallini said, "You are going to do something horrible and you will not tell me what it is."

Mercer put an arm round her and said, "You're imagining things, love."

"I am not imagining. You have spoken in your sleep."

Mercer seemed more amused than alarmed. He said, "What did I say?"

"First you said, 'Bobby' Several times. Then you said, 'Mr. Henderson.' Bobby is Mr. Henderson's friend, is he not? His close friend."

"That's a very delicate way of putting it," said Mercer. "Listen. I think I can hear the car."

He picked up both the large suitcases, one in each hand. They were heavy cases, but seemed to cause him no difficulty. Shallini took the small case, her coat and handbag, and followed him out onto the landing. She took a last look back, switched off the light, and shut the door.

By the time she reached the front hall, Mercer had already put the big cases into the back of the car and had come back and was standing in the open doorway. He stood aside to let Shallini pass. This brought him up against the telephone table. He put one hand out and wrenched the telephone cord out of the wall.

As Shallini climbed into the car, the room door behind him opened and a small man shot out. Mercer's bulk was blocking the front door.

The small man had opened his mouth to say something, when Mercer's hand landed on his chest and shoved him back into the room. Outside in the street they could hear the car starting up.

Mercer said, "Watch it, chum. You were put in here as a spy. Not as a muscle man. There's no call for you to commit suicide." With a final push he propelled the small man into an armchair.

He said, "I imagine you're doing this on commission for old man Henderson. Right?"

The man said, "I can't—"

"No. Of course you can't. Just listen to me. If you value your hide, you'll creep back into whatever hole you came out of and stay there. There's going to be a raft of trouble very soon. Unless you want to get involved in it, get clear and stay clear. It's a last chance. Do you get me?"

The man in the chair seemed to be past speech. His mouth was opening and shutting, but no sound came out. Mercer looked at him thoughtfully.

He said, "What I ought to do is tie you up, cover your face with sticking plaster, and put you in the bath. But it would be troublesome and I don't think it's necessary."

"No need to do that," said the man. "No need at all." His voice rose into a squeak which almost made Mercer laugh. "I'm getting out."

"That's sensible," said Mercer. "Stop here for half an hour. Then you can go."

The man nodded his agreement to this suggestion. He nodded so hard that a handsome top set of false teeth became detached and had to be eased back into place.

Mercer came out of the Bluebell Café and waved a hand towards the battered Volkswagen which was parked opposite the end of Swains Lane with all its windows shut. Then he walked without haste down the street and propped himself up against a garden wall twenty yards farther on. He had timed exactly how long it took Russ to get home from the police station. Seventeen minutes. Unless, of course, he stopped for a drink on the way, but this was unlikely with his supper waiting for him. Five minutes.

He wondered what other men, apart from Banks, Bobby, and himself, Mr. Henderson had put onto the job. He was a person who liked to check and double check all his operations. The fact that he could see no watchers proved nothing.

Ten minutes.

He wondered what Bobby was doing. Fiddling with the safety catch of the P.38 probably. He hoped that he was as good a shot as he thought he was.

Fifteen minutes.

Any moment now. Was that Russ turning into the road? Yes, that was him all right.

Mercer moved deliberately towards him, keeping to the opposite side of the street. As he reached a point across from Russ, he shouted, "Hullo Russo, how's the head?" Russ stopped and swung round. Mercer saw the window of the Volkswagen go down and the glint of a gun. Russ was already halfway across the street. He was limping slightly from the kick he had had in the knee, but that wasn't stopping him.

Mercer shouted, "Dodge, you fool! The car behind you. Dodge or fall down."

Russ jerked his head round. Mercer saw the flash, heard the dull plop of the silenced gun, and saw Russ go down. He wasn't sure whether he'd been hit or was taking evasive action.

At that moment a police car, coming down the main road, squealed to a halt, ramming the Volkswagen as it did so. Two uniformed policemen piled out. Another shot went off. Mercer said, "Damn, the stupid bugger. He's hit one of them."

The driver was out of the police car by now, coming round the far side of the Volkswagen. There was a swirl of bodies, a crash of broken glass, and Bobby was dragged out onto the pavement. One of the policemen had a firm grip of his long blond hair, the other had him by one ankle.

Russ was on his knees, clasping his left shin. Blood was showing through the trouser leg. It seemed to be oozing, not spurting.

"Missed the artery," Mercer thought. As long as Bobby hasn't killed the squaddie, the score to date looked about right. It was time he made himself scarce. He doubled off, fast, down the pavement. Russ shouted something after him. Mercer did not turn his head. Seconds later he was round the corner. As soon as he was out of sight he stopped running and started to walk.

"I told you, quite clearly, that you were never to telephone me here, even from a call box, except in an emergency."

"This is an emergency," said Mercer.

"Oh?"

"The attempt on Russ went off half-cocked. It wasn't anything we could have foreseen. A patrol car came along as Bobby let off the first shot. He winged Russ, all right, then the police tumbled out and there was a scrimmage." Mercer could hear the hiss of indrawn breath.

"Bobby. What happened to Bobby?"

"He got off one more shot. It may have been a mistake. You know what it's like, when you're all struggling together and one man has got a gun."

Mercer was drawing out his words, seeming to speak with conscious deliberation. Mr. Henderson, making an effort at self-control, said, "How long ago did this happen?"

"About an hour ago."

"What!"

"Maybe a little more."

"Then why the hell didn't you ring before."

It was the first time Mercer had heard Mr. Henderson swear, almost the first time he had heard him raise his voice. He said apologetically, "I thought it would be more useful if I scouted round a little first, to find out what they were going to do with Bobby."

"Well?"

"I assumed they'd be taking him to Divisional Headquarters Station and they started out in that direction, but they must have got orders on the car radio. They went to Leaman Street Substation instead. It's the smallest of the Divisional Stations, right down at the end of Leaman Passage. Ten minutes after they'd got there, Superintendent Browning arrived. You know, the one they call Bull Browning."

"Why—?" Mr. Henderson seemed to have some difficulty in getting the words out. "Why should they take him there?"

"Well, it's quiet, you see. If they wanted to give him a bit of a working over. You know how savage they get if a policeman's killed. And Browning's a rough character."

There was such a long silence after this that Mercer thought the man at the other end had gone away. But when Mr. Henderson spoke his voice was under control, cold and clear.

He said, "How many men in that substation?"

"At this time of night? A duty sergeant and one other man probably. Then there would be the men who brought Bobby in. They *could* still be there. And Browning."

"Yes," said Mr. Henderson. "When we remove Bobby we mustn't forget to deal with Superintendent Browning."

"Remove Bobby?"

"You heard what I said. We shall need two cars and six men. Banks, Loveridge, Manton, and Foxwell. And you. Everyone will be issued shotguns and will, of course, be masked. One car to block the end of Leaman Passage and prevent any interference. The second car to go straight in. Understood?"

"I understand the plan," said Mercer slowly, "and it might work, I suppose. Surprise and brutality. But there's just one thing."

"Well?"

"This isn't like robbing a bank or holding up a payroll. It's a direct attack on the police. I think the boys will do it. But they'd feel happier if you were there yourself."

"Of course I shall be there," said Mr. Henderson. "I shall be in the car that goes in. Foxwell to drive. Banks and Loveridge with me. You and Manton to hold the end of the Lane. We meet at Foxwell's garage exactly one hour from now. So you haven't much time."

"Time enough," said Mercer. And again, after he had replaced the receiver, "Time enough." He stood for a few moments without moving. Anyone watching him would have supposed from the absorbed look on his face that he was pondering some difficult problem in philosophy or ethics.

Leaman Street Station was, as Mercer had said, the smallest substation in the Division – indeed, one of the smallest in the Metropolitan area. It had originally been occupied by the Water Guard, who controlled the barge and lighter traffic in the reaches between the Surrey Docks and the Isle of Dogs. When the Guard had abandoned it, the police had taken it over as a useful staging post and a contact point with their colleagues in the River Police. It was not much used. The next economy drive would probably see it abolished.

Sergeant Baxter, who was in charge of the substation and had been looking forward to a peaceful night, was a badly puzzled man.

First, he had been ordered to empty the cells of prisoners. This had been easy, since their only occupant was a drunken Irish coal heaver. Then he had been told to send home Constable Mulligan, who would normally have manned the telephone and kept him company during the night. Finally, he had been given instructions which mainly involved doing nothing, in circumstances in which he felt certain he ought to be doing a great deal.

However, the instructions had been clear and categorical and had come from Superintendent Browning himself.

The Superintendent had arrived at the substation on the heels of those instructions. He had gone straight up to the office on the first floor, presumably to conduct the interrogation of the prisoner who had been brought in an hour before and who was going to be charged, so Baxter understood, with shooting at and wounding Probationary Detective Tolhurst in an affray earlier that evening.

Knowing the Superintendent, Baxter thought he would not like to be in that particular prisoner's shoes. However, the interrogation had appeared to proceed quietly. He could hear the rumble of voices from the upper room, and the only request which had come down had been for a cup of tea. Since the tea had gone up he had heard nothing at all. Taking a soft line to start with, thought Baxter.

It was while he was thinking this that he heard a car coming down the lane. It went past the substation, turned, and came back.

Three men came into the Charge Room. They were all wearing stocking masks. The tall thin man in front had an automatic pistol, an Army issue .455, thought Baxter, who was something of an expert on firearms. The two men behind, who looked to him like typical South Bank toughs, carried shotguns.

"Come away from that telephone," said the thin man. "Sit over there, on the floor. Behave and you won't get hurt."

Educated voice.

Baxter did what he was told. One of the shotgun merchants took post in the street doorway. The thin man, followed, it seemed to him slightly reluctantly, by the second, disappeared upstairs. Baxter watched them go with mixed feelings. The man in the doorway was also nervous. He seemed much more intent on watching the street than the Charge Room. But for his instructions, Baxter would have liked to have made a dive for his legs.

It was while he was thinking about this that there came a single shot from upstairs.

When Mr. Henderson entered the upstairs room he saw, to his surprise, that there was only one man there. It was a bulky, red-faced man, with angry blue eyes, who was sitting on the edge of the table, swinging one leg. He guessed it was Superintendent Browning.

Mr. Henderson said, "I have come to relieve you of your prisoner."

Browning continued to swing his leg.

"And I've no time for argument. If you don't take me straight to wherever you're holding him, I shall be forced to shoot you."

Browning said, without moving, "Your boy friend's not here. He's half a mile away by now."

"You're lying. He is here."

"He *was* here," said Browning. "But we've finished with him. He's tucked up in bed, in a nice cell at headquarters. He wasn't very brave."

Mr. Henderson took a step forward and said, "You damn—"

"Cool it. We didn't have to lay a finger on him. He spilt all he knew in double quick time. It's already been typed and signed."

"Now I know you're lying. Lying and bluffing. He wouldn't open his mouth, whatever you did to him. And I still think he's here. I'll count down to five. No more. Five—"

"You're in dead trouble," said Browning calmly. "All of you. Who's that character behind you with the rabbit gun? It looks like Banks. Can't you make him see some sense, Banks? You're finished. You're blown. There are forty men round this station now."

"Four – three—"

"Look out of the window if you don't believe me."

Banks took a hesitant step towards the window. At that moment a great many things happened at once. There was a crash of glass from the street. A shotgun went off. Banks grabbed Mr. Henderson by the arm and started to say something. Browning had slid off the table and was coming steadily towards Mr. Henderson, who shook off Banks's hand. The gun he was holding went off. The next moment the room seemed to be full of policemen.

First in was a massive and unmistakable figure in a tight blue suit.

Detective Chief Superintendent Morrissey said, "That'll be all for now. Give me that gun."

Mr. Henderson surrendered his gun without a word. Banks had already done so.

"That really turned out very nice," said Morrissey. He was sitting on one end of the bed in a cell at Leaman Street Station. Mercer was sitting on the other end. "Tolhurst picked up the worst wound – bang through the upper arm. Cut an artery. Lucky the boys knew what to do or he might have bled to death. Russ got one in the calf. Bull was the best off of the lot – only nicked his sleeve."

"We were lucky, too," said Mercer. "Lucky he fired I mean. It'll add five years to his sentence."

Morrissey considered the prospect with satisfaction. He said, "Get him up in front of Maxwell or Bligh and he'll be lucky not to get life. All the same, I never thought we'd draw him out. Did you really believe it was going to work? That he'd come out like a mixture between Sir Galahad and the Lone Ranger to rescue his boy friend."

"It was a chance," said Mercer. He sounded very tired. "The only chance there was. He'd got the whole thing so sewn up that we'd never have connected him, in his bijou residence, with the sharp end down here. I don't believe you'll do it even now – without Bobby talking. I don't suppose he has?"

"Not a word – yet," said Morrissey.

"Love's a great thing," said Mercer. He yawned uncontrollably.

"The next point," said Morrissey, "is what are we going to do with you? I think you'll have to stand trial with the others. We'll get you out quietly as soon as the trial's over. Then I think you ought to go abroad for a bit. Any ideas?"

"Pakistan? Shallini would like to see her family again. Do you think the treasury will stand it?"

"I don't know whether they will or not," said Morrissey, "but they bloody well ought to."

Ellery Queen's Mystery Magazine, June 1979.

THE TERRIBLE MRS. BARKER

MRS. BARKER, WHO STRODE into Inspector Petrella's office one morning, was a tall, upstanding woman with the carriage of a guardsman. Her age was difficult to guess. Her apple-red cheeks belonged either to extreme youth or extreme old age, but from her thick shock of iron-grey hair he judged her to be the wrong side of fifty. She was followed by Constable Whitty.

"I told her," said Whitty, "she couldn't come in without an appointment."

"That's right, young man." She turned to Petrella. "The name's Barker. Mrs. Barker."

"I told her—"

"You did your duty." Mrs. Barker dismissed him with a backward wave, and thrust out a large, red hand with so compelling a gesture that Petrella found himself shaking it. The grip was every bit as strong as his own.

"All right, Whitty," he said, "she's got here now. I'd better see her. Sit down, will you?"

Mrs. Barker lowered her weight on to the office chair, which creaked a protest. And as soon as Whitty had closed the door behind him, she turned her light blue eyes on Petrella and said, "I'm being followed."

"I see," said Petrella. "Well, I'd better have your full name and address, then."

"Emmeline Freda Barker," said the woman. "Maiden name, Postgate. Address, 29, Crayborne Street. Six of them."

"Six?"

"Following me," said Mrs. Barker. "Four men and two women. One of the men has lost an ear. There's a bit of it left. It looks as if it's been bitten off."

Petrella got up and moved across to the window. Gabriel Street was not empty, but there was no one in it whose presence he could not account for.

"I don't think they've followed you here," he said.

"They wouldn't be just standing outside. They're too clever for that. Or Bunny may have frightened them away. He gets rid of them for me sometimes."

"Bunny?"

"That's what I call him. He's my boy. Of course, I rely on him a lot. And I've got plenty of friends, too. There's nothing wrong with my disposition."

"Certainly not," said Petrella.

"But Bunny's the only one I can really rely on. I'm afraid he'll find himself a girl some day, and then, of course, he won't be able to look after me. To tell you the honest truth, I sometimes wonder if he isn't a bit soft. I mean, you'd have to be soft to tag around all day after a woman like me, when half the girls you meet would give their eyes for you, now wouldn't you?"

Petrella felt he had to concede that one. Also, he had a lot of work to do, so he reached for the bell under his desk.

"Oh, Wilmot," he said. "This is Mrs. Barker. She has an interesting story to tell us. I'll get her to tell it to you, as I've got to be off now. You can use my room."

He spent the rest of the morning pursuing some inquiries into a case of self-inflicted arson, and had something to eat at a quick-lunch counter with a man who had once been a cat burglar, but had lost his nerve on the roof of a four-storey house, and been rescued by the fire brigade, a blow to his pride which had caused him to abandon crime and become an informer.

At three o'clock he got back to his office and found an indignant Wilmot. Even in uniform Wilmot had never looked much like a policeman. In plain clothes, the resemblance to a teddy boy was startling. Nevertheless, Petrella knew that quite a useful brain functioned under that unspeakable haircut.

"How did you get on?" asked Petrella.

"Fine," said Wilmot. "Fine. I've got it all here. Six pages of it."

"How long did it last?"

"An hour and a half, with me," said Wilmot. "Then I was called out. Luckily Sergeant Shoesmith came along then. He's got some more. She's followed round by six of them. Night and day.

"One of them's lost an ear. And another is coffee-coloured, but he's got six golden teeth. They never leave her. But they're crafty. They keep out of sight almost all the time. And when they crowd her too much, she sends her Bunny after them. He's quite a boy, her Bunny. He soon chases 'em away."

Wilmot looked with distaste at the six pages of ink-stained foolscap. He hated writing. "She's cracked, ent she?"

"Yes. Acute persecution mania. Not uncommon."

"If she's cracked, why did you let her waste my morning?"

"I thought it'd be a useful experience for you," said Petrella.

It was a week later that Wilmot said, "I saw our girlfriend again last night."

"You saw who?"

"Ma Barker. She was eating in Dan's Place. That's a joint I use sometimes down Water Street. And I'll tell you a funny thing."

"No. Let me guess," said Petrella. "She was sharing a table with a handsome boy called Bunny."

"She was all by herself. I kept away. I didn't want her coming over and telling me a lot more stuff. And when I'd finished, I hung back a bit and let her get off first."

"Very wise," said Petrella. "Most persecution maniacs have a strong mother complex. You'd be meat and drink to her."

"That's not half of it. A minute later another man – I hadn't seen *him* before – he must have been keeping out of sight, too – he got up and went out without paying his bill."

"I bet that upset Dan."

"Dan had seen him all right. If this boy had been walking out without paying, Dan wouldn't have been upset. He'd have thrown the cash register at him. But I guessed he'd paid his bill before. And that looked like he might have been waiting for Mrs. Barker to move."

Petrella said, "In those places you usually pay when you get your stuff. There's not much in all that."

"Not taken by itself, there isn't," agreed Wilmot. "The only thing was, I got a look at this boy when he was going out. Coffee-coloured, and a mouthful of gold teeth."

Petrella considered the matter. He did not underrate Wilmot's detective ability, though it was more instinctive than logical. On the other hand, there were thousands of brown men, West Indians, East Indians, Portuguese, Lascars, and all sorts; particularly in the dockside area round Water Street.

And one in three had gold teeth. They seemed to use their mouths as savings banks.

"You'd better keep your eyes open," he said.

But it was Petrella himself who saw her next. He had spent the afternoon and evening talking to the Port and Customs Officers about a case of illegal immigration, and was on his way home when he spotted the figure ahead of him. There was no mistaking the grenadier-like set of the shoulders and the martial stride. As he watched her, she turned in at the door of a café.

Petrella gave her three minutes' start, then went in after her. There was a row of stools at the counter, and Mrs. Barker was planted on one of them. She had ordered herself a mug of coffee and was sitting with her chin in her hands staring at it. Petrella squeezed past, and made for a table near the end of the room.

It was ten minutes before Mrs. Barker stirred a muscle.

Then she straightened up on her stool, grasped the mug of coffee and drained it off, slapped some money on the counter, sprang to her feet, and marched out of the door.

It seemed to Petrella that this spasm of activity was reflected in a series of smaller, reactionary movements inside the room. A man lowered a paper he had been reading. Another got up and walked to the counter. A third, a tall man who had been occupying the table in the far corner, rose to his feet and strolled towards the entrance. The tall man was putting on his hat as he moved, but this did not conceal the fact that all that remained of his right ear was a ragged fringe.

Petrella folded away his own paper and started to move, too. A minute later he was outside. The street was deserted. He stood and listened.

Away to the left he had no difficulty in picking up the drumbeat of Mrs. Barker's tread. He started to run.

At the end of the road he slowed down so that he could turn the corner without apparent haste. He was wearing rubber-soled shoes, and his method of pursuit was simple but well-tried. You waited until your quarry had turned the corner and then ran after him, trusting to catch up before he could turn another. It was an excellent method, provided the streets were all of roughly the same length.

Ferry Street, at the far end of which Mrs. Barker and her shadower were moving, was a cavern of darkness, walled by high warehouses and lit by infrequent lamps. Petrella waited until the two figures were a dim blur at the far end. Then, having much leeway to make up, he started to sprint. He had gone twenty yards when something picked his ankles from under him.

He flew forward through the air, and came down on the unyielding pavement with a force that drove all the air from his body. At the same moment his head cracked up against something hard, and the blackness was prickled with points of light. There was the salt taste of blood in his mouth, and a pounding in his ears.

He got up on to his hands and knees, and let his head hang. Then he realised that the noise he was hearing was not inside his head. The pounding was someone running.

And as the sound grew faint, he realised, thankfully, that they were running away.

Wilmot, who was on divisional night duty at Gabriel Street, tried to conceal his emotions when Petrella arrived.

Petrella said, "You look at me once more like that, Wilmot, and I'll have you booked for insubordination. Get some hot water and the first-aid kit. And I haven't been drinking."

It took ten minutes to make him look roughly presentable. The palms of both hands were raw where he had come down on them, and there was a bruise like a tomato on the side of his head.

"I thought I'd been coshed," he said. "But it wasn't that at all. I hit a fire hydrant when I came down. Luckily not when I was actually diving but when I was rolling."

"He tripped you?"

"That's right," said Petrella. "As neat a trip as you'd ever see at Highbury or the Valley. I flew through the air with the greatest of ease. It was the landing which was the hard part. If he'd wanted to finish me off he could have done it with one hand. I was out. But he ran away."

"Who do you think it was?"

"I can tell you two things about him," said Petrella. "I can tell you what kind of cigarettes he smokes. I found fag-ends in the doorway where he'd been standing. And he'd been there half an hour at least, because I found a number of them."

Wilmot thought this over in silence. Then he said, "So you think Ma Barker—" and stopped.

"It's not easy to swallow," agreed Petrella. "You thought she was crazy. So did I. But if tonight's anything to go by – well, it was a three-man job. Perhaps four. I got the impression there were two of them in the café. And if they had this man posted to pick up the chase, or discourage pursuit – that means three. And since they couldn't know which way she was going, probably a fourth on the other side as well."

"But why?"

"That's what we're going to find out," said Petrella. "We're going to do some work. By which I mean you, not me. I've stuck my neck out too far already. You can have Baldock to help you. Start by getting a candid camera shot of the lady, have it blown up and sent to Central for checking. She might have a record. If not—"

"I know where she lives," said Wilmot. "The woman who keeps the house is a friend of the aunt of the girl I'm going with. She's a great talker."

"Which is?"

"All three of 'em, actually," said Wilmot.

A week had gone, and Petrella was beginning to be able to handle a knife and fork without actual discomfort, before Wilmot reported.

"*She's* clean," he said. "No record. But that's more than you could say for her old man." He paused with the assurance of an actor who has a good line coming.

"Her name's not really Barker at all. Do you know what? She's Mrs. Andy Kelling."

"Good God," said Petrella.

His profanity was excusable. For Andrew Kelling had been, in his own way, a remarkable man.

When, as sometimes happened, houses in the Shires, residences of stockbrokers in Surrey, or villas of City magnates on the middle reaches of the Thames were broken into, and the jewel cases of lady guests were swiftly and silently emptied, the newspapers usually made some references to a "Country House Gang." But the crime reporters suspected, and the police knew, that this was largely eyewash. For Mr. Kelling was a gang unto himself. He was his own Intelligence Service, his own Chief of Staff, his own cracksman, and his own receiver.

He had operated by day a genuine, and indeed profitable, house agency near Staines, and was reputed to have a proportion of his own gains invested in house property. It was these gains, and their precise whereabouts, which had exercised the minds of the police – and certain large insurance companies – when Mr. Kelling had at last been trapped and had walked off, a silent, grey-faced ghost, to begin a long sentence; a sentence which had ended, prematurely, eighteen months later, in the hospital ward at Reading Gaol.

"Yes. I remember he had a wife," said Petrella. "No one thought she had anything to do with his illegal activities. The idea was that he used her as cover. She was part of his respectable background. She didn't know anything."

"It doesn't look as if that's quite right, now," said Wilmot. "At least, the boys don't seem to think so."

"And what do the boys think?"

"It's like this," said Wilmot. "She lives in this house in Crayborne Street, down by the river. She came there about a year ago. It's a sort of boarding house. This Mrs. Williams keeps it."

"Who's a friend of your present girlfriend's aunt."

"That's right," said Wilmot. "And there's no call to say present, as if I changed 'em each week. This one's permanent."

"I'm sorry," said Petrella. "Go on."

"Well, every month or so, Ma Barker gets behind with her rent. Mrs. Williams lets her run a bit, then tells her the old story. How she can't wait for her money for ever, and there's plenty of people would jump at the room, and so on, and Ma Barker says, 'All right, you shall have your money. I'm expecting some dividends in a day or two.'

"And in about a week, sure enough, she comes along and pays everything, in pound notes; only the funny thing is – she never seems to get any letters at all."

"I see," said Petrella. "And do the boys follow her round the whole time, or just sometimes? And which boys are they?"

"It's Larry Michaels – he's the one lost an ear. He was in a circus and had it bitten off by a sealion. And his wife's in it, too. A big girl. I'm told she was the holder-upper of an all-girl pyramid before she retired. The coffee-coloured boy's called Sam Lazzarone, and there's three or four others. The others came in it with Sam, I guess. He was with the Elephants before they got bust up."

"Yes," said Petrella. He knew enough, now, about South London to realise that these Elephants had no connection with sealions and circuses. "Not a very nice crowd."

"And they don't have to watch the whole time, either, because Larry's got a tipoff in the house. An old party on the top floor that Mrs. Williams is sweet on."

"I see," said Petrella. He was silent for a minute, visualising Mrs. Barker, centre of this little net of intrigue; watched by sharp and hungry eyes, waiting for her to lead them to an incalculable prize, nothing more nor less than Andy Kelling's treasure house. What would happen when they got there? The Michaels were an unknown quantity, but if Sam had brought in his Elephant and Castle crowd, there was trouble ahead for all of them.

"Does she know she's being watched?"

"That's just what no one's sure about," said Wilmot. "She doesn't give any sign she knows, but maybe she's not so crazy. She could just be dead cunning. Last two or three times, when she's run short of money, she's started house hunting."

"House hunting?"

"That's right. Her old man was a house agent, remember? I expect his buddies know Ma Barker. I expect they think she's a harmless old coot. They give her orders to view. Last time," Wilmot smiled, "she looked at forty seven different houses – all over the place – some in London, some out of it – forty seven in three days! And when she'd run 'em right off their feet, she slipped 'em, on the third evening. And next day Mrs. Williams got her money."

Petrella said, "If *they* can't follow her, do you think we could?"

"Well, I got an idea about that," said Wilmot. "But I haven't quite worked it out, yet."

"Don't do anything silly," said Petrella.

He had useful contacts himself among the men who let and sell houses, and he spent long hours with busy professionals, poring over their lists and learning something of the ways of their trade.

"Most of us know Mrs. Barker," said Sam Tallybeare, who ran five estate agencies under five different names. "And we knew her old man, too, and liked him. Yes, I know he was a crook. So when his missus wants to go on the prowl, we're willing to oblige.

"She might even buy a house some day. You never know. And she's not just a buyer. She could be a seller. She's got at least three houses of her own. Did you know that?"

"I certainly did not," said Petrella slowly.

"It's not a thing many people know about," said Sam. "And I only know because—" He got up, shut the door, and came back and sat down again at his desk. Petrella divined that he was giving himself time to think.

"Could you tell me the names of the houses her husband owned?"

Again Sam Tallybeare hesitated.

"I've a reason for asking," said Petrella. "And if you can keep your mouth shut, I'll tell you the story. Or I'll tell you as much as I know of it. It's a story without an end, as yet."

When he had finished, Sam waddled across to a filing cabinet, which he unlocked with a key from his own ring.

"In as far as he trusted anyone," he said, "I think Andrew Kelling trusted me. And I'm breaking the rule of a lifetime in giving away what was a professional confidence. However, there's a time for everything. Even for breaking the rules. Here you are. Andy owned three houses at least. One near Heston – when the airport was built, there were a lot of big houses going at knockdown prices. Another's at Chertsey, and the third's at Egham. The first two are pretty useless, in bad repair, and too big, anyway. The Egham one's different. It's actually on the river. I've had a lot of people asking for that, but the old woman won't sell."

"Then they're hers?"

"That's right. He left her everything."

Petrella took further particulars of the three houses and went back to Gabriel Street. He found Wilmot waiting for him.

"I think I've got something," he said. "I told you I had an idea. Well, what it was, my girl's got a bit pally with Ma Barker. Linda says she's not really crazy. Not all of the time. She talks a bit funny, about Bunny—"

"Just who *is* Bunny?"

"He's her son. The only one they had. He died when he was kid. But she never believed he was dead, see? As far as she was concerned, he just went straight on growing up. Sometimes she talks about him to Linda. Tells about how well he's doing now – runs a garage of his own. And how popular he is with the girls."

"He seems to be quite a boy."

"He's all that," said Wilmot. "She told Linda, the other day, that she ought to hurry up and marry him."

"Doesn't she know Linda's engaged to you?"

"She knows that," said Wilmot, "but sometimes I think she thinks

I'm Bunny – sounds mad, doesn't it?"

"Not at all," said Petrella. "She goes for Linda. Linda's the sort of girl she'd like her Bunny to marry. Linda's going to marry you, so you're Bunny. That part's easy."

Wilmot shook his head. "She's certainly fond of Linda. She wants to give her a present. Linda once said something to her about a scarf pin, and now the old girl comes out and says, 'I'll buy you one.' Linda tried to ride her off. She didn't want to take anything off her. Then this morning, she said to Linda, 'I'm taking you out shopping next Wednesday afternoon. See you keep it free.' *Next Wednesday afternoon.* Quite definite."

"That fits nicely," said Petrella. "We're Thursday now. That means she'll probably start going places over the weekend. But that'll be camouflage. She doesn't really plan to go near her cache until – say – Monday. All right? We'll let Larry and his boys get the run around first. Then we'll step in at the finish. And I'll tell you something else. When we do get to the finish, it'll turn out to be Heston, Chertsey, or Egham."

Wilmot stared at him.

"I've been working on this, too," said Petrella, coldly. It turned out to be Egham.

The house stood outside the town at the end of a lane, which is a parking place for picnickers' cars in summertime, but in early spring was nothing but a deserted avenue of dripping poplars bounded on one side by wasteland where the swans nested, and on the other by three large properties, all with their own river frontages. Mrs. Barker's "Green Leas" was the one which lay farthest from the main road; and a bend in the lane hid it even from its neighbour.

"Lovely place for a murder," said Wilmot. He and Petrella, shivering in their raincoats, were occupying a more or less dry ditch on the landward side of the property. They had been there for two hours.

During this time they had seen Mrs. Barker leave the house twice and make her way down to a large boathouse on the river's edge. She had come back, on the second occasion, with an armful of wood; and a trickle of white smoke from the chimney had indicated that she, at least, was contriving to keep warm.

Now that dusk had fallen, a single light twinkled from one of the front windows. The electricity must have been cut off, and Petrella diagnosed a hurricane lamp.

"She making a night of it?" said Wilmot.

"If she does, we do," said Petrella between clenched teeth. "See if you can get a quick look at that boathouse before it's too dark. Go along the ditch and you'll probably find a wooden landing stage; most of these riverside gardens have them. Keep your nose well down and no one will see you."

Wilmot crawled off, glad of the excuse to move. He was away half an hour.

"It's quite a place," he reported. "Keep your voice down." "She can't hear us."

"It's not Mrs. Barker I'm thinking about," said Petrella, his mouth close to Wilmot's ear. "The opposition's arrived. Three of them, in a van. One's sitting in it, up the track. The other two are in the bushes, over on the other side. Now go on, but very quietly."

"It's a sort of boatshed and dry dock," said Wilmot. "I got in a window at the back. It's two levels – a basement and a ground floor, and it's big enough for a motor launch. The bottom part's dry now, like an empty swimming bath, with planks over it, if you follow me."

"I think so," said Petrella. "They'd float the boat in, then shut off the side next to the river, and pump the water out. Did you see anything that looked like a hiding place?"

"There was a lot of wood in the passage. And some steps down and a sort of iron door, like in a ship."

"A bulkhead?"

"That's right. I couldn't open that. Then I looked in the upstairs part. That was empty. Just wooden walls and loose planks over the dock part to stop you falling in. I could have got them up, I expect, but it would have taken a bit of time."

Petrella considered, shifting slowly from one numb foot to the other. It sounded like the makings of a nice hiding place. Supposing you made your cache actually at the bottom of the dry dock. *If a search was threatened, all you'd have to do would be to turn a handle and let the river back in.* Who would think of looking under six feet of water?

He explained his ideas to Wilmot, who said, "What do we do? Go and look?"

"What we do," said Petrella, "is wait. Wait right here and see what happens."

Wilmot groaned softly.

Half an hour later, Mrs. Barker appeared at the front door. She carried a storm lantern in her hand, and came down the steps, and after a moment of hesitation swung round right handed, and made for the boatshed.

"Come on," said Petrella, and, "ouch," as the sudden movement restored the circulation to his feet. "You lead; you know the way."

He followed Wilmot down the ditch and out on to the wooden jetty. Evening had merged into night, and a pale, cold moon shone down on the water which ran by, fast and silent, inches from their noses as they crawled. It was no summer river, but spring water, dangerous and swollen with melted snow and ice.

Wilmot breathed, "That's the window; I left the catch off. Shall I go in?"

Petrella thought about that. He was loath to split his tiny force, but a man inside might be useful.

"All right," he said, "watch your step."

Wilmot disappeared with the speed and silence of a cat into a larder, and Petrella settled down again to wait.

The other two men were not so clever at night stalking, and he heard them ten yards off. As they came out into the moonlight he recognised long Larry Michaels, and guessed that the dark shadow with him was Sam Lazzarone. At the door they halted for a moment and listened.

When the noise came, it broke the silence with startling clarity. Someone was hammering.

The noise shook the two men into action. Larry tried the door and found it locked. That won't stop 'em, thought Petrella. Their blood's really up, now. I only hope they don't come round this end looking for a window.

The moonlight glinted on something in Sam's hand; there was a loud click and the door opened. The two men went in. The hammering had ceased.

Petrella got up again from where he had been crouching and applied his eye once more to the window. A torch came on for a moment from low down, and Petrella saw the iron bulkhead door that Wilmot had spoken of. It was ajar.

Wilmot had said that he had tried to open it and failed. That looked as if Mrs. Barker was now inside the dry dock itself, although the sound of hammering had come from higher up.

For some time nothing happened. The next person who came into view was Wilmot. Wilmot, in that torch flash, had apparently also seen the open bulkhead, and it was clear that curiosity had overcome discretion. He was now inching down the stairs, and soon had his eyes at the opening.

Petrella had stopped calculating; there were too many factors. He had stopped worrying; there was too much to worry about. He almost stopped breathing.

When it happened, it all happened quickly.

From the shadows behind Wilmot arose the avenging form of Mrs. Barker. Wilmot heard her move, jumped to his feet, and swung round. Mrs. Barker hit him a clean, fast, swinging blow under the jaw, and he went down in a heap. Petrella gaped. Wilmot, he knew, had boxed in the professional ring.

Neither pausing nor hurrying, Mrs. Barker stooped, gathered Wilmot by the coat collar in one hand, opened the watertight bulkhead with the other, transferred her second hand to Wilmot, and heaved him through.

Then she shut the bulkhead, stood up, produced a storm lantern, lit it, and stood the lighted lantern on the packing case behind which she had been hiding. She seemed to be grimly satisfied with her work.

From inside the dry dock, but muffled by the intervening bulkhead, came the cries and shouts of men. Larry and Sam had tumbled to their predicament and sounded angry. Petrella hoped they weren't taking it out of Wilmot.

It was at this moment, and not before, that he understood what Mrs. Barker was up to. She had stooped, and taken from behind the packing case a long, iron instrument with a T-shaped handle and a forked end. She inserted this into a square trap, sunk in the concrete floor, and proceeded to twist it.

For a moment there was silence inside the bulkhead. Then cries and shouts, on a new note of terror and panic.

And the sound of water.

For an instant, Petrella's legs refused to obey the urgent orders of his brain. Then he had jumped for the door and burst through it into the shed.

Mrs. Barker looked up. Her colourless eyes gave back the yellow of the lantern light which bobbed and flickered in the sudden draught.

"Open that door," said Petrella.

"Why should I?" said Mrs. Barker.

"You're drowning three men."

"Certainly," said Mrs. Barker. "It seemed the best way."

"I can't allow you to do it," said Petrella. He was moving forward, very gently, judging his distance. His eye was on the iron key which Mrs. Barker still held in her powerful right hand.

"Are you able to stop me?" she said.

"I'm not sure," said Petrella, "but I'm going to try." On the word "try" he jumped.

He caught the key before it could come up, and wrenched it away. The next moment Mrs. Barker had both arms round him, and they had fallen on to the floor. His face was a few inches from the bottom of the bulkhead. Time had spoilt the watertight fit, and water was beginning to crawl out underneath it.

The cries inside had changed to screams.

He hunched his back, drew his knees under him, and bucked. He might as well have tried to shift a mountain. The deadly truth seized him. Mrs. Barker was stronger than he was. Stronger and heavier; and she meant to hold on, and go on holding until the dry dock was full of water; a concrete trap, to the top of which she had, with her own hands, nailed the final boards that evening, sealing the last chances of escape.

He twisted, bringing his head round until he could look into her mad eyes. He controlled his breathing until he could speak, and then he said, "You know, don't you, that Bunny is in there with the other men?"

"It's a lie."

"It's not a lie. That was Bunny that you hit, and threw in. He's probably drowned by now. The other men may escape. They've only got to keep standing. The door's leaking fast, but Bunny will be dead."

He felt her grip slackening. The next moment she was on her feet and fumbling with the iron bolts of the bulkhead door.

The water, which came out in a solid wave, brought Wilmot with it. Petrella got him under the arms, dragged him up the steps and out of the boathouse. Then he turned him on his face and started to work on him.

Out of the corner of his eye he saw two figures grappling on the water's edge, heard a shot and a scream; then a splash. He took no notice at all, but worked steadily on.

Petrella said to Benjamin a week later, "That's that. Now we know. There was nothing in any of the houses except booby traps. The boatshed was in some ways the most ingenious of them, but the one at Heston wasn't bad. A trapdoor in the floor with counterweights, and the lower room sealed up, and a lot of inflammable material collected. If she'd caught them in that one, she was going to burn them."

"A single-minded woman," said Benjamin, "and the money was in a safe deposit all the time?"

"That's right. Three different safe deposits actually. We found the keys in her room."

"How's Wilmot?"

"He's fine," said Petrella. "That boy will take a lot of killing. The only thing he's scared of is someone finding out about Mrs. Barker knocking him out. He'd never live that down. I had to promise him solemnly that I wouldn't open my mouth."

"If you don't talk about it, no one else can," said Benjamin. There was something in his tone which made Petrella look up.

"It's what I came to tell you," said Benjamin. "They found Mrs. Barker this morning. The Thames Conservancy Police pulled her out below Bell Weir lock. Larry Michaels was with her. Her arms were still round his waist. The pathologist couldn't unlock them."

"Nor could I," said Petrella, and shuddered.

Argosy, July 1959.

PETRELLA'S HOLIDAY

THE CONSTABLE ON POINT DUTY in St. Andrew's Circus always has an exasperating time. And this is aggravated when the sun shines, since most of the traffic on the A.2 coastal road passes through the Circus, heading into it by three different routes, then squeezing out through the inadequate width of Vigo Street before attaining the comparative freedom of the Old Kent Road.

Constable Whitty was not only hot. He was rankling under the undeserved rebuke of Sergeant Mortimer. "Keep 'em moving," he muttered to himself. "How the hell can anyone keep 'em moving when there's nowhere for 'em to move to? If this was Russia, now, or America—" He visualised himself, revolver in holster waving a stream of limousines down a four-track highway. "A hundred years out of date. That's what's wrong with this country. I ask you."

A small cart, drawn by a depressed pony, clattered slowly across the intersection, followed by a lorry with an articulated trailer, six girls on bicycles, and a hearse. Time to switch, thought Whitty. Roll on two o'clock.

He raised a hand to halt the oncoming car, turned and beckoned forward the head of the traffic waiting in St. Andrew's Road. A delivery van and an open car got smartly off the mark, followed by a saloon car. The van on the near-side of the car stayed put. Whitty beckoned even more imperiously. The van failed to respond.

"Engine failure," diagnosed Whitty, "near the head of a line of traffic on a day like this. Why does everything happen to me?"

He strode up to the offending vehicle, which was an old, open-backed, Army fifteen-hundredweight truck, and thrust his head into the driver's compartment. "If you can't start her, you'll have to push her," he said.

Then he stopped. The man in the driver's seat was leaning across over the wheel, an empty look on his face, and a neat hole in the side of his forehead framed by a rim of fresh, bright blood.

Inspector Petrella, although he did not realise it at the time, had passed St. Andrew's Circus just before the shooting.

He had not gone through it, but had walked down Dunraven Street, which is separated from the Circus by a large blitzed site. As he went by, he had noticed a line of South Borough Secondary School boys hanging over the wall, and he had observed a game of cricket in progress. The players, as he saw out of the corner of his eye, were young men – indeed, not all that young – probably from the local printing works.

The bowler, who had a shock of red hair, looked up, and it crossed Petrella's mind that he recognised him. He was on his way to an urgent appointment and had no time to stop, but he determined to have a word with Mr. Wetherall, who was the headmaster of South Borough Secondary School, and occupied the flat above Petrella's in Brinkham Road. Some of the blitzed sites were unsuitable playgrounds.

Petrella was on his way to a rendezvous with a man called Roper, who spent his mornings driving a delivery van, his evenings selling newspapers, and the whole of his time keeping his eyes and ears open. For he was a police informer, and one of the most valuable on Petrella's list. His charges were high, but his information was usually accurate.

Petrella waited, with professional patience, for a full hour, and when he stepped out again into the hot street a cruising police car located him and whipped him back to Gabriel Street. There he found his own superior, Superintendent Benjamin, and Benjamin's superior, Chief Superintendent Thorn, in possession.

"I believe," said Thorn – who was half an inch below the minimum height for a policeman, and known to every criminal south of the Thames as Pussy – "that you were using Roper yourself."

"That's right, sir. I was meeting him this lunchtime. He stood me up."

"He had some information for you?"

"He *said* he knew where the Borners kept their bank. He hadn't actually got round to talking terms."

"He'll not talk any more, now," said Thom. "He got an airgun bullet through the side of his head just before two o'clock. A right neat job. I don't know when I've seen a neater. We've got Roper. We've got his van. And about a thousand people to question. And that's all we have got."

"It'll be in all the evening papers," said Benjamin, who had a long solemn face, and hated publicity of any sort. "It's probably on the streets by now."

"It's no bad thing if it is," said Thorn. "We shall have to appeal for members of the public to come forward. We'll draft an announcement for the B.B.C."

"Where are you going to take the statements?" asked Petrella.

"I think we'll use this station," said Thom. "It's handiest, and the best place to see people will be in your office."

Petrella had feared as much.

Stimulated by appeals in the newspapers and on the wireless, the people of southeast London converged on Gabriel Street, for two whole days, in a steady stream. Some of them were cranks, some were liars, and a few of them had actually been in St. Andrew's Circus at the moment of the shooting.

Sergeant Shoesmith, whose methodical habits were invaluable in a crisis of this sort, produced a plan on an enormous scale, which he fastened to the wall, and on it he plotted, in distinctive colours, the position of every witness. In black, if their presence was unsupported; in green if they had been seen by one other person; in red if seen by two or more.

It was late in the afternoon on the first day that a young man arrived, produced an envelope, and tipped out of it a dozen photographs. "I'm from *The Clarion*," he said. "My editor thought you might like to see these. Interesting, aren't they?"

"I'll say they're interesting," said Petrella. "Where did you get them?"

"*The Clarion's* running a series. Black Spots in London's Traffic. We did Charing Cross last week. This week it was St. Andrew's Circus. Rather a coincidence, really."

"Are these actually—?"

"The time of the shooting? Yes. We took one lot between twelve and two. Another lot between five and seven. The last one of the first series would be the one you'd want, I should think. Isn't that your chap, in fact?"

Petrella and Sergeant Shoesmith and Constable Wilmot crowded round the photograph. It was extraordinary. Like having a dream, and then seeing it all in the newspapers next morning. They carried the photograph across to the plan.

"There's that saloon car," said Petrella. "And you can see the nose of the bus, behind. That's Whitty. He's just signalling on the other line of traffic. Looks a bit hot, doesn't he!"

Sergeant Shoesmith said, "I always thought that man with the beard was a liar. He said he was standing under the clock from half past one to half past two. He isn't in any of the photographs at all. There's the little woman who thought it was Communists. And the man with the four dogs."

"Isn't that a bicycle?" said Petrella. "Look, you can just see the front of the mudguard." He looked at the plan. "That must be the schoolgirl. The one who thought she heard a shot. Just exactly where did you take these from? Can you show me on this plan?"

"It was an office," said the young man. "Our chaps usually work from windows. If you stand about on the pavement taking pictures you get a crowd round you. Just about there, I should say. It's a window on the first floor. He used a telescopic attachment. That's why the background's sharp but the foreground's a bit blurred."

"I think they're excellent photographs," said Petrella. "Can we hang on to them?"

"Certainly. We had these copies made for you. Only thing is, if you do get anything out of it, you might let us in on it." Petrella promised to do that.

While Petrella, assisted by Sergeant Shoesmith and Detective Constable Wilmot, was sorting out the eyewitnesses, Superintendent Benjamin was inquiring into the movements of the Borners.

"Curly and me," said Maurice Borner, a handsome, dark-haired, young man with an arrogant Assyrian nose, "was playing snooker at Charley's. Copper was there, too. We started about one, and wasn't finished much before three."

"A long game?" suggested the Superintendent.

"That's the way it is," said Maurice, "when you get interested in a thing."

"Anyone else see you?"

"You know Charley's, Superintendent. It's sort of private. A few of us use it. I believe Sammy did look in."

Sam Borner, fatter than his brother and superficially jollier, agreed readily that he had looked in at Charley's. He had spent most of the lunch hour in his flat with Harry and Nick. They had been having a quiet game of cards. They often had a quiet game of cards at lunchtime.

"It's as clear as the nose on Maurice's face," said Benjamin. "That's the lot that did it. It's not going to be easy to prove. No one's going to be keen on giving evidence against them. They carry too much weight."

"I know the two Borners," said Petrella. "Nick Joel and Harry Hammanight – he's the big ex-sailor, isn't he? Who are the others?"

"Curly's one of the Bassets – the only one out at the moment. Copper's a redhead. He used to be quite a nice boy, and a promising boxer before they got hold of him."

Something in Petrella's memory stirred, but died.

"And it's all very fine," went on Benjamin, "for us to say we know the Borners did it because they'd got their knife into Roper and because they've got an alibi which is so watertight that it sticks – that's not going to cut much ice in court. First thing we've got to find out is how it was done. What the hell are you grinning at?"

"I was just thinking," said Petrella, "that that's one of the finest mixed metaphors I've ever heard."

"Tchah," said Benjamin.

By the second evening Petrella and his assistants were contemplating a dwindling number of possibilities.

"I think," said Petrella, "that we could rule out anyone on the pavement. It would be much too risky."

"Suppose," said Wilmot, who was young and read detective stories, "they had this airgun disguised as an umbrella."

"Why would anyone carry an umbrella on a day like that?"

"Well, a walking stick."

"It's no use supposing," said Petrella. "We know that no one was doing anything of the sort. We know everyone who was on the pavement, on both sides of the road, their names and addresses, and where they came from, and where they were going to. Do you suppose that any of them could have got away with pointing a walking stick at Roper without half a dozen people noticing it?"

"I agree with you, sir," said Sergeant Shoesmith. "Our investigations have definitely ruled out the possibility of any of the passersby being implicated, and the owners of all windows overlooking the scene have been checked and cross-checked."

"Suppose someone got on the roof, went up the fire escape—"

"And shot Roper through the top of the driver's seat without leaving a hole in it?"

"Roper could have been leaning out of the cab."

"He could have been," said Petrella patiently, because he liked Wilmot, "but how could the man on the roof know that he was going to lean out of the cab at just that place and time?"

"I'm inclined to think, sir," said Sergeant Shoesmith, "that it must have been a man in one of the other vehicles. We have established that Roper followed the same route almost every day on the way from his shop to the depot where he picked up his evening papers. And it was inevitable that he would be held up at St. Andrew's Circus. All he had to do was to draw up behind Roper, or beside him, shoot at the moment the traffic was signalled forward, and rely on getting away in the confusion."

"Splendid," said Petrella. "Splendid. Now tell me which of the vehicles you had in mind. We have succeeded in identifying them all, I think."

"Well," said Sergeant Shoesmith, "I admit that's a bit more difficult."

"There were only three possibles," said Petrella. "Unless the killing was done on the spur of the moment, the car must have been in the same stream of traffic as Roper. No one coming into St. Andrew's Circus from another direction could possibly guarantee to be at the head of one line at the precise moment Roper was near the head of the other. Right?"

"Right," said Wilmot. He enjoyed seeing Sergeant Shoesmith put in his place.

"And he must have been beside him or in front of him. The shot couldn't have been delivered from behind. That brings us down to the delivery van immediately in front, the open car to the right front, or the saloon car, level with Roper on the right. We know who they are. They've all come forward, none of them has the faintest connection with Roper, and none of them looks in the least like a murderer. Apart from that"—Petrella prodded a document on the table in front of them—"we've now got the results of the laboratory tests, which show that the bullet went into Roper from the left-hand side, either on the level, or from very slightly above – it would depend on how he was holding his head at the moment of impact. Which makes complete nonsense of the idea that he was shot from a van in front, or from a car much lower than he was and on his right."

"That's right," said Wilmot again. "Real tricky, this one."

"It's no good just saying it's tricky," said Petrella crossly. "We've got to find the answer to it. There's no arguing away the fact that someone put a bullet into Roper's head. He didn't shoot himself."

It occurred to Petrella afterwards that the reason they couldn't see the answer was because they were too near the problem. He took all the photographs home with him that night, and propped them round the teapot while he ate the evening meal he had cooked for himself. And when he went upstairs afterwards to chat with Mr. Wetherall, he took the photographs with him.

Mr. Wetherall, the reigning headmaster of the South Borough Secondary School, was a neat, grizzled man, with a nose reminiscent of the great Duke of Wellington and an all-embracing knowledge of the characters and habits of the South Londoners whom he had taught, as boys, for thirty years, and successive generations of whom he had watched grow up into tough, unpredictable, cheerful, amoral citizens.

"I have no faith," he said, "in amateur detectives who step in where the professional has failed, but if you wouldn't mind handing me that magnifying glass – it is rather a fine one, isn't it? Young Simmonds gave it to me when he left. You may know his father."

Petrella knew Mr. Simmonds well: he was the second most eminent receiver of stolen goods in South Borough.

"This is the photograph that was taken at the moment of the shooting? And the others at short intervals before it?" Mr. Wetherall pored over the photographs, occasionally chuckling to himself as he recognised an ex-pupil in the crowd.

Then he straightened up and said, "Well, really. I'm quite sure you've noticed it for yourself, but that young lady – the one in the final photograph, she appears to be smoking a cigarette. Odd, don't you think, that she isn't doing so in any of the earlier ones? Significant, perhaps?"

"Which young lady?"

"No. Not in the crowd. I mean the young lady in the advertisement on the hoarding. The one advertising SUDDO. *Make Monday Fun-day.*"

Petrella snatched the glass, and focused it. Then, with fingers that fumbled, he grabbed the other photographs and concentrated on each in turn.

What Mr. Wetherall had said was absolutely true. The young house-wife, holding aloft a snowy-white garment, and announcing with a dazzling smile that Monday was Fun-day had, between her teeth, *in the final photograph only* a thin, cylindrical object not unlike a large cigarette.

Early next morning he sought out Mr. Cooper, who was agent for the owner of the bombed site which fronted on St. Andrew's Circus, masked at that side by hoarding, and which ran clear back, behind the hoardings, to Dunraven Street.

"I put this barbed wire up a day or two ago," said Mr. Cooper. "I heard people had been getting down into the site, at the back, playing cricket. We've never had any trouble before. Do you want to go down yourself? It's a bit of a climb."

"See if you can borrow a ladder," said Petrella, "while I shift some of this wire." Half an hour later, with the assistance of a sign painter's ladder, they were standing on what had once been the basement floor of a large building.

"If you don't mind," said Petrella, "I'll do this bit alone. I don't want any unnecessary footprints."

Mr. Cooper looked at him curiously, and said, "This something to do with the shooting the other day?"

"It might be," said Petrella. "Why?"

"I did wonder why anyone would want to climb down here just to play cricket. You can see for yourself. It'd be an awkward place to get at, even without the wire. I suppose I ought to have said something before."

"Yes," said Petrella. "But don't blame yourself. I actually saw them playing, and it didn't occur to me, either. Hold the ladder, would you mind?"

He climbed on the back wall, and made his way across a weedgrown ground floor. Then there was a girder to cross. It had originally been two buildings, he guessed, back to back; one fronting on Dunraven Street, the other on St. Andrew's Circus. He was now in what was left of the larger one. The line of hoardings was above him, their footings at eye level.

Behind them ran the wall which the local authority had put up immediately after the bombing, to prevent people falling into the hole. Petrella looked at the wall cautiously. There was no obvious way up on to it, but there was a pile of rubble at one end which would offer a starting place. And, at the base of the rubble, faint but still distinct, a footprint. Petrella regarded it as lovingly as Robinson Crusoe gazed at the print of Man Friday.

Lucky we haven't had any rain, he thought. Get something to cover it. And have a cast made quick. Better tackle the wall from the other end.

He went back the way he had come, pulled up the ladder, and returned with it to the hoarding. Using a ladder, it was possible to avoid setting foot on the coping at all. He tried to visualise the photographs. Which had been the Suddo advertisement? There was the beer poster on the left. Then the petrol hoarding. Was Suddo next, or next but one?

It was such a neat job that, even knowing what he was looking for, it took Petrella five minutes to find it. A section, twelve inches long by four inches high, had been cut from the woodwork of the hoarding – and cut so neatly that it fitted without any sort of fastening. Petrella prised it out with his fingernails. The space in front of it was blocked by the back of the poster, but a narrow slit had been cut in the paper and pasted over from the back.

Petrella opened it with the tip of his finger, and found himself looking at the face of a bus driver, fifteen feet away and almost exactly on a level with his own.

"It was an ambush," said Petrella to Benjamin. "They knew he went through the Circus every day about that time. Of course, they were bound to be seen getting into the site at the back. They covered that by five of them playing lunch hour cricket while Maurice did the shooting."

"Bit risky," said Benjamin. "Suppose a policeman had gone by and recognised them."

Petrella was still young enough to blush.

He said, "One did. I actually saw them playing, and thought I recognised the one I looked at – it was Copper Dixon, the redhead. I'd seen him once before, in court. It should have clicked, but it didn't."

"I see," said Benjamin. "All the same, you should be able to identify him when the time comes. What about the boys?"

"In the ordinary way, I don't expect they'd be keen to give evidence at all, but Mr. Wetherall – he's their headmaster – tells me that one of them is an Irish boy called O'Connor. The South Bank Irish don't like the Borners. It's a piece of local politics. I don't know the ins and outs of it, but he thinks that O'Connor will give evidence. And if he does, the other boys will follow his lead."

"And they saw Maurice actually climbing down, out of the back part of the building?"

"That's what O'Connor says. And we've got one clear footprint in the rubble he stepped on to get up. And three fairly clear ones on the ledge. That could be useful."

"Unless he's thrown that pair of boots into the river," said Benjamin. "But he may not have done. Even professional criminals make mistakes."

He was turning it all over as he spoke. Petrella would make a good witness, but he had seen only one man. The boys had seen all six, but were dangerous people to put into the box. Scientific evidence of the shoe marks. That might be conclusive. Juries love a bit of science.

"I'll try it on the Director of Public Prosecutions," he said at last. "And see what he thinks."

The case of the Queen against Borner and Others was news at all its stages. The ingenious and coldblooded killing had caught the public attention. Even the hearing in the Magistrates Court produced its quota of sensations.

Such proceedings are often a mere formality, a skirmish preliminary to the main battle at the Old Bailey. But in this case it was clear that the opposition meant to fight the whole way. Maurice Borner was defended by Mr. Walter Frenchman, Q.C., who was old, fat, and experienced; the remaining five by Mr. Michael Harsch, an up-and-coming young criminal advocate of considerable ability.

Thinking things over afterwards, Petrella came to the conclusion that, although he disliked young Mr. Harsch with all his heart, it was old Mr. Frenchman who had done the damage. Mr. Harsch had been too open in his dislike of the police. He had played too obviously to the public gallery. But some of the mud that he slung had seem to stick.

It had not, for instance, taken him long to ferret out the fact that Petrella occupied the flat below Mr. Wetherall, from whose school most of the witnesses came, and he had built upon this fact an impressive edifice of falsehood and collusion.

"And now, Inspector," said Mr. Harsch, when he had exhausted this agreeable topic. "Now we come to the occasion – the remarkable occasion – on which you failed to recognise one of my clients, Mr. Dixon, when you saw him, as is alleged, indulging in a game of cricket, but yet had no difficulty in recognising him afterwards, when it suited your superior officers that you should do so."

This did not appear to need an answer but, as Mr. Harsch had paused for breath, Petrella said, "Yes."

"You agree that it was extraordinary?"

"Do I agree that what was extraordinary?"

"That you failed to recognise this man when you first saw him."

"I recognised him," said Petrella, "but failed to place him."

"Just what do you mean by that?"

"I mean that I recognised his face, but failed to recall his name – at the time."

"When had you seen him before?"

This was a fast one. If Petrella had said, as he very nearly did, "In this court, a month before," it would have been a grave technical error. He blocked it by saying, "I had seen him some time before."

"And how did you recognise him afterwards?"

"Afterwards I was shown certain photographs, and saw the accused himself, and recognised him as the man I had seen."

"In fact, you conveniently recognised him when pressed to do so later."

"Certainly not."

"And you are quite sure that the man you saw, and failed to recognise, was the same as the man you saw later and succeeded in recognising?"

"Oh yes."

"You have, if I may say so, a conveniently selective memory."

Petrella was glad to recall, however, that Mr. Harsch had not had things all his own way. Next in the witness box was Mr. Wetherall, called to speak to the character of the boys concerned.

It was, perhaps, rash of Mr. Harsch to cross-examine, but he had not yet learnt when to let well alone. "I suggest, Mr. Wetherall," he said, "that in a natural desire to speak well of your boys, you have been inclined to somewhat overestimate their truthfulness and powers of observation."

"I'm sorry, Harsch." said Mr. Wetherall, "that you should so soon have forgotten the elementary rules of grammar which I tried for four years to drum into your head. There is no excuse, even in a court of law, for splitting an infinitive."

The press had liked this – *Counsel Rebuked by Own Headmaster.* They had liked it a good deal more than Mr. Harsch himself. Most of his friends at the Bar believed he had been to Marlborough.

Petrella was told that he had behaved himself quite well. In retrospect he was glad of it. There were moments that afternoon when he had despised, in the person of the sleek, young advocate, the whole British judicial system. He had been forewarned what to expect, and was tolerably equipped to deal with it. At the worst it had been a wasted and frustrating afternoon.

But what was a young policeman, whose talents lay in the physical apprehension of criminals, to make of the dialectical hairsplitting of men like Mr. Harsch? And why, in the name of sanity, did the newspapers invariably select for their headline every point made against the police – *Detective Had Convenient Memory, Says Barrister* – and as invariably omit the occasions on which the magistrate concluded the case by exonerating the officer concerned of the suggestions made against him?

Was it because the insults were news and the compliments were not? Or was it, perhaps, because the reporter concerned had been fined forty shillings for a parking offence the month before, and now saw an easy chance of getting his own back?

But these matters were not important. They were pinpricks in comparison with the disaster that had followed.

At the conclusion of the prosecution's case the magistrate had, with apparent reluctance, committed the six men for trial at the Central Criminal Court, but had then been guilty of the outrageous folly, at Mr. Frenchman's request and in the face of the strongest police pressure, of releasing all but Maurice Borner on bail. Useless to point out, as Benjamin did, his long face white with fury, that the backbone of the prosecution's case, so far as the five were concerned, was likely to be the evidence of schoolboys. And that if the gang was allowed to go free between the preliminary hearing and the trial of the case, there would very likely be no case at all. The magistrate had listened, but with a shut mind.

"I might as well have been talking to the backside of my own car," said Benjamin. "If he wants every one of those boys to tell a different story – or no story at all – by the time they get to the Old Bailey, he's going the right way about it."

"Curse the lot of them," said Petrella, sitting on the edge of his bed on a fine September morning, and swinging pyjama'd legs. It was ten o'clock. But somehow he felt disinclined to get up at all. Nor was there any need for him to get up if he did not want to. For he was on holiday.

It was not a holiday that he had sought, for he had no wish to leave Gabriel Street until the Borner affair was settled, but two days earlier Superintendent Benjamin had given him a direct order.

"We've got a bit of a breathing space," he said, "before the case comes on at the Bailey. It can't be in the calendar before October. You're to go off and treat yourself to a holiday."

When Petrella looked mutinous, he had added, "I'm not thinking of you. I'm thinking of myself. If you don't take a breather now, you won't last out the winter. We're too understaffed for me to allow you more than ten days, but ten days you'll take, whether you like it or not."

Petrella had not even the excuse that there was nowhere for him to go. Colonel Montefiore, an aged relative of his mother, had given him an open but explicit invitation to stay at his home in the Chilterns whenever Petrella felt inclined. "Bring old clothes. I can lend you a gun. And you can have your breakfast in bed every day," wrote the Colonel. "And forget about criminals. The only criminals we have round here are poachers, and they're all my friends."

Two days ago the prospect had been attractive. Now, somehow, Petrella was not sure. He felt tired and irritable. At the same time restless, but disinclined for action. He pulled on a dressing gown, and wandered across to the window.

Summer was still to all appearances in full swing. The trees were heavy with leaves, and the sky was blue. A warm summer wind was driving ice cream cartons and scraps of paper along the pavement. In spite of the sun Petrella shivered. His mouth was dry and his feet were cold. He felt disinclined for food, but thought that a cup of strong coffee might do him good.

He was to take the afternoon train, and a bag, half packed, lay on the floor beside his bed. It occurred to him that he was ill-equipped for a visit to the country. It was all very well for the Colonel to talk about old clothes. There were standards to be observed. He would have to do some shopping.

An hour later he left the house. It was a glorious day, and the sun struck down through the leaves. He thought that a gentle walk might do him good, and he set off along Brinkman Road.

He stopped at Spinks', in the Broadway, and bought himself half a dozen handkerchiefs, but thought that Spinks' widely-advertised line in Gent's Genuine Norfolk Jackets was hardly what the Chilterns would expect. He would have to visit the West End to get what he wanted. He decided that the quickest way, at that time of day, would be to cut across to the Surrey Docks Underground Station.

Childers Street is a long and uninspiring thoroughfare. Towards its far end it swings sharply to the right into River Street. Petrella had an idea that, if he kept straight on, there was a back way which must bring him out somewhere near the Docks Station. He realised that he was wrong when the tiny street he was using degenerated into a passage between walls of houses, and ended in a pair of heavy gates which were standing open.

Out of obstinacy he went on through the gates, and found himself on a triangular, cobbled quay which sloped down to the bank of the Surrey Union Canal. The edge of the quay was equipped with a line of iron bollards, and sitting on one of the bollards, smoking a short pipe, was a brown-faced, white-bearded man, whom Petrella recognised.

"Why, hullo, Doctor," said Petrella, "this is a pleasant surprise."

"Good morning, Inspector," said the old man. "Come to inspect my boat?"

"I don't know that I ought—"

The old man looked at him and said. "You look as if a drink wouldn't do you any harm."

His barge, the *Journey's End,* was tied up, fore and aft, to the quay. They stepped on to her iron-plated deck, and made their way astern to the scuttle, which led down into the owner's living quarters, sleeping-quarters, and tiny galley. It looked beautifully snug. Petrella sat down on the spare bunk and watched the doctor pottering about with a percolator, a packet of sugar, a saucepan of milk, and two mugs.

It all took a long time, and before the coffee was ready it seemed to Petrella that he must have slept and woken again. He looked up to see the doctor standing in front of him, a china mug in one hand and a puzzled look on his face.

"You all right, son?"

"Of course I'm all right," said Petrella.

His own voice sounded thick and faraway. "A bit tired, that's all. But I'll be all right. I'm starting my holiday today."

"Let's see you on your feet."

Petrella started to get up. Then the barge was no longer tied up. It tilted alarmingly. He reached out, and caught the edge of the table to steady himself. There was a heavy sea running. And a curtain of mist floated in front of his eyes. Odd that the weather should change so quickly. At that moment he lost hold of the edge of the table, and before he could steady himself the whole barge had tilted back again, and deposited him on the bunk. Then the mist dropped down.

The owner of the *Journey's End* stood for a moment, peering, at this young man who had called to drink a cup of his coffee and had passed out on his spare bunk. Up and down the waterfronts, docksides, and canals of South London, people called him "Doctor." In twenty years it had grown to be a sort of courtesy title. Few people realised that he was, in fact, a qualified doctor, and a man of considerable, if curious, attainments.

He laid his hand on Petrella's forehead, which was damp and hot, felt his pulse, and listened for a moment to his breathing. Then he unlaced Petrella's shoes and took them off, removed his coat and waistcoat, collar and tie, pulled a pillow from his own bunk and put it under the young man's head, and covered him with a couple of rugs.

Minutes, or hours, later Petrella opened his eyes and tried to sit up. The old man jumped up out of his chair and came across.

"See if you can drink this," he said. It was a tumbler of water, into which he dropped a couple of white tablets. "I didn't try to push 'em down your throat when you were out. I've seen people choke that way."

"What is it? What's up?" said Petrella. "Did I pass out?"

"My guess is you've got flu, and a high temperature," said the old man. "Did you say you were starting a holiday?"

"That's right," said Petrella. "Ten days' holiday." He drank up the glass, and went to sleep again. It was a hot, black-and-red sleep, a sleep of aching bones and bad dreams, in which he was endlessly cross-examined by a crocodile in a stuff gown who alternately snapped its yellow teeth and wept over him.

When he finally opened his eyes and started on the slow and difficult job of working out where he was, the first thing he noticed was that they really were afloat. No wild and illusory lurching this time, but a gentle, pleasant pitching of the great, iron coffin in which he lay. He sat up in the bunk too quickly. And lay back again while the world stopped spinning.

Then he propped himself up more cautiously on his elbow and looked round. On the fixed table, in reach of his arm, was a tumbler of water. He picked it up, drained it, was conscious of a bitter, not unpleasant taste, and fell asleep again almost before his head was on the pillow . . .

When he woke next it was night. The cabin was lit by the warm and cosy glow of a paraffin lamp. As he stirred, the doctor got up from behind the table and came over to him.

Petrella found that his head was quite clear. "I'm afraid," he said, "I've been a bit of a nuisance."

"Far from it. I've never had a more docile patient."

"How long have I been here?"

The doctor counted on his fingers. "Two days," he said. "And a little over ten hours."

"Good God." It is always startling when a tiny segment of life goes by default.

"You said you were starting a holiday. I saw no reason why you shouldn't have it on my barge, under the care of a medical practitioner. Qualified, if a bit rusty."

"It's very kind of you," said Petrella. "I was going to stay with my mother's cousin. He'll be having a fit."

"We'll send him a telegram first thing tomorrow morning."

"Where are we? And how did we get here?"

"If you ask too many questions," said the doctor, "you'll put your temperature up again. We're in a stretch of water called the Long Neck, just below Walton. We came here via Greenland Dock, Russia Dock, Lavender Pond, and the open river. Now go to sleep."

When Petrella woke next morning, he felt ravenously hungry and knew that he was well again. After breakfast the doctor went ashore to dispatch a telegram to Colonel Montefiore, at Blagdens Wake, Nettlebed. He wrote it out and handed it, with some misgiving, over the counter of a tiny village shop which called itself a sub-post office. His misgivings were entirely justified, for it never reached its destination, though a Colonel Mountferry of Nettlebed House, Bannockburn, did receive, some weeks later, a telegram which said:

Taken ill suddenly. Will write. Patrick.

The six days that followed were, without any exception, the best that Petrella could remember.

He was steady on his feet by the evening of the first day, and strong enough next morning to help the doctor about the simple manoeuvres of his craft.

He learnt to operate lock gates with a handle like a huge grandfather clock key which lived in the barge's engine room, to steer for long, slow miles through a forgotten waterway, where they might not see a house for hours at a stretch, and their only visitors would be the bullocks who would gallop to the hedges when they heard the *Journey's End* coming, and stand, breathing hard and rolling their frightened, curious eyes until her iron bulk vanished round a bend or under one of the low, stone bridges which had so little headroom that it seemed impossible she should squeeze through them at all.

He learnt to tend the wants of the diesel engine which drove them forward, to trim and fill the paraffin lamps, and to peel potatoes. But it was the evenings he enjoyed most. When the barge was safely tied up, and the lamps were lit; when supper had been eaten and washed up and stacked away, and they settled down to talk before going to bed.

He heard from the doctor something of his curious life. "I was fifty," said the old man. "It was actually my fiftieth birthday, when I stopped being a doctor and became a bargemaster. I'd made quite a lot of money. Those were days when your patients came to you because they liked and trusted you, not because the Government told them to, and a man who was successful in his line could make a reasonable amount of money. I was unmarried, and I calculated that I had enough banked away to keep a man of my frugal habits in comfort for the best part of a century.

"That day I was called to the house of a man I knew well. He was a businessman. Not a tycoon, you understand, just a pleasant person who worked and worried from morning to night to support an expensive wife and three gold-plated children.

"When I reached the house he was dead. Thrombosis. A less fashionable complaint then than it is now. I shut my surgery that very day, sold my practice, and bought the *Journey's End*.

"It's the only decision in my life I've never regretted. I make enough by doing odd jobs to cover running expenses. Sometimes I hear from my stockbroker that my investments have gone up again. I never touch them. When I die they'll go to my old medical school."

It wasn't until the evening of the fourth day that Petrella thought to inquire where they were going. He discovered that their destination was some miles short of Basingstoke, where they were delivering a grand piano, and some harvesting machinery, and picking up two ponies.

It was on the way back that Petrella told the doctor the whole story of the Borners and Roper from beginning to end, and the old man listened in absorbed and judicious silence. He interrupted only once to say, "I knew Copper. He helped me with the barge. He was a nice boy, but too easily led." And at the end of it all he said, "You sound bitter about it. Why?"

"I did feel bitter about it," said Petrella. "I'm all right now. It was just that in the police we do a lot of work, and take a few risks and a few knocks in the interests of law and order, and one would think the law would be on our side."

"The law's on no one's side," said the doctor. "Once it's on anyone's side, it stops being law at all and becomes something cooked up by the politicians."

"Yes, but—" said Petrella.

"If you had the law behind you in the sense that it supported you whatever you did, right or wrong, you'd degenerate into a state security force. Like the Gestapo."

Petrella said mutinously, "I bet when the Gestapo caught half a dozen dangerous thugs the magistrate didn't let them out on bail."

Unknown to Petrella, while the *Journey's End* was nosing her calm path among the water lilies of the Basingstoke and Southwestern Canal, in South Borough events were on the move.

On the morning following Petrella's departure, Mr. Wetherall called on Superintendent Benjamin.

"Patrick and I are great friends," he said. "And I knocked on his door this morning to see if he'd gone. To tell you the truth, I wouldn't have been surprised to find him laid up. He hasn't been looking at all well lately. His room was empty, but there was a suitcase, which he'd obviously been meaning to take with him, on the floor, half packed."

Benjamin had troubles of his own. He said, "He may have been short of time. Suppose it was a question of coming back for his bag or catching the train? Or something like that."

"It doesn't sound like him," said Wetherall. "The breakfast things weren't washed up, either."

"If you're really worried," said Benjamin, "I could get in touch with the people he's meant to be staying with. He left a telephone number."

"If it wouldn't be too much trouble," said Mr. Wetherall.

However, no one was put to any trouble. For at that moment, Colonel Montefiore came through himself.

"Mistake?" he said. "Of course there's no mistake. Patrick told us exactly which train he would catch. I assumed, when he failed to arrive, that he must be ill in bed at home. I think someone should go and see."

Benjamin said he would do what he could, and turned a now worried face to Mr. Wetherall. "There's quite a few things might have happened," he said. "His holiday's his own affair. He could have changed his mind about where he was going. I'll have inquiries made, but we don't want to start a fuss about nothing. Things are rather upset round here as it is."

Mr. Wetherall swears that he said nothing. On the contrary, he asserts that it was one of his own boys that told him the news.

"You know that Inspector," said Martin, who was head of the school that year, and a privileged character. "The young one – Petrella. I heard the Borners done him. They coshed him the night before last. And dropped his body in the canal."

"Where on earth did you hear that?"

"Everyone knows it," said Martin. "What we reckon is, they'll be after Mike and Terry and the others next. Bound to be. After all, they're witnesses, too, aren't they? Some of the boys are forming a vigilant committee – a sort of escort – to protect them till the trial comes on. A good idea, I think, don't you, sir?"

"Good heavens," said Mr. Wetherall. "It's a terrible idea." He cast his mind over the names of the boys concerned. Of the six who had come forward, the leaders had been Mike O'Connor and Terry Shane, both Irish boys, and both members of the large Irish colony which centred on Stafford Street, Latimer Street, and Cutaway Lane.

He remembered hearing that there had been bad blood, even before the Roper killing, between the Borners and the Irish. Something that someone had said in a pub, which had ended in broken glass and blood, and had been stored in the retentive Irish memory. If the Borners and their supporters got it into their heads that O'Connor and Shane were giving evidence out of spite – and if the school got involved – he pictured a battlefield strewn with South Borough Secondary School corpses, and hurried round once again to the police station.

He found that the news had run ahead of him.

"I can't get anything reliable," growled Benjamin. "There's talk of him being seen in Childers Road, and I'm having the bank of the canal there searched. As a precaution, you understand."

"But it's four days now," said Mr. Wetherall. "And he's not what you'd call an inconsiderate young man. Even if he'd gone off—" Then he saw that Benjamin was as worried as he was.

That afternoon a police constable picked up a paper bag, with six handkerchiefs in it, on the wharf at the end of Childers Road. The handkerchiefs were new, and there was an invoice with them, and the invoice had a number on it which indicated the assistant at Spinks' who had made the sale. She remembered Petrella and described him with an accuracy which suggested she had looked at him more than once. "Dark black hair, young-looking, a brown face, very deep blue eyes." She also remembered the raincoat he was wearing; and the fact that he had looked a bit under the weather.

Benjamin gave orders for a search of that section of the Surrey Canal. And sent an urgent message to Chief Superintendent Thorn at District. Dragging operations were carried on by arc lamp all that night; and the next morning a team of frogmen was called in.

More than a hundred South Borough boys were late for school that morning, having stopped to watch the operation, and in the first break O'Connor addressed a mass meeting of his school fellows. He was a thick, stocky, snub-nosed boy with sun-bleached hair, and like all Southern Irishmen he had a grasp of the essentials of mob oratory.

Mr. Wetherall read the portents, and telephoned Superintendent Benjamin, who was even then in conference with his superiors.

"There'll likely be trouble," said Dory, a slow spoken man, who was in charge of the whole of the Division, both uniformed and detective branches. "We'll need a few extra men to carry out a proper search for Petrella. I think I'll ask for them now, just in case."

"It's the boys," said Benjamin. "They've got it into their heads that the Borners have knocked off Petrella to stop him giving evidence. It's a short step from that to the idea that they're planning to knock off the other witnesses too."

"And you don't believe it?" said Thorn.

"No, I don't," said Benjamin. "It's out of character. I'm afraid something may have happened to Petrella. He was looking pretty rotten. Suppose he passed out and slipped into the canal. Or he may just have lost his memory. But I don't believe anyone, even that gang, would be silly enough to knock off a witness, in cold blood. And remember, to make sense of it they've got to get rid of seven or eight boys as well."

He wondered, afterwards, if he had been arguing to convince himself.

It was on the following evening, the sixth after Petrella's disappearance, that the fight occurred in Basset Street. No one quite knew how it started. The fact that it was half past nine suggested that Copper Dixon and Curly had been drinking, but the provocation seemed to have come from a group of schoolboys who had no business to be out at that hour. It ended in Copper losing two teeth from a thrown milk bottle and Terry Shane breaking his wrist in the scuffle that followed. A car load of policemen cleared the streets.

Terry Shane's father was not the person to allow an assault on his son to go unanswered. Micky Shane had had a distinguished career in the all-in wrestling ring, where his speciality had been bouncing his opponents on their heads. He was now growing fat, and a little out of training, but he commanded a considerable following in the Stafford Street area, and on the following evening a party consisting of eight or ten Irishmen paid a visit to the Six Bells, in Carver Street, which was known to be a stronghold of the Borners. Copper, who was the only one of the gang present, got out by a back door, and the Irishmen spent a pleasant ten minutes wrecking the saloon bar.

It is just possible that, left to themselves, the two factions might have felt honour was now satisfied, and called it a day.

The Borners and their mob of followers were beginning to show signs of nervousness. As long as the mob was in being, a powerful and flourishing entity, people had touched their hats to it out of fear of reprisals. Under the stress of circumstances, it was beginning to fall apart.

Had the boys of South Borough Secondary School been prepared to let the matter drop, it might have simmered down. But they were not. On the contrary. Like harbingers of strife, the black-and-red caps blew before the storm, and where they went, fresh trouble was born.

The ninth evening after Petrella's disappearance was warm, even for September. Quiet, overcast, and still. Sammy Borner thought that he would pass the time with a game of snooker with the boys at Charley's. He left his car in the back street outside the entrance to the club, which was in a basement, and approached by a flight of iron steps. When he came out an hour later he found that all his tyres were flat. Not just one, but all four. He also observed five or six boys, one of them a chunky youth with light hair, standing on the pavement, their hands in their pockets, looking at nothing in particular.

"You do this?" he inquired.

"That's right," said the chunky boy, and added, "bloody murderer."

Sammy hesitated for a moment, but the arrival of his friends, Harry, Curly, Copper, and Nick, who were leaving the club at the same time, gave him a feeling of solidarity.

The opposition, after all, was only five schoolboys. They had earned a lesson. Sammy ducked into the back of the car, picked up a jack handle, and moved forward. The chunky boy whistled shrilly, and the next moment the street was full of boys and men.

The riot call reached Dory at Borough High Street Police Station, where he was in conference with Benjamin.

"The Irish have got Sammy Borner and his friends holed up in a snooker cellar in Parton Street," he said. "There's been a bit of bloodshed. If they get their hands on them, in their present temper, they'll finish them."

"And that," said Benjamin, "would break my heart."

Dory was already giving his orders.

Two squad cars and a tender reached the corner of Parton Street together. The air was full of the noise of battle and breaking glass.

"Sounds quite a party," said Dory. He marshalled his forces. "Ben, you stay here with four men, and keep them away from the cars." And when Benjamin protested, "In a mess-up like this, a uniform's worth more than a good character." He arranged the eight men he had chosen into careful formation. "Front two link arms with me," he said. "Use your feet if you have to. And keep together."

They went round the corner like a human tank. It took them sixty highly-coloured seconds to reach the billiard saloon, to push aside the table which was up-ended against the door, and to replace it behind them.

They found four badly frightened men, and a fifth lying on his face in a pool of blood.

"We're in," said Dory. "But that's not to say we'll get out again. They'll be expecting us this time. Wainwright, go and see if you can find a back door or a window or something. Who's this?"

"It's Curly," said Sammy Borner. He looked as if he had been crying. "They've killed him. You've got to do something"

"We're none of us dead yet," said Dory.

There was a splintering crash from the street. The crowd had tipped Sammy's car up on to one side and over into the mouth of the area. The smell of spilt petrol filled the air.

"There is a window, sir," said Wainwright. "But it opens into a sort of little closed yard."

"I don't care if it opens into the back of beyond," said Dory. "So long as it leads somewhere. Hughes and Gavigan, carry this man. And don't drop him. We want him in one piece. Now let's get going."

The window was barely large enough. As they manhandled Curly through, there came from the room they had left a muffled explosion followed by the white glare of detonated petrol.

Dory reformed his force in the courtyard. "Soon as we get round the corner," he said, "we'll be in sight. Make straight for the cars, and don't stop for anything."

Once again the power of united effort, and the drive of a man who knew his own mind, prevailed against disorganised numbers. They tumbled into the cars.

"Make for Gabriel Street," said Dory. "It'll give them farther to go if they come after us."

"They're coming all right," said Benjamin. "So's the Fire Brigade." As they rounded the corner, they heard the bells of the first fire engine.

The *Journey's End* tied up at the Camberwell basin and Petrella climbed ashore. The sky was coal black and threatening.

"Lucky you've got a mackintosh," said the doctor. "Rain soon, and plenty of it, if I'm any judge."

"I don't know how to thank you," said Petrella. "It's been the finest holiday I've ever had."

"Nothing to thank me for," said the doctor. "I've enjoyed having you along. Come again soon."

Petrella said he would; but he knew, even then, that no other trip would be quite like that first one.

He climbed the steps from the dockside up to the level of the Camberwell Road. His first idea was to take a bus home. When he saw the glow in the sky to the northwest, and heard the sound of the fire bells, he changed his mind. He thought he would make first for Gabriel Street, to pick up the news. It was less than ten minutes' quick walk.

He had covered half the distance when, with spectacular suddenness, the heavens were opened and the rain came down. Petrella buttoned up the neck of his mackintosh, and broke into a jog trot . . .

Benjamin and Dory were standing in the first-storey window of Gabriel Street, looking out at the crowd which filled the short approach road. The crowd was mostly men, with a scattering of boys.

It was not doing anything in particular.

"I hope they don't try to get in," said Dory. "That'd mean calling for reinforcements. We've handled them ourselves so far. I'd like to keep it that way."

"They don't know what they want," said Benjamin. "It wouldn't take very much to move them in either direction."

"Thank God it's raining. That'll wash the whisky out of them. What the hell are you laughing at?"

Superintendent Benjamin did not often laugh. Now his long face was wrinkled into folds of genuine merriment.

"I was thinking," he said, "that the Borners have—what's the legal word?—surrendered to their bail."

"They've surrendered to their bail, all right," said Dory. He thought of them as he had left them ten minutes before: Curly still unconscious, being worked on by the police doctor; the other four, white-faced, jumpy even when the cell doors had shut on them.

"Do you think we ought to tell Whitcomb?"

Dory said something uncomplimentary about the Stipendiary Magistrate and went over again to look at the crowd.

"Count your blessings," said Benjamin. "If we can get through without any more broken heads, we'll come out the right side of the ledger. Think of the evidence those boys are going to give after tonight."

Dory said, "I fancy they're moving."

"Moving?" said Benjamin. "They're running away."

There was a disturbance at the mouth of the street. More than a disturbance, a turmoil.

The crowd, which had already started to thin out, was thrown back on itself, as a stream is thrown when it meets a more powerful current. Men moved back on either side, leaving a clear lane in the middle. And down the lane was advancing—

"Good God," said Benjamin. He leaned forward and jerked the window open.

It was hardly Petrella's fault that his long, black hair should have been flattened by the rain over his skull, or that his face, under the neon light, should have taken on a peculiar bluish-white tinge.

Benjamin took a grip of himself. He reminded himself of the unlikelihood – indeed, the impropriety – of the ghost of a Detective Inspector revisiting his old station; and he jumped for the stairs, ran down, and pushed through the crowd.

"Open the door," he said to the station sergeant.

"What about them outside?"

"I don't think we shall have much trouble with them now. Help me with these bolts."

Petrella advanced diffidently into a hushed room. "Good evening, sir," he said. "Good evening, Sergeant. What's up?" He gazed in blank astonishment at the dozen and more uniformed men sitting round on benches. "Why the reception committee?"

"You'd better come upstairs," said Benjamin. And to the Sergeant, "You can send 'em all home, except normal duty men."

Upstairs Petrella found Chief Superintendent Dory lighting a cigarette. He observed that he had a split ear and a black eye.

"Now that you are back," said Dory grimly, "perhaps you'll be good enough to explain what you've been up to."

But Petrella, for once, was unperturbed. He was triple-armed in his own unassailable rectitude.

"I don't know what's been going on around here," he said. "But it can't be anything to do with me. I've been on holiday."

Argosy, September 1959.

THE MAN WHO HATED BANKS

THE DRILL SCREAMED AS IT BIT into the tough metal. The operator, a small man with a sad monkey-face, hummed to himself as he worked. It was the last of eight holes which he was boring, four on either side of the hinge of the strongroom.

When he had finished the drilling, and had checked, with a thermometer, that the surrounding metal had returned to a safe temperature, he filled each of the holes with Polar Ammon gelatine dynamite, tamping the putty-like stuff delicately home with the blunt end of a silver pencil; then he used the sharp end to bore a hole in the middle deep enough to take the tube of the copper electric detonator with its plastic-covered lead of tinned iron.

When all the detonators were in, he collected the eight ends, bared them, twisted them together, and covered the joint with insulating tape. Then he collected a pile of old Army blankets and helped now by a second man, draped them from wires which had already been fixed across the door.

Both men retreated to the guard-door at the entrance of the strongroom lobby. Two of the bars had been cut out. They squeezed through the gaps, dragging the plastic-covered lead behind them.

In the farthest corner of the outer lobby stood an ordinary six-volt car battery. The first man separated the lead wires and twisted one of them round the negative terminal. Both men squatted down, backs against the wall, heads bent forward.

Then the second wire, carefully held in a rubber-gloved hand, was laid on the positive terminal. The shockwave of the explosion pinned them against the wall.

The third man, standing in the doorway of a shop outside, heard the crump of the explosion and swore softly to himself. The next ten minutes were going to be the most difficult.

A newsagent, sleeping four houses away on the opposite side of the street, sat up in bed, and said, "Cor, what was that? Have they declared war?"

His wife said "Wassup?"

"Sounded like a bomb."

"So what?" said his wife. "It hasn't hit us." She dragged him down into bed again.

Eight minutes. Nine minutes. Ten minutes. Eleven minutes. *What the hell are they playing at?* Twelve minutes.

The door of the shop opened and two men appeared. Both had heavy satchels slung over their shoulders. One carried the drill, another had the electric cutter which had been used to saw through the bars. The third man relieved them of drill and cutter and set off at a brisk pace up the street to where the car was parked. Not a word had been spoken from first to last.

Police Constable Owens, of the Gravesend Police, saw the car nosing into the street. He thought it odd that it should have no lights on, and held up a hand to stop it.

The car accelerated. Owens jumped, slipped, and fell into the gutter. He picked himself up in time to see the car corner and disappear.

Police Constable Owens limped to the nearest Police Box.

A pigeon took off from Boadicea's helmet and went into a power dive. It was aimed at the head of a young man with a brown face and black hair, who had just crossed Westminster Bridge. Detective Inspector Patrick Petrella raised his arm. The pigeon executed a side-slip and volplaned off up into a tree. Petrella regarded the pigeon without malice. It was a beautiful day. It was spring. He was starting a new job.

The message which had reached him at Gabriel Street Police Station had not been explicit, but he guessed that his spell of duty in

South London was over. It had spanned three years; and he had enjoyed most of it, but three years in one place was enough.

He pushed his hat a little farther back on his head, and swung in under the Archway and up the three shallow steps into the main building of New Scotland Yard.

The private secretary, a serious young man in horn-rimmed glasses, inspected him as he came into the ante room, and then said, "The A.C.'s ready for you. Will you go in?" Petrella found himself straightening his shoulders as he marched by the inner door into the presence of Sir Wilfred Romer, Assistant Commissioner in charge of the Criminal Investigation Branch of the Metropolitan Police, and – in Petrella's humble opinion – the greatest thief-catcher since Wensley.

"Sit down," said Romer. "You know Superintendent Baldwin, I think."

Petrella nodded to Superintendent Baldwin, big, red-faced, conscientiously ferocious, known to everyone from the newest recruit upwards as Baldy.

Romer said, "I'm forming a new department. It'll be known as C12. And, broadly speaking"—here his face split in a wintry smile—"you're the department."

Petrella managed to smile back.

"You'll have two or three people to help you, but the smaller you keep it, the happier I'll be. First, because we haven't got many spare hands – secondly, because smallness means secrecy. Your first job will be the collection and analysis of information."

As Romer spoke, an alphabetical index of subjects, from Abortion to Zionism upon which this remarkable man might be seeking information, flipped across Petrella's aroused imagination.

"On bank robberies," concluded Romer.

"Yes, sir," said Petrella. "Bank robbery."

"Not bank robbery – in general. It's a particular series of bank robberies that's getting under our skin. Never mind the details now. You'll get those from Baldwin. What I wanted to tell you was this. There's one thing we're quite certain of: there's an organiser. I want him put away. That's your second job."

Back in his own office, Baldwin filled in a few details.

"The bumph's in these folders," he said. "It'll take you a day or two to wade through it all. It goes back about seven years. We didn't know that there was any link up, not at first. The actual jobs are done by different outfits. All pro stuff. Chick Selling and his crowd have been involved. And Walter Hudd. And the Band brothers. We're fairly certain it was them who did the Central Bank at Gravesend last month. You probably read about it."

Petrella nodded. He had heard enough about high-class safebreakers to know that they left their signatures on their job as surely as great artists in other walks of life. He said, "What makes you so certain there's a linkup?"

"Three things." Baldwin ticked them off on the fingers of his big red hand. "First, they're getting absolutely accurate information. They've never taken a bank that wasn't stuffed with notes. And that isn't as common as you might think. You could open a lot of strongrooms and find nothing in them but Georgian silver and deed boxes. Second, the technique's the same. They always work from another building. Sometimes next door. Sometimes as much as three or four houses away . . . that means slicing through a lot of brickwork. They've got proper tools for that too, and they use them properly. Someone's taught 'em. And last, but not least, someone's supplying them with equipment. It's good stuff. So good, it can't even be bought in this country for a legitimate job. When Walter Hudd's boys cracked the Sheffield District Bank they had to cut and run, and they left behind a high-speed film-cooled steel cutter that the London Salvage Corps have been asking for ever since they heard about it. It comes from Germany."

Later, installed in a small room on the top storey of the Annexe into which four desks had somehow been inserted, Petrella repeated much of this to his two aides; the first was Detective Sergeant Edwards, a solemn young man with the appearance and diction of a chartered accountant, who was reputed to be extremely efficient in the organisation of paper work. The second – as Petrella was delighted to note – was none other than his old protégé, Detective Wilmot.

"Who's the fourth?" said Petrella.

"We're getting a female clerical assistant," said Wilmot. "I asked at the pool who it was going to be but no one seemed to know. I don't mind betting though, as we're the youngest department, we shall get the oldest and ugliest secretary. Someone like Mrs. Proctor, who's got buck teeth and something her best friends have got tired telling her about. What do we do next?"

Petrella said, "No one really knows. We shall have to make most of it up as we go along. We've got to have the best possible liaison with the C.R.O. and the Information Room here both on the old jobs, and any new jobs that come along. Then we'll have to circularise all provincial Police Forces, asking for information on suspicious circumstances . . ."

"Such as?" asked Edwards.

"First thing, we might see if we can get the banks to improve the reward system. At present, you only collect the cash if your information leads to someone being arrested. That's not good enough. What happens at the moment is, someone hears a bang in the night . . . Might be something, might not. They go back to sleep again. If there was a reward – it needn't be a big one – say, a hundred pounds for the first man getting on the blower to the police station, we might get some action.

"Next, we'll have to circularise local forces: for information about thefts of explosives; losses of strongroom keys; unexplained caches of notes; suspicious behaviour near banks; bank employees with expensive tastes—"

"Bank managers with expensive mistresses—"

"That'll be enough from you, Wilmot. Do you think you can draft us a circular?"

"Can do," said Edwards.

"The three of us will have to be on the priority warning list through the Information Room here, and the police station nearest our home. We may be called out any hour of the day or night."

"I'll have to warn all my girl friends," said Wilmot.

That afternoon Petrella was sitting alone at his desk staring at the tips of his shoes, when the door opened, a girl looked in, and said, "Are you C12?"

"That's right," said Petrella.

"You certainly took some finding. Nobody seemed to have heard of you."

"We're a very important department. But very hush-hush."

"They haven't given you much of a room. My name's Orfrey, by the way."

"I can't help feeling," said Petrella, "that, as we shall be working together for an indefinite period in a space measuring not more than twelve feet by ten, I shall find myself addressing you, sooner or later, by your Christian name."

Miss Orfrey smiled. Petrella noticed that when she smiled, she smiled with the whole of her face, crinkling up her eyes, parting her lips, and showing small, even white teeth.

"The name's Jane," she said . . .

About a week later, Jane Orfrey said to Wilmot, "Is he always as serious at this?"

"He's got a lot on his mind," said Wilmot. "He might smile sometimes."

"It's make or break, really," said Wilmot. "If we sort out this lot, he gets the credit. If we don't, he gets a great big black mark." "It doesn't seem to be worrying you."

"Paper work doesn't mean a lot to me. I'm what you might call a man of action. What about coming to the pictures tonight?"

"Thank you," said Jane. "I'm going to take some of this paper home."

"It's a serious matter, sir" said Sergeant Edwards.

"What is?" said Petrella, coming up from the depths of his thoughts on the technical construction of strongroom doors.

"Our allowances."

"What about our allowances?"

"Now that we're working at Scotland Yard and on a special job, we ought to get a Special Service increment and a Central London increment.

But the regulations say that where you're entitled to both, you can have the whole of whichever allowance you select, and fifty per cent of the other one. I've been working it out—"

"And I thought you were doing something useful," said Petrella.

Sergeant Edwards looked aggrieved . . .

Two o'clock on a Monday morning, twelve inches away from Petrella's ear, the telephone screamed. He jerked upright, hit his head against the end of the bed, swore, and snatched the receiver off the instrument.

"Job at Slough," said a courteous and offensively wide awake voice. "They've pulled in the men involved: Ronald, Kenneth, and Leslie Band. There'll be a car round for you in three minutes."

Petrella was still trying to fix his front stud when he heard the car draw up.

He finished his dressing sitting beside the driver as they sped along the empty roads towards Slough. The driver didn't seem to be pressing, but Petrella noticed the speedometer needle steady on the seventy mark. At that moment a motorcycle passed them, and he just had time to recognise Wilmot.

Inspector Lansell, of the Buckinghamshire C.I.D., was waiting for them in his office.

"It was the North Midland Bank," he said. "They cut their way through from the cellar of an empty shop next door. Must have started some time on Saturday afternoon. Took all Saturday night and Sunday over the job. Blew the main strongroom door at half past one this morning. A chap living across the street heard it, and telephoned us. We happened to have a patrol car a few streets away, so we got them as they came out."

"Good work," said Petrella. "I'll have a word with them now, if I may."

"They're all yours," said Lansell courteously.

The Band brothers were small, quiet, brown-faced men, all with good records of regular service in the Royal Engineers.

By six o'clock, Petrella had got what he could out of them. It wasn't a lot. They had all been in the hands of the police before. The routine questions had been answered, blocked, or evaded.

Petrella had hardly expected more, and was not depressed. He was particularly interested in two pieces of their equipment: a high-speed, electric drill with an adjustable tungsten-tipped angle bit which had been used to drill a series of holes down either side of the hinge of the strongroom door; and an oxyacetylene, white flame cutter, coupled with a small pumping device which stepped up the pressure and temperature of the flame.

Both were in ex-works condition. The cutter had initials and a number stamped on the base. It looked like shipyard equipment. There was a department in the Board of Trade which would probably be able to identify it for him.

If it had been imported under licence, it could be traced back to its maker.

He had another reason for feeling pleased. The banks, some of which had jibbed at his automatic alarm-reward system, would probably support it now that it had shown results.

He said to Inspector Lansell, "Any idea where my sergeant is?"

"Haven't seen him," said Lansell. "I'll ask."

But no one in the station had seen him. Petrella travelled back to London on a train crowded with coughing and sneezing commuters. He remembered the ice patches on the road and a nagging feeling of uneasiness travelled with him.

In the course of that morning he rang Information three times. No accidents to police officers had been reported.

At two o'clock Wilmot arrived, unshaven but quite unrepentant.

"I've got a feeling," he said – before Petrella could open his mouth – "that maybe we're on to something. It was a turn up for the book. I stopped just short of the High Street to ask the way to the station, and I saw these two in an all-night cafay over the way having a cuppa; and I said, Oi, oi, what are *they* doing?"

"Take a deep breath," said Petrella, "and start again. You saw *who*?"

"Morris Franks and his brother Sammy."

"That pair," said Petrella, with distaste. "What do you imagine they were doing in Slough at three o'clock in the morning?"

"Just exactly what I said to myself. I said, Here's the Band Brothers robbing a bank – and here's two of the nastiest bits of work that ever come out of Whitechapel sitting in a cafay, two streets away from the scene of the crime, drinking tea. This'll stand looking into. So I parked my bike – I reckoned you could get on for a bit without me—"

"Thank you."

"—and I hung around . . . for hours and hours. They must've got through twelve cups of tea, each. Just before seven o'clock they come out, and took a train back to Paddington. I went with 'em. At Paddington they got on the Metropolitan, got off it at King's Cross, and walked towards the Angel. There were quite a few people about by that time. I don't think they cottoned on to me."

Petrella was prepared to believe that. Wilmot's urchin figure would have melted as effectively into the background of King's Cross and the Angel as any animal into its native jungle.

"They fetched up at a big builder's yard in Arblay Street. Jerrold Light & Co. They walked straight in."

"Do you think they work there?"

"It looked like it. But that wasn't all. I hung round for a bit. Half a dozen others went in. I recognised one of them. It was Stoker. Remember him?"

"Albert Stoker," said Petrella. "Yes. Certainly I remember him. He tried to kick my teeth in when I was up at Highside. He was working with Boot Howton and the Camden Town boys."

"If they're all like that," said Wilmot, "they're First Division stuff."

"Mr. Jerry Light would bear looking into," said Petrella.

That afternoon he paid a visit to Arblay Street. Jerry Light's establishment occupied most of the north side. It was the sort of place that only London could have produced. What was originally an open space between two buildings had been filled, in the passage of time, with a clutter of smaller buildings, miscellaneous huts, sheds, and lean-tos, on top of, or propped up against, each other. Such space as remained was stacked, head high, with bricks, tiles, window frames, chimney pots, kitchen sinks, lavatory bowls, doors, pipes, and cisterns. An outside flight of steps lifted itself above the cluster to a door at first-storey level which was labelled, MR. J. LIGHT.

As he watched, this door opened and a man came out. He was a very large man, with a cropped head, a red face, and a closely clipped moustache. A thick neck rose from magnificent shoulders and chest. It was a sergeant major's figure; the sort of figure on which time and inertia would play tricks, reversing the chest and the stomach as inevitably as sand runs through an hour glass.

But it had not done so yet. Mr. Jerry Light was, he judged, not more than forty five and his eyes were still sharp, as he stood surveying his kingdom.

Petrella walked quietly away.

Back at Scotland Yard he said to Edwards, "See if Records has got anything on a Mr. Jerry Light. He runs a builder's yard at Islington, and you can find his full name and details through the Business Names Registry. Wilmot, I think it'd be a good idea if you went along and asked for a job."

"Suppose Stoker recognises me? I had a bit of trouble with him myself at Highside, remember?"

"I'm counting on Stoker recognising you," said Petrella. "Then if you're still given the job, it'll prove that Light's honest. If you don't get it, the chances are the outfit's bent."

"Suppose they drop a chimney on me!"

"Then we shall *know* they're dishonest," said Petrella. He had little fear for Wilmot's safety. Wilmot was extremely well equipped to look after himself . . .

Edwards was the first to report.

He said, "Jerrold Abraham Light. He *has* got a record."

"Bank robbery?"

Edwards smiled, and said, "Not robbing a bank. Assaulting a bank manager. In 1951, he was sentenced to twelve months at the Exeter autumn assizes for waylaying and assaulting the manager of the Exeter branch of the District Bank."

"Robbery?"

"Not robbing, sir. Assaulting. They knocked two of his teeth out, kicked in his ribs, and broke an arm."

"They?"

"There was another man with him. Alwyn Corder. He got twelve months too."

"Why did they do it?"

"No motive was suggested at all. Mr. Justice Arbuthnot in his summing-up called it, 'a particularly cowardly and senseless assault.'"

Petrella's mind wasn't on Mr. Justice Arbuthnot. He had experienced a very faint almost undetectable tremor of excitement; like a patient angler near whose bait a fish had swum, not seizing it but troubling it by his passage.

"Alwyn Corder," he said. "It's not a common name. I could bear to know what he's doing today."

"If he's had any other convictions, he should be easy to trace," said Edwards. "Incidentally, Light hasn't. That's the only time he's ever stepped out of line."

"It's the only time he's ever been caught," said Petrella.

It was seven o'clock that evening before Wilmot returned. C12 kept irregular hours. Sergeant Edwards was filing some papers. Jane Orfrey was filing her nails. Petrella was watching Jane Orfrey.

"Hired and fired," said Wilmot.

"What happened?"

"To start with, it all went like love's old sweet song. Mr. Light said I was just the sort of young man he was looking for; clean, healthy and not afraid of work. He explained how he ran his outfit too. He works for big building contractors; say one of them's doing a site clearance job at Southend, and wants extra help: Light sends a gang down. Half a dozen men – a dozen – however many he wants. Light takes a ten per cent cut out of their wages. They reckon it's worthwhile, because he keeps 'em in regular work."

"What went wrong?"

"What went wrong was, just as I was about to sign on, in comes

Stoker."

"What happened?"

"It was a bit of an awkward moment, actually. Stoker went bright pink, and said he'd like a word outside with Mr. Light. So they stepped outside, and shut the door, and I heard 'em yaw-yaw-yawing. Then Mr. Light came back and said, very polite, that he hadn't got a vacancy right now, but he'd let me know if he had one. So I scampered – keeping my chin on my shoulder, just in case anyone tried to start anything."

"Lucky they didn't."

"I'll say it was lucky," said Wilmot. "Because if they had started anything, they might have spoilt this."

He took his handkerchief out of his side pocket, and unwrapped it carefully. Inside was a lump of cobblers' wax. Impressed in the wax was the outline of a key.

"The key was on the inside of the door," said Wilmot. "I got it out while they were talking. Nice impression, isn't it? I know a little man who'll knock it up for us while we wait."

Petrella said, "Are you suggesting we break into this office?"

"That's right. We could get over the side wall. Borrow a ladder. Plenty of them about."

"You realise that we should be breaking practically every rule in the Metropolitan Police Code?"

"That's right."

"And if we're caught, we shall both be sacked."

"That's why I'm not planning to get caught, personally," said Wilmot.

It was half an hour after midnight when they backed the little van into the passageway behind Light's yard. A veil of drizzling rain had cut down visibility to a few yards.

"Perfect night for crime," said Wilmot. "You hold the ladder. I'll go first. I think I saw some broken bottle on the top of this wall."

Petrella gave him a minute's start, and then followed. Negotiated with care, the ragged cheveux-de-frise presented little obstacle. Petrella let himself down on the other side, and Wilmot's hand grabbed his foot and steered it on to an up-ended cistern.

Five minutes later they were in Jerry Light's office, carefully fastening the blanket, which Wilmot had brought with him, over the only window.

Petrella turned on his lantern torch and put it on the floor.

"Better get cracking," he said. "It looks like a lot of work."

One cupboard contained box files full of bills, invoices, and trade correspondence. Another was devoted to builder's catalogues, price lists, and samples mixed with old telephone and street directories, technical publications, and an astonishing collection of paperbacked novels, mostly pornographic. The desk was full of mixed correspondence and bills. The old-fashioned safe in the corner was locked.

Three hours' hard work convinced Petrella that Mr. Light had a perfectly genuine builder's business.

"There's only one thing here I don't quite understand," he said. "Why should he bother to keep a seven-year-old diary in the top left-hand corner of his desk? Anything you kept close at hand, like that, you'd expect it to be important, wouldn't you?"

"Probably forgot to throw it away."

"But why keep a seven-year-old one, and throw away the other six?" Wilmot came across to have a look.

"There's something else odd about it, too," said Petrella. "Do you see?"

Wilmot shone his torch on to the open book and studied it carefully.

"Doesn't seem to mean a lot," he said. "There's something written on each page. Sort of shorthand. Perhaps it's business appointments."

"That's what I thought at first. But would he have business appointments on Saturday and Sunday too?"

"Doesn't seem likely," agreed Wilmot. "What are you going to do?"

"We can't take it away. If it's important, he's bound to miss it. We'll have to photograph it." He produced from his coat pocket a small black box. "We'll prop it up on the desk. Shine your torch on it, and turn each page when I say."

It took them an hour to finish the job, replace the book, and tidy up.

"If there's anything important," said Petrella, "it's in the safe. I'm afraid that's beyond me."

"You never know," said Wilmot. "I found this key on top of that cupboard. It's just the sort of daft place people do hide their safe keys. See if it fits."

Petrella took the key, inserted it in the lock, and exerted pressure. There was a tiny sensation of prickling in his fingers, and the key turned.

"Nice work," said Wilmot. "Let's see what he keeps in the old strongbox. Hullo! Something wrong?"

Petrella had relocked the safe. Now he walked across and replaced the key on top of the cupboard. He did this without haste, but without loss of time.

"We're getting out of here," he said. "And damned quick. That safe's wired to an alarm. I set it off when I turned the key."

He picked up the torch from the floor, and made a careful tour of the room. There wasn't a great deal to do. But it took time.

"All right," Petrella said at last. "When I turn out the torch, get the blanket down."

"Nick of time," said Wilmot.

They could both hear the car coming . . .

As they locked the office door behind them and went down the steps into the yard, headlights swivelled round the corner throwing the main gate into relief. Brakes screamed; a car door slammed; a voice started giving orders.

Wilmot lay across the wall, leant down and pulled Petrella up beside him. There was no time for finesse. Petrella heard the cloth of his trousers rip on the broken glass as he swung his legs across, felt a stinging pain in his thigh, and the warm rush of blood down his leg. Then he was following Wilmot down the ladder. As he reached the ground, Wilmot's hand grabbed his arm.

Footsteps were echoing along the pavement.

Wilmot put his mouth close to Petrella's ear. "They've sent someone round the back," he said. "I'll have to fix him."

Petrella nodded. He felt the blood running into his shoe.

Wilmot crouched, pressed against the wall. The dim form of a man appeared at the mouth of the passage and came on, unsuspecting.

Wilmot straightened up, and hit him, once, from below, at the exact point where trousers and shirt joined. The man said something which sounded like, "Aaargh," and folded forward on to his knees. As Wilmot and Petrella picked their way past him, he still seemed to be fighting for breath.

"What are these?" said Jane Orfrey.

"They're ten magnification enlargements of microfilm shots of the pages in a seven-year-old desk diary."

"But what do they mean?"

"If I knew that," said Petrella, "I'd know whether I risked my whole professional career last night for something or for nothing. I want you to go through every entry. I expect it's a code. The home-made sort, that's so damned difficult to decipher – where U.J. can mean Uncle Jimmy, Ursula Jeans, *and the* Union Jack. You'll need a lot of patience with it."

Jane said, "We got something useful this morning. Do you remember Mallindales? The hire-purchase house. It was in answer to one of our circulars about marked and series notes."

There were two things, thought Petrella, about Jane Orfrey. The first was that she said *we* quite naturally, identifying herself as a member of the outfit. The other was that she had carried out every job she had been given without once saying, I'm only here to type letters.

He wondered, not for the first time, how they had been lucky enough to get her.

"You're not listening to a word I'm saying."

"I'm sorry," said Petrella. "We've had a lot of answers in to that particular inquiry."

"Mallindales told us they had a special stamp which they used on all their notes. Remember? The point about it was that it didn't appear to mark the notes at all. But if you held one of them flat, and looked across it in an oblique light, you could see the letters M.D."

"I remember now," said Petrella. "They'd paid in a couple of hundred marked notes the day before the Maritime Bank at Liverpool was broken open. They thought we might locate some of them, because the thieves wouldn't realise they were marked."

"We have located one. It turned up yesterday, in the possession of a character called Looey Bell, a small time thief picked up by the Highside police for illicit collecting."

"And this was part of the money he'd collected?"

"That's right. The only person – he says – who gave him a note, was the local parson."

Petrella considered the matter. A clergyman who gave away pound notes to people who came to the door sounded an unusual sort of character. "He might be worth looking into."

"Wilmot's looking into him now."

"He's cracked," reported Wilmot, when he came back after tea. "He tried to give *me* a pound. He said I looked a very nice young man."

"Who is he?"

"The Reverend Mortleman, vicar of St. John at Patmos, Crouch End. When I'd convinced him that I was a police officer and not a good cause, he spun me a yarn about a party who gave him money to give to the deserving poor. Some old girl, with more money than sense, who knew Mortleman when he was an assistant clergyman at St. Barnabas, Pont Street, I gather. He wouldn't tell me her name."

"That sounds plausible," said Petrella. "A lot of rich people go to St. Barnabas. One of them might be sending him money for his local charities."

"I could probably find out who it was if I made a few inquiries."

Petrella considered the matter. He had to be careful not to disperse the efforts of his small force chasing red herrings. "Let it stop there for the moment," he said. "I'll get the local boys to watch out. If they find any more of these M.D. notes circulating in those parts, we'll think again."

The next M.D. note arrived from quite a different source. A waiter at the Homburg-Carleton, going home in the early hours of the morning, started by accusing a taxi driver of overcharging him, then assaulted him, and finished up in custody. The station sergeant, checking his belongings before he was put into a cell, found three pound notes in his wallet, all marked with the Mallindales stamp, and brought them round personally to New Scotland Yard.

Petrella said, "Three of them together! That looks more like it. Where did he say he got them from?"

"He said they were his share of that evening's tronc."

"Then they must have come from someone dining at the Homburg. Good work, Sergeant. We'll follow it up."

Jane Orfrey spent the afternoon with the restaurant manager, and came back with a list of three public dinners, five private dinners, and the names of the eighty-four people who had actually booked tables that night.

"It's impossible to identify their guests," she said. "And there were one or two people who came in without booking."

"It's not so bad," said Petrella. "Agreed, we can't do anything about the people who didn't book. But there weren't a lot of those. And why bother about the guests? Guests don't pay the bill. As for the big dinners, it's only the organisers of those who matter. A bit more work, and we can boil this down to quite a short list."

"Suppose we boil it down to twelve names," said the girl. "What do we do then? Go and ask them all if they know any bank robbers?"

Petrella looked at her curiously. "You need a break," he said. "You've been overworking."

Jane said, stiffly, "It's the most interesting job I've ever done. I don't want to fall down on it, that's all."

"When we heard we were going to get a secretary," said Petrella, "I remember Wilmot said"—at this point, he remembered what Wilmot *had* said, and improvised rapidly—"'As we're the youngest department, we're bound to get the worst secretary.' I think we had a bit of luck there. I think we got the best."

"It's nice of you to say so."

"It must have been a slip-up in the typing pool. They'd earmarked someone like Mrs. Proctor for us, and they pulled the wrong card out of the filing cabinet."

"I don't think the typing pool had much say in the matter," said Jane. "I was posted here direct by Uncle Wilfred."

"Uncle Wilfred?"

"The Assistant Commissioner. He's my mother's brother."

"Good heavens," said Petrella, thinking back quickly over some of Wilmot's strictures on the top brass. "You might have told us sooner."

"You're the only person I have told," said Jane.

Petrella, looking at his watch, was surprised to see that it was nearly half past seven. He was on the point of saying, "Let's go out and get something to eat," when it occurred to him that Jane might think he was asking her out because she was the Assistant Commissioner's niece.

He swallowed the words, and said an abrupt, "Good night."

After he had gone, Jane sat for a whole minute staring at the closed door.

Then she said out loud. "Silly cuckoo. You oughtn't to have told him. Now he's clammed up again."

When Petrella arrived at Scotland Yard on Monday morning, he could almost feel the thunder in the air. He went straight to Chief Superintendent Baldwin's office.

"You got my note?" said Baldwin.

"I didn't get any note," said Petrella, "but I heard the early morning news. It's not too good, is it?"

"It's damned bad," said Baldwin. "Two jobs on the same night. The Manchester one was the biggest haul yet. What was really unfortunate was that the bank knew they were vulnerable – it was one of the payoff days for the Town Centre Reconstruction – and they'd asked the police to keep a watch."

Petrella said, "Not so hot. How did they get in?"

"It was clever. One thing the police were on the lookout for was empty premises near the bank. There weren't any. Just a block of offices, all let. The people who pulled this job must have planned it six months ago. That was when they took this office, two away from the bank. They cut through the wall, crossed the intervening office after it closed on Saturday, cut through the second wall, broke into the bank itself, and opened the strongroom some time on Sunday night. No one heard them. It isn't a residential area."

"What now?"

"Now," said Baldwin grimly, "the local force, prodded by the banks, are asking us to help and when they say help, they mean something more than research and coordination."

"What had they got in mind?"

"Two or three mobile teams of special officers, working on the lines of the murder squad." Petrella felt cold.

"That'll be quite an organisation," he said. "I suppose we should be swallowed up in it."

Seeing his face, Baldwin laughed and said, "It may never happen. But it means we've got to get results, quick. How far have you got?"

It was a question Petrella found embarrassing to answer. It seemed pompous to say, "We're still analysing information. You can't expect results until the analysis is complete." So he said, "We've one definite line. It may lead somewhere." He explained about Jerry Light.

"Do you think he runs the whole show?"

"I don't think so, no. My guess is that he runs the heavy mob. This organisation has its own Flying Squad. When a job's being done, one or two of them will be on hand to get back the equipment, and collect the organiser's share of the loot."

"If that's so," said Baldwin, "there must be a link between Light and the head man."

"We're working on that angle," said Petrella. He thought it wiser not to say too much about the diary, or the circumstances in which it had come into their possession. "Another way would be to trace the equipment, from the factory. It'd mean going over to West Germany."

"That could be fixed," said Baldwin. "We'd need a few days to make the arrangements. You'd go yourself. Do you talk any German?"

"Enough to get on with, *Genug um durchzukommen*," said Petrella.

When he got back to his room, he was tackled by Sergeant Edwards, with a worried face.

"You'd hardly think," he said, "that a man with an uncommon

name like Alwyn Corder could disappear off the face of the earth, would you?"

So much had happened that it took Petrella a moment to think who Alwyn Corder was. Then he said, "You mean the other man who helped Light assault that bank manager at Exeter?"

"Yes. Corder was one of the Joint Managing Directors in a demolition firm. Light worked for the same firm."

"Managing Director? Are you sure?"

"Quite sure. It's all in the Company Office Records. The other director was a Douglas Marchant. Marchant & Corder started the firm just after the war. It went broke in 1952. I've searched every record we possess – not only the Directories, but Electors Registers, Motor Car Licence lists, Passport Office."

"Perhaps he's dead."

"The Register of Deaths at Somerset House was the first place I searched."

"Well," said Petrella. "Perhaps—" and got no further because Wilmot came in like an express train.

"Guess what?" he said. And gave them no time to guess. "A third note's turned up, *and we've got a cross reference.*"

Three heads went up, like three nestlings offered food.

"A jobbing printer in New Cross. Luckily he used the note for a subscription to the local police charity. When they saw the mark, they took it back to him, and he said it was part of a payment he'd had that morning for a job he'd done printing the souvenir menus for a charity dinner"—Wilmot paused with considerable artistry—"at the Homburg-Carleton."

"Good work," said Petrella softly. "Which charity?"

"It's a society which sends kids to the seaside."

Petrella turned up his list. "That's right," he said. "The S.S.H.U.C. They were having a show that night. Can't be a coincidence."

"Who was the organiser?" said Jane. "Mrs. Constantia Velden, O.B.E."

"I'm sure I know the name. Doesn't she do a lot of these things? She's almost a professional organiser."

"Out of my line."

"It's in mine," said Jane. "I did a London season." She departed.

There was a lot of checking and cross-checking to be done, and it was after six before she came back. Sergeant Edwards and Wilmot had gone home. Petrella saw, from the pink patches in her cheeks and the sparkle in her eye, that something had happened.

"I've located your woman organiser," she said. "She lives in a very nice house in St. Johns Wood, with a cook, a chauffeur and three dalmatians. Oozing with money and good works."

"What else?"

"How do you know there's something else?"

"Because you're almost bursting to tell me."

"I've a good mind not to," said Jane. "Well, all right. As a matter of fact, it didn't take very long to find out about Mrs. Velden. And it was a nice day. So I went on up to Crouch End and saw the Reverend Mortleman."

"The devil you did. What in the world did you say?"

"I said I was Mrs. Velden's secretary, and she was a bit anxious, because he hadn't acknowledged the last lot of money she'd sent him."

Petrella stared at her.

"He was most upset. Said he was sure he had acknowledged it. He insisted on me coming in, so that he could find a carbon copy of his letter to Mrs. Velden. He did find it too. So I apologised. Then we had tea together."

When Petrella had recovered his breath, he said, "You were taking a bit of a chance, weren't you? Suppose he'd known Mrs. Velden's secretary by sight?"

"He couldn't have known her new one."

"Her new one?"

"She's been advertising in *The Times.* That's what gave me the idea. Couldn't I answer the advertisement?"

Before Petrella could string together some of the many ways of saying no to this outrageous proposal, she hurried on.

"I don't suppose Mrs. Velden's a master criminal. She certainly doesn't sound like one. But all this money is coming *through* her. She must have some connection with one of the organisers. If I was working for her, and kept my eyes open, I could probably spot—"

Petrella found his voice at last. "You're not even a policewoman," he said. "You're a typist."

It wasn't, perhaps, the best way of putting it. Jane turned dark red, and said, "Of all the stupid, stuffy, ungrateful things to say—"

"I'm sorry . . ."

"Don't you *want* to solve this? Don't you *want* to find out who's running it?"

"Now you're being silly."

"At least I'm not being pompous."

Petrella said, "I'm sorry if I sound pompous, but what you don't seem to realise is that I can't possibly let you take an active part in this, without getting into frightful trouble with the Establishment." He added, hastily, "It's very late, and we're both a bit tired, I expect. Come and have something to eat with me."

"Thank you," said Jane, "but as a typist, I know my place." She made a dignified exit.

Petrella swore, and took a running kick at the metal wastepaper basket. It rose in a neat parabola and broke a window.

Next morning Petrella made a point of getting to the office early. He found Jane alone there, typing furiously. He selected the most propitiatory of half a dozen opening gambits which he had worked out during a sleepless night.

Before he could start, Jane said, "I'm sorry I was stupid last night. Obviously you couldn't do it."

This took the wind out of Petrella's sails so effectively that he could only stare at her.

"As a matter of fact," he said at last, "I had a word with the A.C. – with your uncle, that is – and he said that, compared with some of the things you'd tried to talk him into letting you do, this sounded comparatively harmless."

"Bully for Uncle Wilfred."

"But he laid down certain conditions. First, you're to report, by telephone, to this office every night between five and seven. Use a call box, not a private telephone. Second, if ever you're going out anywhere, you're to let us know where you're going."

"It all seems a bit unnecessary to me," said Jane. "But I'll do it if you insist."

"All that remains now is for you to get the job."

"I rather think I've got it. I went round to see Mrs. Velden last night. It turned out that she knew a friend of a friend of my mother's. We got on like a house on fire." Seeing the look in Petrella's eye, she added hastily, "Of course, if you'd said no, I wouldn't have taken the job. I thought there was no harm in seeing if I could get it. And I'll remember to telephone you."

"It won't be me for the next few nights," said Petrella. "I'm off to Germany."

The Baron von der Hulde und Oberath propelled a cedarwood cabinet of king-sized cigars across the top of his desk towards Petrella, helped himself to one, lit both of them with a long match, and picked up the photograph again.

"Certainly this is one of our drills," he said. "What can I tell you about it?"

"How long has it been in production?"

"Five years. A little more."

"And, in that time, how many would you have exported to England?"

"I should have to consult my records. Perhaps a hundred."

Petrella's heart sank.

"It is a highly efficient drill," said the Baron. "I sent half a dozen the other day to one of your safe deposits."

"Safe deposits?"

"A good safe deposit only possesses one key for each of its safes. If the depositor loses it, the safe has to be broken open. The screws of the hinges have to be drilled out – but it takes an exceptionally good drill to do it. Any ordinary one would break, or melt. A number of cooling devices had been tried before. None successfully. Then we invented this method. It is so very simple. As the drill gets hotter, it sweats. Just like the human body. It exudes its own lubricant. We call it 'film cooling.'"

"I see," said Petrella. "And no one else but you makes these drills?"

"We have the world patent."

"Then you could compile, from your records, a list of people in England whom you have supplied."

"I could no doubt do so. It might take a couple of days."

"It'll be worth waiting for."

"When the list is ready, I will telephone your hotel. The Goldenes Kreuz, isn't it? Take another cigar with you, please. You can smoke it this evening."

Petrella spent the afternoon exploring Dortmund, mostly from the top of a train.

It seemed to him an unattractive city. At seven o'clock he got back to his hotel, and had a bath. Then he set out to have a look at the night life.

First, he stood himself a large, and rather heavy meal at the Barberina. Then he moved on to one of the many beer cellars in the Augusta Platz and ordered a stein of what described itself as the world famous Munchner Lowenbrau; and which tasted no better and no worse than any lager beer he had drunk in an English pub.

On the wall opposite was an advertisement, depicting a man with a monocle smoking a cigar. It looked not unlike a stylised version of the Baron von der Hulde und Oberath. As this thought occurred to him, another one crossed his mind, and he put down his beer slowly.

The Baron had said, "I will telephone your hotel – the Goldenes Kreuz." How did he know which hotel to telephone? Petrella had certainly not told him.

He went back, very carefully, over the events of the morning. He had driven straight from the airport to the headquarters of the City Police, to make his mark with Inspector Laufer, a contact arranged for him by Baldy.

The Inspector had given him the names of the possible manufacturers of drills, of which the Baron had been the largest and the most likely.

Might the Inspector have telephoned the Baron, to tell him Petrella was coming, and might he have mentioned the name of his hotel?

No. That was impossible. For the simple reason that Petrella had not, at that time, chosen a hotel. He had gone to the Goldenes Kreuz after leaving the police station.

It was at this point that his thoughts became linked with a suspicion which had never been quite out of his mind since he had left the hotel.

He was being followed.

It was impossible to say how he knew, but now that he gave his mind to it, he was quite certain. In London, the discovery would not have worried him. Here, in a foreign country, in a strange city, it was less agreeable.

His first idea was to telephone Inspector Laufer, but he dismissed it as soon as he thought of it. There was no explanation he could make which would not sound ludicrous. Dortmund might not be beautiful, but it was a well-organised modern city, with an efficient police force, and well-lit streets. All he had to do was to walk back to his hotel, go up to his room, bolt the door on the inside, and go to bed.

He paid his bill, recovered his coat and hat, and climbed the steps which led up to the street.

A storm of rain had cleared the air, and emptied the streets. He stepped out, briskly. No one seemed to be taking the least interest in him.

Halfway down the Augusta Platz he had to turn right, into the smaller street which would, in turn, bring him to the Station Square. It was at this moment that he heard the car start off behind him. Something in the note of the engine sounded a warning. He jerked his head round, and saw it coming straight at him.

Without stopping to think, he jerked himself to one side, spotted a narrow sidestreet ahead, and ran down it. It was when he heard the car going into reverse that he realised his mistake. He should have stuck to the main street . . .

The sidestreet stretched ahead of him, badly-lit, absolutely empty, sloping steeply downhill. Behind him, the headlamps of the car flicked on, pinning him.

He reckoned he had a good twenty yards start. On his left stretched the unbroken wall of a large building; no entrance, not even a recess. The right-hand side was blocked by a high iron railing.

He put on speed.

There was a T junction at the bottom, and what looked like a rather better lighted road. He swung round the corner. The car, which had been catching up, cornered behind him.

Petrella sidestepped. His plan was to turn in his tracks, and run in the opposite direction before the car could turn. He had reckoned without the driver. As he sidestepped, the car swerved too. The wing caught him in the small of the back, scooped him up, and tossed him against the fence which bordered the road.

The car screamed to a halt, and went into reverse.

Petrella was lying at the inner edge of the pavement, close to the fence. There was a stabbing pain in his chest, and he seemed to have lost the use of his legs.

He could see the driver now, with his head out of the side window. It was a heavy, white, bad-tempered face.

As he watched, the driver manoeuvred the near-side wheels of his car carefully up on to the pavement, judged the distance to where Petrella lay, and started to reverse.

When he's been over me once, thought Petrella, he'll come back again just to make sure. Petrella's legs were like sacks of sand but he still had the use of his arms. Pressing on the pavement, he rolled himself over, and then over again until he was pressed hard against the bottom of the wooden fence.

It was no use. The car was on him now. The near-side wheels were going over him . . . Petrella heaved wildly, felt the skirting board at the foot of the fence bend, and heaved again. There was a dull crack. A complete length of board gave way, and Petrella went rolling, over and over, down a grassy bank to come to rest with a thud at the bottom.

He was on gravel. His groping hand found a wire, and he hurled himself up on to his knees. The fall seemed to have done something for his legs, which were now hurting as much as his chest but seemed to be answering signals again. He crawled forward, pulling himself by the wire.

The fence rocked and splintered as his pursuers, too bulky to squeeze through the space underneath, proceeded to batter it down.

Petrella crawled a little faster

Behind him, he heard the fence go down with a crack.

There was a circular opening on the left. It looked like a drain. He crawled into it, until a bend in the pipe forced him to stop. Footsteps thundered past. Men were shouting. There was a rumbling, thudding noise, which shook the ground; a hiss of steam, and the clanking of iron on iron.

For the first time, he realised that he was on a railway line. The wire he had been following must have been a signal wire. What he was in now was some sort of rainwater conduit. There was plenty of water coming down it, too.

Further voices, angry voices. Official voices. A dog barking.

Petrella pushed himself backwards until he was out in the open again.

Some way up the line an argument was going on. Orders were being shouted in loud, angry German.

Petrella propped himself against the bank, and started massaging the life back into his sodden legs. A dog passed out of darkness, and stood watching him.

"Good boy," said Petrella hopefully.

The dog gave a sharp bark, like a sergeant major calling the parade to attention.

Two men appeared. They were in the green uniform of the railway police. As soon as they saw him, both of them started to shout.

When they seemed to have finished, Petrella said in impeccable German, "Conduct me, at once, if you please, to Inspector Laufer, of the Municipal Police."

Even the dog seemed impressed by this . . .

Constantia Velden was a compulsive talker. She didn't really need a secretary, Jane Orfrey decided. What she needed was a captive audience.

And Jane, for two whole days, had been it.

There were advantages, of course. Within an hour, and without any actual effort on her part, she had learnt almost all there was to know about Constantia; about her late husband, who had been an administrative officer in the Air Force, and had died of hepatitis jaundice in 1955; about her brother, Douglas Marchant, a Wing Commander, D.S.O., D.F.C., now the managing director of a firm making window frames, with a London Office in Lennox Street; about Constantia's charitable enterprises; about the time Constantia had shaken hands with the Queen; about life; about money.

Money came into most of Mrs. Velden's calculations.

Reading between the lines, Jane had deduced that she had inherited a reasonable competence from her late husband, and that she was helped out, where necessary, by her brother. He advised her on her investments and looked after her tax. He had also produced Alex; and probably paid his salary as well.

Alex was the only other resident at the Loudon Road house, and was chauffeur, butler, gardener, and footman combined. A husky, brown-haired, freckled boy, who looked no more than sixteen and was in fact in his early twenties. He did everything that was beyond the strength or capacity of Mrs. Velden and her cohort of daily women.

What spare time Alex had, he spent polishing his employer's car and tuning up his own motorcycle.

He was out with Mrs. Velden now. A lunch date with brother Douglas, she gathered. Jane munched her way through a solitary meal, and wondered, for the twentieth time, what possible connection her talkative middle-aged employer could have with an organisation which robbed banks. Her faith told her that the connection was there. After forty eight hours, her reason was beginning to doubt it.

It was three o'clock before the car reappeared in Loudon Road and Alex jumped out and held the door open for Mrs. Velden. Jane caught a glimpse of her, and of the man who followed her out. So Douglas had accompanied his sister home. Interesting.

Then the drawing room door opened, and he came in, holding it open for his sister and closing it behind her.

He was a man of about six foot, with the round shoulders and barrel chest of a boxer; thick black hair, greying round the edges; a face dominated by a long, straight nose which turned out, suddenly, at the end, over a bush of grey moustache. Like a down pipe, she thought, emptying into a clump of weeds. A disillusioned pair of eyes peered out from under thick black eyebrows.

"Wing Commander Marchant, Jane Orfrey."

"Plain Douglas Marchant, if you don't mind," said the man. "You're my sister's new secretary. Has she driven you mad yet?"

"Really, Douglas . . ."

"If she hasn't, she will. She gets through secretaries at the rate of two a week. She's a Gorgon. She doesn't realise that the days of indentured labour are over. There are more jobs than secretaries. Girls please themselves nowadays. Isn't that right?"

"More or less," said Jane.

"As soon as you present yourself to an agency, they offer you a dozen jobs, and say, take your pick."

"It isn't quite as easy as that."

"What agency do you use, by the way?"

It came out so swiftly that Jane gaped for a moment. Then she said, "As a matter of fact, I got this job through an advertisement."

"But you must have an agency," said Douglas gently. "You'll never get paid properly if you don't."

"Really, Douglas," said Constantia. "Are you trying to lure her away?"

"I don't see why not. I don't mind betting you underpay her."

"Perhaps she doesn't want to work in an office."

"I think it would be terribly dull," said Jane.

"You wouldn't be dull in my office," said Douglas. "Eighteen pounds a week, and luncheon vouchers."

Jane felt it was time she asserted herself. "If I had to work in an office," she said, "I'd choose a professional office, I think. Not a commercial one."

"There, if I may say so, you display your ignorance," said Douglas. "Professional men overwork their staff and underpay them. They operate on too small a scale to do anything else. We're just the opposite. We've got factories all over England. There's hardly a building goes up that hasn't got one of our windows in it."

"You may be right," said Jane. "But personally I find businessmen so boring. They think and talk of nothing but money."

"What businessmen have you worked for?" inquired Douglas politely.

Damn, thought Jane. I walked into that one. Better watch out. He's a lot cleverer than he looks.

"Two or three," she said. And to Constantia, "Should I see if we can raise a cup of tea?"

"Not for me," said Douglas. "I've got to be off. A bit more money-grubbing to do. I'll get Alex to drive me back into Town, if you don't mind."

Jane telephoned Sergeant Wilmot at six o'clock that evening, from a call box on Hampstead Heath. "This is urgent," she said. "See what you can find out about Douglas Marchant. Ex-R.A.F. Runs a business which makes windows. Not widows – windows. The firm's got a head office in Lennox Street and factories all over the place."

"Wasn't he the other director in the firm Light worked for, just after the war?"

"That's right. And he's Mrs. Velden's brother. He gives her money. Any notes she's been passing could easily have come from him."

"I suppose they could have done."

She could hear the doubt in Wilmot's voice, and said urgently, "We're looking for a man who could run a show like this. Well, I'm telling you, Douglas Marchant fills the bill. I can't explain it all over the telephone. But he's big enough and bad enough—"

"A big bad wolf," said Wilmot. "O.K., I'll take your word for it. We'll certainly have him checked up."

"Any news from Germany?"

"Not a word," said Wilmot.

As Jane came out of the telephone booth, she heard a motorcycle start up and move off. When she got back the house was in darkness, and she let herself in with her own key, and went into the drawing room.

She felt restless, and uneasy, and had no difficulty in putting her finger on the cause of it. The powerful and unpleasant personality of Douglas Marchant seemed to linger in the room, like the smell of a cigar, long after its owner had departed. She realised that it was the first time she had been alone in the house.

Leaving the light on in the drawing room, she went along to what Constantia called her business-room at the end of the hall. Her objective was Constantia's desk. She found that all the drawers in it were locked, so was the filing cabinet, and so were the cupboards under the bookcases which lined one wall. The books in the shelves were mostly political and military history, and this surprised her, until it occurred to her that they probably represented the departed Mr. Velden's taste rather than Constantia's.

She took down one of the six volumes of Lloyd George's *War Memoirs,* blew the dust off the top, and opened it.

From an ornate bookplate, the name jumped out at her: Alwyn Corder

Jane started at it in blank disbelief. Then she started taking down books at random. The bookplate was in most of them. For a moment she was unable to think straight. She knew that she had stumbled on something desperately important.

A slight sound at the door made her swing round. Alex was smiling at her.

"Looking for something to read?" he said . . .

Sergeant Edwards said to Wilmot, "It's a big company. Superintendent Baldwin says Douglas Marchant is the Chairman. Leaves most of the work to his staff, and comes up twice a week from the country to justify his director's fees."

"Anything known?"

"As far as Records know, the company and Marchant are both as clean as the proverbial whistle. What have we got on them?"

"What we've got," said Wilmot, "is a woman's instinct. Jane doesn't like his smell. She thinks he's a crook."

"It doesn't seem a lot to go on," said Edwards doubtfully. "When's Petrella coming back?"

"Baldy hasn't heard a chirrup out of him for twenty-four hours," said Wilmot. "If you ask me, he's found himself a Rhine maiden."

It was after midnight when the bedside telephone rang. The red-headed girl, who had been sharing Marchant's flat, and bed, for the past month, groaned and said, "Don't take any notice, Doug. It's probably a wrong number."

"Pass it over," said Douglas, who was lying on his back beside her. He balanced the instrument on his stomach, and unhooked the receiver. As soon as he heard the voice at the other end, he cupped a hand over the receiver and said, "Out you get, honey. It's business."

"This is a nice time to do business."

"Get up and get us both a cup of tea."

Not until the girl had grumbled her way into a dressing gown and out of the room did Douglas remove his hand from the receiver and say, "Sorry, Alex, there was someone here. It's all right now. Go ahead."

His pyjama top was unbuttoned, showing a chest fuzzed with greying black hair. One of his thick hands held the telephone. The other was fumbling on the bedside table for a cigarette. His face was expressionless.

At the end he said, "Let's just see if I've got this straight. Each of the three evenings she's been there, she's been out about the same time and made a call from a public phone box. And this evening, you found her in the library, snooping through a lot of books which had the old bookplates still in them. Damn, damn, *and damn.*"

There was a long silence as if each was waiting for the other to speak.

Then Douglas said, "If she's what we think she is, and if she's got a regular reporting time, she won't pass any of this on until six o'clock tomorrow night. We ought to do something about it before then, I think."

Alex said, "Yes. I think we ought."

"I can't attend to it myself. I'm flying over to Germany tomorrow afternoon. There's been some sort of trouble at the factory. Could you think of an excuse to take her out in the car?"

Alex said, "Suppose I said you had left some papers at the office which had to be taken to the airport – and you had a message for your sister-something like that."

"It's worth trying," said Douglas.

"When I get her in the car – what then?"

"My dear Alex, I must leave all the arrangements to you. A moonlight picnic, perhaps."

As he rang off, the red-haired girl came back with two cups of tea. Douglas drank his slowly. He didn't seem to want to talk. The redheaded girl thought that Douglas, though a generous spender, was a tiny bit odd; and had been becoming odder just lately. Now, the look in his eyes frightened her. At the age of twenty-five she was something of an expert on men, and she made up her mind, there and then, to clear out while Douglas was in Germany – and not to come back.

When, late on the following afternoon, Alex told Jane that he had to collect some papers and take them to the airport, and that Marchant had asked that she should go too so that he could give her a message for his sister, her first reaction was to say no.

Then she reflected that no harm could really be planned on the crowded roads between Central London and London Airport.

"I'll have to ask Mrs. Velden," she said.

"I've asked her. She says the trip'll do you good."

"When do we start?"

"Right now."

"I'll have to get a coat," said Jane.

She ran up to her room and stood listening. The house was quiet. She tiptoed across the corridor and into Mrs. Velden's bedroom. As she had hoped, there was a bedside telephone extension. She grabbed the receiver, and dialled the code number which she knew by heart.

"Hullo," said Wilmot's voice. "What's up?"

"No time to explain," said Jane. "Alex is taking me, in Mrs. Velden's car, to London Airport. We're calling at the Lennox Street office first. Can you put a tail on?"

"It could be done," said Wilmot. "But why—" He found himself talking to a dead telephone. Jane had gone.

It was half past five by the time they reached Lennox Street. Whilst Alex was inside, Jane looked cautiously round to see if Wilmot had been as good as his word. She could see a small green van, apparently delivering parcels at the far end of the road, but nothing else.

By six o'clock, with dusk coming up, they were across Kew Bridge, and had joined the tail-end of the home-going traffic on the Twickenham Road.

"Quicker this way," said Alex, "until they've finished messing about with the flyover on the Great West Road. Trouble is, everyone else knows it too. Let's try a short cut."

He swung expertly across the traffic, and turned into a long road of neat houses, with neat gardens and neat cars in neat garages. At the far end of the road, the street lamps petered out, and they came to a halt in an area of allotments and high fences.

"It's a dead end," said Jane.

"Not the last time I came here, it wasn't," said Alex. "Let's have a squint at the map. It's in the pocket."

As he leaned over her, she felt the needle go into her arm. For a moment, she thought it was an accident – that a loose pin in Alex's coat might have stuck into her. Then she realised what had happened, and started to fight, but Alex was lying half on top of her, his thick leather driving glove feeling for her mouth.

A minute later the boy sat back in his seat, and relaxed cautiously. He had given her a full shot of pelandramine. She'd be out for an hour, and dopey for another hour after that. So, no hurry.

He looked at himself in the driving mirror; and was pleased with the unexcited face that looked back. He stripped off the driving gloves and felt his own pulse, timing it with his wristwatch. Eighty-four. Twelve faster than it should be, but not bad. He took out a comb, and ran it through his hair.

Then he examined the girl. Her mouth was open and she was breathing noisily. Her cheeks were flushed. Anyone looking at her would think that she'd been drinking too much, and had passed out. Just the job.

He felt in the right-hand door-pocket and took out a small bottle of gin. A few drops round her mouth and chin. A little spilt on her dress. Enough for people to smell it, if he was stopped.

He opened the door. There was no one in sight. He threw the gin bottle and the empty syringe over the fence, got back, turned the car, and drove off slowly the way he had come.

The mist was thicker. At the Slough roundabout he took the Staines road, driving carefully now. He crossed Staines Bridge, following the Egham Road. At Egham, the road forked. The main road, with its string of garages, its traffic and its orange neon lighting went away to the left. The right fork, a much smaller road, followed the river towards Windsor. In summer, this road, too, would be crowded with traffic heading for the open spaces of Runnymede Meadow. On a damp February night, it was empty.

Half a mile along, Alex turned out his headlights, and drove very carefully off the road and on to the rough grass. There was some danger of getting the car bogged, but his town-and-country studded tyres would grip on most surfaces. There was a worse danger. Somewhere ahead was the Thames, its bank unprotected by any fence.

Alex stopped the car, got out, and walked forward, counting his paces. It was fifty yards to the bank. He came back, climbed in, and drove the car forward cautiously in bottom gear.

When he stopped again, he was five yards from the edge. At this point, where the bank curved, it had been revetted with concrete bags against the sweep of the winter floods. A yard below his feet the river ran cold, grey and sleek.

Alex walked back to the car. Jane had slumped over sideways, so that when he opened the door she nearly fell out. He got his hands under her body, and lifted her on to the wet grass.

Alone, islanded by the mist, touching the girl's body, moving it, arranging it, gave him a sense of power, near to exultation. He crouched beside her for a full minute to let the singing noise in his ears die down and the lights stop flashing in front of his eyes. Then he got up slowly, went round to the back of the car, opened the boot and took out two fourteen-pound kitchen weights and a coil of odd-looking plaited cord.

With the cord he tied Jane's wrists together in front of her, passing the ends through the handles of the weights and knotting them.

When he stood up, he saw three pairs of yellow eyes looking at him through the mist. He thought, for a moment, that it was his imagination playing him tricks again. Then he heard the engines, growling to themselves, as the cars bumped across the grass in low gear, closing in on him from every side.

He bent quickly, hoisted the girl on to his shoulders and walked to the bank.

A man's voice shouted urgently, and an orange spotlight flicked on.

Alex humped his powerful shoulders, threw the girl ahead of him into the water, and jumped after her. Whilst he was still in midair, a second body flashed past him.

Jane came up out of a tangle of nightmare, of darkness and cold, of lights and noises, into the reality of a hospital bed. The sun was slanting through the uncurtained window, and Sergeant Wilmot was perched on a chair beside her.

"Good morning," he said. "Are you ready to talk?"

"I'm all right," said Jane. "I'll get dressed, if you can find some clothes for me."

"The doctor says he'll let you out in a day or two, if you're good. Let's have the story."

She told him what she could remember, and Sergeant Wilmot wrote it down in his round, schoolboy hand.

"I felt the needle go in my arm," she said. "I don't really know what happened after that."

"Alex took you in the car to Runnymede, and pitched you into the river. Having first tied a couple of kitchen weights on to you. I wonder how many of his girl friends he's got rid of that way before?" He pulled a length of cord out of his pocket. "Simple, but you've got to hand it to him. It's clever. It's made of paper. Twenty or thirty separate strands of it, plaited tight together. Strong enough but it'd melt after you'd been a day or two in the water."

Jane shuddered uncontrollably, and Sergeant Wilmot said, "I never had much tact," and put the cord away.

"Who pulled me out?"

"I did," said Wilmot. "It's the sort of thing you sometimes get a medal for. We were on your tail the whole way. If it hadn't been for the fog and the mess-up on Staines Bridge we'd have been close enough to stop you going in the water."

"What's happened to Alex?"

"He's in the hospital at the Scrubs. In a private room. And that's where he's going to stay until Patrick gets back."

"Haven't we heard anything yet?"

"He's been off the air for nearly forty eight hours. He'll turn up. Don't worry."

"Who said I was worrying?"

"You looked worried. Just for a moment. It might have been wind, of course."

Jane laughed and said, "If I'm going to be kept here, you can do something for me. Get me those photocopies of Jerry Light's diary pages, and a classified directory of London. I've had a hunch and I want to work it out."

When Wilmot had gone, she stretched luxuriously, and then settled down into the warm trough of the bed. She liked the way Wilmot called Petrella, Patrick; and she wondered if she'd ever be able to do it herself. A minute later, she was asleep . . .

At eleven o'clock on the following morning, the door of her room opened. Jane, who was deep in a street directory, her bed covered with slips of paper, said, "Put it down on the bed-table, could you, nurse—" looked up, and saw that it was Petrella.

"Hullo," she said.

"As soon as my back's turned," said Petrella, "you have to go and do a damn silly thing like that."

"Listen, who's talking," said Jane. "What have *you* been up to? And what's wrong with your leg?"

"Someone tried to run me over. I rolled down a bank onto a railway."

"Well I fell into a river. That's not much worse."

They both laughed. Petrella sat down on the end of the bed, and said, "You know why they had to shut your mouth, don't you?"

"Something about those books. I couldn't work it out."

"Listen, and I'll tell you. In 1951 two men were sentenced at the Exeter Assizes for assaulting a bank manager. One was our friend Jerry Light of Islington. The other was one of the Managing Directors of the demolition firm he worked for. A man called Alwyn Corder, who disappeared so efficiently that even our Sergeant Edwards couldn't trace him. Because the simple explanation eluded us all. When Corder came out of prison, *he changed his name to Velden.* All legal and above board, by deed poll, registered in the High Court. I checked it this morning. And in that name, he married Constantia Marchant, Douglas Marchant's sister. It was a business alliance. Douglas was his fellow director in the demolition firm."

"I see," said Jane. "Yes, I see." A lot of tiny little pieces were falling into place, and a certain pattern was appearing.

"There's a lot that isn't clear yet," said Petrella. "But the outline's there. Douglas Marchant and Alwyn Corder, his brother-in-law, now known as Kenneth Velden, and their old foreman, Jerry Light, are the three people who started this racket, and ran it. That's for sure. Then Velden died. The other two couldn't simply hang on to his share. They paid it over to his widow."

"Then Douglas *is* head of the whole affair?"

"It's got to be proved."

"And it would help to prove it, if you could show that he was still keeping in touch with Jerry Light."

Petrella grinned, and said, "Cough it up."

"Cough *what* up?"

"Whatever it is you've discovered."

"All right. It's this diary you found in Light's desk. The entries are meeting places – they're pubs. *Rsg Sn* is the Rising Sun. *Wdmn* is the Woodman, and so on. The letter and numbers after the pub are the postal district, and the last number's the time of day. That's what first made me think they must be pubs, because the times are all between eleven and two, or six and ten."

Petrella got up, and stood for a long moment staring down at her. Then he said, "That's very good indeed," limped across to the door, and went quietly out, shutting the door behind him . . .

"Douglas Marchant," said Petrella to Baldwin, "makes windows. The windows go into new buildings, all over England. In any big building project, the sub-contractors all get paid on the same day in the month. Therefore there must be a lot of money in the main contractors' bank the day before. That's how the intelligence system works. When the bank has been chosen, a gang of specialist safebreakers do the actual work. Jerry Light gives them their instructions, and their kit. And his men collect the appropriate rakeoff after the job's over. That's what the Franks brothers were waiting for, in Slough, that morning after the robbery."

"How are we going to prove all this?"

"*If* we could get one of Jerry Light's boys to sing, he *might* give us Light, *if* we hooked Light, he *might* give us Marchant."

"You don't sound very hopeful."

"They're going to be a tough bunch to drive that sort of wedge into. They've been working together too long, and they know each other too well."

"Have you any better ideas?"

"Yes," said Petrella, slowly. "I have got an idea, but it's so irregular that we're going to need all the backing the A.C can give us. First, I want Jerry Light's phone tapped."

Baldwin made a face. "You know what they think about that, don't you? Anything else?"

"That's just a start," said Petrella. "The next bit really is a bit hot. Now, listen—"

At London Airport the loudspeaker in the Arrival Lounge said, "We have a message for Mr. Douglas Marchant, believed to be travelling from Dortmund. Would Mr. Marchant report to the reception desk?" Douglas hesitated for a long moment.

If things really had started to happen, might it not be wisest to turn straight round and take the next aeroplane back to Germany? He rejected the idea as soon as it occurred to him. It was by abandoning careful, prearranged plans and acting on the impulse of blind panic that people gave themselves away and got caught. He marched firmly up to the reception desk and smiled at the girl behind it.

He produced his passport. "I understand you have a message for me."

"Mr. Douglas Marchant? Would you telephone this number? You can use the telephone in the office, if you wish."

"Thank you," said Douglas. He dialled the number, which he recognised as his sister Constantia's.

"Douglas. Thank heavens, you're back. I didn't know where to get hold of you, so I had to leave a message at the airport."

"What's happened?"

"Alex and Jane Orfrey have both disappeared. And they've taken the car with them."

"When did this happen?"

"Two nights ago. I've been so worried."

"You've told the police."

"Of course. But they've done nothing. They even suggested"— Douglas heard his sister choke—"that they might have eloped together."

"I suppose it's possible."

"Don't be absurd. Alex was a chauffeur – a mechanic—"

"And Jane was your secretary."

"That's different. She was a girl of good family."

Douglas was about to say something flippant, when he realised that his sister was upset; and being upset, might do something stupid.

"I'll make some inquiries," he said. "I'll ring you back as soon as I have any news for you."

As soon as he had rung off, he dialled another number. The girl who answered the telephone said, "Who's that? Mr. Wilberforce. I'll see if Mr. Simons is in." And a few seconds later, "No, I'm sorry. He's just gone out. Can I get him to ring you back?"

"Don't bother," said Douglas. "When he does come back, would you give him a message? Tell him that I got the letter he sent me on the third of March."

"Rightchar," said the girl.

As soon as she had rung off, she walked through to the inner office, and said, "That was Mr. Wilberforce, Mr. Simons. You did say you weren't in if he telephoned."

"That's what I said," agreed Mr. Simons, a short, sharp-looking man in thick bifocals. "And that's what I meant. Did he leave a message?"

"He just said that he got the letter you sent on the third of March."

"You're sure he said the third of March."

"I'm not deaf yet," said the girl.

"All right," said Mr. Simons. "Plug a line through to this telephone, and you can go to lunch."

"'Tisn't lunchtime!"

"Then go out and buy me some cigarettes."

Mr. Simons listened until he heard the outer door shut, drew the telephone towards himself, and dialled an Islington number.

Jerry Light, who answered the telephone, said, "You're sure it was the third of March he said? All right. Thanks very much," and rang off. He opened the drawer of his desk, extracted the diary that lay there, and opened it at the first week in March.

Then he looked at his watch. It was just after twelve. He crammed a hat on his head, went down the outside staircase into the yard, said – "Watch things, Sammy. I'm going out – " to the shaggy young man who was sawing a length of timber, and set off at a brisk pace. He seemed to be walking haphazardly, choosing small empty streets. But his course was steadily northeast.

One o'clock was striking when he went through the door of a small public house in the neighbourhood of Hackney Downs, said, "Wotcher, Len," to the landlord, and walked through the serving area into the private room behind.

Douglas Marchant was sitting in front of the fire, nursing a glass of whisky. He indicated another glass, ready poured, which stood on the table.

Light said, "Ta," took a drink and added, "you saw the news."

"That's why I came back from Germany. All that the papers said was that Alex got out of hospital at the Scrubs yesterday morning and clean away. No details. It mightn't be true."

"It's true all right," said Light. "He telephoned me this morning."

Marchant's lip went up. "At your place?"

"No. He had sense enough not to do that. He got me through Shady Simons."

"Did he tell you how he got picked up?"

"He thinks it was just bad luck. A police patrol car spotted him tipping the girl into the river."

"I don't believe in bad luck like that," said Marchant. "Do you?"

"Not really," said Light. "I think they're moving in on us."

"What did Alex want?"

"A place to lie up in. He spent last night on the Embankment. And for you to get him out of the country."

"Or what?"

"So far, he's kept his mouth shut. If he did decide to talk, he could tell them a hell of a lot they want to know."

Marchant drank a little more whisky. "We'll have to do something about him," he said. "The only place he'd be safe, would be in East Germany."

"I can think of somewhere that'd be a damned sight safer," said Jerry.

A red coal dropped from the fire. The clock on the mantelshelf ticked. In the bar, Douglas could hear the landlord saying, "Nice sort of day for March." He had said it to every customer who came in.

Douglas finished his drink and got up. He said, "I think you're right. We're going to pack up this lark soon. We don't want any loose ends. I've got to go and hold my sister's hand. She's having hysterics. We'll go out the back way."

As the two men emerged from the alleyway, a girl approached them. She had a collector's tray of little red and white flowers. "For the Cottage Hospital," she said. She was a nice-looking girl. Douglas felt in his pocket, found half a crown, dropped it in her tin, and said, "Keep the flower. You can sell it again."

The girl said, "Thank you, sir." Douglas noticed that she had an outsize flower with a black centre pinned on to the shoulder of her dress.

At nine o'clock that night, Jerry Light left his flat in Albany Street and walked to the garage where he parked his car. The attendant said, "She ought to be all right now."

In the act of getting into the car, Light paused, "What do you mean, *now*?"

"Now the distributor head's been fixed."

"I didn't tell you to do that."

"It wasn't us. The man came round from the makers with it. He fixed it himself."

"Oh," said Light. "Yes. Of course. I'd forgotten about that. He fixed it, did he? Come to think of it, I won't be needing the car just now. I've changed my mind."

He left the garage, hailed a taxi, and was driven through Regent's Park to Clarence Gate. Here he dismissed the taxi. Five minutes' quick walk brought him to a row of garages in a cul-de-sac behind Baker Street station.

Light was tolerably sure that no one knew about his second car. It was a new M.G Magnette, with a capacious boot, in which he had stored two bulging suitcases and a hold-all. He had rented the garage in another name, had installed the car in it three months before, and had not visited it since.

The only trouble was that it was now raining so hard that it was difficult to keep observation as he walked. He didn't think anyone was following him, but was not quite sure.

He backed the car out and drove slowly into the park, which he proceeded to circle twice. Headlights showed, blurred by the rain, in his mirror. Cars overtook him. Cars passed him. At the end of the second circuit he was reasonably happy, turned out of the park at Gloucester Gate, and headed north.

"He's making it damned difficult for us," said Wilmot into his car wireless. "I wish he'd used his first car. I'd got that fixed nicely. All we'd have had to do then would be sit back and track him on the radio repeater. Over."

"Count your blessings," said Petrella into his wireless. "If it wasn't raining so damned hard, he'd probably have spotted us already. Over and out."

Jerry Light drove steadily up Highgate Hill, across the North Circular Road, and on towards Barnet. His plan was very simple. He was not a believer in elaboration. His instructions to Alex had been to come by Underground to High Barnet and then to walk out on to the main North Road and along it for a quarter of a mile, past the Golf Course, timing himself to get to the point where the road forked by eleven o'clock. He was to come alone, and make damned sure he wasn't followed.

Light looked at his watch. He was in nice time. Five minutes to eleven, and that was High Barnet station on the right. The rain was coming down like steel rods. Alex must be getting very wet.

Light followed the main road past the Elstree fork. There was very little traffic. A couple of London-bound cars came towards him over the long swell of the hill. There was nothing behind him as far as he could see.

His headlights picked out Alex standing by the roadside.

Light changed down, and crawled to a stop beside him. Leaning across, he turned down the far side window. He used his left hand to do this. His right hand was resting on the floor of the car.

"That you, Jerry," said Alex. "I'm damned wet."

"It's me," said Light. He brought up his right hand, and shot him twice through the chest at point blank range.

Alex jerked back on to his heels, went down on to his knees, and fell forward, his face in the water which was cascading down the gutter.

Resting his forearm on the ledge of the window, Light took careful aim, and shot again.

The repeated detonations had deafened him, and he could hear nothing. The first thing he noticed was that headlights, backed by a powerful spotlight, had come on behind him. He slammed the car into gear, almost lifting it off the ground as he drove it forward.

A siren sounded.

The car behind him was almost on top of him. Light saw, out of the corner of his eye, a minor road to the left, did a racing change-down, and went into a skid turn.

On a dry surface, it would have come off, but the wet macadam was like ice. Instead of correcting at the end of the skid, the car swung wildly out of control, went through the fence, wires twanging like harp strings, turned once right over, and smacked into the concrete base of a pylon, dislocating two of the overhead lines and plunging half of High Barnet into darkness and confusion.

So Petrella came for a second time into the presence of Assistant Commissioner Romer, and came with the consciousness of failure heavy on him.

"I reckoned," he said, "that if we let Alex go, they'd be in a cleft stick. Either they left him in the lurch, in which case he'd split. Or they helped him, and we caught them, redhanded. Now Alex is dead, and Light's dead, and we're further off than ever from proving any connection between the crooks who do the work, and the man at the top, who draws the profit."

"Douglas Marchant?"

"Yes, sir. I've no doubt in my own mind that he's the man who founded the organisation. And who runs it."

"It's not just what's in your mind," said Romer. "There's a good deal of concrete evidence, too. That was a nice photograph our girl collector got of him, talking to Light, outside the pub."

"He could explain that, sir. He's in windows. Light's a builder. It could have been an ordinary business chat."

"Light's a criminal," said Romer, "and a man who committed coldblooded murder a few hours after meeting Marchant secretly at an out-of-the-way public house. I don't doubt that he could explain the coincidence. Most things can be explained, if you try hard enough. Here's another one. Two days ago, Marchant went across to Germany. He visited your old friend, the Baron von der Hulde und Oberath. They had a long talk. The German police have got a man in the packing department. He saw Marchant coming and going, and is prepared to identify him. Last night there was a fire at the factory."

"A fire!"

"Nothing serious. It broke out in the dispatch department, and destroyed all records of dispatches during the last five years."

"I see," said Petrella.

"It's particularly intriguing because our man remembers, four or five days ago, helping to pack and dispatch a drill – to a place called Fyledean Court, near Lavenham, in Wiltshire.

"Did you say a *drill,* sir?"

"Curb your excitement. It wasn't a drill for drilling holes in metal plates. It was a drill for planting seed potatoes. Curious, all the same, that the dispatch records should have been destroyed immediately afterwards."

"It's going to be even more difficult to prove anything now."

"There's one rule I always follow," said Romer. "When you get a smack in the eye, don't sit down. Get up and counterattack at once. I spoke to the Chief Constable of Wiltshire before you came in. He's promised to co-operate with you in every way."

"Co-operate in what, sir?" said Petrella blankly.

"You're going down, with the search warrant which I've secured for you, and you're going to turn Fyledean Court upside down."

"But—" said Petrella.

"But what, Inspector?"

"If I don't find anything, isn't there going to be the most awful row?"

"I'm prepared to accept that risk," said Romer. "He shouldn't have tried to have my niece drowned. I'm rather fond of her."

Petrella drove, while Wilmot read the map.

"We'll go down to Christchurch first," he said.

"I thought we were going to Lavenham."

"We're going to call on Mr. Wynne."

"Who's Mr. Wynne, when he's at home?"

"Mr. Wynne," said Petrella, "was, until he retired, the manager of the Exeter branch of the District Bank."

"The old boy Light and Corder assaulted."

"That's right," said Petrella. "That's where this story began. I want to hear about it, before we tackle Douglas."

It was a lovely day. The early March sun was bright, but not yet very warm. Spring was round the corner, waiting for its cue.

Wilmot abandoned the map and said, "To hell with it! You know what? You ought to do something about Jane."

"Which Jane?" said Petrella, but the car had swerved a full foot to the right before he corrected it.

"Is there more than one?" said Wilmot innocently. "I mean Jane Orfrey, the girl detective, the pride of the Women Police. The one I pulled out of the river a week ago."

"What do you suggest I ought to do about her?"

"You could always marry her, if the worst came to the worst, I mean."

Petrella drove in silence for nearly a quarter of a mile, and Wilmot, who knew him better than most people, began to kick himself for having presumed on it.

At last Petrella said, "I've never proposed to a girl. I wouldn't know how to start."

"Not to worry," said Wilmot, relieved. "It's all a matter of technique. You get in front of her, and work your feet up till you're pretty close. Then you distract her attention – and grab her with both hands. Under the arms, high up, is favourite—"

"You make it sound like unarmed combat."

"It is a bit like that. Mind you, you'll find Jane's got a pretty high standard, now she's been kissed by a real expert."

"What expert?"

"Me," said Wilmot. "When I pulled her out of the water, I had to use the kiss of life technique. Smashing. It'll probably go better still when she's conscious."

"Certainly I remember Light and Corder," said Mr. Wynne. "It's such a beautiful morning. Let's step out into the garden. I have good cause to remember," he went on. "One of my ribs never really mended. I get a sharp twinge there if I stoop suddenly. Particularly when the weather is cold."

He was one of those men who look old when they are young, and young when they are old. The lines on his face were the deep lines of age, but his eyes had the brightness, his skin the pinkness, of youth. He had looked exactly like that, Petrella decided, for half a century; like a tough old tree.

"I read all about the assault those two men made on you," he said, "but what interested me most was the suggestion that your refusal to grant this company credit was based on some sort of personal feeling."

"Personal feeling?" Mr. Wynne drew his lips in sharply, then puffed them out again like a goldfish after an ant's egg. "They must have imagined that. Bank managers aren't allowed much personal discretion. All overdrafts are referred to Area."

"But in this case, it was suggested that you refused to recommend an overdraft, on personal grounds. Some sort of quarrel."

"If there was a quarrel," said Mr. Wynne, "it was very one-sided." He stared up at an aeroplane, from Hurn on the cross-channel run, which was gaining height in a leisurely circle against the pale blue-grey sky. "I can remember the managing director – his name was Marchant, and he'd been in the Air Force – coming to see me in my office one morning. I hadn't quite made up my mind what I was going to recommend. He wanted a very large overdraft, but he had reasonable security, and the company had quite a good financial record. When I said that I should need time to think about it, he got very angry." A slight smile played across the corners of Mr. Wynne's mouth. "Very angry indeed. He said that I'd promised him the money and that I must let him have it."

"And had you?"

"Of course not," said Mr. Wynne. "Are you fond of tomatoes?"

They had drifted to the bottom of the garden. Along the fence which separated the garden from the recreation ground was quite a pretentious greenhouse. The far side was covered with stout wire netting.

"I have trouble with the children, throwing things," explained Mr. Wynne. "Children seem to be brought up without discipline today. I have forced some early Cardinal Joys – they're pentagrams, of course. Would you like to try one?"

"I won't rob you," said Petrella. "You were telling me about Marchant making a scene in your office."

"Yes. He lost his temper, and threatened me. I wasn't impressed."

"When you say he threatened you – do you mean physically?"

"I thought at one moment that he was going to strike me. He went very red, jumped to his feet, and came round to my side of the desk." Mr. Wynne blinked.

"And what did you do?"

"I told him to control himself. After a while he did so, and went away."

"And after that you decided not to recommend him as a suitable subject for an overdraft."

"If you mean that I nursed a grudge against him, you're quite mistaken. I shouldn't allow my personal feelings to enter into a matter like that. It did, of course, occur to me that a man who had so little control over himself might not be the best person to conduct a business. That big fellow there is an Ecballium Elaterium, or Squirting Cucumber—"

"Pickled gherkins," said Wilmot to Petrella, as they drove north to keep a midday rendezvous with the Chief Constable. "Are all bank managers like that?"

"They tend to clothe themselves in the armour of their own rectitude," said Petrella. "But I should think Mr. Wynne is an extreme specimen."

"No wonder Marchant blew his top. Old Wynne would have saved the banks a few shocks in the last seven years, if he'd been a bit more tactful with him, wouldn't he?"

It was nearly four o'clock when they first caught sight of Fyledean Court. They had taken the Tilshead road, across the wastelands which form the central hump of Salisbury Plain. Then they had dropped down off the escarpment, leaving behind them the barren acres of the Firing Range, back to the civilisation of the Lavenham Valley. It was like coming out of war into peace.

Fyledean Court lay at the head of a long, curving, shallow valley. A private approach road ran north from the Lavenham-Devizes road through unfenced fields of stubble, sloping up to a windbreak of black and leafless trees.

At the turn of the road Petrella stopped the car.

"You walk from here," he said to Wilmot. "Keep out of sight over the crest, and work your way in from behind. Pick up anything you can, whilst I keep 'em busy in front."

He gave Wilmot five minutes' start, then drove slowly down the road to the court, and rang the bell. A grey-haired woman answered the door, inquired his name in a broad Wiltshire accent, and showed him into a room which might have been a gunroom or a library according to its owner's tastes. There were a lot of bookshelves, but very few books; a clutter of catalogues, boxes of cartridges, bottles of linseed oil, and tins of saddle soap.

He sat there for nearly ten minutes, listening to the life of the house and farm going on around him. A heavy lorry drove up, discharged some load, and drove off again. Then Douglas Marchant came in.

"My housekeeper tells me that you're a policeman," he said.

"Well—" began Petrella cautiously.

"Does that mean I can't offer you a drink?"

"There's no rule about it, but actually I won't have one just now."

"You don't mind if I do," said Marchant, and opened the cupboard beside the fireplace. There were box files on the lower shelves and a decanter and some bottles and glasses higher up.

Marchant helped himself to whisky, put in a long splash of soda, and said, "Well, now."

Both men were standing.

Petrella said, "I'm a Detective Inspector attached to New Scotland Yard. We've been investigating a number of bank robberies, which seemed to us to be connected – possibly organised by the same people."

"They're smart operators," said Marchant. "I've read about them in the papers."

"And I have a warrant to search your house."

Exactly the correct reactions, Petrella observed. Incredulity, followed by anger, followed by an affection of ridicule. But then, he had had ten minutes to think it all out. That was the difference between searching a slum tenement and a gentleman's residence.

"If it isn't a joke," said Marchant, "and you really do suspect me of being connected with these – these bank robberies, would you spare a few minutes telling me why? If this house is full of—er—stolen goods, they'll still be here in ten minutes' time. Incidentally, I suppose that's one of your men I spotted, leaning over the gate at the back."

Petrella said, "Did you know a man called Light?"

"Jerry Light? Certainly. He was my Squadron Sergeant Major during the war, and came in with me when I started a demolition and scrap metal business after the war."

"Have you seen him since?"

"I see him whenever we happen to work on the same contracts. He supplies labour. I supply windows."

"When did you see him last?"

"Two days ago – in London."

"Why did you meet him in an out-of-the-way public house, and not at his office?"

"I do much more of my work in public houses than in offices."

"I don't suppose you met Baron von der Hulde in a public house?"

Marchant looked surprised.

"You keep dodging about," he complained. "I thought we were talking about poor old Jerry."

"Poor old Jerry," said Petrella softly.

"You must know – he was killed – a motor smash. The night before last."

"I knew," said Petrella. "I was wondering how you did. It hasn't been in the newspapers."

"One of his employees told a business friend of mine. These things get round very quickly in the trade."

"I'm sure they do," said Petrella. "Does everybody in the building trade also know that if Light hadn't been killed, he would have been charged with murder?"

Marchant stood up, his face went red. "If that's a joke, it's in poor taste. I've told you, Light was a friend of mine—"

"So was the man he shot. Alex Shaw."

"Alex."

"Or am I wrong? Wasn't it you who found Alex the job as chauffeur to your sister, Constantia."

"Certainly. But—"

"Into whose hands, incidentally, quite a few stolen bank notes seem to have found their way."

"You're confusing me," said Marchant. "And you're going much too fast. You talk about Jerry Light, and the Baron von der Hulde, and my sister Constantia, and her chauffeur Alex, and stolen bank notes. Are you telling me that Alex was a bank robber?"

"Alex was a very rare bird," said Petrella. One half of his mind was occupied with what he was saying. The other half was noticing that Marchant was still standing up, and had put down his empty whisky glass on the table. "He was a professional killer. Not just a muscleman, like the Franks and Stoker and the other simple hooligans Light employed to run your dirty business for you."

"My business?"

"Yes. *Your* business. And that's really the oddest twist in the whole affair. Because, as far as I can see, you made bank robbery your business from motives of personal spite. You had a good, legitimate business, and a bank killed it, so you decided to get your own back on all banks."

Marchant walked over to the cupboard, which still stood half open, took out the decanter, poured himself a second whisky, and then said politely, "Please go on."

"There's not a lot more to it. You were well placed, of course. As a demolition expert you knew all there was to be known about cutting through brickwork and steel. Light, I imagine, was your contact with the professional criminal element. You supplied the equipment, mostly from Germany, organised the whole show, and took"—Petrella's eye wandered round the room for a moment—"I would guess, a very handsome share of the profits."

Marchant said, "Is that your curtain line? I'm sorry. Really I am. I haven't met anything more fascinating since I stopped reading comics. Now – get on with your search, apologise, and be off with you."

The door opened, and Wilmot looked in.

"Sorry to interrupt," he said. "But I thought you ought to have this at once," and he thrust a piece of paper into Petrella's hand.

Petrella read it and said, "Thank you, Sergeant. Don't go away." And to Marchant, "That potato drill *that's just been delivered.* When you declared it at the Customs, did you tell them about the other piece of machinery?"

"What other piece?"

"Sergeant Wilmot hasn't had time to make a close examination, but he says that there appears to be a second piece of machinery screwed to the framework, inside the larger piece, and painted to resemble it. It looks like a high-speed metal drill. Curious requirement for a farmer."

"If there is, I know nothing about it."

"It would be an excellent way of bringing stuff into the country. You'd need some co-operation from the German manufacturer, of course."

"On a level," said Marchant, "with your other fairy stories." But he was sweating.

He's getting ready to jump, thought Petrella. But which way? There are two of us here, now. I'm nearer the window. Wilmot's between him and the door.

"If you'd care to look at the declaration that I made to the Customs—" He opened the cupboard door, and took out a box file. The whole of the back of the cupboard hinged inwards. Marchant went through it, and slammed the door behind him.

Petrella jumped at the same moment, but he was a fraction of a second too late. The cupboard door was shut, and immovable.

"Out into the passage," he said.

Wilmot grabbed the handle, and pulled, but that door was fast. The mechanism at the back of the cupboard must have bolted the passage door as well.

"Damn it," said Petrella. "He had that lined up, didn't he?" As he spoke, he was looking round for a weapon. There was a poker in the grate, but it was too small to be much use. He opened a long cupboard and found a twelve-bore gun in it. He made sure that it was unloaded, then grabbed it by the barrel and swung the butt at the window. It was a narrow, leaded casement, and it took five minutes to beat an opening through it. Wilmot went first, and dragged Petrella after him. As they reached the farmyard, they heard the aeroplane, and saw it taxiing out of the Dutch barn two hundred yards away.

"It's a Piper Aztec," said Wilmot. "Lovely little job. I spotted her as I came in. Take off and land on a tennis court."

"We ought to have thought of that," said Petrella. "With his record – an aeroplane was the obvious thing."

They could only stand and watch. The silver toy swung round, nose into the wind; a sudden burst of power, and it was away.

"We'll try the telephone, but I don't mind betting it's disconnected. The whole thing was laid out like a military operation. He went twice to that cupboard. Twice, in front of my eyes, to put me off my guard."

The plane was circling to gain height, and swung back almost overhead.

"Once he gets to Germany we can whistle for him. Come on."

Wilmot didn't seem to hear him. He was still staring after the dwindling plane. "He won't get to Germany," he said. "I emptied his main tank. There'll be enough in the starter tank and Autovac to get him airborne. He'll be lucky if he gets as far as the coast."

The dipping sun touched the starboard wingtip of the plane, and a tiny spark of light winked back at them.

Petrella cut out the extract from the New Forest Advertiser, and pasted it carefully into the guard book.

UNEXPLAINED FATALITY The Piper Aztec two-seater aircraft, registration G/XREZ, which crashed on Tuesday evening at Christchurch has now been identified. The pilot, who died in the crash, was Wing Commander Marchant, D.F.C., of Fyledean Court, who has been farming in the Devizes locality for some years. Wing Commander Marchant was a popular figure locally and a generous contributor to Service charities.

The cause of the accident has not yet been ascertained, but eyewitness' accounts speak of the engine having cut out, which would suggest a mechanical defect or fuel stoppage. The pilot was evidently trying to land the aircraft on the local recreation ground. Tragically, he failed in the attempt by a few yards only, and crashed in the back garden of a Christchurch resident, Mr. Alfred Wynne, a retired Bank Official. His extensive tomato and cucumber house was entirely demolished.

This appeared on the same day that Petrella announced his engagement to Jane Orfrey.

Argosy, September and October 1964.

MICHAEL GILBERT

CLOSE QUARTERS

An Inspector Hazlerigg mystery

It has been more than a year since Canon Whyte fell 103 feet from the cathedral gallery, yet unease still casts a shadow over the peaceful lives of the Close's inhabitants. In an apparently separate incident, head verger Appledown is being persecuted: a spate of anonymous letters imply that he is inefficient and immoral. When Appledown is found dead, investigations suggest that someone directly connected to the cathedral is responsible, and it is up to Hazlerigg to get to the heart of the corruption.

'…brings crime into a cathedral close. Give it to the vicar, but don't fail to read it first.' – *Daily Express*

THE DOORS OPEN

An Inspector Hazlerigg mystery

One night on a commuter train, Paddy Yeatman-Carter sees a man about to commit suicide. Intervening, he prevents the man from going through with it. However, the very next day the same man is found dead, and Paddy believes the circumstances to be extremely suspicious. Roping in his friend and lawyer, Nap Rumbold, he determines to discover the truth. They become increasingly suspicious of the dead man's employer: the Stalagmite Insurance Company, which appears to hire some very dangerous staff.

'A well-written, cleverly constructed story which combines the unexpected with much suspicion and dirty work.'
– *Birmingham Mail*

Michael Gilbert

The Dust and the Heat

Oliver Nugent is a young Armoured Corps officer in the year 1945. Taking on a near derelict pharmaceutical firm, he determines to rebuild it and make it a success. He encounters ruthless opposition, and counteracts with some fairly unscrupulous methods of his own. It seems no one is above blackmail and all is deemed fair in big business battles. Then a threat: apparently from German sources it alludes to a time when Oliver was in charge of an SS camp, jeopardizing his company and all that he has worked for.

'Mr Gilbert is a first-rate storyteller.' – *The Guardian*

The Etruscan Net

Robert Broke runs a small gallery on the Via de Benci and is an authority on Etruscan terracotta. A man who keeps himself to himself, he is the last person to become mixed up in anything risky. But when two men arrive in Florence, Broke's world turns upside down as he becomes involved in a ring of spies, the Mafiosi, and fraud involving Etruscan antiques. When he finds himself in prison on a charge of manslaughter, the net appears to be tightening, and Broke must fight for his innocence and his life.

'Neat plotting, impeccable expertize and the usual shapeliness combine to make this one of Mr Gilbert's best.'
– *The Sunday Times*

Michael Gilbert

Flash Point

Will Dylan is an electoral favourite – intelligent, sharp and good-looking, he is the government's new golden boy.

Jonas Killey is a small-time solicitor – single-minded, uncompromising and obsessed, he is hounding Dylan in the hope of bringing him into disrepute.

Believing he has information that can connect Dylan with an illegal procedure during a trade union merger, he starts to spread the word, provoking a top-level fluttering. At the crucial time of a general election, Jonas finds himself pursued by those who are determined to keep him quiet.

'Michael Gilbert tells a story almost better than anyone else.'
– *The Times Literary Supplement*

The Night of the Twelfth

Two children have been murdered. When a third is discovered – the tortured body of ten-year-old Ted Lister – the Home Counties police are compelled to escalate their search for the killer, and Operation Huntsman is intensified.

Meanwhile, a new master arrives at Trenchard House School. Kenneth Manifold, a man with a penchant for discipline, keeps a close eye on the boys, particularly Jared Sacher, son of the Israeli ambassador…

'One of the best detective writers to appear
since the war.' – BBC

Printed in Great Britain
by Amazon.co.uk, Ltd.,
Marston Gate.